GALANTY SHOW

By the same Author

INSANITY FAIR

DISGRACE ABOUNDING

NEMESIS?

A PROPHET AT HOME

ALL OUR TOMORROWS

LEST WE REGRET

Play

DOWNFALL

Novel

THE NEXT HORIZON

GALANTY SHOW

by

DOUGLAS REED

JONATHAN CAPE
THIRTY BEDFORD SQUARE
LONDON

FIRST PUBLISHED 1947

PRINTED IN GREAT BRITAIN IN THE CITY OF OXFORD
AT THE ALDEN PRESS
BOUND BY A. W. BAIN & CO. LTD., LONDON

GALANTY SHOW

I

I SAW the telegram (which began it all) arrive at Seven Priscilla Grove, for I was looking out of my top-floor window, before turning to my typewriter, when it came.

My day's work always begins with this proprietorial glance at the agreeable morning scene outside. On the level of my room London's rooftops, warm in the rising midsummer sun, stretched away to the Thames and vanished in a blue haze beyond. Below, Lady Cynthia was washing down the steps (for this was not Mrs. Barnes's Day) while three of her guests, Lord Bloomsbury, Edith Wilstan and M. Piôřřič, strolled towards the Brompton Road and their daily labours. My own, I usually approach with reluctance, being indolent by nature, and the appearance of the post office boy, who came past them as they went round the corner, gave me the idler's excuse to tarry a moment more at my window, my back to the implacable sheets of paper which I should have to fill during the day. He approached on the opposite pavement, looking from side to side until his gaze fixed on the word 'Seven', painted on the twin columns above Lady Cynthia's head. Then he came across and stood uncertainly behind her.

Lady Cynthia, breathing hard and rubbing vigorously, did not hear him. Busy with her bottom step, she was bent nearly double and thus displayed the better half of two shapely legs between knee and thigh (as I knew, having come on her from the same direction one morning). She was blissfully unaware of this, never having realized how skirts had shortened since she first let down her own, when she was about fifteen. Now that she was fifty the world saw what it had missed in her youth, which was much, for Lady Cynthia was still beautiful and looked far less than her years. From the messenger boy's angle she appeared younger still, and I saw that he was held in a kind of trance, both bashful and gleeful. I coughed.

Lady Cynthia looked up, waved her cloth and smiled brightly.

'Now then, lazybones,' she said, 'you should be at work.' I pointed with my head and eyes at the boy. She looked round, jumped, and exclaimed 'Oh!' (I wondered why women, who have a sixth sense for what goes on around them, so seldom have eyes in the back of their heads for a bulging skirt-seat, a crooked seam, or an inquisitive male.) The messenger of destiny handed over his telegram and began to remove his disturbing presence from the cloistered peace of Priscilla Grove. Lady Cynthia, wiping damp hands on her apron, opened the envelope and read. A feeling of good and exciting news ascended to me. In the pleasurable hope of delaying my appointment with my typewriter a little longer, I leaned farther out. Smiling happily, she looked up, but her glance, as it travelled to me, was intercepted by Lady Bloomsbury, who put her head out of the window below mine.

'Oh, Doris,' called Lady Cynthia. 'What do you think? I've let the first floor! Isn't it grand!' She showed the telegram.

'Oh, lovely,' said Lady Bloomsbury. She perceived from Lady Cynthia's divided smiles that someone else was sharing the news, twisted her neck until she lay nearly on her back, and performed the remarkable feat, in that position, of bowing upward to me. 'Good morning, Mr. Grame.' She uncoiled herself, with some trouble, until she faced the earth again. 'Have you just heard then, Cynthia?'

'Yes. This telegram's from your Harold. . . .'

'From Harold?'

'Yes, isn't it thoughtful of him? He's sending me two Americans.'

'Americans! Oh. That's good, Cynthia. You'll be paid this time.'

'I know. I was so afraid I should get some more White Ukrainians, or something. Isn't it good, Mr. Grame?'

'Fine,' I called down. 'When are they coming?'

Lady Cynthia looked at the telegram. 'They'll be here on Thursday. A Mr. and Mrs. Vanderboom.'

'A married couple. How exciting,' said Lady Bloomsbury. 'Ah wonder if they're honeymooners.'

'I don't know. Harold doesn't say. He sends you his love, Doris.'

'Oh, Ah must see the telegram. Ah'll come down.'

'No, don't. I'll run up.'

Lady Cynthia tripped up the steps, leaving small shoeprints on the moist surface. Lady Bloomsbury's head withdrew. I took a last look round, seeking another excuse to dawdle. None offered. Someone turned the corner, but it was only Mr. Alistair Jene, Lady Cynthia's husband, returned by homing instinct from the shops with the household rations in a string bag and followed by his aged and temperamental Aberdeen terrier, Peggy. He was talking to himself, as always. 'A shocking thing, a shocking thing,' I heard him say of some calamity in his dream world. They entered the house, adding his shoeprints and Peggy's paw-marks to Lady Cynthia's tracks on the moist steps. Priscilla Grove was its placid self again, quiet and empty. Reluctantly I turned to face my typewriter, thinking all excitement done.

II

THERE are quiet backwaters in the upper reaches of the river Thames which inseparably belong to raging oceans far away, for even from these secluded pools a few drops of water go out to join distant tempests, and in course of ebb and flow return again. Similarly, Priscilla Grove belongs to London, and must even be very near to the fiercely beating heart of London; the map of the city says so. Yet I shall never be quite sure that it is in London, or even that it exists. I know that it is an enchanted glade; it may be a dream. Sometimes, when I listen to Mr. Alistair Jene, I am sure it is one.

The great traffic river that has its source at Piccadilly Circus and rolls westward, roaring by day and glittering by night, widens at Hyde Park Corner, surges down Knightsbridge and there divides into two lesser, but still stately streams. One of these, the Brompton Road, bears to the south-west and throws off tributaries and branches to left and right as it goes, and if you steer your bark into the third or fourth (or is it the fifth or sixth?) of these another wide and navigable and apparently endless prospect opens, thronged with human craft. A hundred yards along it, however, there is a little opening on the left – unless I dream it. Perhaps I do, because nearly all pass it by and few perceive it. But *if* you are able at that point to fall asleep and enter dreamland, you may turn aside, pass through the little opening, and enter Priscilla Grove. There is no stir or bustle here by day and little light at night: footfalls and voices lose their sharp edge and some magic deadens the noise from the surrounding city; the place is as hushed as the Forest of Arden.

Priscilla Grove runs for about fifty yards and ends in a brick wall. (This, again, makes me doubt whether Priscilla Grove really exists. If it does, it should have made up its mind to go on and lead somewhere, like all the other Streets and Roads and Crescents and Places hereabouts; the brick wall is the sort of thing that pops up in dreams, especially the ones in which you are being chased.) There are twelve houses, which face each other in two rows, Numbers One to Eleven, and Two to Twelve; or rather, there were once twelve houses. If Priscilla Grove is a dream, it is a lifelike one: Number Eight, which should face Number Seven, appears to have been cleanly removed by a bomb. That greatly improves the view from my top-floor window.

The remaining eleven houses, though they have a dreamlike quality, are solid and substantial. The steps run up to columned porches, and the front doors that gleam inside these have all been painted different colours: green, cream, red, pale blue, royal blue, and so on; at some period this pleasant vogue ran through Priscilla Grove. There are little gardens in front and behind, but as gardeners, with servants, have vanished like elves at the coming of dawn, most of these have been paved and made into small courts and terraces, with pot plants and shrubs to soften their angularity. Trees have been left unfelled in some of the gardens, and these are tall, gnarled and very old; they must have been there when this was just a grove, and not Priscilla Grove.

Each house has three storeys above the ground floor, and a basement beneath it. In the top floors maidservants used to sleep, and in the basements they used to work, but now only one servant remains in Priscilla Grove: old Mrs. O'Bourke's old Mrs. Miggins at Number Twelve. Those two have been there since young Mr. O'Bourke, now gone, brought home his bride in 1880; they have been there so long together they would not know what to do without each other and without Priscilla Grove.

To-day only the dreamer's eye may perceive ghostly cooks and butlers in the basements, ghostly dinner-parties behind the ground-floor windows and ghostly tea-parties above, ghostly children at the nursery windows and ghostly maidservants laughing down from the topmost ones. All the houses (save Mrs. O'Bourke's) have been divided and partitioned and sub-divided into small and smaller flats, of which the biggest has four rooms and the smallest one room. With the help of a host of Daily Women, who Oblige for two or three hours each morning, the owners eke out a livelihood by letting these, preferably to Single Gentlemen; if needs must to Single Ladies; and occasionally to Married Couples Without Children. The charm and relative cheapness of Priscilla Grove, to which the native Londoners mostly remain oblivious, have been discovered by more enterprising visitors, and Numbers Two, Four and Six (which are jointly owned) are packed with the more poorly paid attachés of the Styrian, Illyrian and Transirian Legations. At certain times of the day, and in certain lights, they impart something of Montparnasse to Priscilla Grove. They have a lean and hungry look, a dark and conspiratorial air, and develop five o'clock shadow after breakfast. The artists at the end house on our side, Number Eleven, also help to create this illusion. When they first face the day, about noon, and in the evening at the hour when the Bunch of Grapes opens, they emerge from

Number Eleven, good-looking girls in trousers and pretty youths with long hair and sandals, in such numbers that you wonder how they can all stow away in the one house. Indeed, the ten other houses look askance at Number Eleven, because it is known chiefly to contain one-roomed flats, which implies much propinquity, and the artists, somehow, do not *look* married. We others do not even know that they are artists. We know there are artists in these parts and give them the benefit of that doubt, if we cannot acquit them of the other. In any case they deserve sympathy: they are not really happy despite their insouciant bearing; for they are exiles from their hunting-grounds, Priscilla Grove being at least eight hundred yards from Chelsea and the King's Road.

Number Seven holds the acknowledged rank of first among equals in Priscilla Grove, for several reasons. For one, its population is small, quiet, and predominantly native. For another, it is the only house, save for old Mrs. O'Bourke's (which in the circumstances is but the husk of a house) still in the original ownership; all the others have changed hands, most of them several times. Lady Cynthia was born in Number Seven, left it only to be married, and inherited it with its furniture. This was lucky, because Mr. Jene absent-mindedly put his money into a timber project in Eastern Poland and lost every penny when war broke out again in those parts; we think that his more explosive and baffling ejaculations probably relate to this affair. Lady Cynthia, undismayed, returned to Number Seven with him and there defied the war, including the bomb, while their son, Oliver, commanded a destroyer and at long intervals came to spend his leave with them. At the end she sat indomitable beneath plasterless ceilings and behind paneless windows; found that she and Mr. Jene had but a few hundred pounds in the world; and decided to let her house support her by opening it to paying guests. What seemed a startling innovation in Priscilla Grove quickly became the rule, for none of her neighbours returned to it, and the newcomers who bought the vacant houses all had the same plan.

By a stroke of that good fortune which attends the brave, Lady Cynthia's former maid, Mrs. Barnes, lives just round the corner (in the Fulham Road) and was willing to oblige four mornings a week, so that Lady Cynthia hardly ever has to wash the steps or perform the heavier housework, and is left ample time for cooking. Better still, Mr. Barnes, a builder and decorator in a small way, very cheaply worked such wonders with paint and plywood that half the big kitchen, the pantry and the cook's sitting-room were transformed into a comfortable basement flat for Lady Cynthia and her husband. Working at dead of night or crack of dawn (for fear these crimes might be observed by the eye of the law, which dislikes to see houses under repair) Mr. Barnes, while Lady Cynthia trembled, put back a window-pane here and a little plaster there; found and installed second-hand bathtubs and washhand-basins; and one foggy evening recklessly painted the front door. For his wife and Lady Cynthia he soiled the clean record of a blameless life and risked ruin and imprisonment. I betray his crime here only because I think I have covered up the trail that leads to Priscilla Grove — if the place exists at all.

At last all was ready. Lady Cynthia, her Alistair, and Peggy were snug in the basement. Above them the dining-room remained the dining-room, with the big oval mahogany table still in it; but the study behind had been made into a common sitting-room for the guests-to-come. The first floor, where the great drawing-room and big bedroom had been, was a comfortably spacious flat of sitting-room, two bedrooms and bathroom. The next floor was a flat of the same kind, but with smaller rooms. On the top floor were three small bed-sitting-rooms and a common bathroom. Looking furtively behind him, Mr. Barnes loaded the last debris on to his barrow and departed. Lady Cynthia stood at her cooker in the basement, ready to receive boarders.

I was her first guest and am now her oldest inhabitant. I have said that I am still not sure how, or even if, I came to her; but unless she vanishes into air one day, and I wake up, I shall stay with her for ever, for I could not be happier anywhere else. I like quiet for the bit of writing that I do; but not the quiet of the countryside. Priscilla Grove and Lady Cynthia gave me the urban peace I need (at any rate, until the telegram arrived, and I hope that all the commotion to which it led has now passed away, never to return). She had great fun, she said, settling me into my room, with plenty of shelves for my books and a great desk before the window, from which I can look over London and watch the sun rise and fall. When she was finished she stood in the doorway with a pleased air, said 'There, now I think you'll do,' and left me to my work.

That night we dined in state at the big table, Lady Cynthia leaving me alone with Alistair Jene while she ran down to the kitchen to hoist the food in the service lift, and running up again to meet it as it arrived and put it on the table. Alistair first planted in me the feeling that I might be under a spell, or living a dream, so remote was he from the world about him. As Lady Cynthia left us to propel the soup upwards he spoke for the first time. Gazing fixedly at me he said serenely, 'Queer looking chaps, writers.' I realized later that he was unaware of having said anything, then and at most times.

After that the big table, and the house, filled quickly. First came the Bloomsburys. Lord and Lady Bloomsbury, of the 1946 creation, and their son, Harold Biggs, took the second-floor flat. Lord Bloomsbury had been a school-teacher, a trade union secretary, and a Socialist Member of Parliament, before he was made a peer to swell the governmental forces in the Upper House, and consequently he resembles a porpoise, but beneath all his bewilderment he has a rugged integrity and a dogged good humour which gain respect. He has a puzzled air, and may be wondering why he is Minister for Jet Propulsion; but the trade union newspaper insists that he is the best man for that post. I feared for him, and for Lady Cynthia, who was highly pleased by the coming of the Bloomsburys, on their first evening at dinner, when Alistair, looking gravely towards him, said courteously, 'Lord Bloomsbury, forsooth. I don't know what we're coming to.' But Lord Bloomsbury merely said, 'No more don't I, laad,' of which retort Alistair remained as unconscious as of his own remark, and all was well.

Lady Bloomsbury, who, though married in London, had spent the greater part of her youth in the provinces, from the first insisted on sharing the cooking with Lady Cynthia, whom she called 'pet', until the pet, lost for a reciprocal endearment, suggested 'Cynthia' and 'Doris'.

This new recruit in the kitchen was sometimes a clear gain to the household, for Lady Bloomsbury is a queen of cooks in her own field, has a magician's touch with dried eggs, and can make tinned beef taste like tinned salmon; but it became a doubtful blessing when the cosmopolitan atmosphere of Priscilla Grove laid its spell on her and she began to ransack the bookshops for second-hand treatises on foreign cooking. We never knew what to expect when Lady Bloomsbury set out to make a Georgian refugee feel at home. She tried also to share the step-washing with Lady Cynthia, on Mrs. Barnes's absent days, but this Lady Cynthia, who venerated precedence and knew that Doris should go into dinner before herself, if dinner in this sense had not become an extinct function, would never allow.

I saw with affection that Lady Bloomsbury felt herself in wonderland in Priscilla Grove (as indeed she may be). Number Seven owed her coming to the fact that the Bloomsburys were provincials; Londoners, as I say, were wont to pass without noticing it. The Bloomsburys added to its charm. Their son Harold, however, marred it. He was, I felt, of those whom only a mother can love. Lady Bloomsbury adores him. He is a tall, gangling, pallid and toothy young man, up to the neck in causes and movements and dogmatic about them all. He talks loudly and often about Rusher, a country I chance to know, though he does not. He is an official in, and a poor advertisement for, the Ministry of Family Planning, and I rejoiced when he obtained three months' leave to go on a lecture tour in America, whence he sent the fateful telegram.

The Bloomsburys introduced Edith Wilstan to Seven Priscilla

Grove but I, who often saw most of the game, felt that it was mainly on account of Harold that she came, and entered into one of the two vacant rooms on my floor. Though they were not engaged Harold had given her every cause to think that an unspoken understanding existed between them. Sometimes he took her as often as three times in a week to Communist discussion-group meetings, and we all saw that this swept Edith off her feet, as it would any woman, of course. Edith is what kindly dowagers used to call 'a fine gel', when they could think of nothing better to say. She *is* fine; that is, in parts. ('Hm, a buxom wench,' Alistair remarked on her first appearance at table.) She has the ruminant's eye, and it rested worshippingly on Harold when he was with us and held forth about Rusher. She encouraged him, and I held that very much against her, because he is a great bore without any encouragement. Sometimes when I hoped he had stopped he would catch that eye and start off all over again. Tact and finesse are needed to hold in check the combination of Harold, his mother and Edith, or our evenings at the big table and in the sitting-room afterwards would become intolerable. I was surprised at first, and then intrigued, sometimes to find an ally in Lord Bloomsbury. He is not so soft, I decided, as he looks. He sees through his Harold.

The coming of Edith left empty only the top-floor room next to mine and the big first-floor flat. Up to this point all had gone well with Lady Cynthia. Now all went agley. She could not let the single room at all; she let the big flat too often, and each time was worse deceived. The message 'Lady Cynthia has a flat to let at Seven Priscilla Grove', might have been heliographed from Durazzo to Tiflis, so thickly did Balkan exiles, Georgian princes, Ukrainian chieftains and mysterious Odessans press on each other's heels to take it. Her first tenant, an Albanian prince, stayed a month and then left without paying his rent before Lady Cynthia would heed my mild warning that there were no Albanian princes. He was followed by a Hungarian count and countess of the utmost charm who within a week had eight other Hungarian counts and countesses sharing the two bedrooms with them, brewed coffee for all, day and night, in the gas water-heater, and at the end had to be removed, in hysterics, by the police, while all the Styrian, Illyrian and Transirian attachés from Numbers Two, Four and Six shouted abuse or applause, according to their countries' relations with Hungary.

After these experiences with the Transdanubian nobility Lady Cynthia welcomed a plain Soviet Russian, who was understood to be something in the Kremlin, with open arms. 'Harold will be *such* good company for him,' she told Lady Bloomsbury. Harold, when he came home and heard the news, behaved like a young girl who feels the first excitement of love; a rapt and infatuated look spread over his pale face. The news of the Commissar's coming disturbed Priscilla Grove in many ways. It upset the Styrians, Illyrians and Transirians at the corner, who all held strong opinions about the Commissar's country. They strolled to and fro before the house in twos and threes, talking volubly and staring through the windows. It also reached and fluttered the artists at the other end. The young men put on the reddest of their lumbermen's shirts, the girls tied kerchiefs round their heads, and they gathered in adoring groups before Number Seven, hoping for a glimpse of him.

Having scores to pay off against Harold, I prepared to mix matters a little by telling the Commissar that he was a Trotskyist. This, however, proved unnecessary; the Commissar's suspicions needed no prompting from me. A remarkable figure, he was nearly seven feet tall and his head was shaven to the quick. He arrived with his wife, a frightened-looking woman in sackcloth, and one much-battered suitcase. He was eagerly awaited by the company assembled at table that night, but when he came down showed great alarm at the demonstration outside; the artists were singing the Red Flag, while the Illyrians and Transirians were having a free fight about some obscure point of Communist doctrine. The Commissar seemed in fear of his life and insisted on having the blinds down.

From that moment the party never recovered. He behaved with extraordinary reserve, refusing to answer such questions as 'How do you like our English weather?' and warning his wife also not to commit herself. When Harold, in the manner of Left-Understands-Left, confidently intervened to draw him out his manner changed from passive mistrust to angry suspicion. He glowered at Harold, made transparently rude remarks about him in Russian to his wife ('I thought I heard him say something about Trotskyists,' I told Harold casually afterwards) and seemed on the verge of violence. Then he suddenly jumped up, dragging his wife after him, strode out, and later informed Lady Cynthia, through a door held just ajar, that he would take his meals in his room in future. The next morning, however, when she went up with a tray, she found the door locked. Knocking was answered by loud and obviously menacing shouts from within, and Lady Cynthia went hurriedly downstairs to hold a council of war with her Doris and Mrs. Barnes.

Just then, looking from my window, I saw two blue-jowled men on the opposite pavement talking and glancing at Number Seven. I thought nothing of it, taking them to be two of our Styrians, Illyrians or Transirians, and was about to begin work when loud explosions sounded from below, and the two ran off as fast as their legs would take them. A moment later the Commissar, shouting threats and brandishing a revolver, rushed out of the house and after them, followed by his wife. All four disappeared round the corner and there, I assume, vanished into air, for we never saw or heard of any of them again, and the suitcase was found to contain only newspapers. There was endless discussion about this strange affair in Priscilla Grove, and for some days knots of disputing attachés and artists made it look more like Montparnasse than ever before. There were many different theories. Harold explained it all by saying that the Commissar was really a Trotskyist renegade, while the two men were Soviet agents sent to watch him. But I still think I recognized in them the First and Second Secretaries at the Transirian Legation, and one day shall inquire there whether any such are missing. I feel I owe this to any kith and kin they may have left behind. There are so many Transirian Secretaries at Numbers

Two, Four and Six that the absence of two will never be noticed unless I do something about it.

After this Lady Cynthia became morbid about the first-floor flat. 'I begin to think there's a curse on it,' she said to us all that night at dinner, 'or perhaps it's a judgment on me for making Mr. Barnes put in that second-hand pink washhand-basin he found for me.'

'Pink washhand-basin?' I said. 'Why, if this is retribution for the washhand-basin there's more to come. What about the bathtub and the black-and-white tiles. That ought to be worth a Mad Mongolian Mullah at least.'

'Oh, don't, Mr. Grame,' said Lady Cynthia, trembling. 'I'd forgotten those.'

'Don't frighten her, Mr. Grame,' said Lady Bloomsbury. And don't you worry, Cynthia, pet. Ah'm sure you'll get somebody nice soon.'

I said no more, but I wondered. I thought by this time that anything was possible in Priscilla Grove. Also, I was coming to feel that I had a personal interest in the matter. I had never believed myself to be temperamental, but somehow I could not shut my mind to what was happening in the first-floor flat when it was undergoing one of its crises. The disquiet and unrest that germinated there seemed to spread themselves throughout the house and make all work impossible; at any rate, for me. Thus in one way and another, between the Albanian prince, the Hungarian count and countess and the Commissar, I had lost a large number of working-days, and I felt that the first-floor flat owed me something for my shattered peace.

After the episode of the Commissar, however, life seemed to settle down at Number Seven. Trouble threatened when another sufferer from five o'clock shadow presented himself as a candidate for the vacant top-floor room next to mine. When she learned that he was from the Bulgoslav Cultural Society Lady Cynthia nearly shut the door in his face, but before she could do this he produced a recommendation from Harold. Watched with apprehension by all of us at first, M. Piôťřič proved harmless, and became known as Em Porridge, which was the best Mrs. Barnes could do with his name. He had a radio and a telephone installed in his room and spent much time there, listening to the one or having violent altercations through the other. I learned a lot of Bulgoslav from Em Porridge's radio and his telephone conversations, which came clearly to me through the wall. It sounded an easy language, and soon I felt that I could myself have made a speech in Bulgoslav. The Bulgoslav mind seemed to run in a narrow groove. '. . . Bulgoslavsky politik oojovitch' (Em Porridge or his radio would say) 'Da, da. Nichy, nichy. Hellenski politik nichy demokratiki. Oh da! Da-da-da-da. Narodny russki demokratiki. Angliski ut amerikansko fascisky. Da, da! Dobro, dobro. . . .'

As time passed, then, and the memory of her initial troubles faded, a well-balanced little community grew up round Lady Cynthia, and life at Seven Priscilla Grove, as I have shown, became the gracious and peaceful life of a typical English household. The only flaw in our content was the persistently empty space on the ground floor, which meant a gap in Lady Cynthia's bookkeeping. Because it worried her, whom we loved, it worried us all.

And now, at last, it was let again, and this time to good tenants: to friends of Harold!

III

THE news of the telegram was conveyed to Lord Bloomsbury, Edith and Em Porridge when they returned to Priscilla Grove that evening, and in the course of the day even penetrated Alistair's consciousness, so that we all gathered for dinner in glad good humour. The sense of loss which Harold's empty seat caused in his mother was clearly sweetened for her by the thought that he was to be the instrument of filling the other vacant places at the big table.

'Ee, Cynthia, pet,' she said, 'Ah'm that glad you're going to have some good folk in the big flat at last. It'll be a weight off your mind.'

'Yes, it will, Doris,' said Lady Cynthia, 'and I can't tell you how grateful I am to Harold. It's most thoughtful of him.' She smiled happily, but I saw that she was not unreservedly giving herself to hope. The Commissar had unnerved her. Besides, she was a devoutly religious woman and I guessed that the bath-tub lay heavy on her conscience. Having sinned so much, she could not believe that retribution had finished with her.

'Yes, our Harold's a good boy,' said Lady Bloomsbury. 'A couple of rich Americans is just what you need, loov.'

'Steady on, Doris,' said Lord Bloomsbury, 'don't run away with yourself. Lady Cynthia's had enough disappointments. How do you know they're rich?'

'Oh, all Americans are rich.'

'Well, how do you know they're Americans?'

'They must be. Harold says they're from New York.'

'From what I remember of New York, that makes it most unlikely that they're Americans.'

'Is that really so, Lord Bloomsbury?' said Edith, earnestly. 'How strange.'

Alistair, though he showed no sign of having awakened, appeared to have understood the conversation. 'You might as well look for English people in Swiss Cottage,' he said, 'as for Americans in New York.'

'Why, aren't there any English people in Swiss Cottage?' said Lady Bloomsbury in surprise.

'Of course not. They're all – er Swiss, or something.'

'I hope you're not anti-Swiss, Mr. Jene,' said Lord Bloomsbury. 'I happen to know the Government lays great importance on good relations with Switzerland.'

'Harold is very strongly opposed to Swiss-baiting,' said Edith.

Em Porridge's eyes glittered behind his spectacles. 'Pleess,' he said, 'since I am in England I meet many Swiss. In Bulgoslavia we have not Swiss. I am much interest for this question. In Soviet Russia . . .'

Lady Cynthia intervened tactfully; since the days of the Commissar, the fighting attachés and the singing artists, she liked to keep Soviet Rusher out of the conversation as much as Harold would let her. 'Now, don't let's start all that again,' she said. 'This is our Bulgoslav evening. We've a surprise for Em Porridge. Will you all go into the dining-room? Come on, Doris.'

'Yes, loov, Ah'm coming.'

Excitedly they went downstairs, and, led by Edith, we took our places round the mahogany table. Em Porridge looked bashfully pleased. 'The Lady Cynthia,' he said, 'she has a surprise for me? What is he, a Bulgoslav evening?'

'Ah, you must wait and see,' said I. But I was already mourning for my dinner. I had previously known a Hungarian evening and a paprika goulasch which had greatly surprised the Hungarian count and his countess. Doris was, in English, an unusually good plain cook. Her excursions into Continental cooking I distrusted. Presently there was a creaking of ropes and the service lift rumbled up while Lady Cynthia's and Lady Bloomsbury's footsteps mounted the stairs and the ladies entered the dining-room.

Em Porridge was first served, as befitted the guest of honour. He looked at his plate, grinned politely, and said, 'Ah!' It might have meant anything.

'Good God!' said Alistair.

'It looks delicious,' said Edith.

'What *is* this, Doris?' said Lord Bloomsbury.

'Stuffed vine-leaves! Em Porridge's national dish! Isn't she *clever*?' said Lady Cynthia triumphantly.

'Ahh! How you call him?' asked Em Porridge, hiding bewilderment behind his most dazzling smile.

'Stuffed vine-leaves,' said Lady Bloomsbury. 'Ah believe you eat practically nothing else in Bulgoslavia. . . .'

'No wonder they don't stay there,' said Alistair charmingly.

'. . . but Ah couldn't get vine-leaves, so Ah used cabbage-leaves. And Ah couldn't get any rice, so Ah used split peas. But Ah'm sure you won't know the difference, eh Tom?'

'I hope he won't,' said Lord Bloomsbury.

'I think it's *lovely*,' said Edith, 'so *different*. I *love* Continental cooking.'

'He is very good,' said Em Porridge. 'I have never taste anything like him. And you make him for me?'

'Now hurry up,' Lady Bloomsbury ordered us, 'there's better to coom. Ee, you'll know this one, Em Porridge.'

'Yes?' inquired Em Porridge anxiously. 'What is he?'

Fixing him with an eye that defied him to plead ignorance, Lady Bloomsbury uttered one word. 'Shashlik,' she said.

The effect on Em Porridge was immediate. 'Ahh, *shashlik*,' he said, and rose reverently to his feet; had he worn a hat, I felt, he would have raised it, and in the silence which followed I expected to hear the Angelus. 'Shashlik!' And he sat down again, as if there were nothing more worth saying. Great joy was in his eyes, and the memory of many feasts. 'Shashlik,' he murmured. We were all impressed. This time, we felt, Lady Bloomsbury had scored a bullseye. While she, Lady Cynthia and Edith collected the plates and went downstairs we plied him with questions.

'What is shashlik, Em Porridge?' asked Lord Bloomsbury.

'Ah, he is meat,' said Em Porridge, rolling his eyes, 'meat with a sewer.'

'Oh, Lord,' said Alistair.

We heard the creaking and the rumbling and the mounting footsteps, and the three women, all rather red in the face, came in again, collected the dishes from the lift, and served them. I saw the light fade and die away in Em Porridge's eyes. But gallantly he rose and bowed to Lady Bloomsbury.

'There,' she said, 'now see what you think of that, Em Porridge. Ah must tell you others that shashlik is pieces of meat, with onion and seasoning, grilled on a skewer. But Ah hadn't any meat, so Ah used corned beef, and Ah hadn't any skewers, so Ah threaded them on blind-cord. But they'll taste none the worse for that. The secret's in the sauce and the flavouring. And there's pancakes to follow.'

'Pankicks?' said Em Porridge faintly.

'Yes, *you* know, Em Porridge – *bliny*!'

'Ah, *bliny*. Ah, da, da, he is very fine.'

'Palmerston wouldn't have stood it,' said Alistair courteously and distinctly, 'neither in Poland nor in any other damn country.'

We others understood that Alistair's mind had returned to his lost plantations, but Em Porridge was always puzzled by these mysterious allusions. Poland appeared to play an important part in his thoughts and the mere mention of it seemed to provoke him. He clearly felt that Alistair harboured some valuable information about that country, if it could only be extracted, and I suspected that he wrote long memoranda, interpreting Alistair's hints, which by way of the Bulgoslav Cultural Society reached Comintern headquarters in Moscow. Lady Cynthia frequently had to head Em Porridge away from the subject of Poland, too.

'Pleess,' said Em Porridge eagerly, turning his gleaming lenses on Alistair, 'you say Poland. I am much interest for this question. . . .'

'Mr. Jene was thinking about an investment, Em Porridge,' said Lady Cynthia firmly. 'Do tell us what you think of your *shashlik*.'

Em Porridge reluctantly but politely abandoned his quest. 'She is wonderful,' he said.

'*It*, Em Porridge.'

'Yes, yes, I it.' And he ate, voraciously, having been bred in the law that to devour your host's offerings is the first rule of civility among guests. I admired his spirit, and understood why many centuries of alien conquest and rapine had failed to make his race extinct.

When the *bliny* had come and gone we all repaired to the common sitting-room to finish off the Bulgoslav evening with Turkish coffee, made by Edith, who is a coffee-snob, as are so many fine gels. It proved to be two solid inches of finely-ground coffee, with an eighth of an inch of liquid atop and Alistair, who absentmindedly took a gulp of it, emerged yelping with a thick black rim round scalded lips. Conversation was usually difficult at this hour because Em Porridge at ten-minute intervals insisted on listening to the day's news from Radio Moscow, Radio Belgrade, Radio Cracow, Radio Batum and Radio Astrakan, and the air was filled with sounds like the sharpening of rusty knives, from the box by which he sat crouched. Even Priscilla Grove could not soften the edge of these menacing noises; 'Polski', 'Russki', 'democratski', 'fascisky', 'communisky' darted like hornets in and out of our dronelike talk.

Lady Cynthia lit her pipe (she smokes nothing else, having acquired the habit during a sojourn among the Sioux Indians of North America, and it has become so much a habit with her that she is always taken aback if anyone else shows surprise at it). 'I wonder what they'll be like,' she said.

We all knew whom she meant. 'Mr. and Mrs. Vanderboom?' said Lady Bloomsbury. 'Ee, Ah'm sure they'll be very nice.'

'The usual combination,' I ventured, 'a Southern gentleman with a Northern factory and a New England wife with an Old England complex.'

'What *do* you mean, Mr. Grame?' said Edith.

'I'm not sure that I know,' I said, 'but it sounded good.'

'I wonder if she's young?'

'If *they're* young, you mean.'

'American husbands never seem young, somehow.'

'Edith,' I said, 'that's very profound of you. In my experience they hardly ever seem to be there at all. They are almost invisible. But their wives make up for what they lack in physical substance and youth.'

'Ssh, pleess, a moment,' said Em Porridge. We hushed a moment. A terrible voice said, 'Amerikanski ut angliski plutokratski nichy nimmovich demokratny.' He nodded, looking at us. We nodded. He turned off the radio. We relaxed.

'Ah expect she'll be an aluminium blonde,' said Lady Bloomsbury.

'Or a silver-mauve,' said Edith

'I'm dreading the first sight of her stockings and shoes,' said

Lady Cynthia, puffing at her pipe. 'I am *not* an envious woman, but they do pile on the agony for us.'

Lord Bloomsbury cleared his throat and we waited. 'These American girls,' he said pontifically, 'are all as like as peanuts in a packet.'

'Well, I like peanuts,' said Lady Cynthia, 'and I'd quite like to be like Hedy Lamarr.'

'God bless the four kingdoms of Old Habsburgia,' I said. 'She's not noticeably American.'

'Oh, isn't she?' said Lady Bloomsbury. 'Ah thought she was a typical American.'

'Ask Em Porridge,' I said, craftily. (I knew he had a tale to tell, having heard it before.)

'Ah, the Hedy Lamarr?' he said, eagerly. 'No, no. He is from Europe. I see him many years ago, in my own country, in a film, *Ecstasy*. He have nothing on. . . .'

Lady Cynthia interrupted firmly. 'Oh, in that case she *is* typically American, from what I know of the films. It is quite extraordinary how those Hollywood girls contrive to look naked in a dinner gown and a mink coat. Doris, what on earth shall I give them to eat?'

'Ee, Ah must get a book on American cooking.'

'Now, that's where I think you're wrong, Doris,' said Lord Bloomsbury. 'Why don't you stick to the thing you're best at? Give them good plain English cooking.'

'On a basis of corned beef and dried eggs,' I prompted.

'Americans love coffee,' said Edith. 'I'll make a big pot of coffee before I go each morning, Lady Cynthia, and you can heat it as they want it. And they love doughnuts, but not the doughnuts we have. They like them with a hole in the middle.'

'I must see if that shop in the Brompton Road can't let me have a few doughnuts the day they arrive, just to make them feel at home. I'll cut out the middle, to make the hole.'

'But that's the part where the jam is, Cynthia, pet.'

'Where the jam used to be, you mean. But perhaps Americans don't like the jammy part; that's why they have the hole in the middle. They're so odd. What with jamless doughnuts and lynching, I sometimes wonder if they're quite *civilized*.'

'You don't need to worry about feeding them, Cynthia,' said Alistair, awakening. 'Americans carry their own rations. They have their pockets full of things called life-savers, and chewing-gum. Feed them a little ice-cream between whiles and they can go on indefinitely, like camels.'

'But we haven't any ice-cream,' said Lady Bloomsbury.

'Well, then, just . . . er, stop somebody and buy some,' said Lord Bloomsbury, irritably. 'There's no use making difficulties.'

'Ee, well, I wish our Harold were coming with them,' said Lady Bloomsbury.

'I suppose he didn't say when he was coming?'

'No, Edith, he didn't. But he won't be long now, I expect.'

'Ssh, pleess, a moment,' said Em Porridge, from the radio.

We paused while a large number of Chinese crackers exploded in the instrument. When it was finished the party began to break up. Edith went to her room, and Em Porridge to his. I tarried a few minutes, knowing there would be no sleep for me until he had heard the ten o'clock news from Cracow and telephoned to his office, for relay to Moscow, a brief report of Alistair's allusion to Poland. Lady Cynthia was looking worried. Her past ordeals, I saw, prevented her from feeling completely happy about the new tenants of the first-floor flat, and the bathtub lay like lead on her soul.

'Cheer up,' I said, as she knocked out her pipe, 'I'm sure all will be well.'

'Well, we shall soon see, anyway,' she said doubtfully, 'only two more days to Thursday. I do hope they won't be mixed up with the Ku Klux Klan or something.'

'They're much more likely to be good supporters of the Democratic Party,' I said.

'What, *terrorists*? Oh, don't, Mr. Grame, that would be too dreadful.'

'You misunderstand me. I said Democrats, not Republicans.'

'Oh, I see. Is that better?'

'It couldn't be worse. It's probably just the same thing.'

'You mean, like our Conservatives and Socialists? But I do wish we could keep politics out of Seven Priscilla Grove.'

'Perhaps we only imagine that they come here, Cynthia. Perhaps all life is politics; perhaps life is all a dream. Good night.'

'Just look how the British Government acted in the case of John Brown's ear,' said Alistair. 'There was no nonsense then.'

'Oh, come on, Alistair,' said Lady Cynthia. 'Good night, Mr. Grame.'

IV

ON Thursday morning Seven Priscilla Grove was in a mood of expectant excitement. A stranger's eye would have seen nothing uncommon in the company gathered at the breakfast table, but its members all felt that this was a day different from other days.

'Well, they'll soon be here now, Cynthia, pet.'

'So Harold's friends are arriving this morning, Lady Cynthia.'

'The American lady and gentleman, he come to-day, yes?'

Had we needed reminding, the noises off would have reminded us that they were coming. Overhead, bangs, bumps, the intermittent hum of a suction cleaner, and Mrs. Barnes's coloratura rendering of 'One Fine Day', announced that the empty first floor was being made ready. In her youth, when she had laboured in the basement and lived in the top floor of Number Seven, Mrs. Barnes had had to repress a violent impulse to sing her only song, 'One Fine Day'. Now she over-compensated this early frustration. She had little faith in, indeed she distrusted, the great levelling that had since occurred in the world, and had not allowed it to change her own behaviour in any respect, save this one: she felt, and who could gainsay her, that democracy had liberated her to sing 'One Fine Day' whenever and wherever she wished, and the pent-up song of her girlhood gushed forth in an endless torrent. On this Thursday morning her top note, unbelievably mournful, caused Peggy to howl, a cracked breakfast cup to spring asunder, and Lady Cynthia to start nervously. Racked with foreboding, and tormented by memories of the Commissar, she found a sinister meaning in Mrs. Barnes's dirgelike warning that one fine day somebody would come along.

'I don't think Mrs. Barnes should sing that this morning, of all mornings,' she said, 'it seems like an omen. And I do wish I knew what time they were coming along. It's very awkward. I must help Alistair with the shopping this morning. He's so absent-minded and the shopkeepers unload on him anything they can't get rid of any other way. We've a shelf full of tins of pilchards which we shall never use.'

'Ee, don't you worry, pet, Ah'll use them for clam chowder. They'll never know the difference. The secret's in the flavouring. Ah found such a good recipe in a cookery book I bought. Ah'd look after them myself, if they come while you're away, but Ah've to go out this morning.'

'Oh, have you, Doris? Never mind. Mr. Grame, I don't suppose they *will* come while I'm out, but if they should, and if you should happen to be looking out of the window, will you give Mrs. Barnes your moral support?'

'Leave it to me,' I said. 'Whenever anything happens in Priscilla Grove I'm always looking out of the window.'

In fact, I had no intention of leaving my window until they arrived. It is not every day that something happens in Priscilla Grove, and the odd things that do occur, once in a long while, heighten the charm which its normal uneventfulness has for me. Also, I deserve an occasional respite from my work, and I felt this was the time to take one. So I lit my pipe, leaned my arms on the window-sill, watched the Bloomsburys, Edith and Em Porridge, Lady Cynthia, Alistair and Peggy vanish round the corner, one after another, and waited. There are a Jekyll and a Hyde in all of us; and if Jekyll had resented the successive disturbances, the Hyde in me had much enjoyed the Albanian prince, the Hungarian count and countess, and the Commissar. I felt an agreeable curiosity about the future.

Priscilla Grove that morning looked more than ever like the first scene in an operetta, disclosed by the rise of the curtain. The solid white houses, shining in the sun, seemed ethereal, as if they were painted on a backcloth. The green tubs of geraniums, begonias and nasturtiums, in the little forecourts, might have been stage properties. Mrs. Barnes appeared and knelt on the bottom step below me. On the opposite side of the street old Mrs. Miggins pushed old Mrs. O'Bourke along in her bathchair: 'Street Scene', my mind's eye read from a programme. At one corner a little group of artists, unwontedly early afoot, stood before Number Eleven; at the other a few swarthy Transirians from Number Two appeared to be plotting an assassination. This was the moment when, I thought, as the curtain rose, the artists should advance to the centre of the stage, singing 'We live for our art, in the Quartier Latin'; and then retire, while the assassins advanced, singing '*We* live by the knife, and spaghetti au gratin'.

On to the stage drove a taxi-cab and stopped upstage centre: that is, before Number Seven. From it stepped a woman, who waited on the pavement, tapping her foot. Now, I thought dreamily, I *know* that this is an operetta, or a dream. Everybody else in sight behaved like the members of a chorus. The slouch-brimmed hats at one end, the long-haired heads at the other, all turned towards her, and their owners stood transfixed. The sad music of 'One Fine Day' broke off abruptly, like a rusty knife scraping on a plate, as Mrs. Barnes turned on her step and seemed unable to move. Mrs. Miggins, and with her of course Mrs. O'Bourke, stopped to look. None of them would stir, I thought, until the leading lady, thus entered, had sung the first verse of her song; then all would join in the chorus.

For myself, when I saw her, I nearly gave out that 'phew-whew' which is the soldiers' tribute to beauty. She was superb. She was even the exaggeration of perfection: too lovely, too beautifully dressed, too cold, too oblivious, too disdainful. She was like a film-star overplaying a part, a mannequin over-acting aristocratic poise, or a dressmaker's wax figure imbued with just enough life to move about. She was very dark and, I thought, about eighteen. She wore simple things: a beige linen suit, tan shoes, bag and shirt, and a straw hat; but they were exquisite and she wore them exquisitely. The Jekyll in me grieved, and the Hyde gloated, at the thought of the effect she would have on Lady Cynthia, Lady Bloomsbury and Edith. It was just as well, I thought, she was married.

The little toe went on tapping, as Priscilla Grove stood still. I saw that the foot and the leg to which it belonged were contained in a shoe and a sheer silk stocking which would infuriate every other woman in Priscilla Grove. The small head, on its perfectly moulded marble column, turned languidly from side to side as its owner surveyed the stricken groups of artists and assassins at either corner. Even from that height I could see how long the black eyelashes were, and as I watched they were raised and the gaze of two dark eyes travelled up to meet mine. They held the arrogant indifference of a cat looking at a saucerful of water. The Hyde in me winked. They passed on, as if unseeing. Hyde recoiled, baffled and snarling.

Then the spell that lay over Priscilla Grove suddenly broke, as her companion climbed painfully out of the taxi-cab: Mrs. Barnes rose, the groups at the corners relaxed, the taxi-driver jumped down and began to carry up the steps bags marked in big white letters 'Senator A. A. Vanderboom', and old Mrs. Miggins resumed her arduous journey with old Mrs. O'Bourke. Senator Vanderboom, as he laboriously undid himself, emerged as a tall and portly man in a frock-coat, and I saw, with hilarious apprehension, that he was old enough to be his wife's grandfather. He was sixty-five at the least. He had a florid, beaming face and flowing white hair beneath a hat which, had it grown a little more, would have been a sombrero. Mrs. Barnes waited, cringing affably. The taxi-driver returned and touched his hat. ''Arf a crown, guvnor, please,' he said.

'Ah, and how much is that in your English money?' I heard the Senator say.

'Two and a tanner.'

'H'm, yes. I have only dollar bills. My good woman, perhaps you will pay the driver, until I can change some money. Come, my dear.'

I saw Mrs. Barnes fumble beneath her apron and beauty ascend the steps, followed by the Senator. I judged it time to go downstairs and do the honours. 'One fine day she'll come along', I hummed happily as I went. I rather regretted that impetuous wink.

V

WHEN I arrived the taxi was departing, Mrs. Barnes was coming up the steps, and the Senator and his wife were in the hall. Or rather, he and the hall were behind and around her; she made it and him seem like background. I am an admirer of loveliness in women and consequently perceive first those good points which they are always at pains to lay stress on. By practice, however, I have come to observe almost simultaneously those which they would prefer should pass unnoticed. The thick ankle, the incorrigible little bulge below the belt, the refractory wisp, the prominent tooth, the pallid eyelash, the chubby knee: there is nearly always something to enable their sorrowing sisters to say, 'She's such a lovely girl; isn't it a pity that . . .'

Mrs. Vanderboom (save for her name, I reflected) was shockingly flawless, a provocation to others of her sex. Her lovely throat ran without shadowed hollow into her shoulders; her small waist set off a bosom and thighs that adequately, but not too amply, filled her clothes; her legs, from knee to ankle, were perfectly turned; she moved gracefully and carried her head like a queen. Having noted those essential things, I examined her face. It was heart-shaped, and showed level teeth between parted lips. A slight duskiness lay on her skin, like the bloom on a peach.

Looking at her, I held out my hand to her husband. 'I'm pleased to meet you,' I said, thinking to get that one in first.

'How do you do?' he boomed. I turned to her. 'How do you do?' I said. 'I'm pleased to meet you,' she said, tonelessly. Her hand lay listlessly in mine. I tried to see in her eyes if Hyde's wink were forgiven. I could find neither recognition nor recollection in them; I had seldom felt so non-existent, even in Priscilla Grove. She either was, or pretended to be, a statue. I started as the Senator's voice boomed in my ear.

'Are you Lord Jene?' he asked.

'Er, no,' I said recovering myself. 'Lady Cynthia did not know at what time to expect you and has had to go out, with Mr. Jene. She asked me to see you were made comfortable if you arrived before she could get back.'

'Did you say *Mr.* Jene?'

'Yes. Lady Cynthia has a title in her own right. Her husband is a commoner.'

'Indeed. Is that . . . um . . . usual?'

'Oh, it's quite in order, I assure you.'

'Hm, I trust so. Harold did not make the position clear to us. I should not like to think he had concealed anything from us.'

'You'll want to go to your room,' I broke in. 'Everything is ready. Mrs. Barnes, will you show the way.'

'Yes, sir. Will you follow me, Mum?'

Mrs. Barnes, whose mind was clearly filled with questions, with difficulty tore her eyes from the silent Mrs. Vanderboom and toiled upstairs. The girl passed me as if I were not there; the Senator bowed and followed. I stood a moment, watching, and then went down to the kitchen. I thought I would like to hear Mrs. Barnes's report. After a few minutes she came.

'Everything all right, Mrs. Barnes?' I said.

'I 'ope so, sir,' she said, darkly. 'Lady Cynthia had the one big bedroom ready for them, but they're going into separate ones.'

'Aha!' I said.

'Yes, and if you ask me, sir, it's just as well. I do 'ope Lady Cynthia 'asn't caught another tartar. Do you think they're really married, sir?'

'If they're not, I don't see that separate bedrooms in the same flat are going to make an honest household of us, Mrs. Barnes. But they must be. They're friends of Mr. Harold, and he himself cabled to Lady Cynthia to take the rooms for them.'

'Well, it looks very funny to me, sir. She doesn't speak a word, unless he says something to her, and then it's only "Yes, Senator" and "No, Senator". That's queer, between husband and wife. And he's so old.'

'A young wife and separate bedrooms are the respective privileges of age and youth in America, Mrs. Barnes,' I said. 'There's nothing unusual in that.'

'Well, I do 'ope Lady Cynthia 'asn't fallen into it again,' she said. 'It seems like a case of Crippen and Miss le Neve to me. My 'usband was on the jury in that case, and 'e told me all about it.'

'I don't see the comparison,' I said. 'Miss le Neve was a girl who masqueraded as a boy when she ran away with Mr. Crippen. I feel quite certain that Mrs. Vanderboom is a woman, whether she's Mrs. Vanderboom or not. I don't think I could be mistaken about that, somehow. And isn't she lovely?'

'Lovely she may be, but she gives me the creeps,' said Mrs. Barnes, 'and so does 'e.' She was busy at the cooker. 'I must take up the coffee now, sir. Lady Cynthia said I was to give 'em coffee the moment they came. Oh dear, I'm that agitated.' And in sign that she was, she pressed too hard on the cardboard disk inside the milk bottle she was trying to open and a white column shot up and hit her full in the eye. 'Oh, drat it,' she said, wiping her face with her apron, 'I believe they've brought bad luck in the 'ouse again.'

'Mrs. Barnes,' I said, 'I think I'll go and meet Lady Cynthia on her way home. Perhaps she ought to be prepared. You take them lots of coffee in the meanwhile, and if they vanish into thin air or anything, give me a wink when I come in.'

'Oh, don't sir,' begged Mrs. Barnes.

So I went and waited about at the entrance to Priscilla Grove until Lady Cynthia, Alistair and Peggy approached. When she saw me Lady Cynthia's face paled a little and she quickened her step. 'Have they come?' she said. 'Is everything all right?'

'Yes, they've come,' I said, 'and I'm sure everything's all right.'

'Oh, dear,' she said, 'that means that everything isn't all right. What's happened?'

'Nothing,' I said, 'they just drove up in the usual way, and Mrs. Barnes put them in their rooms and is now plying them with coffee. They're a remarkable couple, an elderly Senator, about seventy. . . .'

'Senator?' said Lady Cynthia. 'Oh dear, how Roman. I hope he's not a Fascist. We've had everything but that, and the Illyrians opposite are so sensitive.'

'To say nothing of the artists down under,' I said, 'but whatever he is I shouldn't think he's that: he looks like the Archangel Gabriel in modern dress. His wife's very young.'

Lady Cynthia stopped and looked accusingly at me. 'How young?' she asked.

'I should think about eighteen,' I said.

'Oh, horrors,' she said, 'and what else?'

'She's extraordinarily beautiful.'

Lady Cynthia groaned. 'I had a presentiment,' she said. 'I knew something terrible would happen.'

'But surely there's nothing terrible about being young and beautiful?'

'It all depends,' said Lady Cynthia darkly. 'Is that the worst?'

'Well, there's just one thing,' I said, 'and I thought I'd better prepare you.'

'Mr. Grame, it's *not* another Trotskyist renegade?'

'No, but Mrs. Barnes thinks perhaps – just possibly, you know – they may not be married.'

'Ooh,' cried Lady Cynthia, 'how could Harold do that to me? Why does she suspect that?'

'Well, the difference in their ages is rather noticeable, even for Americans, and they've taken separate bedrooms. Personally,

I think that's the proof they *are* married, in the circumstances, but Mrs. Barnes has old-fashioned ideas and has decided they are a guilty couple.'

'I had a foreboding about them,' cried Lady Cynthia. 'It's a judgment on me. I should never have persuaded Mr. Barnes to put in that black-market bathtub. I must see what's happening,' and she broke into a run.

I followed more slowly. Behind me I heard Alistair say, 'Arbitration? Nonsense. Send a couple of cruisers and a twenty-four-hour ultimatum, it's the only way to do business with people like that.' Peggy growled. It sounded so much like a comment on Alistair's remark that I looked round. But it was a Transirian, just emerged from Number Two; Peggy does not like Transirians.

VI

WHEN I reached Seven Priscilla Grove Lady Cynthia, with a nonplussed look on her face, was in the hall, talking in whispers to Mrs. Barnes, who carried a tray with a cooling pot of coffee on it.

'What now?' I asked.

'Oh, Mr. Grame,' said Lady Cynthia, 'we don't know what to do. There's a card with "Red Star Line: Do not disturb" hanging on the door of the Senator's room. You don't think he's going to barricade himself in, like the Commissar, do you?'

'Oh no,' I said. 'I suppose they just want to rest after their journey.'

'But what has the Red Star Line to do with it? Is there some sinister meaning in that? I do hope we're not going to have more politics in the house.'

'No, no,' I said, reassuringly. 'I expect he's a snapper-up of unconsidered trifles. Did you try the door? Was it locked?'

'No, I didn't, and Mrs. Barnes didn't, either. We didn't dare. You can't imagine the intimidating effect of that "Do not disturb!" Not even "Please". It makes me feel quite like an intruder in my own house. If I dared I'd take the card away. I'm so afraid the artists will get to hear of it and come singing the Red Flag outside again.'

'I shouldn't worry,' I said, 'they're just lying down, I expect. They'll be down later. I should forget about them until then.'

'If I only could. Mrs. Barnes, does Mrs. Vanderboom wear a wedding ring?'

'Never took 'er gloves off, my lady,' said Mrs. Barnes gloomily. 'I stayed as long as I could, but she kep' 'em on. Just mooned about like a ghost, looking in the mirror and looking at the furniture, and never took 'em off, while I was there.'

Behind us Alistair appeared in the doorway with Lady Bloomsbury, who had caught him up. Courteously murmuring, 'I always said that damned Welsh lawyer would be the ruin of us,' he drifted dreamily past and vanished into the basement. Lady Bloomsbury excitedly joined us.

'Have they come, Cynthia, pet?' she asked.

'Well, I don't know,' said Lady Cynthia doubtfully, looking at me.

'You don't know?'

'Oh, I don't know what to think, Doris. You know I'm superstitious about the first-floor flat. All I know is there's a card with "Don't disturb" on the door. I haven't *seen* anybody.'

'But, Cynthia, loov, you must know if there's somebody there or not!'

'No, I don't. Mr. Grame *says* he saw somebody arrive. . . .'

'Mr. Grame!' said Lady Bloomsbury, looking at me accusingly.

'It's all right, really,' I said, hastily. 'I'm sure I saw somebody. At least, I'm as sure of it as I'm sure of anything that happens in this house.'

'Oh, please, Mr. Grame,' said Lady Cynthia nervously.

'Well, ask Mrs. Barnes, then. She was there.'

'Yes, m'm,' said Mrs. Barnes, 'there's A Couple up there.' She put such meaning into the word couple that Lady Bloomsbury's curiosity became almost frantic.

'You see, Doris,' said Lady Cynthia, 'if they really are there they came while I was out, and I'm so worried. Er, Mrs. Barnes, will you take the coffee down and keep it hot? We don't know when it may be needed.' Mrs. Barnes, who clearly felt there was still much she could contribute to the discussion, reluctantly withdrew. 'Come into the lounge, Doris.'

Lady Bloomsbury was obviously torn between the delightful prospect of being able to console a friend in trouble and the duty to deny that anything in which her Harold had a hand could lead to trouble. She followed Lady Cynthia. I thought I would give them a few moments and strolled upstairs to look round. All was still and on the door to the first-floor flat hung the Senator's warning. I went down again, and into the lounge. In the corner Lady Cynthia and Lady Bloomsbury sat with their heads together.

'Well, Ah think it's all nonsense, Cynthia,' said Lady Bloomsbury loudly, as I came in. 'You're overwrought, that's what it is, what with that Commissar and now Mrs. Barnes getting ideas into her head. Ah'm sure our Harold wouldn't . . .'

'Ssh, Doris,' said Lady Cynthia fearfully, casting her eyes to the ceiling, 'they might *hear*.'

'Our Harold,' continued Lady Bloomsbury, in a whisper, 'wouldn't dream of sending you anybody who wasn't right.'

'But Mr. Grame says he's seventy. Don't you, Mr. Grame?' whispered Lady Cynthia.

'I'd swear to sixty-five,' I whispered.

'And she's only eighteen.'

'Not a day over,' I agreed, softly but firmly.

'Well, what of it? When men pass fifty they'd all keep harems if they could. As they can't, they get married. They're all the same, aren't they, Mr. Grame?'

'Undoubtedly,' said I.

'And what's she like?'

'She's the most beautiful thing I ever saw,' I said, with the air of one anxious to put in a good word and smooth things over, if he could. I perceived, however, that Lady Bloomsbury's reaction, like Lady Cynthia's earlier, was one of immediate hostility. I pondered the queer ways of womenfolk; the lovely young wife above already had two severe critics below, though neither of them had seen her.

'Oh, *is* she?' said Lady Bloomsbury, sharply. 'In that case, perhaps you're right to be on your guard, Cynthia, pet.'

'Merely because she's beautiful?' I asked, artlessly.

'Now, don't start twisting what Ah said, Mr. Grame.'

'I wonder how we can find out if they're married,' said Lady Cynthia, filling and lighting her pipe.

'Well, there's the usual way,' I said, 'you bide your moment and then ask her, "Have you been married *long*, Mrs. Vanderboom?"'

'She'd be ready for that and have her answer pat,' said Lady Bloomsbury.

'Then there's the old-fashioned method,' I said, 'of the direct approach: "Excuse me, but this is a respectable house and I must ask to see your marriage lines".'

'I couldn't do that,' said Lady Cynthia.

'Ee, well, Cynthia, pet, I expect we'll have to be satisfied with a wedding ring, if she wears one.'

'But surely even that wouldn't be conclusive,' I said, 'if she's what you fear she may be. What a pity, Lady Bloomsbury, that Harold isn't here. He could set all Lady Cynthia's fears at rest. I'm sure he must know them well.'

I thought both ladies looked at me rather sharply, as if I had expressed their own thoughts. Or perhaps (who knows?) I put the thought into their heads.

'When is Harold coming back, Doris?' asked Lady Cynthia.

'Ah don't know exactly. Very soon now, Ah believe, perhaps next week or the week after. Ah haven't heard from him lately.'

'Oh, we *shall* have a houseful if he comes next week. Oliver's due on leave then, too.'

The two ladies looked at each other. 'Ee, Ah'm anxious to meet this young lady,' said Lady Bloomsbury, with apparent inconsequence. 'Ah wish our Harold had written to me about her, I mean, about them. Don't you fret yourself, Cynthia, pet. Ah'm certain you've nothing to worry about. We'll just behave as if there was nothing amiss and enjoy ourselves. Ah've thought what to give them this evening. Fried chicken! Ah'm told they just croon with joy when they see fried chicken.'

Lady Cynthia has the palate and stomach of an ostrich and really believes that her Doris is a genius of the kitchen. 'Oh, Doris, how clever of you,' she said happily. 'How did you get the chicken?'

'Ah didn't. Ah could have, if Ah'd been silly enough to pay five shillings a pound for a tough old boiler. Ah got a rabbit from that little man off the Fulham Road. But they'll never know the difference beneath the breadcrumbs. The art's in the cooking.'

VII

AN uneasy feeling of frustrated feminine curiosity hung over Seven Priscilla Grove for the rest of that day. Lady Cynthia, Lady Bloomsbury and Mrs. Barnes (who was Staying On until dinner) lay impatiently in wait, but lunch-time came, and tea-time, and there was not a sound from the first-floor flat. Looking lazily down from my window, as evening approached, I saw Lord Bloomsbury, Em Porridge and Edith turn the corner, one after another, and pass into the house, and let my fancy loose on the still invisible Senator and Mrs. Vanderboom. The Jekyll in me decided that they had dematerialized themselves after hanging out the 'Don't Disturb' card; the Hyde, that they were dead. I heard Em Porridge enter his room on one side of mine and (after an interval during which, I guessed, she had garnered what news there was) Edith arrive and enter the other.

Then, suddenly, a stir ran through the house. There were faint, distant sounds, then mounting footsteps and a knock at my door. I opened it and saw Mrs. Barnes, red-faced and breathing hard from excitement and exertion.

'Mrs. Barnes,' I said, 'what *have* you got on your head?'

'Me cap, sir,' she said.

'But why are you wearing a cap indoors?'

'It's one of them caps we used to wear indoors, sir, and me streamers, too. Lady Cynthia found them in an attic somewhere, and she says it's dress to-night, sir, and will you have a word with her.'

'Dress!'

'Yes, sir.' And Mrs. Barnes, like a frigate under full sail, tacked to starboard and bore down on Edith's room. I went downstairs, past Lady Bloomsbury, who was wrestling with a revoltingly naked rabbit in the kitchen, and into Lady Cynthia's sitting-room. She had a pair of trousers stretched on the table and a large pair of scissors in her hand.

'Oh, Mr. Grame,' she said, 'you must all rally round tonight. Mrs. Barnes just took the coffee up and found the Senator in full evening dress and she had a glimpse of Mrs. Vanderboom apparently getting ready to be presented at Court and dripping with diamonds, and we just can't let them down. You know how feudal these Americans are. We must respect their convictions and make them feel at home. So we're all going to dress.'

'Great Scott,' I said, 'was that why Mrs. Barnes was disguised? But I haven't any evening clothes. I don't think any of us have, except Em Porridge, of course.'

'Oh, we can all manage somehow. Alistair has his 1914 tails. They're as good as new except that the trousers won't meet by six inches, but I'm going to cut a slit at the back, because that won't be seen and they'll meet in front then,' and saying this, she gashed Alistair's trousers down the back seam. 'There!' She stepped back with an admiring air. 'I've a long black silk skirt, very smart, but no suitable upperworks. I'm torn between one of Alistair's dress-shirts, with a lace ruffle, and my squirrel-dyed-ermine bolero, held together at the throat by my diamond clip. That would probably look most recherché. The only trouble is, I'm afraid I might show an inch or two of tum. But from what Mrs. Barnes saw of Mrs. Vanderboom some of us will have to show something if we're to keep our ends up against her. Lady Bloomsbury has something in dove-grey, a giving-away dress she wore at her niece's wedding in 1938, I believe, and when I've finished with Alistair's trousers she's going to cut off the sleeves and shoulders. Lord Bloomsbury has the dress clothes he had to buy second-hand in Covent Garden when he was sent on a mission to Moscow, and I know Edith has a semi-evening frock of some kind. That only leaves you.'

'Oh, if it's like that,' I said, 'count on me. I've my double-breasted blue suit. It's very dark and will pass for black if you don't turn on many lights. I've an only just off-white shirt and collar, and I'll ink out the dots in my blue polka-dot bow tie. Then I'll hide behind Em Porridge as much as I can. I do hope we shan't make the Senator and his lady feel dowdy.'

'Oh no, I don't think so,' said Lady Cynthia. 'Well, hurry along then, Mr. Grame. Oh, and warn Em Porridge, will you?'

I had a little difficulty in making Em Porridge hear (he was listening to Radio Kharkoff) and then, when he did appear at his door, in making him understand. 'Evening dress,' I said, gesticulating. 'Tails. White tie. Abendanzug. Toilette de soirée. Tuxedo. Smockang.'

'Ah,' he said, and a bright light came into his eyes. 'Smockang!'

'Yes,' said I, 'with tails,' and I flapped my hands about behind.

'Aha,' he said, and smiled hugely. 'Gala! Yes, yes. I come.'

The polka dots were slow to dry and he was ready long before I was, as I knew by a sound, like the clashing of cymbals, from his room. It was made by his decorations striking against each other as he revolved before the mirror. At last I was dressed, and knocked on his door. Em Porridge appeared. I had the impression that he was brilliantined from head to foot, suit, shirt and all. He wore an orange order, nine inches broad, across his shirt-front, a diamond eagle on a scarlet ribbon round his collar, four glittering stars on his left breast and one on his right. In him the chivalry of Bulgoslavia found its perfect flower.

Edith emerged from her room at that instant, and Em Porridge, exclaiming 'Beeyutiful,' bowed and kissed her hand. I said nothing, refusing to join the long line of Edith's best friends who had never told her. She wore something which had once been of black velvet, but which now appeared white in the two places, fore and aft, where Edith is most plentiful, and she was tied round the middle with a tarnished silver sash. 'Well, I hear they've come, Mr. Grame,' she said, brightly (Edith is always bright and unless someone warns her will one day be winsome). 'Have you seen her?'

'Her, Edith?' I asked. 'You mean them. Yes, I have seen them. In fact, only Mrs. Barnes and I have seen them.'

'And what do you think of them?'

'Them, Edith,' I said. 'Ah, you mean her. She is unique.' And before she could ask anything more I placed her arm reverently in Em Porridge's and followed them downstairs.

In the lounge a scene of great elegance awaited the Senator and his wife and I felt that they would be agreeably surprised by their first evening in a typical English home. For an instant I was startled by Lady Bloomsbury's *décolleté*; I thought she had perhaps gone too quickly from the skinning of the rabbit to the curtailment of the dove-grey gown, and had used on the second the heavy hand undoubtedly needed for the first; but then I reflected that Mrs. Vanderboom might welcome a little competition, and in Lady Bloomsbury would find a lot. Lady Cynthia had decided on the squirrel-dyed-ermine bolero and I guessed, after a surreptitious glance, that it was fixed to the skirt, and the inch or two of tum thus covered, by a concealed arrangement of safety pins. The total effect was stately, and was enhanced by Lady Cynthia's pipe, which, as I say, surprises only those who do not know her. Alistair was less absent-minded than usual. An anxious expression clouded his face and his hand continually wandered, beneath his coat-tails, to the back of his waist. Lord Bloomsbury looked at Lady Bloomsbury as if he were trying to remember where he had seen her, or perhaps so much of her, before. Em Porridge shone brightest of all, and I kept near to him, hoping that the dazzling radiance he gave off would blind all beholders to my blue suit.

We were grouped round Our Sherry, three bottles of which Lady Cynthia had one day borne home in triumph from the wine merchant in the Brompton Road. The label bore merely the words Sherry (in large letters), Type Wine (in smaller ones) and Made In London (in minute characters). We had all hailed the coming of Our Sherry, drunk from it, and thereafter shunned it, one glass of it having produced the most diverse symptoms in various inmates of Number Seven: Alistair was stricken with an ailment resembling enteric, Em Porridge was left stone deaf for three days, and Peggy, having licked a few drops which spilled on to the parquet, squinted for weeks afterwards. I took the precaution of a mild emetic, and suffered less. My own guess, in the absence of any formula on the label, was that it was a compound of syrup of figs, lime juice and lighter fuel, with a shot of prussic acid.

On the whole, we made a picture of refined luxury which might have pleased the eye of a Gainsborough, and the feeling of almost unendurable feminine suspense which slightly marred its repose was ended by the sound of descending footsteps. The Senator opened the door and held it while his wife passed through. Again there was the tangible pause which had attended her appearance in Priscilla Grove in the morning. She wore an emerald crinoline frock, cut so low that the promise of better things to come, which I had seen earlier in her exquisite throat, was more than fulfilled, and a diamond necklace and earrings. Her black hair was swept up, in the Victorian manner, and cunningly brought out the full shapeliness of her face and head. I noticed again her strangely lifeless expression; she reminded me of the doll in *Tales of Hoffmann*, and I almost expected the Senator, hovering behind, to wind her up. I felt, rather than saw, three pairs of feminine eyes dart towards her left hand; unforgivably it and its companion were covered by elbow-length green gloves. Behind her the Senator loomed bigger and portlier than I had thought; I had never seen so vast an expanse of shirt-front outside clowndom.

Although I had prepared her, this apparition unnerved Lady

Cynthia and she almost forgot to take her pipe out of her mouth as she advanced, tittering slightly and with less than her usual self-command, to do the honours. 'How do you do, how do you do?' she said, pointing to each of us in turn in the manner of an auctioneer, 'Lady Bloomsbury, Miss Wilstan, Lord Bloomsbury, my husband, Em Porridge, Mr. Grame.' The Senator beamed and nodded; his unsmiling wife bowed gravely round the circle. 'I do hope you had a good journey. Will you have a glass of sherry?'

'Ah, thank you, my ladyship,' said the Senator. I beat Alistair to the bottle and poured out several glasses. The ladies all declined, while Alistair, Lord Bloomsbury, Em Porridge and I made pretence of sipping ours, pending an opportunity privily to give it to Lady Cynthia's cactus plants, which had grown an inch after a previous dose. The Senator put his glass to his lips and with a quick movement of his head drained it to the dregs.

'A beautiful dry wine,' he said sonorously. 'I see you English gentlefolk still keep good cellars, my ladyship.'

'Yes, isn't it good?' said Lady Cynthia, delightedly. 'Do have some more. And please call me Cynthia. Everybody does.' I filled the Senator's glass. 'Now, *are* you quite comfortable, and have you everything you want? I just wanted to warn you about the hot water. That brown colour is only coffee.'

'Coffee?' said the Senator.

'Yes, Countess Jerkesy, who had your rooms before, used to make coffee in the water-heater. She had a gipsy band there one evening and I think they all became so nostalgic that they put too much coffee in. You know what the Hungarian aristocracy are for gipsy music and coffee, Senator, ha-ha? I think we've got most of it out now. But I must warn you to turn the heater off *at once* if you find the water doesn't run. That means that the pipe is clogged with coffee grounds and the whole thing will blow up if you don't turn it off. I don't suppose it will happen. We've taken several pounds of coffee grounds out and I don't think there can be enough left to stop it again. I was so glad the Commissar had just left when it blew up last time.'

'The Commissar?'

'Yes, although he really ought to have turned it off before he went. I did warn him. I don't think you should drink the water, unless you particularly like the taste of coffee.' Lady Cynthia's voice was pitched on a higher note than usual and I felt that the memory of past ordeals, and her misgivings about her new guests, were making her slightly hysterical. Glancing aside I saw that Lady Bloomsbury and Edith were feverishly plying Mrs. Vanderboom with small talk; she responded only with monosyllables and inclinations of the head. Em Porridge was drawing nearer to her with tigerish intent in his eye. Lord Bloomsbury and Alistair were edging towards the cactus plants on the window-sill. The Senator drained his glass. I thought I saw his left ear twitch violently. I refilled his glass. He raised it to his lips, then paused.

'One moment, my lady Cynthia,' he said.

'Oh, just Cynthia, please.'

'One moment, Cynthia, Ma'am. What is that?'

All heads turned towards him and we listened, obeying his upraised hand. From below came the unearthly top-note of 'One Fine Day'.

'Oh, that's Mrs. Barnes,' tittered Lady Cynthia nervously.

'Indeed. What a magnificent voice. Is she another of your guests?'

'As a matter of fact, she's my daily woman.'

'A servant? Remarkable. Genius in the scullery.' Another howl ascended to us, and Peggy whimpered. 'What glorious cadences! Is that not superb, my dear?' An automatic movement of a lovely head gave silent assent.

We looked in horror at the Senator. We knew that Our Sherry was potent and incalculable, but had not believed it capable of this. I saw Lord Bloomsbury and Alistair take a stealthy step backwards and with trembling, furtive hands tip the liquid on to the cactus behind them. Em Porridge, who had never entirely recovered from his deafness and did not hear Mrs. Barnes, looked around in perplexity. The Senator drained his glass. There was a tense pause while we waited to see him reel. Nothing happened. Then Lady Cynthia sprang into the breach.

'Now, come along,' she said, 'it's time to eat.'

When we were seated at the big oval table I had cause to be thankful for my plebeian rank which, though it placed me between Lady Bloomsbury and Edith, left me almost face to face with beauty in green. I stared my fill, unashamedly, and again found that, although her eyes sometimes met mine, she seemed unaware of me. Em Porridge, too, as he bent over her from the right, failed to capture her attention, for all his glittering accoutrements. I felt, however, that she turned with a certain trustfulness to Alistair, on her other side, and that with her near him he was less remote from worldly affairs than usual. There was some Algerian wine, red and raw but harmless enough in itself, though it was as dynamite to detonator when added to Our Sherry. He filled her glass and his own and drank.

'Your health, my dear, and welcome,' he said.

'Thank you,' she said, sipping. She did not smile, but looked towards him, I thought, with liking and interest.

'Isn't she lovely?' I murmured to Edith. 'I like Harold's taste in friends.'

'I don't know why you need put it like that,' she said coldly, ignoring my question.

Before I could answer (I confess that I find both Edith and Harold unsympathetic) the creaking and rumbling began and Mrs. Barnes came pounding up the stairs to meet the service lift. She was made nervous from the start by the Senator's ejaculation, 'Ah, here is our singer. Remarkable!' which greeted her; she handed the soup with uneasy mien. She, too, remembered the Commissar. When she was gone the moment came which I had been awaiting. Lady Bloomsbury leaned forward and began the ordeal by question and answer.

'Ee, it's nice to meet friends of our Harold,' she said. 'How was he when you saw him last, mah dear?'

'I think he was very well, Lady Bloomsbury,' answered Mrs.

Vanderboom, uninformatively. It was the first sentence she had uttered and everybody stopped to listen. She spoke with a precise enunciation, as if she had been tutored in elocution, and with hardly any American accent, and again she reminded me of someone: of Eliza in *Pygmalion*, whom an experimenting professor transformed from an aitchless drab into an ornament of high society. I began to wonder about Mrs. Vanderboom's past, and the part the Senator might have played in it. She seemed so much a product, and so noticeably lacked human warmth and spontaneity. I guessed, at random, that she might be from some American small town; that she had come into the Senator's orbit, perhaps, by way of chorus or film-extra parts; and that he had had her expensively 'finished', as elderly husbands sometimes do. She was suspiciously guarded.

'Have you known him long?' persisted Lady Bloomsbury, while Mrs. Barnes removed the soup plates and began to distribute the fried rabbit.

'No, not very long.'

'Ah suppose you have mutual friends in New York?'

I saw that Lady Cynthia and Edith were both straining to hear the answer above the conversation between the Senator and Lord Bloomsbury, but before it came Alistair intervened. His mind had left us again and he said, clearly and charmingly, 'I expect the damned things will go pop all down the back at any moment.'

'Oh no, they won't, Alistair,' called Lady Cynthia, 'I've put a gusset in. Do stop worrying.' Mrs. Vanderboom looked from one to the other in mystification. Lady Bloomsbury, with some impatience, resumed her quest.

'Did you meet Harold through mutual friends?'

'Oh no. We met at a cocktail party.'

'At a cocktail party!' Edith's tone said plainly. 'I knew it.'

'Yes. At the Institute.'

'Ah see,' said Lady Bloomsbury, who obviously did not see. 'Er, the Institute . . .'

'The Institute of Selective Parenthood.'

'Oh. Ah see. Something like our Marriage Advisory Council, Ah suppose, of which Lord Bloomsbury is chairman. But Ah don't think they give cocktail parties. In fact, Ah've always understood they're strongly opposed to alcohol. Are you, er, interested in this Institute?'

'Oh, the Senator is president of it. Aren't you, Senator?'

'What's that, Semmy, my dear? Oh, the Institute. Yes, Lady Bloomsbury, I am its president.' The Senator leaned forward and looked towards Lady Bloomsbury. I had noticed him drink three glasses of Algerian wine and glanced at him apprehensively. I saw with satisfaction, being jealous for Our Sherry, that although his speech was clear his hair was standing on end and he was squinting. One eye was fixed fiercely on Lady Bloomsbury's face and the other on her corsage, and it was impossible to know which was under his control. I saw a blush begin at her plimsoll line and mount upwards until it reached her hair. She gave a little shrug, which was intended unostentatiously to stow her cargo more neatly below decks, but had the opposite effect. In her first fine careless rapture, fresh from the rabbit, she had undoubtedly cut freely at the giving-away dress; it was now giving all too much away. Lady Cynthia, remarking her plight, came to the rescue.

'Lady Bloomsbury was talking about her son, whom you met in New York, Senator.'

'Ah, Lord Biggs. A fine young man.'

'Well, not *Lord* Biggs. The Honourable, if you like.'

'The Honourable Biggs?'

'No, just Mr. Biggs. Actually, everybody calls him Harold.'

'Really? It's very confusing. Is there, ah, any *doubt* about the title?'

'Oh no, it's just the way these things work.'

'Ah! Well, he's a very fine young man, anyway. Of course, his measurements are not as good as they might be . . .'

'His measurements?' said Lord Bloomsbury.

'His measurements?' said Lady Bloomsbury.

'Yes. We are bound to attach great importance to measurements, at the Institute. But I hold that in the long run brain is as important as brawn. Perhaps more important. Breeding, brain, brawn: those are the Institute's three golden rules, aren't they, Semmy?'

'Yes, Senator,' she answered.

There was a baffled silence, broken only by the clatter of plates as Mrs. Barnes removed the remnants of the rabbit. 'What is he talking about?' murmured Edith to me. 'I think it's the sherry,' I whispered. 'I knew it would do the trick. I bet you he'll stand on his head in a moment.'

'Oh don't,' she returned, 'do think of poor Lady Cynthia.'

That lady rushed into the silence again. 'Senator,' she said, with the air of one resolved to be gay at all costs, 'I must tell you, on behalf of us all, how lovely we think Mrs. Vanderboom is.'

For the first time I saw a sign of life in the face opposite me. An expression of surprise passed over it, and the lips shaped themselves to speak. But the Senator spoke first.

'*Mrs.* Vanderboom, Cynthia, Ma'am?' he said. 'You mean *Miss* Vanderboom.' I felt Lady Bloomsbury and Edith tauten.

'Oh, now isn't that silly?' cried Lady Cynthia. 'You know, Senator, I must admit that I just *wondered.* You see, the telegram said Mr. and Mrs. Vanderboom. I suppose it was one of those stupid telegraphic mistakes. Of course, now everything's clear. We thought you were husband and wife. How foolish of us not to guess that you are father and daughter.'

'Miss Vanderboom, Ma'am,' said the Senator, squinting hideously, 'is my ward. The child of my brain, perhaps, but not of my loins. Ha-ha.'

'Loins,' said Lady Cynthia faintly.

'Cynthia,' said Alistair urbanely, 'you're showing your tum.'

'Oh,' said Lady Cynthia, composedly. It was true. The hidden contrivance of safety pins had long since parted (as I and others had observed) and beneath Lady Cynthia's bolero showed a narrow strip of tum. 'I wondered where that shocking draught was coming from. I must pin it up. Excuse me a moment, Senator. Mrs. Barnes, please serve the sweet.'

'Yes, M'm,' said Mrs. Barnes.

But the sweet was never to be served. As Mrs. Barnes took the plates from the lift and turned towards us the hatch-door fell with a guillotine-like clang, pinning her by the streamers. Pulled up abruptly in her progress, two helpings of pink jelly shot from the plates and fell on the floor. Alistair imperturbably rose and went to free her. The hatch-door was stiff; as he bent his weight to shift it there was a sharp rending sound and two sundered trouser legs, in concertina-shape, slid towards his feet. Looking as if this happened to him at every meal, Alistair stooped, hoisted them, and holding one in either hand, with absent-minded dignity left the room. His mien was that of a man whose thoughts were in Poland.

'Oh dear,' exclaimed Mrs. Barnes, tugging at her streamers. Lord Bloomsbury, Em Porridge and I rose to help her, but the Senator, under the invigorating influence of Our Sherry, was first. He stood up briskly. He should not have done. Our Sherry does not allow liberties to be taken with it. I was vividly reminded of a moment I had once experienced in a Canadian forest, when the tree-fellers stood back and a great pine came thundering to the ground. The Senator swayed an instant and then dropped full-length backwards, with a crash that shook the house and, as we afterwards found, brought another pound of coffee-grounds out of the water-heater upstairs. Peggy, who was licking up the jelly, left the room without touching the floor once, as far as I recall, and was discovered later cowering in the coal cellar. The Senator lay as peaceful as a stone Crusader on a tomb, and looked rather like one, save for the squint.

He was a heavy man and by the time we had carried him to his room the evening was irretrievably spoiled. I went up to bed and met Edith on the landing.

'It's a pity the party broke up like that,' I said. 'It was just getting interesting, wasn't it?'

'I'm glad you found it interesting,' she said. 'I thought it was all very mysterious. That's what happens when an inexperienced young man like Harold goes abroad.'

'Edith,' I said, 'what on earth do you mean?'

'Ward!' she said, looking at me with every sign of loathing. 'You men are all alike.' And without another word she went into her room and banged the door.

VIII

THE next day disquieting vibrations filled Number Seven and even reached out into Priscilla Grove. From my window I saw the artists and the assassins gazing expectantly at the house and wondered if this were merely because they wanted another look at Miss Vanderboom or if their instinct told them that some new surprise was brewing within. They had come to expect much of us. Old Mrs. O'Bourke, too, I saw, as she was pushed past in her bathchair, point at Number Seven with her stick and make some remark, accompanied by a mournful shake of the head, to old Mrs. Miggins, who responded with an equally mournful nod.

Inside the house the 'Don't disturb' card was up again and the Senator, abed, was being tended by his ward. Mrs. Barnes, after taking up breakfast, reported that he had a lump on his head as big as a duck's egg, but we did not know if she had in fact seen it, or merely yielded to wishful thinking. When she went out to wash the front steps I saw from my window that suspicion was expressed even by that part of her which she presented to the world when step-washing. She had undertaken for the time being to Oblige every day, ostensibly from devotion to Lady Cynthia, but more probably, I surmised, in the determination to be present when the worst happened and the police arrived to remove those in whom she saw the reincarnation of Dr. Crippen and Miss le Neve.

I worked quietly in my room all day; or rather, I tried to work quietly, for the feeling of arrested crisis in the house was distracting. Edith's very footsteps, as I heard her go out, expressed defiance of and contempt for mankind, particularly, I thought, myself; although I could not imagine what cause I had given her. Em Porridge's gleaming spectacles, turned backwards towards Number Seven as he directed himself towards the Bulgoslav Cultural Society, revealed a more baffled perplexity, at the company and the surroundings in which he found himself, than even Alistair's dark allusions habitually caused in him. Lady Cynthia was busy in the basement ministering to Peggy, who, whimpering quietly in a cushioned basket, was recovering but slowly from hysterics brought on by the shock of the evening before. I saw Lady Cynthia go out once, with anxious face and hurried footsteps, and return soon afterwards, and guessed that she had been to the Brompton Oratory to pray for guidance and intercession. I half expected to see Mr. Barnes arrive and remove the fatal bathtub.

I lunched alone, in an atmosphere of doom, and met no other member of the household until the evening, when I found Lady Cynthia in the lounge before dinner. I wore my blue suit, to be on the safe side, but she was in day clothes.

'Aren't we dressing to-night?' I asked.

'Oh no, I had to stop that,' she said. 'Alistair's trousers are beyond hope, so I crept up and slipped a note under their door. I was very quiet about it. I suppose that wasn't disturbing them, was it?'

'No, I shouldn't think so, if you did it stealthily enough,' I said. 'What did you say?'

'I said, "Dear Senator, we won't dress this evening".'

'Did you! Er, I suppose they won't take that literally, will they?'

'Oh, Mr. Grame, don't. I never thought of that. Well, if they do, we must just pretend not to notice anything, that's all. We can't pander to them in everything. There are limits to hospitality.'

'True,' I said, 'still, I shall be interested to see. I might bring myself not to notice the Senator, but I can't make any promises about Miss Vanderboom.'

Lord and Lady Bloomsbury came in. 'Well, Cynthia pet, how are our new friends to-day?'

'I don't know. I haven't seen them.'

'Tom,' said Lady Bloomsbury, suddenly, 'how do men get wards?'

'Wards? I don't know.'

'Some achieve wards and some have wards thrust upon them,' I said.

'Ah wonder what he meant last night, when he said she was the child of his brain, not of his loins?'

'I wondered what he meant by that,' said Lady Cynthia. 'It sounded so . . . anatomical.'

'Ah wish Mrs. Barnes hadn't got caught up in the service hatch just at that moment. And Ah wish he hadn't fallen down afterwards. Ah was dying to ask him what he meant.'

'But it's so difficult to pursue the subject when an old gentleman starts talking about his loins like that.'

'I don't think I should reopen the matter,' I said. 'It might make him think of loincloths. Lady Cynthia has already put a note under his door telling him not to dress for dinner.'

'I say, Grame, you don't really think . . .' said Lord Bloomsbury, uneasily.

'I don't know. Personally, I'm ready for anything. Lady Cynthia says we must just pretend not to notice anything if they do. You know, carry it off with a quip and a jest.'

'No, I didn't suggest that, Mr. Grame,' said Lady Cynthia firmly. 'Nothing about quips and jests. I just said, pretend not to notice anything, and I'm sure that's the best way.'

'Ah only hope Ah'd be equal to it,' said Lady Bloomsbury. 'Ah've been trying to cultivate an aristocratic calm, ever since we got the title, but Ah don't know if Ah could quite rise to that. Ah never expected to be put to such a test.'

'Oh, there's a famous precedent,' I said, 'and at a royal court, too.'

'Well, I doubt if they'll go that far,' said Lord Bloomsbury judicially. 'If you ask me, he didn't know what he was talking about last night. It was Senator Sherry talking. He was blotto.'

'Anyway, Ah hope they'll come down soon. Ah'm determined to find out what their relationship is, at all costs.'

'Surely his white hairs put him above that suspicion, Lady Bloomsbury,' I said.

'Ah don't see that at all. Most men of that age haven't any hairs at all, and Ah never heard that bald heads are above suspicion.'

'Oh, Doris,' said Lady Cynthia, pulling agitatedly at her before-dinner pipe, 'do you think they're . . .?'

'Ah don't think anything, but Ah might if they hadn't been sent by our Harold. Even so, Ah wish he'd written and told us more about them.'

Edith and Em Porridge came in. Faintly we heard a bell in the basement, and then Mrs. Barnes's footsteps mounting to the first-floor flat.

'We were just talking about wards, in a general way, Edith,' I said.

She gave me another inexplicably hostile look. 'There are some things better not discussed in polite society,' she said.

'Edith! Ah think you should remember that they're our Harold's friends.'

'Well, I know, Lady Bloomsbury, but I think they're very queer, and after all, Harold *is* inexperienced and impressionable.'

'Harold!' said Lord Bloomsbury.

'Harold!' said Lady Bloomsbury.

'Harold!' said Lady Cynthia.

There was a pause, of the kind that attends the birth of an idea. Then we heard Mrs. Barnes's footsteps again and she opened the door.

'They're not coming down to-night, M'm,' she said, with righteous gloom. 'The gentleman's not feeling well enough.'

Lady Bloomsbury gave the 'tut!' of a baffled investigator. We trooped into dinner and I sat down next to Edith. 'I think you've started something,' I murmured to her.

I can never understand the effect I have on Edith. She turned a glance like a stiletto on me and was about to say something when Em Porridge broke in. Leaning across the table towards her, his glasses beaming and his teeth gleaming, he said, 'Pleess, Miss, I am interest for this question. "Polait socaity" – what is he?'

IX

NEXT morning was Saturday and we were a full company at the breakfast table save for the still invisible occupants of the flat above. As Lady Bloomsbury came in she picked up several letters from her plate, thumbed them over rapidly, and extracted one with an exclamation of triumph.

'It's from our Harold!' she said. 'Now we'll see what's what.' Laying the others aside she slit it open, took out the letter and began to read. We all waited expectantly, save Alistair, who broke the silence by saying pleasantly, 'What an ass!' Lady Bloomsbury looked up.

'Who is?' she said, sharply.

'Who is what?'

'Who is an ass?'

'I don't know. Who is?'

'But you said, "What an ass!" I thought you meant Harold.'

'I? I didn't speak. Why should I call Harold an ass?'

'Oh, it's all right, Doris,' called Lady Cynthia, 'it's only Alistair. Do tell us what Harold says.'

'Extraordinary,' murmured Alistair. Lady Bloomsbury returned to the letter. 'He's very well,' she said, 'er . . . hm, yes . . . h'm . . . oh yes, he's very well . . .'

'You said that before, Doris,' said her husband.

'. . . er, he hopes we are all well . . .'

'Yes, yes. What about the Senator?'

'. . . er . . . (turning the page) . . . he's enjoying himself very much . . . lectures a great success . . . a wonderful country, America, but he fears it is reactionary at heart . . . "Have made many good progressive friends, however" – isn't that interesting?

. . . oh, just listen to this, he's coming back on the 29th – why that's next Tuesday, isn't it?'

'Yes, dear, so it is. Isn't that lovely? It will be nice to have him with us again. You'll be back just in time to meet him.' The Bloomsburys were going away for the week-end. 'Er, what does he say about *the Senator*?'

'Er . . . just a moment . . . h'm, h'm . . . no, he doesn't say anything about the Senator.'

'Nothing! How very odd.'

'Oh well, Ah suppose he thought he'd explained everything in the telegram. He's so forgetful. Anyway, he'll be here soon and we can ask him all about it.' Lady Bloomsbury folded the letter, put it in its envelope, and began opening the others. I felt Edith, beside me, relax with the cautious scepticism of a cat as the dog next door passes. I wondered a little about the letter. It seemed to me that Lady Bloomsbury had only read out a very little of what ran to several pages. I thought I might tarry a little over my toast and marmalade. I was right, for when Edith and Em Porridge had departed she took out the letter again and leaned mysteriously towards Lady Cynthia.

'Ah didn't want to read it all in front of Edith, Cynthia, pet,' she said, 'but our Harold does say something about the Senator and Miss Vanderboom, and Ah don't quite know what to make of it. Listen: "I know Lady Cynthia is anxious to have trustworthy tenants for the first floor and I was very glad to be able to send her some really nice people, a Senator Vanderboom and his ward, whom I have come to know here. I very much want you to meet . . ." and there he's written "her" and crossed it out and put "them". "I very much want you to meet them. He's a big man in the Selective Parenthood movement here" – that's right, Cynthia, they mentioned that on Thursday night, didn't they? – "and she's his triumph. She has to be seen to be believed. Of course, the diehards would be shocked at the circumstances of her birth, but our friends of The Movement here regard her as the queen of the progressive cause."' Lady Bloomsbury laid down the letter and looked at us. 'Now what on earth does all that mean?'

'Oh dear,' said Lady Cynthia.

'Is that all he says?' asked Lord Bloomsbury.

'Yes, that's all.'

'I don't like the sound of "queen". I didn't think Harold would pick up American expressions.'

'Ah don't like the sound of any of it. What do you think of it, Mr. Grame? Ah don't mind discussing these matters before you. Writers always seem like doctors to me.'

'I was just marvelling at the intuition of women,' said I. 'Edith spotted it at once.'

'Edith?'

'Yes, don't you remember, last night, how she spoke about Harold? "Inexperienced and impressionable".'

'Doris, I hope the young fool hasn't been making a fool of himself,' said Lord Bloomsbury. 'I didn't like that bit where he crossed out "her" and put "them".'

'I think Edith might put the worst complexion on the piece about Miss Vanderboom being the Senator's "triumph",' I said. 'I wonder what that means?'

'Ee, our Harold's got such a funny way of putting things, sometimes. Ah don't suppose it means anything. But "the circumstances of her birth"; Ah smell trouble there.'

'Oh, I don't suppose that means a thing, dear,' said Lady Cynthia. 'Why, in our family, farther back, every heir was found to be a changeling, or changed for a foundling, or something. It's all too tortuous. I haven't the least idea who I am.'

'Ee, well, there's never been anything like that in *our* family,' said Lady Bloomsbury, grimly, 'and Ah don't think it's respectable. Ah'm frankly worried about Edith. She and Harold are so well-matched. Ah'd pretty well made up my mind to it.'

'I hope you didn't think you'd made up Edith's mind to it, Doris,' said Lord Bloomsbury. 'Have you been raising her hopes?'

'Harold raised her hopes! Didn't he take her twice to Blackpool for the Trade Union Congress? She naturally assumed his intentions were honourable.'

'But after all, we don't *know* that Harold has been caught by this girl, Doris,' said Lady Cynthia, 'and anyway, there's no formal engagement between him and Edith.'

'Ah very much fear Edith thinks there's an understanding. Harold is so impassioned when he talks about collectivization and the aristocratization of the proletariat – it's enough to put ideas into any girl's head.'

'Even that doesn't amount to a formal declaration,' said Lord Bloomsbury. 'Matters may not have gone as far as you think.'

'Ah hope not. Ah was very anxious when they were working together at the Ministry of Information. You know how erotic the atmosphere was there.' Lady Bloomsbury dabbed the eye of a disappointed mother with a handkerchief.

Lady Cynthia tried to soothe her. 'Now, now, Doris,' she said, 'you're probably upsetting yourself for nothing. I don't suppose for a moment there's anything between this girl and Harold. Put your hat on and let's go and have a cup of coffee at Harrods.'

But Lady Bloomsbury was not to be consoled. 'Ah don't think Ah could stand the excitement,' she said rising and hurrying from the room.

X

DURING the week-end, while they awaited the return of Harold, the ladies of Number Seven showed signs of that nervous impatience which attends the search for the lost key to a locked door. Edith wore a martyred look and Lady Bloomsbury, when she left for her visit, a grim one, while Lady Cynthia sharpened the edge of their fears by overplaying the part of the reassuring friend; Peggy, though convalescent, was wan. We saw nothing of the Senator (though Mrs. Barnes, descending with empty trays, brought news that the bump was subsiding) or his ward.

Sunday was especially trying. It was always a quiet day in

Priscilla Grove, but on this Sunday the great heat produced a listless languor in everybody which deterred the artists and the assassins from shaving and caused them to drape themselves over, instead of leaning against the gateposts, balustrades and railings of their houses. From my window, they looked dead, and I wondered lazily if this were the instant before the moment when Priscilla Grove would dissolve like the mirage I half believed it to be. Within the house was a deep hush. Even Mrs. Barnes was silent. She is a deeply religious woman of good, English, Godfearing stock, and does not sing 'One Fine Day' on Sundays.

But on Monday morning all this changed. Even in Priscilla Grove Monday always brings that intangible stir which says that another working week has begun; that, somewhere or other, whether we in Number Seven believe it or not, shops are opening, offices filling, voices speaking into microphones, ears listening at telephones, rehearsals beginning and models disrobing. Before breakfast Mrs. Barnes's coyote-like howling announced that One Fine Day he would come along. At breakfast she told us that the Senator, though asleep, was much better; that he would later get up, and then come down.

The nearness of these coming events produced a glint in the eyes of the ladies at the breakfast table. I could almost hear the buckling of swords and girding of armour, and looked forward with professional zest to the day's battle. When breakfast was over, and I was again in my room, I felt that I should be able to fill no paper and made myself comfortable at my window. I saw, as the morning passed, that the artists and assassins, when they emerged, turned curious glances towards Number Seven. None could have told them that it awaited Harold's return, or that great issues depended on this, yet these choristers seemed to divine that this was but a pause between episodes upstage, to be ended soon by some new incident there, and instinctively fell into their apt groupings.

About eleven o'clock I was startled out of my reverie by the appearance of Miss Vanderboom, who came out of the house and turned towards the corner. I seldom leave Priscilla Grove, for it is my world, and when I do, it is only to assure myself that the outer world is still there; but now I ran downstairs and followed her. When I emerged she was out of sight; when I reached the Brompton Road she was a little ahead of me. She wore a white frock and a big white hat. I saw, again, that she was city-trained; her gait and carriage were perfect. She looked casually at the shop-windows as she passed, then at the Brompton Oratory on the other side. She hesitated; then crossed and went in, and I followed.

Standing by a pillar to one side, I watched her as she knelt, a white figure beneath the lofty dome in the almost empty church. In remote distance, it seemed, priestly shapes moved before the great altar, an invisible acolyte lit tall candles, and hushed voices sang responses. Against the great dim background her lovely, bowed head and profile sprang into sharp relief. After a little while she rose and went out, turned to the left, and paused by a leafy, shady passage. I quickened my step.

'I'd like to show you this,' I said, 'it's worth seeing.' She looked at me without surprise and, I saw, without interest, but she fell into step with me. We went past another church. Behind it were old, indecipherable tombstones, ranged against a mellow brick wall, a circle of great, ancient trees, and, in their centre, a green lawn, with some wooden seats and two children, playing. They and the birds made the only sounds in this quiet place. We had come a hundred yards from the great traffic stream, but two hundred years in time. We sat down, beneath a huge elm, and I turned towards her. I took a long look and for the first time regretted my years.

'Welcome to London,' I said. 'Did you expect anything like this?'

'No,' she said, 'it is so peaceful. There is nothing like this in New York.'

'I saw you come out, and followed. I wanted to talk to you and it didn't look as if I would ever have a chance back there.'

She turned her strangely unlit and impassive look on me. 'I have never been out alone before,' she said.

'What?' For a moment I suspected her of the cheapest kind of coquetry.

'The Senator does not allow me to go out alone. He was asleep, and I came out. He will be very cross.'

'Are you serious?' I asked.

She looked faintly surprised. 'Of course. I am always serious.' She dismissed the subject and looked at the playing children. 'What lovely children those are. I wonder where their mother is.'

I glanced at them. They were self-confident, townbred children; probably, I thought, from the little row of mews-cottages nearby. 'Oh, they're well able to look after themselves. They'll run home when dinner's ready. Do you like children?'

'I would like to have children like those. I would not let them play alone if I were their mother.'

'Your mother must have been very proud of you,' I said.

'I never knew my mother.'

'Oh, I'm sorry. Your father, then?'

'The Senator does not like me to discuss these things,' she said, rising. 'I must go back now. I am sorry. It is lovely here.'

Feeling baffled, I walked beside her in silence. As we turned into Priscilla Grove the Senator and Lady Cynthia were standing outside Number Seven, looking left and right. When they saw us they stiffened with surprise, and as we approached I saw that the Senator's squint, though less, was still with him, a fact I noted for the treatise on the effects of Our Sherry which I was compiling.

'Semmy,' he said, as we approached, 'what is the meaning of this?'

'I hadn't been out for three days,' she said, with the faintest hint of mutiny, 'and you were asleep and it was such a lovely day.'

'This is the first time I have known you disobey me.'

'How could you, Mr. Grame!' said Lady Cynthia.

'Me?' I said, innocently. 'Why, we met in the Brompton

Road.' Lady Cynthia looked unconvinced; she knows that I do not often go out.

'Come with me, my dear,' ordered the Senator. 'I must speak seriously to you about this.'

As they disappeared upstairs Lady Cynthia turned to me; less with reproach, I saw, than with curiosity.

'What is she like?' she almost whispered.

'Absolutely lovely,' I said.

'Tchah,' she said impatiently, 'I know all about that. I mean, what did she tell you?'

'Absolutely nothing.'

'She must have said *something*.'

'Well,' I said candidly, 'the solitary piece of information was that she'd never been out alone before.'

Lady Cynthia looked almost vixenish. 'What!' she exclaimed. 'She said *that*! Poor Lady Bloomsbury.'

'What on earth has that to do with poor Lady Bloomsbury?'

There was another 'Tchah!' of vexation. 'You men are all so stupid. Never been out alone before, indeed!' and Lady Cynthia hastened towards the basement. Halfway down the stairs she stopped and turned. Raising her voice to make herself heard above Mrs. Barnes's top note, which came at that moment, she said, 'I don't believe it was a chance meeting. I believe you took her out.'

'Lady Cynthia!' I said, shocked, and her head disappeared. The top note died away, leaving mournful echoes in the empty hall. Behind me I heard brakes, and turned round. Harold was halfway out of a taxi. For a moment I thought it was an apparition.

'Harold!' I said, going to meet him. 'What a surprise! It's grand to have you back.'

He paused in paying the fare to look at me inquiringly. I had not always shown such happiness in meeting Harold.

'Are you all right?' he said.

'All the better for seeing you,' I said. 'Welcome home. Come in.'

'Well, I'm coming in, aren't I?' he said. 'What on earth's the matter with you?'

'Nothing,' I said, 'nothing at all. Everything's fine.' I reflected that I had never really liked the look of Harold and that he had not improved during absence. His hair seemed thinner on his high forehead, and longer over his collar, than it had been three months before. The fervour of many Causes glistened damply through his pallor. I did not admire his sea-green pullover or his baggy grey trousers or his long thin wrists.

'Come along, Harold,' roared the Hyde in me, slapping him on the back, so that he coughed a little, as the taxi drove away, 'we're all waiting for you. Except your parents, of course.'

'My parents,' he said, 'aren't they here?'

'No, they're away for the week-end. They didn't expect you until the 29th.'

'But this is the 29th.'

'Harold,' I said, 'I hope you'll be more careful about your dates when you come to be Prime Minister and declare war, or peace, or something. This is the 28th. Anyway, all the rest of us are waiting for you. Lady Cynthia and Alistair, and Em Porridge, oh, and Edith, of course.'

'Edith?' he said, vaguely.

'Yes, you haven't forgotten Edith, Harold, have you?'

'Oh, of course, Edith,' he said.

'Why it hasn't been the same house without you,' I said, wringing his hand.

'Is the Senator here, and Miss Vanderboom?' he broke in, taking it away and rubbing it.

'Yes, yes, they're here, too.'

'Grame,' he said, fixing me with pale eyes behind thick lenses, 'isn't she marvellous?'

'Miss Vanderboom? Well, we haven't seen much of her yet. The Senator had a slight accident—just fell and grazed his head, you know—and they've been very much in their rooms.'

'My dear man, you don't need more than one glimpse of Miss Vanderboom to know that she's marvellous. Haven't you any eyes?'

'Now that you mention it, Harold,' I said, reflectively, 'she is rather good-looking.'

'Rather good-looking! She's unique. But there's much more to her than that. She's the living embodiment of Progress.'

'Oh, in that case,' I said, 'she must be unique, of course. I hadn't realized that.'

'Grame,' he said, like a man unable to contain his secret any longer, 'I'm going to marry that girl.' And he wiped his glasses, which become moist when Harold is moved by any strong emotion.

'You are?' I said. 'Really! Do your parents know?'

'Not yet,' he said, 'and I don't want you to say a word until it's announced. They may make difficulties. I'm afraid they live a bit behind the times. . . .'

'Not quite progressive enough?' I suggested.

'Exactly,' he said, 'and there are unusual circumstances.'

'You mean about Miss Vanderboom's birth?'

'Well, yes. How did you know?'

'I think you gave a hint in your letter to your mother, and she wondered. In fact, we all wondered. What *are* the circumstances?'

'They're really quite normal, for a progressive. Or rather, they should be the best possible recommendation, to anybody but a crypto-reactionary. . . .'

'You know, Harold, I'm afraid you will scare your mother if you put the case like that.'

'It may take me a little time to bring them round to my way of thinking, but they won't change my mind, in any case. It's all fixed up between the Senator and me.'

'Between the Senator and you?' I said. 'He didn't mention anything about it.'

'No, I told him not to until I arrived.'

'And what does Miss Vanderboom say about it?'

'She hasn't been told yet. But of course she will do what the Senator says.'

'Will she? Well, that's fine. We *will* be a happy household when the good news is out. I can't say how glad I am to hear it and to see you.'

While Harold struggled with his suitcases I went to my room. The Hyde in me rubbed gleeful hands as I climbed the stairs.

XI

I KNOCKED on Edith's door before dinner that evening, thinking it would be kind to prepare her, if nobody else had done so, for an unexpected meeting with Harold, but there was no answer and I went down. In the lounge I found Lady Cynthia puffing furiously at her pipe, while Alistair read the paper. She looked round nervously as I came in.

'Well, have you learned all you want to know from Harold?' I said.

'Nothing whatever, beyond what he said in his letter,' she answered. 'It's most frustrating. I only saw him for a few minutes and he seemed in a very odd state. He kept babbling about the Senator being a great man and Miss Vanderboom being unique. He hardly seemed to know whom I meant when I said Edith was looking forward to seeing him.'

'I noticed that, too,' I said. 'By the way, did you ask him about the circumstances of Miss Vanderboom's birth?'

'I didn't get a chance. He rushed upstairs and he's been there ever since. I do wish Lady Bloomsbury were here. It's all so mysterious. I have a most unpleasant feeling that something dreadful is going to happen. Oh, here they come.'

The door opened, and the Senator held it while his ward entered. If they had ever misunderstood Lady Cynthia's request not to dress for dinner, Harold had explained it to them. The girl wore an astonishing frock of silver sequin, with a great scarlet flower in her hair. The Senator's pink face was deeply tanned, and I was surprised at this, since he had been indoors since his arrival, until I recalled that there was still a good deal of coffee in his washing-water. On the back of his head a small square of lint was held in place by strips of sticking-plaster. His ward's complexion was unchanged; her room has no water-heater.

'Ah, Cynthia, ma'am,' he said, coming forward like a battleship steaming into action, 'how are you? Good evening, Mr. Jene, sir, and Mr. Grame. Sit here beside Lady Cynthia, my dear. Cynthia, ma'am, may I beg a glass of that excellent sherry we had last night?'

We gasped. 'Last night,' said Lady Cynthia, faintly.

'Yes, do you not remember? Before we went in to dinner.'

'Oh yes, of course. Alistair!' Alistair came reluctantly out of a brown study and went to the sideboard. I made a mental note for my treatise: we had not known that Our Sherry could produce amnesia, but three nights and days had clearly been wiped from the Senator's memory. We watched as he drained his glass and looked longingly at the bottle. I glanced involuntarily at the cactus; it had grown another inch.

'Thank you,' said the Senator, as Alistair, oblivious to optic telegrams from Lady Cynthia, refilled his glass. 'Ah, I regret to learn from our young friend here' (Harold entered as he spoke) 'that Lord and Lady Bloomsbury are away. I had a leetle surprise for them, ha-ha.'

'A surprise?' said Lady Cynthia eagerly. But she was fated to be thwarted in her quest. The Senator drained his second glass and as his head returned to the horizontal she saw that he was squinting again, and squinting, moreover, in the direction of the bottle. She vainly tried to catch Alistair's unseeing eye; like a sleepwalker he moved again towards the Senator's glass. Fortunately, at that moment, Em Porridge came in. She rose brightly and said, 'Ah, here is Em Porridge. I don't think we can wait any longer for Edith, she's very late sometimes. We'll go and eat now.'

Reluctantly the Senator put down his glass, exclaiming, 'A wonderfully smooth wine, smooth as silk. I have fallen among connoisseurs, I see,' and followed her, while his hair began to stand on end. As we sat down I looked curiously across at Harold and Miss Vanderboom. I wondered whether she had by now been informed of her coming happiness, and what she thought about it. I could not catch Harold's eye, which was fastened in surprise on the Senator's mahogany complexion and squint.

I saw, however, that the girl appeared no more aware of Harold than of anyone else and doubted whether she had been told. But in that case, I thought, how could he and the Senator be certain that she would fall in with their plan. Harold was no great catch, surely; unless the Senator had his eye on the title. But the girl's submissiveness remained a mystery. Looking at her, I had an idea: I wondered if hypnotism were the answer. It was a feasible explanation. It would account for her listlessness, her docility, and her mechanical responses when spoken to. If she were under the power of the human eye, I reflected, the Senator would have to go easy with the sherry or lose his victim; he would not be able to practise hypnotism with that squint.

Suddenly I realized, with a pleasant feeling of power, that I knew more than anybody else about what was afoot. I knew that Harold meant to marry her, and besides myself only Harold and the Senator, I guessed, as yet knew that. I knew that Edith was considered by herself and Lady Bloomsbury to be as good (or as bad) as engaged to Harold; the Senator did not know that and Harold seemed never to have realized it. My mind began to play with the possibilities of the plot.

'Now, Senator,' said Lady Cynthia, as the rumblings in the service lift began and Mrs. Barnes entered, 'you were saying something about a surprise.'

'Ah yes,' roared the Senator, 'a leetle surprise.'

I looked hard at Miss Vanderboom, but there was not a flicker of comprehension or complicity in her eye. I was sure that she did not know. Harold was looking at her in fascination, as, indeed, were Em Porridge and Alistair (and so was I).

'Yes, ma'am, an announcement. But you must not press me

now. It is to be a leetle surprise for Lord and Lady Bloomsbury, when they return. I want to make it a gala occasion. I propose that we have a party. You shall all be my guests at the Opera and at supper afterwards.'

'Oh, how exciting! It would be lovely. But I don't know if the Opera is open at this time of year.'

I thought I might put in a helpful word. 'Oh, there's always *something* going on there, Lady Cynthia,' I said, bending forward. 'Last week there was the International Esperantists Rally and the Polar Societies Congress. . . .'

'Pleess,' said Em Porridge, earnestly, 'I am interest for this question. Polar Societies – what is he?'

'Polar, Em Porridge, not Polish. Polar societies concern themselves with celestial poles, not political ones.'

'So!' said Em Porridge, suspiciously, 'he is not political. But how can this be? I am unconscious that there are not-political Poles. . . .'

Leaving him to thrash it out with Harold, I resumed. 'And this week I believe there is the Royal Arsenal Co-operative Society's dance. . . .'

'Splendid, splendid,' cried the Senator, 'a ball! A Crown occasion?'

'Well, let us say a half-crown occasion,' I said, 'and I'm almost sure there is the Basic English League's jamboree.'

'Magnificent,' thundered the Senator, who was busy with the Algerian wine, 'I am a passionate lover of good music. Though I shall always maintain that the United States is the greatest country in the world, I must admit that London is still the metropolis of culture and refined gaiety. Mr. Grame, you understand these things. You might do me the favour to reserve a box for me at the Opera on Tuesday evening.'

'Yes, I might,' I said, thoughtfully.

'You will of course acquaint me of my indebtedness to you.'

'Yes, I will,' I said, firmly.

'And do me the kindness to engage a private room for supper afterwards at the Alhambra.'

'The Alhambra?' I said. 'I fancy it's a picture theatre now, but I think there's a café. They might run us up something appetizing in baked beans.'

'Luscious. Wherever you think best – the Cremorne, the Vauxhall, anywhere, I leave it to you.'

'Thank you,' I said, 'I'm sure I've seen a restaurant in London somewhere. I'll find out.'

'Oh, how delightful,' exclaimed Lady Cynthia. 'I haven't been anywhere since the W.V.S. dance for pen-pals during the war, in the black-out. It was *too* motherly. I shall enjoy myself.'

Alistair had been giving signs of regaining consciousness. Now he spoke. 'Cynthia,' he said, 'I will not put those damned pants on again.'

'No, I'm afraid they're past mending, anyway. But you can wear your grey flannels, dear. Nobody will see them if you're in a box. And you look very nice in the coat.'

'What about supper afterwards?'

'Oh, well, you must just hurry in and sit down at table quickly. I'm sure nobody will notice. Don't *make* difficulties.'

'Well, what about you then? Your tum will show above the table.'

'Oh, I've decided not to wear my ermine. Safety pins are not what they were, and besides, there was such a draught. I shall wear one of your dress-shirts with a little lace at the throat and wrists.'

'If I may say so, Cynthia, ma'am,' shouted the Senator, 'I thought the confection which adorned you last night was extremely elegant. The art of self-revelation without immodesty is one in which, may I say, the ladies of your English nobility are supreme. If you wish to crown beauty with beauty, my ward will gladly lend you a tiara or two.' He paused, swayed a little, and put a hand to his head. 'Ma'am, if you will excuse me I must go to my room an instant. The heat is excessive. I shall be back immediately.'

The Senator drained his fourth glass of Algerian wine and we watched in terror as he stood up. Beads of sweat stood on his brow and he was squinting outwards, instead of inwards, but he did not fall. He strode towards the door and met Edith, who came in at that moment. The Senator stopped and squinted fiercely at her.

'Poor measurements, poor measurements,' he said, 'but plenty of brain. Nothing that couldn't be put right,' and the door closed behind him.

Edith looked at us with indignant surprise, which cleared as she saw Harold. She went towards him with the trustful air which seemed to say 'Oh, you big, wonderful man!' and which once had so inflated him.

'Hullo, Harold,' she said. 'We didn't expect you until Tuesday.'

'Oh, hullo, Edith,' he said aloofly. 'There was some mix-up about the dates. How are you, all right?' and he sat down again. Edith's face clouded as she looked at Miss Vanderboom, sitting next to him. She came round to her own empty place, next to me.

'Your guardian is a very rude old gentleman,' she said spitefully to Miss Vanderboom.

'Edith!' said Harold.

'Oh, Edith, he didn't mean anything. The Senator's not very well,' said Lady Cynthia.

I saw a look of faint but genuine surprise pass over Miss Vanderboom's face. 'Rude?' she said. 'Oh no, the Senator is never rude. He is most polite, always.'

'Well, if you call it polite to look at someone you hardly know and shout "Poor measurements", I don't.'

'But he say you have plenty brain,' urged the maladroit Em Porridge.

'I'm not interested in his opinion of my mental powers.'

Harold rushed in once more. 'You see, Edith,' he said loftily, 'the Senator looks at everybody from a biological point of view....'

'I dare say. All men do that, but they don't say it. He can keep his thoughts to himself.'

Even Miss Vanderboom seemed to be slightly affected by the acerbity around her. 'But you do not understand, Miss Wilstan,' she said graciously, 'the Senator is always like that. It is well known. He was just summing-up your qualifications.'

Edith, with the air of a goaded tigress, slowly put down her knife and fork. She was obviously loading and aiming her retort, and there was an awful hush like that before a great howitzer is fired. In the nick of time, moved by the inherited instinct of many generations of tactful ancestresses, Lady Cynthia hurled herself into the breach.

'Oh, Edith,' she said rapidly, with terrible cheerfulness, 'what-do-you-think-the-Senator-is-taking-us-all-to-the-Opera-to-morrow-night-and-to-supper-afterwards.'

'I shall not be there,' said Edith crisply.

'He-says-he-has-a-little-surprise-for-us-all.'

Edith hesitated and looked towards her. 'A surprise?'

'Yes. I can't think what it is, but isn't it exciting?'

Edith's gaze turned towards Miss Vanderboom and found only tranquil candour in that lady's eyes. It moved to Harold. I do not believe Harold can blush, but he blinked behind his spectacles, and his hand made a nervous movement to his tie. I felt that I was no longer alone in my secret knowledge. Edith now shared it with me. I waited for an explosion.

It came. There was a loud report from above, followed by a thud and lesser noises. Exclaiming, 'Oh bother, the water-heater's blown up again,' Lady Cynthia rushed from the room, followed by Mrs. Barnes. Harold seized the opportunity to go and stand by the door, looking up the stairs, as if this were helpful. We heard agitated voices and hurrying footsteps. After a little while Lady Cynthia and Mrs. Barnes came down again.

'It might have been worse,' said Lady Cynthia. 'The Senator was bathing his forehead, and there was a blowback. There's a lot more coffee on the floor, but fortunately the carpet's brown, and if we wait until it's dry I think we can get most of it up with the Hoover and it will hardly notice.'

'What about the Senator?' I asked.

'Oh, I'm afraid he's got a black eye, and I think he's a bit browner than he was, but he seems quite cheerful.'

'I will go to him,' said Miss Vanderboom listlessly, rising.
'I'll come with you,' said Harold, quickly.

The evening lagged after this, for every word and look of Edith's carried a heavy load of accusation, the greater part of which she distributed between Em Porridge and myself, while she kept a little over for the wondering Lady Cynthia and the oblivious Alistair. Though we were blameless of whatever she suspected, she succeeded in inflicting a heavy feeling of guilt on us: many women have this gift. We broke up early, and I went up the stairs with her.

'I wonder what the surprise is going to be, Edith?' I said, casually.

She stopped and transfixed me with a barbed look. 'I believe you know all about it,' she said.

'I?' I said. 'I know just as much or as little about it as you.'

'You ought to have been a woman, Mr. Grame,' she said. 'You have . . . er . . .'

'A nasty mind,' I prompted her.

'No, a feminine intuition.'

'That's a great compliment.'

'No, it isn't. A feminine intuition is only becoming in women. It's revolting in a man. You . . . er . . .'

'I know too much?'

'Exactly.'

'Well, I think I know *one* thing, Edith,' I said. 'I believe you wish it had been her.'

'Wish what had been whom?'

'I believe you wish the water-heater had blown up on Miss Vanderboom, instead of the Senator.'

'Oh, you're impossible.' And Edith slammed her door. I was going into my room when I remembered something, and went down to the basement, where Mrs. Barnes, having washed up, was putting on her hat to go home.

'Mrs. Barnes,' I said, 'did the Senator pay you that half-crown for the taxicab?'

'No, he didn't,' she said. 'I suppose he'd like us to believe he's forgotten that, too.'

'Thank you, Mrs. Barnes,' I said. 'I just wondered. I'll see you get it.'

As I pulled the clothes round me and turned out the light I thought I heard a sound like a wet hiccough. I listened. I had the impression that Edith was crying, next door.

XII

THE next morning, having given all these strange events a certain amount of thought, I went out and made my way to Harrods; to be more precise, to the theatre-ticket office of that emporium. Behind the counter a pretty girl with a radiantly faraway look in her eyes tapped her teeth with a pencil, and I placed myself humbly before her.

'Do you,' I asked, 'procure seats for the Opera?'

'For Covent Garden?' she said. 'Oh, yes. I'm not sure what's on there now.'

'It's for to-night,' I said.

'To-night,' she echoed, and ran her finger down a list. 'Oh yes, it's the Basic English League's Congress. I believe it's *very* good.'

'Not to be missed?' I inquired.

'The chance of a lifetime, I hear,' she said; she was a trained saleswoman. 'Of course, I expect they're sold out. Would you like me to see if I can get you something?'

'If you could bear to,' I said. 'In point of fact I want a box, a very large box.'

'A box,' she said, doubtfully. 'Are there any boxes at Covent Garden?'

'Of all kinds, I imagine,' I said, 'from orange to stage. Do try.'

She manipulated the dial with her pencil and communed, in

tones of foregone hopelessness, with some distant informant. A look of surprise spread over her face and she turned to me, holding the receiver at the ready.

'It's a free evening,' she said disappointedly. 'You just go in and take a seat. They don't expect to be crowded out.'

'Ah,' I said, 'but I particularly want a box.'

'The gentleman says he particularly wants a box,' she conveyed, and listened to what seemed to be a long and amusing answer. Then, to me, 'She says the congress is only using the floor of the Opera, but she doesn't see why you shouldn't have a box if you really want one. In fact, she says if you care to make a donation to the Opera House Benevolent Fund you can have the Royal box.'

'Put me down for five pounds,' I said.

'Yes, sir,' she said, and then into the receiver, briskly, 'Book Royal box, to-night, Joan. Name, sir?'

'Biggs,' I said, 'the Honourable Harold Biggs.' She put down the receiver, wrote out a ticket and handed it to me.

'Put the five pounds down to my account, will you?' I said (I knew by chance that Harold had one). 'Oh, and will you arrange with your car-hire department for a car to call at Seven Priscilla Grove this evening about seven o'clock? A large car, for a large party. A big Rolls-Royce might do.'

'Certainly, sir,' she said respectfully.

'Then that's that,' I said. 'Good morning.'

When I reached home (after engaging a supper-table at the Ritz by telephone) I looked into the lounge in quest of any news there might be. Lady Cynthia was there, busy with something at the window. She had her back to me and started guiltily as I came in. 'Oh, Mr. Grame,' she said, 'you made me jump. I thought it might be the Senator.'

'Cynthia,' I said sternly, going to her, 'what are you doing? What are you hiding behind your back.'

She brought forth the bottle of Our Sherry. 'I was just going to give it to the cactus,' she said. 'I'm terrified that the Senator will get at it again. I was going to fill the bottle with weak tea, flavoured with ginger-beer. The colour would be right, and they say ginger-beer is slightly alcoholic.'

'You mustn't do that. The shock to the Senator's constitution might be fatal. Besides, this cactus has had enough.'

'Do you think so?' she said. 'It seems to thrive on this sherry. I thought it would be glad of some more. After another bottle I might win first prize with it at the Cactus Show next month.'

'I'm surprised at you, Cynthia,' I said, gravely. 'Safety comes first. Do you want to have blood on your hands? Are you prepared to risk human life for the sake of a first prize at the Cactus Show? This cactus is getting out of hand. I'm almost certain I heard it growl at the Senator last night, as it is. It may be tractable with you, because it knows you, but you should think of others.'

'Well, what should I do?' she said.

'Give me the sherry,' I said. 'I have a use for it. That's right. By the way, it's all fixed for to-night. I've booked the Royal box.'

'The *Royal* Box! Oh dear, then I shall have to borrow one of Miss Vanderboom's tiaras.'

'Better make it two and be on the safe side,' I said, 'and there's a car calling for us at seven o'clock.'

'But all this will cost a fortune.'

'That's all right,' I said, 'it's the Senator's party. By the way how is he this morning?'

'Oh, he's in bed again, trying to get his black eye well in time for to-night. Harold looked in for a moment and told me. He was up there for hours and then he rushed out, saying he had something important to attend to. He seems so conspiratorial since he came back. I wonder what they're brewing up there. You don't think this surprise of the Senator's is going to be anything dreadful, do you?'

'Oh no, probably a pearl necklace apiece for you, Lady Bloomsbury and Edith, or something. You know how Americans love scattering largesse.'

'Well, I'm not so sure. I still have a feeling that I haven't been sufficiently punished for that bathtub.'

Lady Cynthia wandered unhappily towards the basement and I went up to my room, where I decanted the sherry into two hip-pocket flasks which I have picked up at some point in my travels. Then I went down and paused a moment before the 'Don't disturb' card outside the Senator's flat. Yielding to an impulse, I knocked softly. After a moment the door opened. Miss Vanderboom looked at me impassively.

'How is the Senator?' I whispered.

'He is asleep,' she said.

'Then come downstairs. I want to talk to you.'

'Oh no,' she said, 'I cannot do that. You know the Senator does not permit it.'

'The Senator is asleep, the Senator won't know, and blow the Senator,' I said, 'this is very important.' And to test my theory about hypnotism I glared at her fiercely.

For the first time she smiled, very faintly. 'What a funny face you are making,' she said. 'Why do you look like that?'

'Oh, it was just an experiment,' I said; and then, trying another tack, 'I must speak to you. It's about you and Harold.'

This time she showed some interest and seemed undecided. 'About me and Harold?' she said doubtfully. I gently took her hand and drew her out. 'Come on,' I said, softly closing the door. Obediently she came with me. We went into the empty lounge and sat down.

'My dear,' said I, and as I said it I reflected that of all sad words of tongue or pen the saddest are 'My dear', spoken by a man past lover's age to a girl like this, 'my dear, do you know if you are going to marry Harold?'

'Why do you ask?' she said.

'Well,' I said, 'some very odd things have been happening in this house, and some of the oddest since you came. Er, will you do something for me?' I pointed to my right index finger, on which several revolting hairs sprout between knuckle and joint. 'Will you pull one of these hairs out?'

She pulled hard. 'Ouch,' I said, 'thank you. That's all right, I just wanted to be sure that this is all real. Now, do you know if you are going to marry Harold?'

'Yes, I am,' she said, 'the Senator told me so this morning.'

'And what do you think about it?'

'I? I think nothing about it. I must follow my destiny.'

'And why do you think Harold is your destiny?'

'I do not. The Senator does.'

'Do you always do what the Senator says?'

'Of course. The Senator, and the Committee.'

'The Committee?'

'Yes. The Committee of the Institute. The Senator is president.'

'Look here,' I said, 'this is leading us nowhere. Are you fond of Harold?'

'No.'

'Do you like Harold?'

'No.'

'Well, I'm glad about that, anyway,' I said. 'I was beginning to wonder if there was something wrong with me. I didn't see how anybody could like Harold. But Edith does.'

'Miss Wilstan?'

'Yes, that's what I was working up to. I thought you ought to know that there was a sort of understanding between them, when Harold went to America. She certainly considered herself engaged to him.'

'But why do you tell me this? What has it to do with me?'

'Well, I just wondered, since Harold means nothing to you, and he means something to her, whether you ought to marry him. I thought you ought to know the facts.'

'I have told you that it is nothing to do with me,' she said, rising. 'It is the Senator's wish.'

'But what is all this about the Senator and the Committee and the Institute? Why do they decide everything for you?'

'You must ask the Senator,' she said. 'I have told you before he does not like me to talk about these things or to have to explain them. I am going now.' And with that she went.

I am not easily deflected from trying to make everybody in Number Seven happy, and I hung about waiting to waylay Harold on his return. A little later he appeared and I intercepted him as he was about to run upstairs. I examined him with curiosity, trying to find some hidden charm which might induce a girl like Miss Vanderboom to yield to her guardian even in this matter. I failed. From his damp forehead, all the way through his loose clothes to his large feet, he was as unsympathetic as a slug.

'Ah, just a moment, Harold,' I called.

'What is it?' he said. 'I'm in a hurry.'

'Just a word,' I said. 'Come in,' and I led him into the lounge. 'First, I've got it all fixed for to-night. I've booked the Royal box, and a Rolls-Royce to take us all to Covent Garden, and a table at the Ritz afterwards.'

'You have!' he said, staring. 'That's going to cost a lot, isn't it?'

'It is,' I said, cordially, 'but the Senator obviously doesn't want to spare expense.'

'Oh. Well, I must go.'

'Half a second, Harold,' I said. 'There's one other thing. Is the great surprise, by any chance, going to be the announcement of your betrothal?'

'If you must know, it is.'

'I just wondered,' I said, 'if it wouldn't be better to prepare your parents for it first. Is it quite wise to spring it on them like that?'

'Really, Grame,' he said, 'that's my affair. As a matter of fact we've discussed it most carefully, the Senator and I, and we've decided that the best thing *is* to present them with a *fait accompli*. You can't get away from it, they're old-fashioned, although they've been in The Movement so long, and they'll probably make a fuss about the circumstances of Miss Vanderboom's birth.'

'But, for anything's sake,' I said, 'what *are* the circumstances of her birth? You're making everybody frantic with all this mystery. Why do you keep throwing out hints?'

'It's no concern of anybody but Miss Vanderboom and myself,' he said, 'and my parents will be informed after the announcement of our engagement. That will cut short any inquests.'

'Will it?' I said. 'I wonder. There's just one other thing, Harold.'

'Look here,' he said, 'I'm busy. I've been rushing round inquiring about licences and I've got to go and see the Senator.'

'Only a moment,' I said. 'Do you think you are being quite fair to Edith?'

'Edith!' he said. 'What has Edith to do with all this?'

'Well, I feel pretty sure, and your parents also feel, that she thought there was an understanding between you both when you went away.

'Between me and Edith?' he cried. 'Rubbish. What an interfering old busybody you are, Grame. Who put that idea into her head?'

'She thought you did.'

'What nonsense. Why, her measurements are quite impossible,' and he disappeared up the stairs.

I strolled out on to the front steps for a breath of air. Priscilla Grove lay dozing in the noonday sun. It was a lovely day, full with the promise of a glorious evening to come: a perfect evening for the Opera.

XIII

AT seven o'clock that evening Number Seven recaptured the forgotten splendours of the grand houses of London during the great times of the 'nineties. There was that aura around it which, I am told, used to surround Holland House and Lansdowne House on the night of a society ball. The artists and assassins were gathered in full strength outside. Either their sixth sense had told them that some exceptional event again impended at Number Seven, or they had seen the glint of tiaras on every level from the basement to the attic. Lady Cynthia, with the equalitarian instinct of the *grande dame*, had borrowed three from Miss Vanderboom, one each for herself and the other ladies. The Bloomsburys, returned about tea-time, were still agitated from the shock of finding Harold already there and of the surprise party which had been prepared for them. Harold was keeping out of their way, in the pretence of having to get everything ready.

Just before seven we began to foregather in the lounge, under the admiring eye of Mrs. Barnes, who found repeated pretexts to come in and look at us. Lady Bloomsbury had filled in her too-open spaces with a fichu; she and Edith carried their tiaras rather like ladies who are being taught deportment by walking with books on their heads. I wondered a little about these tiaras, which were clearly worth some millions if they were real. However, their sparkle was dazzling. Alistair's grey flannels and Em Porridge's decorations enlivened the otherwise sombre dress of the men; I had re-inked the dots in my blue bow-tie. When Miss Vanderboom, the Senator and Harold joined us we reached resplendence, tempered by taste and dignity. Only in London, and in London nowhere but in Priscilla Grove, I thought with avuncular, almost paternal pride, could anything like this be found.

Miss Vanderboom, in an exquisite white gown, with a coronet on her black hair, was the loveliest creature I had ever seen. I noticed that the other ladies, glumly, shared my opinion; that Alistair became wide awake as he looked at her, and that Em Porridge, who in his undemocratic youth had grown up in a part of Bulgoslavia where the Mahommedan faith still prevailed, salaamed deeply three times.

The Senator was the perfect foil for her. His great size, his mahogany hue, his vast shirtfront, his beplastered head and his black eye all combined to lend emphasis to her delicate grace and beauty. The Bloomsburys, who had not seen him for some days, looked at him with mild surprise. He came in with an expansive smile.

'Ah, Lady Bloomsbury, Lord Bloomsbury,' he said, 'how delightful to have you back with us. Cynthia, ma'am, tell me something. I have heard strange things about these old manorial residences. Is your house by any chance haunted?'

Lady Cynthia jumped. 'Oh!' she said, 'I hope not. It's the only thing I've been spared. Whatever makes you think it might be?'

'An extraordinary occurrence, ma'am. I woke this morning with a black eye. Do you think you might have a poltergeist?'

There was a brief silence, and I made another mental note: total amnesia after *two* glasses. Then Lady Cynthia, with a smile of hideous gaiety, said, 'Oh, I don't think so, Senator. Perhaps you did it in your sleep; these utility pillows are so bumpy.' The Senator looked round thirstily. 'Do have some sherry.'

I filled his glass. The Senator drained Lady Cynthia's cold tea and ginger-beer and staggered. 'Strange,' he said, 'a very raw, crude wine. Surely it is not the one I had before. That was as soft as silk.'

'Oh, it's a new bottle.'

'Ah! You should have warned me. I am not used to these fiery spirits.'

I saw the Rolls-Royce drive up outside. 'Here's the car,' I said. 'I think we should go.'

We went, and there was a deep and reverent hush among the throng outside as we appeared on the steps. The driver took one look and then jumped out to hold the door open for us; he knew quality when he saw it. Lady Cynthia went first. I stopped her as she was about to enter the car.

'Cynthia,' I said, 'the pipe. Chic, of course, but do you think, on this occasion? I believe they have introduced some stupid rule about pipes at the Opera.'

'Oh, sorry,' she said, and knocked it out, absent-mindedly, on the heel of her shoe. All the others followed her into the car. I leaned to the driver. 'Is there interior lighting in this car?' I said. 'Certainly, sir,' he said, and touched a switch. A bright illumination suffused the group behind him. I climbed in. We drove away amid loud cheers, and as we looked back on the waving crowd of artists and assassins I was struck once more by the stage-like air of Priscilla Grove. Our progress through Knightsbridge and Piccadilly was a sensation. It was obvious from the looks and the remarks which accompanied our passing that we brought a long-lacking touch of colour and old-world pageantry into the drab lives of the citizenry. At Piccadilly Circus a flower-seller tossed a bunch of violets through the open window, which the Senator graciously accepted and presented to Lady Bloomsbury, asking Harold to pay the man as he was still without the local currency.

At the Opera House, too, we were received with all the honours. A slightly bored-looking girl in the box office became alert (indeed, she seemed almost alarmed) when she saw us, but appeared at a loss when I asked to be led to our box. 'Jack,' she called to a surprised-looking male attendant who was watching us, 'here's a party wants a box. *Are* there any boxes?'

'I think there are some somewhere,' he said. 'I seem to have heard something of the kind. I'll go and fetch old Joe. He'll know.'

He vanished into the depths of the Opera House and presently returned with a frail old man, whose rheumy eyes lit up with gladness when he saw us. He thought the great days were come again. 'I know where they are, sir,' he quavered proudly. 'They think old Joe's a bit simple, but 'e knows a thing or two that they don't. My memory's all right. I'll show you. You just come with me. Why, I remember . . .'

Mumbling tales of olden glories, he tottered off and led us up great winding staircases and through long, dim corridors. It was very quiet, and we went on tiptoe, out of reverence for the past. After five minutes he stopped before a door, said 'This is it. No, it isn't,' and went on for another minute, eventually coming to a halt before a second door with the words, 'Here we are, ladies and gentlemen.' When we were all inside we heard a cough and, looking round, saw that he had come in too, and was standing near the Senator with clear meaning in his clouded gaze.

'Ah, yes,' said the Senator, 'er, Mr. Grame, have you a coin? I have yet to visit my banker.'

'Oddly,' I said, 'I've only a hundred-pound note. Em Porridge, have you any change?'

'Change? What is he, pleess?'

'Oh, all right, never mind,' I said. 'Lord Bloomsbury . . .'

'Doris,' said Lord Bloomsbury firmly, 'you forgot to put my money in my dress clothes.'

'Yes, Ah did,' said Lady Bloomsbury, with equal firmness.

'Perhaps you, Harold . . .' I said, still more firmly, drawing well away from the old man.

Harold, who had drawn even farther away, came reluctantly back, took out a compartmented purse in pigskin, searched it, and produced a shilling. The old man looked at it lying in his palm, and then raised his palm close to his eyes, as if he knew that they were not trustworthy. Having made sure of the truth, he distributed a bleary look among us all and spoke.

'Toffs!' he said. 'I don't think.' And the door closed behind him.

We all crowded to the front of the box. I had not realized there were so many boxes at the Opera. There seemed to be hundreds of them, all empty save our central one. It was rather like being in the moon, and looking out into immeasurable space. The effect of our appearance resembled that which would be produced if the Koh-i-noor were placed on a large black velvet cushion in an empty shop-window.

The effect we achieved in the Opera was immediate and gratifying. Far away in the nether gloom a number of people, mostly bald, were in the stalls. On the stage, facing them, a line of bald gentlemen sat at a table. In their midst one was standing and appeared to be speaking, though at the great distance it was impossible to be sure. However, as the lights went on in our box and we appeared he looked up, paused uncertainly, and then said something to those on either side of him. They looked up and rose, also. Meanwhile in the auditorium more bald heads had been turning, and now their owners similarly stood up and turned towards us. The central figure on the platform bowed; they all bowed. We bowed back. Then they began to sing.

I listened closely for some time before I could understand what they were singing. I had a feeling that few of the delegates to the Basic English League's Congress spoke English as their native tongue, so that strange accents and intonations obscured the words of their song. After a little time and much concentration, however, I deduced that they were singing the National Anthem in Basic English.

> Divinity salvage the sovereign
> Divinity salvage him, do

was what I understood, though of course I may have been wrong. Presumably because these words did not fit the original melody, they sang them to the tune of 'My Bonnie lies over the Ocean'.

It was a memorable moment, and I congratulated myself on having enabled Miss Vanderboom and the Senator to gain another glimpse of the best side of English life and customs. When the singers had finished they bowed again, we bowed back, and the entire company, including ourselves, sat down. At this moment I felt glad that the box was a box and not a boat, else it would have listed hard over; Miss Vanderboom, in one corner, was in the position of the football in a scrum, the members of which were Lord Bloomsbury, Alistair, Em Porridge, Harold and myself, while the Senator and the other three ladies were left, loosely arranged, in the remaining space. Em Porridge, a much younger man, beat me to the seat next Miss Vanderboom, while Alistair and Harold took firm grips on the back of her chair. Thwarted of my objective, I took the Senator by the sleeve and drew him out of the fray.

'Come with me,' I whispered, and led him into the little retiring-room, where there were chairs, a sofa, table and mirror.

'You mustn't miss this,' I said. 'This is the Royal retiring-room, last used when Queen Caroline had the vapours on seeing Mrs. Fitzherbert in a neighbouring box at the first night of *Gone with the Wind.*'

'Really?' he said. 'Was that so long ago?'

'Oh, longer,' I said, taking one of the flasks out of my hip-pocket and pouring him a glass, 'you know how wind goes.'

'Remarkable,' he said, draining it and looking around. 'I am indebted to you for this privilege, Mr. Grame.'

'Oh no, you're not,' I said. 'It's all in the price of the box. Now, won't you have a glass of sherry?' This was an experiment; I wished to see if *one* glass would produce amnesia.

'I thought I had one,' he said, vaguely.

'Oh no,' I said, 'here it is.'

'Ah, now that's the *old* bottle,' he said, drinking it and looking at me cunningly. 'I can tell it at once. As gentle as a babe it is.' I saw, with the scientist's thrill of fulfilment, that his squint was returning and his hair rising.

'Now we must rejoin the ladies,' I said, and led him back. He went straight to the edge of the box and would have dived over it but that I had hold of his coat-tails and arrested him. He then leaned over, clapped loud and long, and roared, 'Bravo, bravo!' The delegates rose and bowed. I pressed him gently into a seat between Lady Cynthia and Lady Bloomsbury, who were watching with that air of tortured ecstasy which, in the English of all classes, conceals total incomprehension of Art. The figure on the stage appeared still to be speaking, but at our distance no sound broke the deep silence, save a hum of conversation from the other end of the box, where Miss Vanderboom was beleaguered.

'Isn't it nice?' said Lady Cynthia to Lady Bloomsbury.

'Ee, Ah think it's very good indeed,' said Lady Bloomsbury. 'Are you enjoying it, Senator?'

'Magnificently, ma'am, magnificently. Ah, is it not surprising that ours is the only box occupied?'

'It's an old English custom, Senator,' I said. 'Our way of

paying a modest compliment. When distinguished visitors from abroad are here, none venture to seat themselves on the same level.'

'Ah, these grand old customs. Good republican though I am, I confess I have a weakness for the aristocracy of manners. On normal operatic occasions, then, I assume *all* the boxes are filled?'

'No, I think they are then *all* empty,' I said, 'that is another old English custom.'

'May Ah ask what is the name of this opera, Mr. Grame?'

'It's the very latest thing in operas, Lady Bloomsbury, a mixture of the Greek drama, the surrealist and the implicit. Words without Songs, I believe it's called. Most of the singers, as you see, are in the auditorium, not on the stage.'

'Ee, but they're not singing.'

'That's just the point,' I said, 'this is the New Opera.'

'Oh, of course,' said Lady Cynthia.

'Yes, yes, Ah understand,' said Lady Bloomsbury.

'Most interesting, most interesting,' said the Senator.

'But they *did* sing once, Mr. Grame,' said Lady Cynthia.

'That was the opening chorus, to let you know what the opera is about,' I said, 'they won't do that again.' And as I spoke the people on the stage and in the auditorium rose, bowed to us, and went out. For the first time I understood the meaning of the term, splendid isolation.

'Oh, they're going out,' said Lady Cynthia. 'Is it over?'

'By no means,' said I, 'this is the most significant part of the opera; this is the silence that says more than any words – the interval. It is something that was never thought of before. It is called Trottelstein's Theory . . .'

'Trottelstein?' said the Senator.

'The composer,' I said, 'a genius. He is really the Einstein of music. He is the first man to apply the theory of relativity to opera.'

'Er, how *does* it apply?' asked Lady Cynthia.

'In the relation of sound to silence,' I said. 'Trottelstein saw that by increasing the proportion of silence the dimensions and significance of opera could be completely revolutionized. It is odd that no one thought of it before, but then, as you know, all these great discoveries are made by chance. If da Vinci had not seen the apple fall we might never have had the steam-engine. Trottelstein happened to be present at a performance in Milan when the diva was stricken with laryngitis in mid-aria, so that the wider she opened her mouth the deeper the silence became. He immediately saw the enormous possibilities of the thing. I believe his masterpiece, *Geigenschweigen*, is in rehearsal now; it will be performed without artists, orchestra or audience and probably without an opera house and all the leading personages in music have consented not to be there. It will be a unique occasion and I can't tell you how much I am looking forward to not hearing it.'

'A superb conception,' said the Senator, 'for culture one must still come to Europe.'

'Well, hardly that,' I said. 'I believe the first night is not to be at the Metropolitan Opera in New York. Unhappily that will prevent me from not being present at the first non-performance.'

'Oh, I see,' he said. 'In that case, one more distinction is ours. Culture is seeking refuge in the New World.' He stirred, I thought a little restlessly. 'Ah, Mr. Grame, you haven't another glass of that excellent sherry?'

I caught Lady Cynthia's accusing eye on me. 'Sherry,' I said, hastily, 'what sherry?'

'I thought,' he said, vaguely, 'I could have sworn . . . in the retiring-room just now . . .'

'No, no,' I said, firmly, 'that was *last* night, Senator, you remember?'

'Indeed,' he said. 'Ah, then I must do without it.' He rose and stood with his back to the theatre. 'And now my friends, before the opera resumes, I must crave your attention, all of you, for my leetle surprise. The time has come. Semmy, my dear, come here. Harold.'

I saw Lord and Lady Bloomsbury look at him with rising unease as he took his ward and Harold by the hand and stood between them, facing us. We were grouped around them in a half-circle. I could feel Edith unsheath her claws and arch her back, though I did not look at her. Em Porridge looked on with the expression of helpless bewilderment which had become habitual in him since his arrival at Seven Priscilla Grove. Alistair leaned languidly on a chair-back. Lady Cynthia absent-mindedly took her pipe out of her handbag and began to fill it, but there was anxiety in her gaze.

'Lady Bloomsbury, Lord Bloomsbury,' said the Senator, squinting hard and rocking backwards and forwards from heel to toe (whether this was his platform manner or the result of the sherry, I could not guess), 'I have the honour, indeed the privilege, to inform your ladyship and lordship that the Honourable Harold has requested the hand of my ward, Insemnia, in holy wedlock . . .'

'Harold!' said Lady Bloomsbury.

'What!' said Lord Bloomsbury.

'Harold, is this true?'

'Yes, mother, it is.'

'Then Ah'd like to ask why you choose this extraordinary way of telling us?'

'There are Reasons, mother,' said Harold, loftily.

'Reasons! What reasons can there be for behaving to your mother like this?'

'I shall explain . . .' began Harold, when the Senator's booming voice broke in on him. The Senator was rocking violently and seemed to be only dimly aware of what went on around him. His eyes wandered at random (and in two different directions) in space.

'. . . in holy wedlock, ma'am, I said, in holy wedlock. Ah, where was I? Ah yes, in holy wedlock. And I have had the privilege, in fact the honour, of consenting on behalf of my ward. Ah, Lady Bloomsbury, Lord Bloomsbury, this is a great occasion. She is the firstborn of our cause, the predestined mother of a new race of supermen and superwomen. . . .'

Alistair and Em Porridge were quicker than I and just managed to catch the Senator's legs as he rocked himself so violently that he fell backwards out of the box into the huge black void (for at this moment the lights went out). Lord Bloomsbury, Harold and I joined them and took some of the strain, but the Senator was a very heavy man, and it was not until the four ladies came to the rescue by pulling on our coat-tails that we were able to hoist him aboard again. As he slowly came back over the edge the door of the box opened and the old man appeared.

'Ain't you got any 'omes?' he said. 'Everyone else 'as gorn, an' your car's outside blazing with lights like the Lord Mayor's coach, an' 'undreds of people round it. I don't know 'ow you'd ever 'ave got out if I 'adn't come an' fetched yer. Old Joe's the only one left who knows 'is way about this place. They may think I'm a bit soft, but I do know where the Royal box is and that's more than any of 'em can say.'

The Senator, groping with his unruly eyes for the place whence these sounds came, moved past me with the stately grace of a poplar in a high wind. 'Ah,' he said, 'the ancient servitor, the devoted retainer, the confidant of kings. Invaluable man, invaluable. Harold, have you another coin, perhaps? These thousand-dollar bills are an embarrassment. Ladies, come. To the Ritz.'

From the box, the glory departed. Harold fumbled, but not deeply enough, and escaped. I gave the old man a note, and followed. I heard him mutter, behind me, 'Now that's like the old times.'

XIV

OUR reception at the Ritz surprised even me, since I had made no arrangements for our coming to be publicly known and consequently was not prepared for the thunderous ovation we had from a large crowd of men in evening clothes, who carried what seemed to be banners, and were grouped on either side of the main entrance. The Senator, too, was startled.

Is this customary, Mr. Grame?' he said, vainly struggling to undo his squint.

'No,' I said, 'the populace only gives a welcome of this warmth to visitors of the first importance either from Manhattan or Moscow.'

'Remarkable!' he said. 'While I cannot approve of your imperialist policy, I confess I admire some of your British institutions.'

'We do our best,' said I.

As I climbed out of the Rolls-Royce I saw that in fact the deafening cheers had been given in error. There had evidently been a sudden strike of waiters, and this accounted for the evening clothes, which otherwise are rare in London. The banners, on nearer inspection, were picketers' placards, with such injunctions as 'We also wait who only stand and serve', 'We've got to get rid of the Ritz', and 'Waiters of the world, unite!'

Their mistake was natural; I saw at once what had happened. From the elegance of our equipage, our evening clothes, and the quiet magnificence of our attire in general they had assumed that we could only be Socialist Ministers, come, with our ladies, either to show sympathy for their cause, or to lead an assault on the establishment. Miss Vanderboom, in whom, as I gathered from murmured remarks, they thought to recognize the Ministress for Austerity, shared the loudest cheers with her guardian, who by chance bears some resemblance in build and fine raiment to the Minister for Indigence and Travail. When the others had passed, bowing backwards, through the portals I said a few words to the crowd.

'Comrades,' I said, and paused. There was silence, and I realized that few of them understood English. I resumed. 'Mes camarades,' I said. 'Kameraden' (terrific applause) 'wir sind einig mit Euch. Nous sommes d'accord avec vous. Courage, amigos. Der Tag kommt bientôt, sogar pronto, hombres. Zeit wartet auf niemand; warum solltet Ihr? Vive Cyprus et Malta. Banzai!'

A roar of cheering followed me though the doors. Inside I

found my party grouped in a vast, dim and unpeopled hall. Towards us advanced an anxious-looking man in day clothes.

'Ah, Maurice,' I said (I had never seen him before, but all *maîtres d'hôtel* seem to answer to this name).

'I'm not Maurice,' he said. 'Maurice has gone.'

'Guglielmo, then?'

'No, he's gone, too.'

'Well, Siegfried.'

'No, they're all out.'

'Then who are you?' I said.

'I'm the chairman of the board,' he said. 'I couldn't bear to let you down, Mr. Biggs, so I stayed to look after your party. I've got all the iron shutters closed, so I think we'll be all right. I'm afraid the banquet's off and I can't really do your guests justice. I can lay my hands on a few dry biscuits.'

'Excellent,' I said, 'garnish them with a little parsley, and that sort of thing, and I'm sure nobody will notice the difference. Oh, and put out a bottle of sherry.'

'Leave it to me, Mr. Biggs,' he said. 'Of course, there'll be a slight extra charge.'

'Will there?' I said.

'Yes,' he said, 'danger money.'

'Oh, of course,' I said, 'that'll be all right. Put it on the bill.'

'Come this way,' he said, and led us to a large table in the middle of an enormous, and deserted, dining-room. He produced a bottle of sherry and while the others placed themselves ('You sit here, my dear' – 'Oh no, I'll sit *here*, you sit *there*' – 'Oh, perhaps Miss Vanderboom should sit *here*') I poured out a glass apiece, three parts from my flask and one part from the bottle. The soup was delicious, the biscuit having dissolved completely in the hot water, and by the time the next course arrived, covered with parsley, I felt sure that our chief guest, at any rate, would not remark anything unusual.

'The Ritz is noted for its *vol au vent*,' I said, bending over my plate.

'Delicious,' said the Senator, taking a mouthful of parsley and attacking his biscuit fiercely with his knife and fork, so that a large piece shot across the table and spiked itself on one of Em Porridge's decorations. The sherry by this time had produced in all present, save myself, that state of impaired perception which is the most remarkable of its effects. All ate with enjoyment and a silence fell, broken only by sharp sounds as knives cut biscuits, forks attempted to pierce them, and flying fragments found their marks. Then Lady Bloomsbury, with an air of determined happiness, sat back and spoke. Our Sherry never strikes twice in the same place; the visible symptom it produced in her was that she gaily tore off her fichu and mopped her forehead with it.

'Well, mah dear,' she said to Miss Vanderboom, 'Ah suppose Ah'd better call you mah dear now that you're engaged to our Harold. Ah must say Ah think this is a queer way for him to tell his mother and father about it.'

'Well, you know what these Americans are, Doris,' said Lord Bloomsbury, as if none other were present. 'Hup. Pardon.' Though otherwise normal, he was coming out in hiccups.

'No, Ah don't,' said Lady Bloomsbury, grimly. 'Ah'd like to know a lot more. Ah'd like a nice chat with you when we can have a moment together, mah dear. If we ever can have a moment together.' She blew her nose indignantly on her fichu.

'I shall be very glad, if the Senator approves, Lady Bloomsbury,' said Miss Vanderboom. I saw that this extraordinary girl seemed immune to the workings of Our Sherry; she remained as clear, and as lifeless, as a crystal.

'Oh, I'm sure the Senator will agree, mother,' said Harold. He fingered his bow-tie, and when he had finished its hands stood at six o'clock, instead of a quarter to three.

'Ee, Ah should just think he *will* agree,' said Lady Bloomsbury. 'Ah'll see to that. Ah was just telling your ward that Ah'd like a little talk with her, Senator.'

'What's that?' barked the Senator, trying vainly to get Lady Bloomsbury in focus. 'Ah yes, my dear lady, we shall have much to discuss, much to discuss. We must have a leetle conference, to-morrow perhaps.'

'Hup. Pardon,' said Lord Bloomsbury, vacantly. 'Conference? What conference?' The word conference is to Lord Bloomsbury, even when his mind is clouded, as the smell of battle to a war-horse.

'Well, in mah young days the conference came first and the engagement afterwards,' said Lady Bloomsbury. 'Ah think you've picked up some very odd ways in America, Harold.'

Lady Cynthia felt it was time for tact. 'Oh, autres pays, autres mœurs,' she said, sending out a smile like a baited hook in the direction of Miss Vanderboom. 'N'est-ce-pas, er . . .?'

'Je m'appelle Insemnia, madame,' said Miss Vanderboom.

'Comment? Oh bother, I mean, *what* did you say?'

'In-sem-ni-a.'

'Insemnia? What an unusual name. Very pretty. I wonder what its origin is. I always think the study of names such a fascinating subject, don't you?'

'What does it *mean*?' said Edith loudly. We all jumped. Our Sherry had struck in yet another place: Edith's voice had dropped an octave. It came out in a deep bass.

'Good Lord,' said Alistair, like a man startled from sleep. 'Was that you, Edith?'

'Was what me?'

'I thought you said something in a very deep male voice. There must be a ventriloquist among us. Em Porridge, are you pulling our legs?'

'Pleess,' said Em Porridge. He spoke with difficulty because, as I saw, his wide smile had become fixed and he could not get it back; I was a little worried about lockjaw.

Alistair looked at him in alarm. 'What on earth are you making that face for?' he said. 'Is that how you hide the movement of your lips?'

'Pleess,' said Em Porridge, with the corners of his mouth almost touching his ears, 'I do not make him. He is make like theess.'

'Extraordinary,' said Alistair, 'I didn't see any sign of movement.' Had he known, Em Porridge's tautly stretched lips were incapable of any. 'Is it very difficult to learn?' A sound like the booming of a great bell made him shoot round; it was Edith saying, 'Nonsense.' 'There, he's doing it again.'

'He isn't doing it,' said Edith, on the deepest note of the famous drinking song, 'I'm doing it. Will you kindly allow me to speak?'

'But why speak like that?' said Alistair, reasonably.

'Well, why are you talking like that?'

'Like what?' asked Alistair. Though he did not know it, he used a shrill falsetto.

Edith ignored him. 'You were telling us all about the Institute, and your meeting with Insomnia, Harold,' she said, gruffly.

'Insemnia, ma'am,' thundered the Senator, turning his squint towards her, 'Insemnia is the name.'

'Well, Insemnia, then.'

'Yes, come on, Harold. Ah'm still waiting to hear all about it.'

'Well, there's not a lot more to tell, mother,' said Harold, fingering his bow-tie; he seemed to think it was slow and put it forward from six o'clock to ten past eight, 'we just met.'

'Oh, but how did it all *happen*, Harold?' cried Lady Cynthia, deftly patting her hair and giving her tiara a list of forty-five degrees. 'You can't fob us off like that. We want to hear all about the *romance*.'

'Romance!' said a sepulchral voice in disdainful accent.

Not even Our Sherry can thwart Lady Cynthia's tactful impulses. 'Was it love at first sight?' she hurried on.

'*Selection* at first sight, Lady Cynthia,' came in cool tones. We all turned towards Miss Vanderboom.

'Selection,' came the voice from the grave. 'And who selected whom?'

'Oh, the Senator, of course. He selected Harold, after full inquiry and consideration.'

'You see, mother,' explained Harold, correcting his tie to five past seven, 'Insemnia is the firstborn of the Institute, and the whole future of the Cause naturally depends on the choice of a suitable mate for her.'

'Mate! Harold, Ah don't think you need be quite so ... nautical.'

'And the Senator did me the honour of choosing me.'

'The Senator did?'

'Yes, ma'am, I did. A special meeting of the Committee was called at once and unanimously approved. The Committee, of course, is guided by the advice of its president – myself.'

'The customary democratic procedure,' I ventured.

'As you say, Mr. Grame,' said the Senator, beaming at but missing me.

'Ah don't understand a word,' said Lady Bloomsbury. 'Ah don't know whether it's the heat.' She frisked the back of her neck vigorously with her fichu.

'I was just thinking it was a bit hot, Doris,' said Lord Bloomsbury. 'Hup-hup. Pardon! I can't make head or tail of it, either. Now, look here, Harold. ...'

There was an interruption; the next course arrived and I refilled the glasses. I thought I noticed Miss Vanderboom shiver a little when I handed hers to her. 'Are you cold?' I murmured. 'It *is* a little cool in here,' she said casually. 'You *are* human, I suppose?' I whispered. She glanced at me indifferently. 'Naturally,' she said, and drank her sherry without turning a hair. Wondering, I returned to my place. The chairman of the board had excelled himself. The biscuit was done to a turn, I judged that it had been softened in water, then lightly grilled on both sides, and served with bread-sauce and a little greenstuff from one of the floral arrangements in the lounge.

'Is the bird to your taste Senator?' I asked.

'Perfection sir,' he volleyed back.

'Not too high?'

'Simply perfection.'

'Good. Look out for the wishbone, all.'

'Er, what shall I serve to follow?' whispered the chairman.

'Oh, biscuit *glacé*, I think,' I said.

He looked at me with an eye which seemed to convey speechless admiration, nodded, and went away. In the distance I saw him placing small lumps of ice on some more biscuits.

This, I knew, was the critical moment in the life of the party. Everybody was in or past the third glass of sherry, and I calculated that amnesia should be near, if it had not already set in. I looked round the table and saw that, with the exception of Miss Vanderboom, who seemed as unruffled as a boxer before the fight, all present were struggling to remember what it was that they were so curious to know, or reluctant to explain. Lady Bloomsbury, who was beet red, had a determined but baffled look.

'Now, Senator,' she said, 'Ah would like to ask, if Ah may, why you selected our Harold to become engaged to the Institute.'

'Hup,' said Lord Bloomsbury. 'Yes, and there is this mystery about her birth. I would like to know about that, Senator, if you will be so good. Hup. Pardon.'

'Berth, sir,' cried the Senator, 'berth! There is no mystery, Lord Bloomsbury. She had no berth. She had a stateroom, on the *Empress of Poland*.'

Em Porridge turned quickly towards the Senator and spoke, painfully, through his frightful grin.

'Pleess,' he said. 'You say Empress of Poland? But Poland, he is now free and democratic. I am interest for this question. . . .'

Alistair leaned forward and looked closely at Em Porridge's face; indeed, he almost rubbed noses with Em Porridge. 'Fantastic,' said Alistair, 'not a movement of the lips. Do it again.'

Lady Cynthia, I saw with great admiration, was keeping that tight hold on herself which befitted the daughter of a long line of three-bottle ancestors. She was determined not to lose track of the conversation, or to miss any chance of giving it tactful guidance.

'Born in a stateroom,' she said. 'Oh well, if that's all the mystery it's no mystery at all. Good gracious, you should know of some of the things that happened in my family. Stateroom! Why, that's nothing. Stables, stalls, stirrup-rooms – it's all *too* equestrian, my dear. . . .'

If Lady Bloomsbury should ever lie at death's door, which I doubt, the faintest echo of a vulgar allusion will bring her back to life and indignation. Lady Cynthia's remarks pierced the mists which were gathering round her. 'Well, there's been nothing like that in mah family, Cynthia, pet,' she said, 'and Ah'd sooner not hear about it in others.'

'Ladies, ladies, I beg you.' The Senator rose and stood, quite firmly but noticeably aslant, like the leaning tower of Pisa. 'I must remind you that my ward is not accustomed to lewd talk. Insemnia, my dear, you must forget what you have heard. You know what these limeys are.' (The Senator, too, I gathered, was a little overcome). 'Lady Bloomsbury, I am a leetle surprised at you. I should not like to think that the mother of my child, ah, I mean, the mother of my child's husband, that is, the mother of my ward's future husband . . . Ladies and gentlemen, I give you a toast! To Insemnia and Harold, and their children, the supermen and superwomen of the future! To Selective Parenthood!'

'Super bunkum! Selective poppycock!' said a voice that seemed to come from the tomb.

The Senator, thus interrupted, hesitated, blinked, and was lost. As long as he could cling to a train of thought he was safe. Deprived of it, he was as a tightrope walker from under whom the tightrope is suddenly drawn. There is an instant during which he seems able to continue walking without the rope, but that is an illusion. The Senator toppled slowly over. The leaning tower collapsed.

He is, as I have said, a heavy man, and we had to enlist the help of the chairman of the board to carry him to the car. The crowd outside, thinking when we reappeared that their favourite Minister had been murdered within, turned ugly for a moment, and shouted 'A mort! A bas les assassins! Muy cochinado! Schweinerei!' and other such fierce cries, which in this island, from the days of the Tolpuddle Martyrs, have been handed down from martyred father to rebel son. However, I contrived to calm them with a few well-chosen words, telling them that their comrade, the Minister for Indigence and Travail, had merely been tipping his elbow rather too often and had passed out. Not knowing the Cretan or Neapolitan for 'tipping' I used the English word, which happened also to be the only English one they understood, and at the sound of it they broke into frantic applause.

It was now quite dark, so that our illuminated chariot gleamed even more brightly in Piccadilly than it had shone earlier in the evening, and if the people in the streets were fewer, their admiration was greater, as we passed. Lady Cynthia's tiara, having fallen off and been hastily restored, was being worn back to front. Lady Bloomsbury, whose grasp on events was now a little uncertain, was waving her fichu in a way that resembled the first movement in the dance of the seven veils. Em Porridge appeared radiantly happy to all beholders; in fact, he was in great pain from the prolonged and obdurate distension of his mouth.

The Senator was not with us in the flesh; we knew he lived, from his stertorous breathing, but he had the rigidity of death, so that, being unable to bend him and get him into the car, we had strapped him on the roof, hoping that the night air would do him good.

At Number Seven Mrs. Barnes, Peggy (who fled yelping to the basement when she saw us), and a few of our picturesque neighbours still waited to see our return. The sound of cheering accompanied us as, with the help of the driver, we carried the Senator upstairs.

Mrs. Barnes watched us with the gloomily contented mien of foreboding fulfilled. 'I knew it,' she whispered to me. 'It's Crippen all over again.'

I was kept awake for some time by sharp sounds that rose to me from the flat below. 'Hup, hup,' I heard. 'Pardon!'

XV

NEXT day an unusually deep peace filled the house. Indeed, it was more than peace; it was a deathly hush, and had I known Number Seven less well I might have thought that all in it were dead save myself. By an occasional glance from my window I saw that we were still the centre of curiosity and conjecture for the other dwellers in Priscilla Grove, who showed a vulgar tendency to form chattering groups outside. When Mrs. Barnes brought me something on a tray at midday she reported briefly, 'They're all dead to the wide. I don't know what you can have given 'em, Mr. Grame.' It was only in the early afternoon, when I went down to see if I could get a cup of tea, that I heard faint signs of life, and presently the sufferers began to gather in the lounge.

Lady Bloomsbury, carrying smelling salts, was the first, and she was closely followed by Lady Cynthia; a moment later the door opened again and a faint 'Hup. Pardon!' announced Lord Bloomsbury. They were all pale and sank listlessly into chairs.

'Cynthia, pet,' said Lady Bloomsbury, 'Ah don't know what it is, Ah think Tom and Ah must have eaten something that disagreed with us during the week-end. Ah really don't think Ah feel well enough to come to the Opera to-night.'

'No more do I,' said Lord Bloomsbury. 'Hup.'

'That's very funny,' said Lady Cynthia, filling her pipe, looking at it with distaste, and putting it away again, 'I was just thinking the same thing myself. I feel very low, I can't imagine why. I think I shall have to ask the Senator to excuse me.'

'Don't look now,' I said, gently, 'but you've been.'

'Been? Been where?'

'To the Opera. Don't you remember? Last night. We had the most terrific party.'

'Mr. Grame!' Lady Bloomsbury sat upright. 'Is this true?'

'Perfectly.'

'Tom, you must have had too much to drink again.'

'Well, if I did, you must have, Doris. I don't remember a thing. Do you, Cynthia?'

'Nothing whatever. Oh, this is one of Mr. Grame's silly jokes.'

'Then it's in very bad taste. Hup. Pardon!'

'Ah wish you'd stop making that noise, Tom. What are you doing it for?'

'I'm not doing it for anything. I can't help it. I think I must have eaten something.'

'Doris!' Lady Cynthia also sat up sharply. 'I wonder if it's true? I couldn't make out why I was wearing a tiara when I woke up this morning. Mr. Grame, are you joking?'

'No, I'm not,' I said. 'We had a wonderful evening. We went to the Opera first and on to supper at the Ritz afterwards.' And, keeping to the facts in general but embroidering the details, I told them the story of the lost evening. Gradually incredulity gave way to doubt and then to reluctant belief on their faces.

'Well,' said Lord Bloomsbury, when I finished, 'I never heard such an extraordinary thing. Why should three grown people in their right minds be afflicted like this? I hope to goodness they won't get to hear of it at the Ministry. It would never do for me to forget where I'd sent the Air Force to, or something.'

'Doris,' said Lady Cynthia suddenly, 'it's the sort of thing that only Our Sherry could do.'

'Oh, it can't be that,' I said, quickly. 'You gave it all to the cactus yesterday. Don't you remember?'

'Mr. Grame,' Lady Bloomsbury looked at me suspiciously, 'have you told us everything?'

'Everything?'

'Yes. Did we enjoy ourselves? Did we behave ourselves? Did anything particular happen?'

'Oh, you enjoyed yourselves rapturously. You behaved as only the members of this household can behave. The solitary other thing that happened was that the Senator announced Miss Vanderboom's betrothal to Harold.'

'What!'

'To our Harold!'

'Mr. Grame!'

'Yes, he did,' I said firmly.

'Did we give our consent?'

'I'm not quite sure about that. It seemed to be rather taken for granted. You had some difficulty in getting to grips with the subject. Is Harold up?'

'No, he's still asleep. Well, Ah never heard anything to equal it. Ah never expected to wake up and find a stranger wished on to me as my daughter-in-law. Did the Senator explain the mystery of her birth?'

'He said it wasn't a berth. It was a stateroom.'

'Really?' said Lady Cynthia eagerly. 'Is it a secret of state? I adore low life in high places.'

'Cynthia,' said Lady Bloomsbury heavily, 'Ah must ask you not to be loose in your talk about our Harold. Ah don't know whether Ah dreamed it, but Ah could swear Ah had to remind you about that before. You should be thankful that your own child never went to America.'

'Oliver? Oh, he's coming on leave this week.'

'Ah suggest that you should tell him to stay away. Was that *all*, Mr. Grame?'

'Yes, I think so. Oh, the only other detail was that the Senator told us Miss Vanderboom's first name.'

'What, Semmy? Ah always thought it was short for Semiramis.'

'No, it's Insemnia.'

'Insemnia Vanderboom! What a hideous name!'

'That's a funny monniker. Hup. Pardon.'

'Well, whatever she's called, Ah feel Ah'm in a most peculiar position. Ah don't know who she is or what she is or if Ah've given mah consent.'

'Well, for that matter I don't know if I've given mine, Doris.'

'That's different. Men are hopeless in these things. Cynthia, Ah feel as if Ah'd been trying all mah life to find out who this woman is.'

'*Woman*, Lady Bloomsbury!'

'Ah said woman.'

'It's remarkable what malice women can put into the word woman, Grame. It's the most scathing term of abuse they know.'

'That's enough, Tom. Ah wish Ah could think of a worse one. Ah've never felt so thwarted in mah life.'

'I tell you what,' I said, 'I bet the Senator's still out for the count, er, I mean, still asleep. I'll go and bring Miss Vanderboom down, and you can ply her with questions.'

'Ah doubt if she'll come.'

'Leave it to me,' I said, and ran up the stairs. In answer to my knock the girl appeared, cool, indifferent, and lovely in a pale yellow frock with a big green flower at the neck.

'The Senator is still asleep?'

'Yes.'

'Then come down to tea,' I urged.

To my surprise she seemed to want to. There was the faintest note of mutiny in her voice. 'Yes, I think I will,' she said. 'The Senator has forbidden me to go anywhere without him, even downstairs, but he sleeps so much. I shall be imprisoned here for life if this goes on. I never knew him sleep like this before and I am so bored with these rooms.'

I made up her mind for her by taking her hand and drawing her with me again. We went downstairs and into the lounge.

'Here she is,' I said. 'The Senator is very tired, and still asleep.'

'Ah, how nice to have you for a moment at last,' said Lady Cynthia, skilfully piloting the girl to a seat between herself and Lady Bloomsbury, who bridled and paused a moment, in the search for a conversational opening which would not give too much away.

'Well, mah dear,' she said guardedly at last, 'did you enjoy yourself last night?'

'Oh yes, thank you, Lady Bloomsbury, very much. Of course, it was all very strange and different from what I expected, but then I have never been out in the evening before, let alone in a foreign country. It was all most unusual.'

'Ah! Er, what did you find so *unusual*, mah dear?'

'Well, I did not expect we should be the only people at the Opera and at the Ritz, though Mr. Grame explained that, of course. And there was Em Porridge's ventriloquial act, when he made Miss Wilstan talk like a man and Mr. Jene talk like a woman; I thought that was very amusing. But what really surprised me was when we brought the Senator home on top of the car; I did not know that was customary.'

There was a strained pause and three pairs of eyes looked viciously at me; I had not mentioned every trivial incident. Then Lady Bloomsbury resumed.

'I see. Er, you *remember* everything, of course?'

'Of course.'

'I was afraid of that. Hup. Pardon!'

'Tom, do stop making that noise.'

'Why should I not remember everything, Lady Bloomsbury?'

'Oh, naturally you remember everything, mah dear. I was just wondering – it was so hot. Ah, so you and Harold met in New York.'

'Yes, as he told you, at the Institute.'

'H'm, yes. Tell me, mah dear – we have had so little time for a nice chat, since you arrived, and Ah don't *think* we went into matters very deeply last night – tell me all about yourself.'

'But I have.'

'Well, not very much, dear, have you?' put in Lady Cynthia. 'Or have you?'

'All there is to tell.'

'*All?*'

'Yes. What more can I tell you?'

Lady Bloomsbury restrained herself with a great effort, and sought for a new opening. 'Well, for instance, your parents, mah dear. I don't think we touched on that matter last night, or did we?'

'Oh no. We didn't talk about *that*.'

'Ah!' In Lady Bloomsbury's exclamation was the tone of victory bells: now I'm off, she plainly said to us others. 'I was so sorry to hear about your parents, mah dear. You have lost them *both*?'

'No,' said the girl, 'I have not lost them. I never had them.'

'Really!' Lady Bloomsbury seemed to me to assume the grim, grey shape of a destroyer coming in for the kill; I saw the men standing by the torpedo tubes. 'Forgive me if Ah ask you these things, but Harold is my only son and this is all so sudden – were they separated?'

'No. They were never joined.'

'Indeed! Who were . . . er, who *are* they?'

'Ah, I never knew them. You must ask the Senator.'

There was a protracted pause, broken only by 'Hup. Pardon!' from Lord Bloomsbury, while Lady Bloomsbury fought to keep her self-control, covering up the struggle by a long sniff at her smelling-salts. On Lady Cynthia's face was that most agonizing of feminine expressions; the look of a woman who thinks she could quickly get at the truth if she were allowed, but does not feel she is entitled to poach on another's ground. Then Lord Bloomsbury rushed in.

'The Senator!' he said, with overwhelming tact. 'My poor child, are you trying to tell us that the Senator is really . . .'

'No, of course not,' she said.

'Well, then, but who *is*?' burst from Lady Bloomsbury. 'You say you never knew your parents. Either – er, I mean, *neither* of them?'

'But naturally I never knew them,' said Miss Vanderboom.

'*Naturally!* But were they *both* dead before you were born? Oh dear, that couldn't be, of course. Ah'm getting so confused. Had they separated before you were born?'

'They never met,' she said patiently, as if stating the obvious to the unteachable.

'They . . . never . . . met! Mah dear. . . what *is* your name?'

'Insemnia. I am sorry if you do not understand, but I cannot make myself any clearer. It is all quite simple. I have no parents but the Institute. It made me, and gave me my destiny and my mission.'

'Some unusual kind of orphan, Ah suppose,' said Lady Bloomsbury with awful composure (I marvelled that she did not burst and admired her iron will), 'but may Ah ask what you mean by your destiny and your mission?'

'To found a new race of men and women based on scientific selection,' said Insemnia, as if reciting a well-learned part.

'What is all this about?' broke in Lord Bloomsbury impatiently. 'It all sounds like politics to me.'

Lady Cynthia could hold herself no longer. She felt that she held the key; that the right question put in the right way would solve all mysteries.

'Look, dear,' she said, leaning forward and touching the girl's knee, 'I think it's all a little misunderstanding. We're probably not talking about the same thing at all; I expect we're at cross purposes. Perhaps the word parent is one of those which mean something different in America . . . like, er . . . suspenders. Now, when Lady Bloomsbury asks about your parents she means your father and mother. . . .'

At this moment there was a thump upstairs which shook the house. We all knew, without asking, that the Senator had fallen off the bed. Miss Vanderboom rose.

'I must go and see if that has wakened the Senator,' she said. 'I am sorry if you are puzzled. It all seems so clear to me. Perhaps you will ask the Senator.' And she went.

I never knew so dreadful a moment as that, in which we waited for Lady Bloomsbury to go off bang. Trembling, we watched the struggle. Slowly she conquered herself. She was a woman in a million, and I understood how and why her man had become Minister for Jet Propulsion. At last she spoke.

'Ah'll get to the bottom of this,' she said, 'if Ah have to go and dress the Senator and bring him downstairs myself.'

'Oh, Doris, *please* don't do that,' said Lady Cynthia nervously, grasping an occasional table in both hands. She is a firm believer in touching wood.

XVI

AFTER this storm among the teacups I felt that if Lady Bloomsbury's health were not to suffer permanent damage her tormenting uncertainty would need to be quickly ended, and resolved to do what I could to hasten those explanations which alone could reassure her. I am the last man to interfere in the affairs of others, unless I am convinced that I can be of help, in which case nothing can deter me from good deeds. I left the room unobtrusively, went upstairs, and hammered on Harold's door until he opened it. He looked dishevelled and heavy with sleep.

'Harold,' I said, 'I'm worried about your mother. She feels you have treated her badly by not asking her consent before you became engaged to Insemnia.'

'But how does she know about it?' he said, stupidly.

'You told her last night. At the Opera. Or the Senator did.'

'The Opera? What opera? We're going to the opera to-night.'

'Harold,' I said gently, 'you overdid it. Far be it from me to begrudge a young man his wild oats, but you went too far. I only hope the policeman will not trace you to this address.'

'The policeman?'

'The one you debagged in Piccadilly. You should be more careful, Harold; you don't know your own strength.'

'I say,' he said, wildly, 'is this true? What else did I do?'

'That was the worst. Let us leave it at that. After all, there's no use crying over spilt blood.'

'Blood!' he said.

'Well, it was only a little blood, and I don't *think* you killed him,' I said. 'Of course, it's the internal bleeding that's dangerous.'

'Oh dear,' he said, 'who was it?'

'Don't ask me more, Harold,' I said, covering my eyes with my hand. 'Some poor nameless creature of the streets. You said he reminded you of Lenin.'

'*Lenin!*' he said. 'You mean Trotsky.'

'You didn't know what you were saying, Harold,' I explained. 'You clearly *said* Lenin.'

'Goodness gracious,' he said, 'if this gets known I shall be ruined.'

'Don't worry,' I said, 'it won't. Your secret is safe with me. I got you away before you could be recognized. But your mother is our immediate anxiety. You must go to her, Harold. She is in the lounge. Lady Cynthia is looking after her.'

'Oh, dear,' he said, 'all right, I'll come as soon as I'm dressed.'

On the way down I tapped at the Senator's door and Insemnia opened it. 'Ssh,' I whispered, 'I must have a word with the Senator.' With the faintest look of surprise she led me in. The Senator, in a vermilion dressing-gown, was sticking plaster on his face, before a mirror.

'Senator,' I said, 'I would like a word with you. As man to man. You understand?'

'Perfectly, sir,' he said courteously, 'pray proceed.'

'The fact is,' I said, 'that a very curious thing has happened. Your guests of yesterday evening remember hardly anything about the Opera and the Ritz.'

'The Opera?' he said. 'The Ritz?'

'Oh course,' I said, 'you and I remember everything that happened, but frankly I fear the others drank too much. You follow me?'

Clouds of suspicion and doubt chased each other across his face and were followed by a counterfeit of bland comprehension. 'Ah!' he said. 'That is the sure sign of a decadent aristocracy—a weak head. I like a man who knows when he has had enough. Personally, I can take it or leave it alone.'

'Exactly,' I said. 'Well, the trouble is that Lord and Lady Bloomsbury have retained only the most muddled recollection of what you told them about your ward's betrothal to Harold and her origins. They seem to think you said she was born in a stable as the illicit offspring of a Hungarian hussar officer and a milkmaid, and as good Socialists they feel they could not possibly consent to the introduction of any cavalry blood into their family.'

'What, our Insemnia!' he cried. 'Monstrous! I said nothing of the sort.' He paused. 'Er, I *didn't*, did I, Mr. Grame?'

'No, no,' I said, 'but Lady Bloomsbury is much upset, and she is a very delicate woman. She is devoutly religious and the mere mention of the word cavalry offends her deepest convictions. I think you should put matters right. She is in the lounge now.'

'Of course, of course,' he cried. 'I'll be right down. Thank you, Mr. Grame. I shall not forget this.'

'Are you sure?' I said.

'Certainly I am sure,' he said, and then added, as if to himself, 'Hungarian hussar? Why, we never had one on the books.'

Though I was a little puzzled by this remark I forbore to answer and left him. In the lounge I found Lady Bloomsbury, still simmering but just off the boil, with her husband and Lady Cynthia. By dint of small talk in a light vein, which I always believe to be soothing to ladies, I kept her entertained until we heard the sound of descending footsteps and Harold opened the door, holding it for Miss Vanderboom and the Senator to enter. The Senator, looking bronzed and fit, as they say, came in with his arms outstretched in an all-embracing gesture. Then he joined them and rubbed his hands, beaming at us.

'My friends, my friends,' he cried, 'this is a joyful day. What a glorious evening that was! What singing! What food!'

Lady Bloomsbury and Lady Cynthia exchanged the glances of allies in adversity. They saw that the Senator had a long start of them and, remembering his earlier lapses of memory, they looked unhappily surprised to find him so far ahead.

'Lady Bloomsbury,' the Senator continued, 'this is a more than usually happy meeting. I was touched by your delight when you heard of the young people's betrothal.'

There was a wary pause. Then, 'Er, *were* we delighted?' said Lord Bloomsbury, cautiously. 'Hup. Pardon!'

'Tom,' said Lady Bloomsbury, 'stop making that noise. Ah can't bear it.' She fanned herself with her fichu, which I surmised still remained in her hand from the evening before. 'Senator, Ah don't think you're quite right in saying we were delighted. Of course, Harold is old enough to know his own mind, but Ah believe we felt we should have been told more about the circumstances.'

'Mother,' said Harold, in his most objectionable manner (which is that of a man crushing a solitary heckler at a packed meeting of the Friendship With Rusher Society), 'I don't think you should use a feudal tone in these times.'

'Don't talk to your mother like that, Harold,' said Lord Bloomsbury. 'Hup.'

Harold's mouth opened for a further reproof when the Senator intervened. 'Now leave this to me, Harold,' he said. 'You young aristocrats are too impetuous. You must control yourself. Lady Bloomsbury has a perfect right to all information. I thought the matter was fully explained last night, didn't you, my dear?'

'Completely,' said Insemnia, who was sitting between the two ladies.

'But if there is any small detail I can supply, why, of course, I am only too glad. Now, if you are alluding to the circumstances of Insemnia's birth, Lady Bloomsbury, I must make it plain to you, ma'am, that there is no truth whatever in the story of the Hungarian hussar.'

'Hussar?'

'Yes, ma'am. Not a word of truth. I don't know,' proceeded the Senator warmly, 'who puts these rumours about. The villain, whoever he may be, should be prosecuted. There was *no* Hungarian hussar, ma'am.'

'Ah,' said Lady Bloomsbury, uncertainly, 'well, Ah'm relieved to hear that, Ah suppose.'

'Yes, ma'am. Indeed, I can give you the fullest assurance that there is no cavalry strain whatever in Insemnia's blood.'

'You see, mother,' said Harold, reproachfully.

'You see, Doris,' said Lady Cynthia, 'I knew everything would be all right.'

Lady Bloomsbury looked as if she were in danger of suffocation. Lord Bloomsbury laboriously made his way into the discussion, with the air of a committee-chairman used to reducing tangled debates to a brief, clear and simple issue. 'I think what we're really trying to get at is this, Senator,' he said. 'Hup. Pardon! We don't want to be unreasonable, but we feel it would be interesting to know a little *more* about the circumstances of Insemnia's birth.'

'My dear sir, of course, of course. I merely thought I had explained that fully. Am I not right, Mr. Grame?'

'Certainly,' I said. Three pairs of self-distrustful eyes turned towards me.

'And, I must say, I thought Insemnia would by now have explained the matter herself. Why didn't you, my dear?'

'But I did,' she said, distantly.

'And you, too, Harold. I think you owed it to Lady Bloomsbury and Lord Bloomsbury to tell them all.'

'But I have.'

'Ah, I thought so. Never mind, let us state the facts again. There's no harm in repetition; the important thing is to make everything quite clear. Insemnia, Lady Bloomsbury, ma'am, is the firstborn of our Institute. . . .'

Lady Bloomsbury broke in with a worried look. 'That's very odd,' she said. 'Ah've heard those words somewhere before. Ah think Ah must have read them in a book or something.'

'That's funny. I seem to remember them, too,' said Lady Cynthia. 'I wonder if they were in that book by James Joyce I lent you, Doris?'

'Ah didn't read that book,' said Lady Bloomsbury firmly, 'so they weren't in that.'

Lord Bloomsbury, taking a firm hold on himself, made another effort. 'Senator, I hope this isn't asking too much,' he said, and then he turned to Insemnia, 'Forgive me, my dear, if we talk across you, but the Senator seems to know so much more about you than you do. Senator, do you think . . . er, could you tell us who were *Insemnia's parents*?'

'Ah do not expect to be listened to,' said Lady Bloomsbury, 'but Ah ought to warn you, Tom, that it is quite impossible to gain any information on this point. Insemnia herself told me she had had no parents. Ah am still trying to account for her presence here.'

'No, I did not say that,' intervened Insemnia indifferently. 'I explained everything clearly. I do not know why I am not understood when I speak.'

'Perhaps it's the language difficulty,' I suggested. 'It always was a barrier between the English-speaking peoples.'

'That's not funny, Grame. Mother, I think you are being most unreasonable.'

'Harold, I've told you before not to speak to your mother like that. You must have a little more consideration for her.'

'A little *more* consideration,' said Lady Bloomsbury in stifled tones. 'Ah pray Ah may have patience.'

'Harold, please leave this to me. I am disappointed in you. Lady Bloomsbury, I apologize. If in spite of my efforts there is still some small doubt in your mind, let me go over it all again. Insemnia's father, ma'am, was a French prizefighter . . .'

'Ee,' said Lady Bloomsbury.

'. . . who was chosen for his measurements.'

'His measurements!'

The Senator paused while Insemnia yawned, daintily. For some reason we all watched in fascination. The archer's bow, which her lips formed, was pulled full stretch; then, the shaft of boredom dispatched, the bow reappeared. The Senator coughed.

'Ah, where was I? Ah yes, his measurements. Yes, ma'am, for his measurements. You see, Insemnia's mother was adamant about his measurements. She made it a condition of her great sacrifice for our Cause that the father, whom she would never see, of the child she would never know, should have the measurements of the Apollo Belvedere.'

There was a pause, while blank incomprehension filled Lady Bloomsbury's, Lady Cynthia's and Lord Bloomsbury's eyes, like water being poured into six glasses. I thought I would keep the conversation going with a helping hand. 'But if your Cause sets such a high physical standard,' I said, 'where does Harold come in?'

Harold turned on me with unusual warmth. 'There are *other* qualifications,' he said, 'muscle isn't everything.'

'Exactly,' said the Senator, 'in the second generation, Lady Bloomsbury, the Committee places the emphasis on intellect and birth, not physique.'

'So now you understand, mother,' said Harold, 'the honour which I was paid by the Committee.'

'Of which,' the Senator added quickly, 'I am the president.'

Once more Lady Bloomsbury fought her battle and won. 'Ah hope Ah'm not dense,' she said in a strangled voice. 'Ah always thought that was a common fallacy about women, but Ah begin to have mah doubts. Ah just don't know what you're all talking about.'

'Really, mother, this is intolerable.'

'Harold, Ah warn you!'

'Harold, I don't want to have to tell you again not to speak to your mother like that. Senator,' said Lord Bloomsbury, with the irritability of a much-baffled man, 'I hope I'm not, hup, pardon, hard of understanding, but it is a fact that there is a good deal of difference in the English language as spoken on both sides of the Atlantic; I've noticed it in the pictures. Sometimes I miss whole sentences. Why, only the other day,' he continued with a reminiscent look, 'at Forever Amber . . .'

'Tom! There's bits that you ought not to understand in any language.'

'Oh, ah, h'm, well, what I mean, Senator,' said Lord Bloomsbury, enunciating his words very slowly and distinctly, 'Can . . . you . . . tell . . . us . . . who . . . is . . . er, was . . . Insemnia's . . . mother?'

'Ah yes, indeed, sir. A wonderful woman, a wonderful woman. I was much reminded of her by the glorious singing we heard last night. She was a famous opera singer, an American lady of the Jewish community . . .'

'Ee,' said Lady Bloomsbury.

'. . . who was filled with a noble belief in her mission to mankind. Insemnia,' he added reverently, 'is her offering to the future of the human race. Aren't you, Insemnia?'

'Yes, Senator.'

'There's a progressive for you,' said Harold. 'Now in Soviet Rusher . . .'

'Oh, please, Harold,' said Lady Cynthia, 'you know how superstitious I am,' and she reached out and touched the wood of the occasional table.

'And is Insemnia's father dead?' asked Lord Bloomsbury, feigning comprehension.

'Unfortunately, sir, yes. He died of overstrain.'

'Ah. Caused by prizefighting, I suppose?'

'No, Lord Bloomsbury, he was a martyr to our Cause. The Institute – that is to say, of course, the Committee, at my recommendation – posthumously awarded him its Order of Merit, First Class.'

At this point Insemnia yawned again. It had the same hypnotic effect on all of us as the first yawn. When she finished there was a perceptible pause while we gathered our wits.

'Ah do not wish to be indecently inquisitive, Harold,' then said Lady Bloomsbury resolutely, 'but have you yet met your future mother – Ah mean, mother-in-law?'

'Insemnia's mother, ma'am,' said the Senator mournfully, 'died tragically in Philadelphia many years ago. I fear she was herself to blame. She broke with the traditions of her profession by taking a curtain call in an interval and failed to notice that the descending curtain was the iron safety one, not the plush. I hope we need not discuss her further just now. The thought of her end always upsets Insemnia. Doesn't it, Insemnia?'

'Yes, Senator,' she answered automatically.

We were fated – or perhaps I should say Lord and Lady Bloomsbury were fated, for after all it was no concern of mine – to suffer many interruptions in the quest for the facts about Insemnia. At this moment Edith and Em Porridge entered. Edith said, 'Hullo' in a voice which, though it was higher than it had been, was still deep enough to make those jump who had forgotten the banquet at the Ritz. Em Porridge was unlucky enough to knock the last spar from beneath Lady Bloomsbury's tottering self-control. Though the corners of his mouth had retreated a little from his ears, his smile was still unusually wide, and a little unnerving to those who had not met it (or did not recall meeting it) before. With his usual politeness he advanced towards the senior lady present, bowed, and grinned horribly at her. Lady Bloomsbury, already much confused, thought he was delighting in her misfortunes. It was a natural mistake; none among us had seen such mirth before.

'Ah don't see what there is to laugh at, Em Porridge,' said the overwrought lady, in tones of trembling indignation. 'Cynthia, Ah must go to mah room. Ah've had enoof for now.'

Em Porridge looked after her as she swept tremulously out. He could not show surprise, poor fellow, however much he felt, and he must have felt some, knowing as little as he did of what was going on – for his deafness, too, had recurred. Lord Bloomsbury, saying to Harold, 'Now you see what you've done!' pursued his wife. Harold and the Senator, on propitiation bent, hurried after him; Insemnia, with an air of crushing ennui, followed them.

Lady Cynthia took out her pipe and looked helplessly at me. 'Oh dear, that bathtub,' she said. 'I know now just how the Lady of Shalott felt when the mirror cracked from side to side. What *is* it all about, Mr. Grame?'

'If you ask me,' I said, 'the clue's in the name.'

'The name?'

'Yes. Insemnia. Artificial insemination.'

'Artificial insemination. But what has all this to do with drowning?'

'Try the dictionary,' I suggested.

'But I can never understand dictionaries. They always say, see something else. And when I look at something else they say see something different. Oh dear, I suppose I ought to run up and tell poor Lady Bloomsbury what you say.'

I was left with Edith and Em Porridge. Peggy, who had not ventured upstairs from the basement for some days, put her head round the door to see if a dog's life could be called its own again. The first thing she saw was Em Porridge, with all his teeth, and much of their gums, bared in what must have seemed to her a snarl of death. She returned rapidly to the basement. The shock broke the spell which lay on Em Porridge; I heard a distinct snap, and his lips closed like a piece of elastic, released. Rubbing his face, he looked at us with more bewilderment even than usual.

'I go to my room,' he said, fingering his mouth. 'He hurts.'

He went and I was alone with Edith.

XVII

I FELT more strongly still that the time had come for me to try and help all these good people in their perplexity and distress. Lady Bloomsbury, in particular, needed a respite and time to quieten down; while Edith was far too much indoors for a girl of her age. I do not like to see women suffer; and in Seven Priscilla Grove one woman was like to lose a son and another an almost-captured husband, to say nothing of the miseries which Peggy was enduring below-stairs. They all needed taking out of themselves, as the good old saying is; at least, it is an old saying and therefore is presumably good.

'Edith,' I said, 'I think this house needs an airing. The old folk should be left to themselves a bit. They've had too much excitement. Let us young people all go out somewhere.'

'*Us* young people?' she growled.

'Yes,' I said, ignoring the wound, 'you and I and Harold – and the Senator and Insemnia.'

'What, go out with that girl? Are you trying to be funny, Mr. Grame?'

'Far from it, Edith,' I reassured her. 'The fact is,' and I looked over my shoulder and whispered, 'I very much want a word with her myself. Er, I think I could contrive to get the party split up and leave you and Harold alone.'

'Oh, Mr. Grame,' she said, and her voice rose a couple of tones at the happy prospect, 'do you think you could?'

'I'm sure of it.'

'But why do you want to talk to her?'

'As a matter of fact I want to see if I can't find out something about the circumstances of her birth.'

'Do you mean birth or berth?'

'Birth,' I said, 'the kind that is accompanied by *mal de mère*.'

'But what about the Senator? Why bring him?'

'I don't think she'd come without him, but you can leave him to me. I'll see that he doesn't get in your way.'

'Where shall we go?'

'Oh, I'll think of something. We'll show them the sights of London, if I can find someone who knows where they are. Now, look, Edith, you run upstairs and persuade Harold to come. He won't want much persuading, but Lady Bloomsbury might need coaxing to let him go. You murmur in her ear that you're going to find out from him everything she wants to know about Insemnia; that'll fix it. I'll go and round up the Senator and Insemnia.'

'All right,' she said, and then paused. 'But why are you doing this, Mr. Grame?'

'Very largely for you,' I said.

'It's not like you.'

'Fie!' I said. 'Edith, you have never understood me. Now, trust to me and all will come right.'

'Very well,' she said. 'I wish I could believe it, though.'

She ran upstairs and I heard her knock on the Bloomsburys' door as I tapped on the Senator's. He was striding up and down with an air of preoccupation; Insemnia was invisible and, I assumed, in her room.

'Ah, Mr. Grame,' he said, 'I am still puzzled about this story of the Hungarian hussar. . . .'

'Oh, I wouldn't be,' I said. 'I'm sure you explained everything.

Senator, I think you should see the sights of London. I am impatient to make some return for your magnificent hospitality of last night.'

'My hospitality?' he said warily.

'It was sumptuous,' I said, dismissing the subject. 'I should like to show you and Miss Vanderboom something of the London which visitors to our shores seldom see.'

'That is most courteous,' he said. 'What would you suggest?'

'Well, there's a quaint old church,' I said, 'St. Paul's it's called, I believe, or the Tower of London, which is used for the incarceration of beefeaters – the only ones now left in this island, Senator, a very rare sight – or Madame Tussaud's. . . .'

'The famous waxworks?' he said, eagerly. 'I have heard of that. I should like above all things to see Madame Tussaud's.'

'Fine,' I said. 'What could be better? I think there's a bit of it left from the bombing, and we shall just have time before dinner. Let's go. But first . . .' and I handed him my second pocket flask.

He took it with a surprised look and drank. 'Ah,' he said, 'that is extremely mellow brandy. What is it?'

'Sherry,' I said. 'Have another.'

'Thank you,' he said, and took another, murmuring, 'a suave cordial, my dear sir, suave.'

'A little one for the road,' I suggested.

'Thank you,' he said, and I saw with satisfaction that he began to squint and that his hair rose. Suddenly, without warning, he roared, 'Insemnia!' so that I jumped.

She appeared in the door. 'Yes, Senator?'

'We are going out, my dear. Mr. Grame is most kindly taking us to see the famous waxworks.'

'The sights of London,' I put in.

'Make yourself ready quickly, my dear.'

She did, and when we went downstairs Edith and Harold were already waiting; Harold, I thought, with a mixture of relief and impatience. We strolled out into Priscilla Grove, bowing to the guard of honour of artists and assassins which now seemed permanently to be posted before the house, and when we emerged into the Brompton Road took a taxi.

We found Madame Tussaud's full of people, with whom we mingled in a loose group. I watched for an opportunity to give the Senator a little more sherry and was fortunate enough to find one when we reached the tableau of the death of General Gordon. I contrived to leave Insemnia, Edith and Harold in contemplation of the murder of the two little princes in the Tower, while the Senator and I merged ourselves for a moment among the crowd of waxen Egyptians whose spears, for so many decades, have been levelled at the hero of Khartoum. When we returned to the world of living beings I judged that the Senator was ripe for my purpose; he absent-mindedly borrowed and put on one of the Egyptians' turbans, which I had to restore rather quickly to its owner's head. Then I led them to the Chamber of Horrors, planted the Senator firmly in front of Landru and left him. I knew Our Sherry to a nicety by this time and calculated that he would not be able to move from the spot until I fetched him. I caught Edith's eye (it was an easy catch) and deftly steered Insemnia away, leaving Edith alone with Harold, who happened to be looking at Charles Peace at the moment. I wanted to give Edith plenty of time to get clear, so I took Insemnia into a secluded corner and showed her the deathmask of Murat.

'Who is that?' she said.

'I think it must be the President of the French Institute of Selective Parenthood,' I said.

'But why is that knife sticking in him?'

'Oh, they do these things better in France,' I said casually.

'I think you are not telling me the truth,' she said, coldly; she was a serious young woman, I reminded myself. 'Why is that?'

'I'm sorry,' I said, 'I suppose it's a habit I've picked up.'

'Where is the Senator?'

'He's all right. He's round the corner.'

'I think we should go to him.'

We went back and I saw, with gratification, that Edith and Harold had disappeared. The Senator still stood where I had left him, immovable and staring hard at Landru. I tiptoed up to him and peered into his face; he did not stir. I passed my hand gently before his eyes; he did not blink.

'Ah,' I said, 'just as I thought. He's off.'

'Off?'

'Yes. This model is evidently lifelike. It was always thought that Landru had hypnotic powers, you know. That was supposed to be how he gained his influence over women. But it was only a theory. Now I have proved it. It is a great triumph for me. The world of criminology will ring with my name to-morrow. You must be the first to congratulate me.'

'But what about the Senator?'

'It will be best not to disturb him now,' I said, 'a sudden awakening is not good in these cases. We will leave him here a little longer.'

'Won't he be in the people's way?'

'True. He might be. I think we can remedy that.' I took the Senator's arm and found that, with a slight impulse, he moved easily. I gently made him mount the platform beside Landru and turn round; then I took a numbered card from another figure (I did not notice whose it was, as steps were approaching, and I had to hurry) and hung it round his neck. 'There. Now he'll do. Come along.'

'But ought we to leave him like that?'

'Oh, yes, it's frequently done – it saves left-luggage fees, you know. Have you never left him like this before?'

'No, never.'

'How odd. Well, come along; this is no time for idle prattle.' We went past two or three groups of figures and round a corner and there I checked her with a touch. Voices sounded in the vicinity of the Senator and I wanted to hear what they said.

''Oo's that, Elsie?'

'Stalin, I think.'

'Go on, 'e wouldn't be in the Chamber of 'Orrors.'

'Oh no, nor he would. I dunno. 'Orrible looking feller, ain't he, Bert?'

'I wonder 'ow many 'e done in.'

'Well, if you'd bought a programme, like I said, we'd *know* 'oo it was.'

'I don't *want* to know 'oo it is. The look of 'im's enough for me. Aren't 'is eyes awful . . .?'

'Oh, look here, Peter, here's Landru. You remember, the French Bluebeard.'

'Oh yes. Isn't it extraordinary that a bald man can have so much hair on his chin? I say, Joan, I wonder what they do with a beard like that when you're being guillotined. Do you think they tuck it up so that it shan't suffer or just let matters take their course?'

'I can't *think*. Oh, and there's Crippen. Isn't he a duck, Peter? So astigmatic. Who's this, between them? What does the programme say? No. 64 – Miss le Neve. Good gracious, that's Crippen's girl friend. But she's twice as big as Crippen, and *so* unwomanly. What an odd pair they must have made. No wonder the ship's captain spotted that they weren't father and son, or whatever they made out to be. Why, she looks old enough to be Crippen's grandfather. And not a trace of sex appeal.'

'Revolting old tart, isn't she? Boss-eyed, too. Well, there's no accounting for tastes. What's the sticking-plaster on her head for, anyway?'

'Perhaps he used to beat her. She's got the remains of a black eye, too. I wonder why she's so sunburned. I suppose they had very hot weather crossing to America. . . .'

Beside me I heard a strange noise. I turned and looked at Insemnia.

'Was that *you*?' I asked.

'What?'

'I thought I heard a giggle. You can't giggle, can you?'

'I did smile. I very seldom smile; the Committee does not like me to. But I thought of the Senator standing there and something suddenly made me smile. He would be very angry if he knew. So would the Committee. But it came of itself. Is not that strange?'

'Amazing,' I said. 'Come with me.' I took her small hand in mine, I am still rather good at absent-mindedly taking small hands in mine, and led her up the stairs into the great hall where the kings and queens stood about, with dusty evening sunbeams striking diagonally between them. I had known these kings and queens long, long ago, as a boy, and they were my friends, like Gordon, with the spears at his throat; and King Harold, with the arrow in his eye; and the little princes, with the stranglers bending over them; and Nelson, with his shot-torn chest; and all the others there. They smiled fixedly at me when I was a child, and I had been their adoring liege, and I was rather proud now to pass between them with this lovely girl. I could have sworn I saw a glint in Charles II's eye as she passed him. I played for an instant with the fancy that she belonged to me and I to her; that we would presently find a vacant place and mount a little dais and live in waxen happiness, hand in hand, for ever after. Then we reached the end of their line and the pretty dream drifted away into the sunbeams. I led her to my best and oldest friend, the wonder of my childhood.

'Oh,' she said, 'she is beautiful.' She leaned over the cot and my mind's eye, as I watched her, saw her one day bending thus over a cradle. A woman's head never sits with such grace on its neck as in that age old movement, and this was an exceptionally lovely woman. I saw her baby, that child yet unthought of, as clearly as I saw her.

'Isn't she?' I said. 'See how she lives, although she does not live.' Beneath the lace the sleeper's bosom gently rose and fell.

'She is beautiful. Who is she?'

'She's Sleeping Beauty. I think she's you. She breathes, but she isn't alive.'

She looked at me, and I saw a faint cloud of resentment fill her eyes. 'Please do not talk as if there was anything *different* about me. It is very bad for me. It excites me. The Committee always warn my visitors to behave quite naturally.'

I thought for a moment, wondering if and how I could ever get past the Committee and the Senator. To one side, almost hidden by Henry VIII and his wives, I saw a red plush settee with a high back. I took her to it, and we sat down; I turned towards her and tried to strike a note which would disarm, and not alarm, her.

'My dear,' I said, 'you *are* different; you can't get away from it.'

'I am *not*,' she said, impatiently. 'I am a woman like every other woman.'

'Hath not Insemnia eyes, organs, senses, dimensions?' I said. 'For that matter, Sleeping Beauty over there appears like every other woman. Nevertheless, I think you are different. For one thing you are lovelier than almost any other woman.'

'You think I am lovely?' she said, indifferently. 'They all say that.'

'The deuce they do,' I said, nettled. 'I thought you'd never been alone with anyone before.'

'Nor have I. But the Committee says so, and the reporters. The women columnists are the worst; they say it as if they wished to insult me. It is very boring.'

'Boring! Women usually like to be told they're lovely. But that's just it; you aren't usual.'

'Why does Lady Bloomsbury ask me so many questions and pretend not to understand when I answer them?'

'You mean about your parents?'

'Yes, and why they were never joined.'

'She doesn't pretend not to understand. She just can't make head or tail of it. These progressives are always so backward.'

'I think she is mad. I think everybody in that house is mad.'

'Oh no. You're just outside Lady Bloomsbury's ken. She's never before met anybody who was . . . er, artificially produced. She'll probably have a seizure soon, from trying to grasp it.'

'She seems almost frightened of me.'

'No, not quite that. She's worried about her Harold.'

'Harold! It is a great honour for Harold to marry me. When the news becomes known in America he will be a public hero there.'

'That's something I want to ask you, my dear. Why did you pick on Harold? He's a walking tract. If you marry him all your troubles will be little pamphlets.'

'But you know I did not choose him. The Senator chose him.'

'How long have you been in the clutches . . . I mean, how long has he been your guardian?'

'How long? Always. Since I was born. He made me.'

'*Made* you! Good gracious, I'm just beginning to realize the implications of all this. No wonder Lady Bloomsbury couldn't get anywhere with it.'

'Why do you stare at me like that, as if you had never seen anything like me before?'

'Well, I'm just awakening to the fact that I never have seen anything like you before. I feel like Adam when he first saw Eve – er, almost. And you never knew your parents?'

'They never knew each other.'

'Gosh!' I said, slowly. 'Now I begin to see. I suppose I ought to say, isn't it wonderful what they can do nowadays? The old gentleman sees himself as a lord of creation. There's no end to the vanity of mortals, is there? Napoleon, Lenin, Mussolini, Hitler and all the others were modest men, small-time gangsters, compared with him. He has a really big idea. And you were never outside that Institute before?'

'No. It is my home, my destiny and my mission.'

'I suppose the Committee dandled you on its knee as a baby?'

'Yes. They have watched over me from the moment I was born.'

'And now they're going to marry you off. But still I don't understand why they picked on Harold to help you fulfil your mission. Why on earth Harold?'

'For his intellect and noble birth.'

'Noble birth! But Harold isn't . . . Ah, now I see daylight. The Senator thinks Harold comes of an old aristocratic line?'

'Of course. That was what he sought. Pure descent is most important. That is why he chose Harold for his second great experiment; I am the result of the first.'

'I see. Wouldn't it be a joke if some third party took a hand? I've a mind to try and promote the cause of selective parenthood according to my own ideas. Look out!'

I had heard the voices of Edith and Harold, coming nearer. They stopped and sat down on a settee the other side of Henry VIII and his wives. Fortunately Anne Boleyn gave us ample cover.

'I think you've been very unkind to your mother, Harold,' said Edith's voice, 'springing all this on her.'

'Edith, I must ask you not to interfere. This is my affair.'

'Well, I think it's my affair too. Before you went away we were practically engaged.'

'Practically engaged! I never mentioned the word.'

'What a cowardly subterfuge! What do you imagine I thought when you took me to all those Communist discussion-evenings about free love? They made me feel quite naked. I was so ashamed, I had to pretend we *were* married.'

'Edith! How could you dare?'

'Well, I dared, and so what?'

'Don't use those beastly Americanisms.'

'Then don't bring your beastly Americanisms home with you.'

'Edith!'

There was a sharp report, as of a face being smacked, and then the sound of Edith's footsteps, indignantly retreating, and of Harold's voice, pursuing her with expostulations. These noises faded in the distance, and all was quiet. It was nearly closing-time and we were the only people left among the waxworks. In the silence I thought I could hear the faint noise of the machine that made Sleeping Beauty breathe. Insemnia yawned slightly.

'Does Miss Wilstan like Harold?' she said. 'How strange. His measurements are so poor. I do not know how anybody could like Harold.'

'H'm,' I said, 'well, I suppose we'd better go. But before we go I am going to kiss you.'

'Why?'

'Because I want to and because I probably won't be able to again.'

'I have never been kissed.'

'Oh, go on. Not even by the Committee?'

'Least of all by the Committee. They have taken great precautions against my being kissed.'

'How do you feel about it?'

'I do not feel anything about it.'

'You're not afraid of it?'

'Oh no. Why should I be?'

'You shouldn't be. Nobody ought to be afraid of a first kiss. It's the last kiss that one ought to fear, if any. This is probably my last one.' So I took her in my arms and kissed her very hard and very long, observing in myself again that the inner man remains for ever twenty. It was an enormous temptation to run off with her there and then, and I do not know to this day whether it was principle or merely the waning energy of later years that prevented me. She neither yielded nor resisted. At last I let her go.

'Ah well,' I said, 'I wish we could both have been turned into wax at that moment; it would have been the happy ending. Did you like it?'

'No, I do not think so.'

'Dislike it?'

'No.'

'It just didn't mean anything?'

'No, I think not.'

'I was afraid of that. Adieu, youth. Come on, we'll go.'

'But the Senator?'

'Oh, lord, yes. I'd forgotten about him. We'd better collect him.' So we went back and down the stairs to the Chamber of Horrors. Ahead of us went an old attendant, who was looking round before closing for the night. He saw the Senator just before we reached him, gazed an instant, yelled, and staggered backwards into a chair, covering his eyes. I went to him and put my hand on his shoulder.

'What is it, friend?' I said. 'Are you unwell?'

'Look over there, sir,' he said. 'Do you see anything?'

I looked. 'Crippen,' I said. 'Landru.'

'Nothing between 'em?'

'Nothing,' I said. 'Why?'

'You don't see Jack the Ripper?'

'Jack the Ripper?'

'Yes, with a black eye, and 'is 'air standing on end, and plaster on his face?'

'Now, take it quietly,' I said. 'Keep calm. You are ill.'

He trembled violently and clutched my sleeve. 'I'll never touch another drop,' he said. 'Fifty years, man and boy, I've been 'ere, and never given way before. I've stared 'em out and defied 'em to get me down. I've laughed in their faces, I 'ave, many a time. They can't frighten me, I've told my missus, time and again. And now it's come upon me. I can see Jack the Ripper as plain as I can see you. 'E was destroyed by the bomb; blown to bits, 'e was, years ago. I used to snap my fingers in 'is face. And now 'e's come back to 'aunt me. 'E's there again, mocking me, squinting at me.'

I handed him my flask. 'Take a mouthful of this,' I said, 'and we'll go out together. You'll be all right in the morning.' He drank deeply; the sherry brought on a violent paroxysm of coughing. While he gasped for breath I leaned towards Insemnia. 'I think we'd better leave the Senator here for to-night,' I murmured, 'perhaps it's better so. He looks so peaceful. It would be a shame to disturb him now.'

'Is it usual?' she said.

'Oh, perfectly,' I said. I heard something and looked at her sharply. I was almost certain it was a tiny giggle.

Taking the old attendant firmly by the arm, I supported him up the stairs. We only left him when we were all three outside and he had turned the key in the lock.

'Thank you, sir,' he said, 'thank you. I don't know what might 'ave 'appened if you 'adn't been there.'

'Don't mention it,' I said. 'You'll laugh about this in the morning.

'I only 'ope so,' he said, and tottered away.

'INSEMNIA,' I said, 'it's a lovely evening.' It was. It was that magic hour before the dusk when the life of London takes on a new note; when the working day is done and the evening not yet fully begun, when the town empties before it fills again, when many are hurrying homeward and the others are not yet hurrying townward, when there is a slowing of traffic, a lessening of hubbub, a change of time in the city symphony. 'Let's go and dine. I refuse to part with you yet. These hours are like good wine. I want to sip them long and slowly before I turn down the empty glass.'

'You talk in quotations,' she said.

'A writer is but a walking book,' I said. 'You have read a lot then?'

'There is little else to do at the Institute,' she said, 'and the Committee wishes it. But should we not go home?'

'If we go home,' I said, 'there will be Questions, endless Questions, and you will not be able to say, "Ask the Senator," because the Senator will not be there.'

'I should not like that. We will go and dine. But when shall we fetch the Senator?'

'Leave that to me,' I said. 'He is very well where he is.'

So we walked down Baker Street and Oxford Street and Regent Street, and for the first time I noticed a quickening of interest in her. She looked eagerly about her, let me show her the shop windows and chattered, for her, quite vivaciously.

'You like this?' I said.

'Yes, I am enjoying myself,' she said. 'It is very exciting. I think I like being with you.'

'I'm only afraid it isn't being with me so much as doing something you've never done before.'

'Whatever it is, I like it very much.'

I looked at her walking beside me. Her loveliness sprang sharply out against the blurred background of half-seen faces, figures, shops. No doubt about it, she was more alive than I had ever seen her. What a treasure, I thought, for a man who could take and keep her at this moment, and watch her bloom in his hands like an opening flower. So much to show her, share with her, teach her – life would not be long enough.

'I'm glad you do,' I said. 'If you only knew what a temptation you are to me. I didn't feel it so much in Priscilla Grove; out here in the real world it becomes acute.'

Remarks like this she did not understand and she made no reply. I guided her through the doors of the Café Royal and up the stairs to one of the tables-for-two, with rose-pink shades, in the balcony. Aeons ago, it seemed to me, when I was in uniform, during some war or other, I had sat here with girls. Where were they now? I thought, and tried to recapture their faces from the past: Joan, Betty, Chrissie, Stella and the others. It was no use; with her before me, memory would not yield them. They might have been a dream. While the waiter served us we looked down on the company below. Sadly changed it was, I thought; or was the change in me? Surely I remembered people keener, happier, more alert, better-dressed than these? Sad folk they looked, like officials, all; repressed, furtive, featureless. I took my eyes away from them. But for Insemnia I would have hastened to Priscilla Grove.

'Tell me some more about you?' I said.

'What do you want to know?'

'About your childhood and your girlhood.'

'Ah, are you going to start questioning me about all that again. I cannot understand why everybody looks at me in such a strange way and asks these questions. It is all so dull. It is all so uninteresting.'

'But not to me,' I urged her gently. 'Did you never know your parents at all?'

'No, I don't think they ever saw me.'

'Oh, your mother must have seen you at least once,' I said. 'You can take my word for that.'

'Well, if she did I know nothing of it. I only know what the Senator told Lord and Lady Bloomsbury. I only remember the

Institute and nurses and governesses and drawing-teachers and music-teachers and language-teachers, and always the Committee, saying Insemnia must do this or Insemnia must not do that. I am treated with great respect, because I am the firstborn of the Institute, and all its other children are taught to look on me as a kind of princess.'

'It sounds like the life of the queen-bee in the hive,' I said. 'The Senator seems to think of everything; I wonder if he has arranged for Harold's end after his, er, wedding with you. I believe the lot of the bee-bridegroom is sad.'

'I once got hold of a book about bees, by Maeterlinck,' she said. 'It was very exciting. The Committee was angry that I had it, and it was taken away. They said it was reactionary. But I had nearly finished it.'

'H'm,' I said, 'and what else goes on in the Institute?'

'Well, there are lectures about selective parenthood, and we are taught the evils of the old system of uncontrolled choice, and always I am in a throne on the platform, near the Senator, because I was the first of the Institute's Selected Children and am to be the mother of the new race, based on controlled selection. And we have concerts and plays and there are visitors and they stare at me. It is the staring that upsets me. Especially when foreign scientists and journalists come. One day the President of the French Academy poked me in the ribs to see if I was real. They look at me as if I were a freak, and I cannot understand this, because the Committee teaches us that it is the children of the old-fashioned, *laisser-faire* marriages who are the freaks. It makes me very nervous.'

'It would,' I said, 'well, well. By the way, what about that cocktail party where you met Harold? That doesn't sound like the Institute at all.'

'Oh, that was my coming-out party. I wore a crown. It wasn't really a cocktail party at all, but the Senator had some cocktails behind a screen and the screen was knocked over, so he had to turn it into a cocktail party and pretend they were meant to be there. The Senator was cross. The Committee had some and behaved very strangely. They made a great noise. There was never any noise in the Institute before.'

'Did you have a cocktail?'

'Oh no. I am not allowed to taste alcohol.'

'What!' I said. 'Why, you had three glasses of Our Sherry the other night and you were the only one who didn't turn a hair.'

'Was *that* alcohol? I didn't know. It was rather bitter.'

'Well, blow me down,' I said. 'I wonder if they mixed a little blotting-paper in the ingredients when they were . . . er, manufacturing you, my dear. Anyway, you *are* different, whatever you may say. You can't deny it; I know now.'

'Why?'

'Oh, didn't you notice that the others behaved a little strangely?'

'I did wonder once or twice. But I thought those were old English customs. You said so. And I've never been out before.'

'It must be wonderful to be so new to the outer world. And yet, in a way, you miss a great deal. There are no surprises for you.'

'Why,' she said, irrelevantly, 'did you kiss me?'

'Ah, now that *is* an old English custom. I suppose the Committee didn't tell you anything about kissing?'

'Oh yes, we have lectures about it, and diagrams. Unplanned osculation was one of the worst features of uncontrolled parenthood, in the old days. We are trained to find it amusing. We always laugh in chorus when we hear the word.'

'Great Scott,' I said, 'then why did you let me kiss you?'

'I don't know. I was curious to know what it was like.'

'But, my lovely Insemnia,' I said, 'that's just exactly what any normal, non-prefabricated girl would say! Good Heavens! Think of all the years of training that have been squandered on you! Think of all those wasted lectures! This would break the Senator's heart. And were you disappointed?'

'I suppose I was. I hoped it was going to be exciting.'

'You *hoped*! Then you are lost. In you the best-laid plans of the Senator and the Committee have gone agley. You are just like other women.'

'Oh, *am* I?' she cried, her eyes sparkling for the first time. 'How lovely!'

'Ah, then you are not,' I said, 'because any other woman would detest that remark.'

'But I *want* to be like other women,' she said. 'I tell you, it upsets me very much to be told I am not, and stared at as if I were something strange.'

'I wouldn't worry too much about that,' I said. 'I think you'll find you'll always be stared at as if you were something strange. At any rate, for many years yet. And when you've been kissed once or twice more, by other men than me, and told why, by other lips than mine, you'll realize *why* you are being stared at and you'll rather like it.'

'But I shan't be kissed by any other men,' she said. 'The Committee will never allow Harold to kiss me. I shall never see him after we are married. I must go back to the Institute to fulfil my destiny.'

'Oh lord, the queen-bee-and-bridegroom theme again,' I said. 'I suppose you'll be allowed to see Harold *while* you are being married to him?'

'Yes, I think so. It is to be in Westminster Abbey.'

I sat up. 'Is it, though?' I said. 'Only in Westminster Abbey? No little-church-round-the-corner for you and Harold. Whose idea is this? The Senator's?'

'Yes. He thinks the publicity will bring in a lot of new subscriptions.'

'Ah! I wondered when we should come to that part. So the Senator likes subscriptions?'

'The Institute needs them, of course. He advertises for subscriptions in all the leading newspapers. Sometimes he will not accept a donor without a large subscription.'

'How do you mean, accept a donor?'

'A parenthood-donor. There is much competition to be a parenthood-donor. It has a great publicity value, and their pictures appear in the honours lists of Selected Parents. They are called Gold Star Fathers, because they give their sons, and the Senator makes them pay for the privilege.'

'Insemnia, have mercy on my innocence. He makes them pay for *that*!'

'For their sacrifice to the Cause? Oh yes. The Senator feels very strongly that they should give their all. I think he sometimes takes their subscriptions and does not make use of their donations at all. He tells them they have fathered a new offspring of the Cause, and they are pleased, but they haven't really, and I'm afraid the Institute's accountants are very inaccurate in their net-population certificates. I think it is very wrong of him. But it's all for the Institute and the Cause.'

'That's a very smart business idea. Of course, he can't very well play that trick on the mothers. A way hasn't yet been found to prevent them knowing whether they've had a baby or not, has it?'

'I don't *think* so. But he does very well from the fathers. He has just built a new wing to the Institute.'

'H'm. He should be a wealthy man.'

'Somehow he always seems to be worrying about money.'

'For the Institute?'

'Oh, of course, for the Institute. He is selfless.'

I felt now that, at last, I knew something about Insemnia, and sat silent a few moments, twiddling my glass, while I let my fancy play around the possibilities. Frankly, I was happy that it was none of my business, for it was a tangled skein. I could not imagine how Lady Bloomsbury, or for that matter anybody else in Seven Priscilla Grove, unless it were Edith, whose desire to believe the worst sharpened her wits, could ever be made to understand the position. I pictured myself explaining it to Lady Bloomsbury and Lady Cynthia and finding that they moved ever farther from the facts, the more I sought to clarify these. I could not believe that even Harold really knew what he had let himself in for; his head was always buzzing with so many bees that simple truths seldom penetrated it. No, on the whole, anxious though I was to help anybody who was in need of succour, I was relieved to think that it was no affair of mine, and glad that I had never been of a meddling disposition. So I put all other thoughts out of my mind and gave myself to the contemplation of my lovely companion; reflecting a little ruefully that, had I been younger, I would undoubtedly have found a way to solve the problems of all others concerned to my own satisfaction at least.

As the darkness deepened and the lights grew brighter she took on the different loveliness which a lovely woman gains at that hour; her skin became a little duskier, her eyes and teeth picked up new glints. We sat a long time, as long as we could, and I saw that she did not tire, but seemed rather to enjoy the experience and my talk more as the hours passed. At last the place was empty save for us. For once, I had no wish to go back to Priscilla Grove.

'Insemnia,' I said, on an impulse, 'we'll make a night of it. We have none to consider but ourselves. No wife waits for me with barbed questions ready in the bow. The Senator is comfortable. We shall go to a night-club. Why do you smile? Does the idea please you?'

'Oh yes, it does,' she said, 'but I was smiling at the thought of the Senator. It is very wrong of me. He has always been so good to me; but for him I should never have been born at all. And yet something makes me smile when I think of him standing there.'

'I could snigger a little myself,' I said, 'but what weird ideas you have. But for him you'd never have been born at all! You have a lot to unlearn, my dear. You were obviously standing in the wings of time somewhere, just waiting for your cue. You had to be, Senator or no Senator. There couldn't not have been a you. Sometimes I wonder if the Senator had anything to do with your being made. You've only his word for it, you know.'

'And the Committee's.'

'Oh, blow the Committee,' I said.

The midsummer's night was perfect. The spangled sky lay like sequined gossamer above the dark roofs and the empty streets were shiny, like still waters: into their polished surfaces the red and amber, green and yellow lights cast coloured curlicues; it only needed gondolas to come gliding round the corners of these quiet canals and the carnival-makers to romp, singing, along the pavements. In the soft warm air Insemnia's beauty was disquieting. I felt the quickening of the pulse which such companionship, at midnight, must bring, even at my age. The Mayfair Follies, I thought, could wait a while; the night was young yet. Slowly we walked along Piccadilly; then beneath the great trees in the Green Park to Hyde Park Corner, where we turned back. Her arm lay in mine and I pressed it. I thought there was a faint responsive pressure. Around us was the elusive scent of limes; it recalled to me Vienna, a place I seemed to have known in some other dream or former life, and a girl called Gretl. I stopped abruptly and took her in my arms.

'All right, then,' I said, resignedly, 'once more. I'm even going to say all the old ridiculous things: how lovely you are, how rare, how appetizing. They were always true, but never so true as now. Come here, darn you.' And this time I really kissed her. She looked surprised when I let her go.

'Why are you so . . . disturbed?' she said.

'Because of you,' I said. 'What did you think of it this time?'

'It was a little more exciting this time,' she said, a trifle uneasily. 'It is very funny. It is not what I expected at all.'

'Ah, you have so much to learn, my lovely,' I said gently. 'I hope you find the right teacher.'

The Mayfair Follies was crowded, dim and smoky. The Hyde in me chuckled as we entered, for the Jekyll had many years ago sworn never to waste an hour in one of these morbid dens again. Now I found that I had done them an injustice. Insemnia showed an eager interest that was indistinguishable from happiness; I discovered once more that there is no woman so old or so young, so poor or so rich, so plain, comely, bright or dull, but loves a night-club, and the dirtier, the noisier, the murkier, the better. With the help of a bottle of champagne we became quite animated; and with the aid of a second, the end of the floor-show, and the exhaustion of most of the other guests, which left a little space on the floor, I astounded myself by deciding to dance.

'Come, my dear, we'll dance,' I said, rising.

'But I have never danced,' she said, sitting still.

'What! With all those tutors and mistresses, you've never learned to dance. No, don't tell me, I know: the Committee disapproves of dancing. Come along, I'll teach you.'

Docile as ever she came, and I took hold of her. 'Now, just let your body and your legs respond to the pressure of my right hand, in the middle of your back, so,' I said, 'and I'll guide you with my left. You'll find it quite easy.'

She danced perfectly. That is, she did exactly what I wished her to do, and I am told that I dance well (or rather, I was told so, when last I danced, which, now that I come to think, was some time since).

In order to make it as simple as possible for her, I used a good deal of pressure with my right hand, and after three dances found, with gratified resignation, that I was enjoying myself very much indeed; the more so, in that she loved every step and moment.

'Oh, I like this very much indeed,' she said, looking up at me without a smile, but with a something in her eyes I had never seen, or expected to see there. I pressed her gently, to announce a somewhat complicated step. To my surprise she pressed me quite hard and smiled.

I suddenly lost my avuncular feeling towards her. I realized that, without intending to, I had carried the education of Insemnia much farther, that evening, than I had ever dreamed of. After all, we had been in each other's company for many delightful hours. She had never been out with a man before; I had never expected to take out a girl again. We had drunk the worse part of two bottles of champagne and, like a thief in the night, its effects had crept upon us. There was a great exhilaration in me; there was great content, and I guessed, some feeling akin to gratitude in Insemnia. She was irresistibly desirable, and yielded to my arms; meaning nothing thereby, I knew; but still . . .

I looked down at her, and thought I would have to let this midsummer night's dream carry me on and do what it would. What was I doing here with this girl? It must be a dream; then let the dream dream itself out. Feeling hilariously happy, I raised my eyes and came to earth with a jolt as I looked into the astonished ones of Oliver Jene.

I like and admire Oliver. He is what I should like my son to be. His philosophy of life and his tactics at sea are similar, simple and Nelsonian. Believe in God and go for the enemy (he holds) and you will have the best of both worlds; for a straight course is the shortest distance between two points, and by following it you not only come quickest on the foe, but also offer the smallest target. He follows these rules with great success in love and in war; he won a D.S.O. at Matapan and nearly always has some smart little prize in tow when he comes on leave. Harold scorns him as an ignoramus, yet he seems to me to know much more than Harold. He dances as only destroyer commanders can, who in my experience are surpassed alone by destroyer petty officers and seamen. He looks good, having a clean skin, a clear eye and a firm jaw.

As I say, I like Oliver, and it happened that he had been in my thoughts for some days, since I heard that he was again due on leave. Though I greatly dislike people who poke their noses into the concerns of others, it had faintly occurred to me that he might be interested in meeting Insemnia and that, if anything hampered this, it would be courteous of me to help, if I could. Nevertheless at this particular moment his appearance at the Mayfair Follies was most unwelcome to me. Indeed, for an instant I wondered if I could successfully pretend not to see him, and I took Insemnia two or three times more round the floor. But as the place was now empty save for us this harmless deception proved beyond my powers; also, there was a compulsion in his riveted stare which was irresistible. With a sigh I gave Insemnia a last squeeze, which meant much more than she could know, murmured to myself 'Hail and farewell', and led her to him. The midsummer night's dream faded; I guessed that, outside, the dawn was come.

'Hullo, Oliver,' I said, 'it's good to see you. Let me present you to Miss Vanderboom. Insemnia, this is Commander Jene, Lady Cynthia's son.'

'How do you do?' he said. He appeared not to see me and held her hand while he looked at her. After waiting a little I gently unhooked them and we all sat down. Now that we were three Insemnia reverted to her aloof and oblivious manner.

'It's grand to see you back again, Oliver,' I said. 'Commander Jene is in the navy, Insemnia; he's just come on leave. Miss Vanderboom and her guardian have taken the first-floor flat, Oliver.'

'Yes, it's a good floor,' he said, absently, staring at her, 'good band, too.'

'Oliver,' I barked, as from the bridge, 'action stations!'

He jumped. 'Oh, sorry,' he said, 'I am afraid I wasn't listening.'

'Indeed you weren't,' I said. 'I was just telling you that Miss Vanderboom and her guardian, the Senator, are staying in the first-floor flat.'

'What, at Number Seven!' he said, and I saw a look come into his eyes; the kind of look, I surmised, that would enter them if an enemy submarine surfaced a league ahead and he gave the order to ram. 'Why that's marvellous.'

'Yes, you'll like the Senator,' I said.

'The Senator?' he said, vacantly; his eyes were on Insemnia again.

'Miss Vanderboom's guardian,' I explained patiently, 'I was just telling you.'

'Ah yes. Er, where is he?'

'We've left him at the waxworks. We're going to collect him later.'

'Oh yes, of course. Will you dance, Miss Vanderboom?'

'Oliver,' I said, still patiently, 'I don't think Miss Vanderboom would enjoy it without music, and the band's gone home. In fact, everybody's gone home but our waiter and he's clearly going to stiletto us if we don't leave. Let's go and have breakfast, and we'll pick up the Senator afterwards.'

He seemed in a kind of trance and rose. As we walked along Piccadilly, Insemnia between us, I saw that the sun was well up and calculated that if we ate our one piece of controlled toast slowly we should be just in time for the opening of Madame Tussaud's. I had never known Oliver behave so strangely and wondered if the sea air had begun to affect his mind. He did not open his mouth, save to put toast in it, while we breakfasted at the Corner House, and I longed for the time to pass. The magic of the night was gone, and only a glass slipper was left in the house of my dreams. With Oliver there, Insemnia was no longer mine alone. The coldly indifferent girl was back. And anyway, I am no longer twenty, and I was not feeling at my best.

'Well, now we can go and collect the Senator,' I said, looking at my watch.

'Yes, I think we should now,' said Insemnia.

Oliver spoke, still looking at her. 'The Senator?' he said.

'Now, look here, Oliver,' I said, 'I've told you twice. The Senator is Miss Vanderboom's guardian and we left him at the waxworks. Pull yourself together, my dear boy. What's the matter with you?'

With an effort he collected his wits. 'Oh yes, of course,' he said, 'the Senator. You left him at the waxworks? What an excellent idea. I never could understand why more people aren't left at the waxworks. Let's go and fetch him.'

I looked at him admiringly. 'That's my Oliver,' I said, 'that's the hero of Matapan. Come on.'

We took a taxi and let it wait while we entered Madame Tussaud's. The doors were just opening, and the girl at the box office looked a little surprised as we shot through them almost before they were apart. 'You're early, aren't you?' she said.

'What's the hurry?' 'Oh, we do this every morning,' I said. 'We refresh ourselves with a look at the Cabinet before we go to the Ministry. We find it sets us up for the day.' She seemed doubtful, but we hurried on. I was a little anxious lest the Senator should have been covered with a dustsheet and suffocated. However, it was all right. He was still there.

'Is that him?' said Oliver keenly. 'What do we do, carry him out?'

'No, wait a moment,' I said. 'I can manage this, I hope.' I made a series of quick passes before the Senator's eyes. To my dismay he remained immobile. I tried again; there was no result. 'Oh dear,' I said to Insemnia, 'this is a nuisance, we may have to leave him until you return to America.'

'Oh, I don't think we ought to do that. Please try again.'

'Hold on a moment,' I said. 'I think I know a way.' I took out my pocket flask; there was but a drain left in it, but the smell was, if anything, stronger than ever. I decided that the formula must include a dash of ammonia, and made another note for my treatise. I held the flask under the Senator's nose. To my delight he shuddered violently, blinked several times, and then beamed on us.

'Extremely interesting,' he said loudly. 'Now Mr. Grame, I should like to see the famous Chamber of Horrors.'

'I think we've hardly time left, Senator,' I said. 'We have to get back for dinner. Oh, this is Commander Jene – Lady Cynthia's son, you know.'

'Ah, how do you do, my dear sir?' shouted the Senator, looking at Oliver approvingly. 'I didn't see you come. A good type physically,' he remarked to Insemnia in brackets, 'extremely fine measurements, hasn't he?'

'Yes, Senator.'

I took him by the arm and found that, save for some rigidity, he was quite normal and mounted the stairs without difficulty. Halfway through the long hall, we met the old attendant of the night before, coming to his labours. He did not notice us at first, having paused to remove a speck of dust from the Pompadour's nose, but when he turned and saw us advancing on him with the Senator between us he let out a loud scream and disappeared at speed in the direction of the Historical Tableaux. The Senator stopped in surprise.

'Why did he do that?' he inquired.

'Oh, I think he was trying to get us to play hide and seek with him,' I said. 'I shouldn't humour him, Senator.'

'Certainly not, sir,' replied the Senator, resuming his march. 'I deeply disapprove of games of chance.'

The girl at the pay-desk also appeared perplexed, so much so that she tried to put her head out of the little hole and stare after us: being unable to get it back, she remained in that position, looking like Mary, Queen of Scots, on the block; a kind of living sample, for other visitors, of the delights within.

The taxi-driver was waiting, and bore the look of martyrdom habitual in waiting taxi-drivers. I found, as I had rather expected, that the Senator could not bend, and saw that we should have to transport him in a standing position. I asked the man politely if he would be good enough to lower the hood.

He looked at me with amazement and hatred. 'Put the hood down?' he said, in a voice choked with horror. 'Why, the hood's never *bin* down since I've had this cab, and I've had it seventeen years.'

'I know,' I said winningly, 'but it's a lovely morning, and this gentleman can't bend. He has to travel standing.'

The driver's face went quite purple, and his cheeks distended, with suppressed imprecations. Making inarticulate noises like a woman in labour, he got down and tried to shift the hood. Oliver and I helped him, and at length, with rusty protests, it gave way and collapsed in a musty heap at the back of the cab; a swarm of moths fluttered out and flew away.

We made the Senator comfortable; that is, we planted him firmly in the cab and his head and shoulders rose above it like the conning-tower of a submarine. Thus we drove, in some state, back to Priscilla Grove, the driver in front muttering, 'Put the . . . hood down, 'e says!' to himself in the manner of a Greek chorus.

I felt that for years to come this tale would be told in tones of envenomed reminiscence, by taxi-cab men gathered over their dinners in those little wooden huts, scattered about London, where taxi-cab men, when they can bear the sight of their fares no longer, meet, eat and relate the miseries of the day.

All went well at Number Seven, save that the ill-fated Peggy, who had just put out a trembling nose for a much-needed sniff of restorative fresh air, saw us levering the Senator out of the cab ('To you, Oliver, from me') and sought the basement with such velocity that she knocked Mrs. Barnes over backwards, who was coming up. Supported on either side by Oliver (who was a little awkward about it, because his head was turned towards Insemnia) and myself, the Senator mounted the steps, rather stiffly, like a wooden soldier.

Outside I heard the taxi-driver throw in his gear with a crash like a collision of express-trains and drive away, muttering, 'Would you kindly put the . . . hood down, 'e says!'

XIX

INSIDE Number Seven, that usually quiet and well-ordered house, there was a certain confusion. We saw Lady Cynthia's back vanish down the basement stairs: alarmed by the noise of somebody falling, and by Mrs. Barnes's cries from below, she was too agitated to notice our entrance. Lady Bloomsbury and Edith put curious faces out of the dining-room door; I warded off the questions they seemed likely to ask with a warning look, which might have meant anything, but which they clearly interpreted to mean a great deal, and we marched the Senator upstairs, leaving Insemnia with him.

'Nice old boy,' said Oliver, as we came downstairs again, 'makes a wonderful waxwork, doesn't he?'

This is one of the many things I like about Oliver. Having sailed all the Seven – or however many they may be – Seas, he seems used to curious sights, and if he saw Davy Jones riding round the Sargasso Sea on the sea-serpent's fourth hump he would, I feel sure, make a brief entry in the log ('Object, appearing to be Davy Jones on sea-serpent, sighted off Sargasso Sea') and order another pink gin. I suppose it is the naval training. He is not always wanting to know the why of everything; still less does he think, like Harold, that he knows all the answers to all the whys. However, even he had one or two questions.

'I say, Grame,' he said, 'what did he mean about my measurements?'

'I'm not quite certain,' I said, 'but I think he was looking at you as a prospective bridegroom.'

'Bridegroom? Not for that glorious girl?'

'Well, that's just the point,' I said. 'I believe he reserves the right to select your bride, whom you would never see.'

Oliver, as I say, does not fall into the easy error of dispersing his attack. He keeps to one objective. My remarks aroused no curiosity in him. His thoughts were with Insemnia.

'Isn't she the loveliest thing?' he said. 'Tell me about her.'

'She is rather pretty, isn't she? There's some slight mystery about her birth, I understand.'

'What on earth does that matter with a girl who looks like she looks?'

'I believe,' I said casually, 'she's engaged to Harold.'

'What! To that weed! She couldn't be.'

'Well, I really know very little about it, and as you know I make it a rule never to mix in matters that do not affect me, Oliver.'

'No, I didn't know,' he said candidly. 'Look here, Grame, you can't dodge me like that. I want to know everything about her. After all, you were out with her, you crafty old rogue. I'd like to know how you managed that. Tell me about her.'

'This is not the time,' I said. 'Judging by the noise below your mother needs you, Oliver. Go to her in her need, and get your hammock slung. You haven't even said hullo to her yet.'

'Well, I didn't know I was going to meet this girl, did I?' he argued reasonably. 'Mums can wait, I've often seen her before.'

However, he went downstairs and I entered the lounge, where Lady Bloomsbury and Edith, who were deep in mutual commiseration, turned indignant looks on me. Edith opened her mouth, but I forestalled her.

'Edith,' I said, 'I fear the Senator is deeply hurt about the way you and Harold left us in the waxworks.'

Edith's eyes opened wide. 'Well, I like that,' she said. 'We looked everywhere and couldn't find you. We thought you'd gone without us.'

'Did you look behind Anne Boleyn?' I said.

She was about to speak when she caught my eye, and blushed. 'We looked all round,' she said, briefly, 'and there was no sign of you. We saw a figure in the Chamber of Horrors looking remarkably like the Senator.'

'Ah yes,' I said, 'I observed the resemblance myself. That was Miss le Neve. She was a very large woman. Oh well, it can't be helped. The Senator will be down to dinner in a moment.'

'To *dinner*!' they said.

'Yes. You mustn't notice anything. I'm afraid he was much upset and it's affected his memory. These things happen, don't they, Lady Bloomsbury?'

Lady Bloomsbury opened and closed her mouth several times; I saw that she still struggled against stubborn adversity. Eventually she made up her mind to let things be and changed the subject.

'Ah'm very much puzzled, Mr. Grame,' she said. 'Lady Cynthia brought me a message from you about artificial respiration. Ah've looked in all the dictionaries and Ah can't find out what artificial respiration could possibly have to do with Miss Vanderboom's birth. Ah'm more mystified than ever.'

'But, dear Lady Bloomsbury,' said Edith, 'haven't you been able to get any information from Harold? She must have *some* background. She can't just have sprung from the earth.'

'Ah wouldn't be too sure, Edith. They can do such extraordinary things nowadays, what with . . . um atomic energy and all these artificial fertilizers. Ah can get no farther with

Harold. The more he tells me the less Ah understand. As far as Ah can make out she's some kind of foundling – something to do with twilight sleep, and wishful thinking, Ah imagine.'

'Excuse me, Lady Bloomsbury,' I put in, helpfully, 'I think Lady Cynthia misunderstood my well-meant effort to be of assistance to you. I said artificial insemination, not artificial respiration. I think the clue is in Miss Vanderboom's first name – Insemnia.'

'Yes,' said Edith, excitedly, 'that's it, of course. It means she was artificially inseminated.'

'Edith! Ah hope you don't know about such things.'

'Oh yes, Lady Bloomsbury, in The Movement we keep abreast of all scientific progress.'

'Ah don't know what you mean, but Ah think it's disgusting. Ah did think you would have helped to keep The Party clean, Edith. Men ought not to be allowed to go to America, they always discover something. If only Columbus had left well alone.'

'I suppose Harold is infatuated with her,' said Edith miserably.

'Well, of course, she is rather attractive, in a repulsive way. But as a matter of fact our Harold doesn't seem to think so much about her as about The Cause, as he calls it, and The Movement, and Progress, and Scientific Selection. Ah sometimes wonder whether Ah should have let him read the *Daily Worker* when he was so young.'

'I'm sure she only picked on him because she's after the title.'

'Now, there you're wrong. We must be just, Edith. Ah gather the Committee selected our Harold, at this bottle party at the Mothercraft Centre, or whatever it was . . . Oh, it's no use tutting, Edith. Harold seems to think there's no appeal from the Committee's verdict.'

'But that's absurd, Lady Bloomsbury. They can't do that.'

'As Ah said before, mah dear, you don't know what they can do these days, with all these emergency powers and whatnot. Ah sometimes wonder if The Movement isn't going a little too far.'

'I shouldn't interfere, because it's nothing to do with me at all,' I said, timidly, 'but there was one little thing I heard. It's probably of no importance, but perhaps you ought to know, Lady Bloomsbury.'

'Ee, go on, Mr. Grame,' she said, impatiently.

'Well, I seem to remember the Senator or Miss Vanderboom the other evening – when it was so hot, you remember? Yes, of course you do – well, I think one of them made some allusion to Harold's noble descent.'

'They probably think our title goes back to the Doomsday Book,' said Lady Bloomsbury gloomily. 'These Americans are so baronial.'

'But don't you see, dear Lady Bloomsbury,' said Edith quickly, 'that might make a difference? This girl might change her mind if she knew Harold wasn't of noble descent.'

'You mean the Committee might change its mind? Ah wish Ah could believe it. You know, mah dear, Ah always had such hopes for you and Harold – excuse me, Mr. Grame.'

'Not at all,' I said. 'My sympathies, if I were to allow myself any in an affair that does not involve me, would be all with Miss Wilstan. Wouldn't they, Edith?'

She gave me a look that contained little nourishment. 'They might be,' she said, briefly, 'if it suited your book.'

'As Ah was saying, Ah had mah hopes, ever since you were boy and girl together at the London School of Economics, Edith. Did our Harold never *say* anything?'

'Oh, he never said anything definite, but you know how he looks at you when he talks about The Future Belonging to Youth. I was just a silly girl, and believed it all. . . .'

'Mah poor child. Ah dreamed for you, too. Ah had dreams of a quiet wedding at the Caxton Hall and afterwards a small reception, for just a few nice people of our kind, at the offices of the Fabian Society. And then – a little home of your own. . . .'

'With a little room upstairs – for Harold to keep his collected works of Lenin in and write his letters to the *New Statesman* . . .'

'Oh lovely dream,' I said.

'. . . and now he's going to marry this abandoned creature,' and Edith burst into tears.

'Who doesn't even know where she was abandoned,' said Lady Bloomsbury, fumbling for her handkerchief.

'Or by whom,' I added, coughing to hide my emotion.

They were weeping on each other's bosoms as Lady Cynthia entered. 'Oh dear,' she said, nervously, 'whatever's wrong now?'

'Oh, it's nothing very much,' I said. 'I'm afraid it's your fault, in a way, Cynthia. You meant well, but you mentioned the words artificial respiration to Lady Bloomsbury, and you know how she dislikes loose talk about sex.'

'Oh, I am sorry,' she said, going to them; with a pat here and a pat there, in the way such women have, she managed to break their clinch, sit them up and dry their tears, 'but you told me to, Mr. Grame.'

'No, I said artificial insemination.'

'Is that different? How stupid of me. Now, don't upset yourself any more, Doris. Mr. Grame, I've been hearing the most extraordinary things from Oliver. He says he met you and . . .'

I stopped her with a warning gesture. 'I shouldn't say any more now, Cynthia,' I said mysteriously, 'there have been misunderstandings. These are delicate matters. A word at the wrong moment might do much harm.'

'Oh, gracious,' she said anxiously, 'is there going to be more trouble? Mrs. Barnes swears she has concussion; she's in my bed and I don't know where I'm going to sleep. I always fall out of Oliver's hammock, so it won't be any use his giving it up to me. And she fell on Peggy. I can't find anything broken, but Peggy looks much *flatter*, somehow. I do think Mrs. Barnes might be more careful. I shall have to serve breakfast myself.'

She had hardly gone when the Senator came in. He looked very well; either his good night's rest or the morning air had clearly benefited him, and his deepening tan added to his appearance of robust health. He looked more alert and businesslike than he had looked, or possibly, than he had been allowed to look, since his arrival among us.

'Ah, good evening, good evening,' he trumpeted. 'It keeps very light, doesn't it?'

'The nights are very short in these latitudes, at this season,' I said. 'In fact, we sometimes miss one altogether.'

'Indeed,' he said, 'ah well, no matter. I am very hungry.'

The creaking and rumbling began in the service hatch and Lady Cynthia entered. The Senator looked in mild surprise at his cup of tea and meagre plateful of something called Barley Bits, described on the packet as a cereal food packed in Chicago.

'Ah,' he said, 'this is one of your meatless days, I see.'

'Ha-ha,' tittered Lady Cynthia apprehensively.

'As a matter of fact, Senator,' I said, 'this is a fast day.'

'Oh, I should have known,' he said, examining the sawdust-like mess. 'Ah, it's not Lent, is it?'

'No. Lease-lent, I think,' I said, 'much the same thing.'

'I find it a little dry,' said the Senator, speaking with some difficulty through his first mouthful. 'Would there be any cream?'

'Cream!' said Lady Bloomsbury, Lady Cynthia and Edith together.

'The Senator means milk, Cynthia,' I explained. 'Cream is one of those words which mean something different in America, like . . . er, suspenders, you know. Cream, Senator, is with us the fatty upper substance which by law has to be removed from the milk before the milk is withheld from the population. By that means there is much more butter to be withheld.'

'Yes, yes,' he said with his usual air of *rien comprendre est tout pardonner*, 'I understand. I must say that you are far more progressive than we on the other side, in many things.'

'Ah'll fetch you some of mah milk substitute, Senator,' said Lady Bloomsbury. 'Ah make it with corn-flour; Ah'm told you can't detect the difference.'

'That's perfectly true,' I said, as she went downstairs. 'Having forgotten the taste of milk, we can't.'

'Charming woman, charming woman,' said the Senator; and then, as she returned, 'Thank you, ma'am, a thousand times. Delicious!' he said after tasting it, and laid down his spoon. 'I wonder where my ward is.' His eyes rested on Edith, who was opposite him, and he paused. Then he leaned forward, and said earnestly, 'Young lady, I have been studying you. You interest me greatly in my professional capacity. As I go about I am always on the look-out for promising types, you know, ha-ha. My records are unique in The Movement. Allow me to make a few notes.' He took out a notebook and pencil and wrote, looking from Edith to the book and murmuring, as if to himself, 'H'm, intellectual type; brain-power good; bloodstrain needs strengthening; measurements poor; suggested donor, say, Spanish bullfighter.' He closed the book. 'Young lady, if ever you contemplate planned maternity, my Committee will be most happy to serve you. We must have a word some time. Pardon me, ladies, an instant. I must see what my ward is doing.' Absent-mindedly laying the notebook on the table, he left us, a trifle stiffly.

'Well . . .' said Edith, very red.

'What did he mean?' said Lady Cynthia.

'Ah daren't think,' said Lady Bloomsbury, 'but Ah strongly advise you not to meet his eye, Edith.'

'Not meet his eye! Why not?'

'Ah believe it's all done by the power of the eye. You'll notice that Ah never meet his eye.'

'Doris!'

'And Ah implore you not to have anything to do with his Committee, mah dear, or you may find yourself in trouble.'

'In *trouble*!' said Lady Cynthia, trembling. 'Oh dear.'

'Look at the trouble it's brought on me. Ah could slap the Committee.'

The three ladies started as the door opened, but it was Harold. Harold always looks indignant about something, and until now the something had generally been a new affront to Soviet Rusher, but now he looked more indignant than usual and was clearly in the grip of strong emotion.

'Oh, hullo, everybody,' he said. 'Mother, father's being quite impossible. I was just telling him that the Senator wants the wedding to be at Westminster Abbey and he said the Dean wouldn't allow it. I met the Senator on the stairs and he was furious. He threatens to complain to the American Embassy. I must say I agree with him.'

'In ... Westminster ... Abbey!' said Lady Bloomsbury faintly.

Lady Cynthia perceived an occasion for tact. 'Oh, but Harold,' she said, 'surely there *might* be difficulties.'

'Why should there be?' said Harold loftily. 'We are not living in feudal times any more.'

'But, mah dear boy, wouldn't the Dean want at least a birth certificate? Ah don't think he would accept Insemnia's incubation card, or whatever she has.'

'Mother, you talk as if Insemnia had been hatched from an egg.'

'But *isn't* that the procedure in these cases, Harold?' asked Lady Cynthia timidly.

'How can you be so unenlightened? I really believe I should be blackballed at the Left Book Club if this were known. Don't you agree, Edith?'

'No, I don't. I entirely agree with Lady Bloomsbury.'

'Et tu, Edith!' said Harold austerely. 'Are *you* flirting with reaction?'

'Rubbish,' said Edith, 'you must be mad.'

'Oh, Edith,' said Lady Cynthia soothingly. 'Harold, this is rather a surprise. Don't you think a wedding in Westminster Abbey would be an ... exaggeration, in the circumstances?'

Harold looked as dangerous as Harold can look. 'What "circumstances", pray?' he inquired.

'Well, Insemnia's escutcheon *is* rather blotted. ...'

'Blotted! I think it's all blot and no escutcheon,' said Edith cattily. 'Why not have the wedding at the Foundling Hospital?'

'Mother, did you hear that?'

'Well, Harold, Edith is upset. The Senator was just making the most wounding innuendoes about her and some Spanish bullfighter.'

'Spanish bullfighter!'

'I ought to have smacked that horrible old man's face. If he comes in again I will,' said Edith.

'Oh, Edith, dear, *please*,' said Lady Cynthia.

'What *is* this about you and a Spanish bullfighter, Edith?' said Harold peremptorily. 'Bullfighters are a most reactionary crowd.'

'You imbecile,' said Edith.

'Edith, I hardly know you. You're talking like a Fascist.'

'And you're talking like a fool.'

'You've been deceiving me. I believe you're a Fifth Columnist.'

'After I've wasted the best years of my life listening to all your drivel about planned economy, and thinking you meant it,' said Edith, bursting into tears, 'you bring home this half-hatched octoroon. . . .'

'You'd better be quiet, Edith. I shall never trust a comrade again. As Insemnia's husband I shall have a unique standing in The Movement. Selective Parenthood is the greatest progressive experiment of the century, and I'm honoured that destiny has chosen me. . . .'

'Destiny!' said Edith, emerging from her handkerchief. 'Destiny has nothing to do with it. That . . . foundling chose you because she thinks you come of an old noble line, and you don't, and you haven't told her. All right then: marry her. Tell her all about planned economy. See if you can eat planned economy, or sleep with it. I'll send back all your presents.' She leaned across the table and smacked Harold's face, hard; then, diving into her handkerchief, she flung to the door, opened it and turned. 'Fool!' The door slammed, just missing Alistair, who came in at that moment, appeared to notice nothing, and sat down, urbanely murmuring, 'Curzon Line! I'd give 'em Curzon Line.' In one of his rare moments of wakefulness, he saw that Harold was rubbing his face. 'Toothache?' he asked, sympathetically.

The door opened again and Lord Bloomsbury, the Senator and Insemnia came in. The two men looked startled. Insemnia, who was obviously incapable of being startled by anything, calmly sat down next to me.

'Cynthia, Doris,' said Lord Bloomsbury, in more agitation

than I had ever seen him show, 'the most extraordinary thing just happened. We passed Edith on the stairs just now and she looked at the Senator, said "Spanish bullfighter", and smacked his face.'

'Obviously insane!' roared the Senator. 'Homicidal mania! It was the greatest shock of my life. It just shows how careful the Institute needs to be in the selection of parents. I could have sworn that she was a perfectly normal type; a little overbrained and undermuscled, perhaps, but nothing that an infusion of the right blood could not remedy. Some unsuspected mental taint might upset the whole of our work. I must amend my notes about her. Where is my book? Ah, here it is. Now, that's very strange! I find that I had tentatively prescribed a Spanish bull-fighter as the suitable corrective for excessive mental and inferior physical development in a Nordic type.'

'Telepathy,' I suggested. 'She must have read your thoughts and didn't like the idea.'

'Ahrrm,' coughed Lord Bloomsbury, who often makes a conversational bridgehead in this manner. 'Well, Doris, the Senator and I have been talking things over and I think I'm beginning to get the matter clear in my mind. It seems that this, er, young lady is the fruit . . .'

'Fruit!' said Lady Bloomsbury keenly.

'Well, er, the product, that is, the child of a union . . . er, no that's not right. Not a union, ah, let us say, a *transaction* between her parents . . .'

'Who never knew each other,' remarked Lady Bloomsbury crushingly.

'That's right, now you're beginning to understand . . .'

'Ah'm farther from understanding than Ah ever was.'

'Now, please, Doris, just listen closely. I gather that the parents were most carefully chosen . . .'

'From 20,000 parenthood-donors, who offered themselves from all parts of the world,' put in Harold proudly.

'And who had to pass the severest tests of health, physique and intellectual attainment,' added the Senator sonorously. 'I may claim that Insemnia is the result of the most remarkable process of elimination ever known.'

'So now you see, Doris.'

'That's the position, Mother.'

'Ah pray that Ah may have patience,' said Lady Bloomsbury between clenched teeth, 'Ah can see no hope of ever being told the truth about this matter. Ah feel that something is being kept from me. Ah will say no more, but Ah must insist on a clear answer to one simple question. Is she . . . were they . . . is it *legitimate*?'

'Mother, please don't start all that reactionary stuff again.'

'Harold, I pray you, leave this to me. Legitimate, ma'am? In science there is no legitimacy or illegitimacy. This is Progress.'

'Planned Parenthood,' I put in helpfully.

'Precisely. You are extremely apt in your choice of words, if I may say so, Mr. Grame. A trained mind, a trained mind. I could wish your measurements . . .'

'Oh, they don't matter. I'm not a candidate.'

'Ahrrm,' said Lord Bloomsbury. 'Apparently it's all quite normal and natural in America, Doris. You know what these . . ahem, I mean, of course, the whole thing is very odd by our old-fashioned notions.'

'It's not odd, it's double dutch,' said Lady Bloomsbury, 'but Ah will not give up the attempt while breath remains in mah body. Senator, Ah address mahself to you. Is this all?'

'All, ma'am?'

'Has anything irrevocable been done?'

'Irrevocable?'

'This is intolerable, Mother. What are you driving at now?'

'Harold, I've told you before, I will not have you talk to your mother like that.'

'What Ah wish to know, Senator, is: have there been any of these telepathic transactions, or whatever they are?'

'My dear lady! My dear ma'am! The Institute would never countenance such a thing. We have a tradition of propriety second to none in the world. Only after the ceremony at Westminster Abbey does the process of controlled, indirect parenthood begin, in all its majesty and beauty, under the supervision of the Institute.'

'Would it be wise, Lord Bloomsbury,' I suggested, 'to inquire whether the child, or children, become the property of the Institute?'

The point seemed to be worth investigation in the interests of all concerned, or I should not have intervened. Unhappily this new idea seemed to upset Lady Bloomsbury; exclaiming, 'Ah don't know what mah poor mother would say if she knew,' she burst into tears and once more tottered from the room. Lady Cynthia sped after her with compassionate noises; Lord Bloomsbury and Harold would not, I think, have followed but that she drew them with a look of reproach that was like a grappling hook. I was left with the Senator, Insemnia and Alistair, who was contentedly talking to himself; a mouthful of toast made his words difficult to understand, but I thought I heard something about Pilsudski.

The Senator looked after Lady Bloomsbury in bewilderment and then turned to me. 'Mr. Grame,' he said, 'I have no wish to pry into the secrets of your old nobility, but I know, of course, that the thinning of the bloodstream through intermarriage sometimes produces ill effects. Lady Bloomsbury's behaviour seems to be somewhat strange. Tell me, sir, is there any mental disequilibrium in that quarter?'

'None at all,' I said, 'at any rate, hardly any. I believe the ladies of Lady Bloomsbury's family have always been highly strung since the fourteenth earl was hanged at Tyburn, but it is nothing of account, Senator, nothing.'

'And Lady Bloomsbury's powers of comprehension are normal?'

'Fully up to the standard of to-day.'

'Then why,' said the Senator, at a loss, 'is she unable to grasp the simple facts of Insemnia's birth? And why should she oppose a wedding at Westminster Abbey? I understand it is a highly respectable church.'

'Oh, I think it's all a little misunderstanding. I never like to push myself forward, or I would offer to have a word with the Dean myself; we were at night school together.'

'Do that, my dear sir,' said the Senator warmly, 'do that. After all, we must consider what is due to Insemnia's rank.'

'Of course,' I said, 'don't worry, Senator. I am sure all will be arranged. Er, there is one other little matter, though . . . but it's no business of mine. . . .'

'Speak, Mr. Grame, speak,' he cried. 'What is it?'

'Well,' I said, deprecatingly, 'if you do not find in Lord and Lady Bloomsbury that ready assent, that ecstatic joy, which you anticipated, at the prospect of this match, I think I might guess the reason. They are old-fashioned folk, Senator, quietly proud of their birth and breeding, and I believe they disapprove of the French prizefighter. They feel that a union between their son and the, er, fruit of a French prizefighter would be a mesalliance.'

'What!' he said, staring. 'First the Hungarian hussar, now the French prizefighter! Is there no pleasing them? What more do they want? His measurements were unique.'

'I know, I know,' I said. 'It is an absurd prejudice, perhaps, but there it is.'

'They object to prizefighting?'

'Not that so much, I think. Their ears blush at the word French.'

'Oh, if that's all, I could have made him a German prizefighter.' I looked at him with speechless reproach. 'Ah, that is to say, Mr. Grame, I could have concealed his nationality, had I but known. Now let me see.' A cunning look, I fancied crept into his eyes. 'So the dame doesn't want a French prizefighter,' he said, as if to himself. 'Okay, I guess I can fix that.'

'Senator!' I said, in surprise.

He appeared to pull himself together. 'I mean, my dear Mr. Grame,' he boomed, 'I think I can overcome all Lady Bloomsbury's misgivings.'

The door opened and Oliver came in, shouting, 'Breakfast

ahoy!' The words died on his lips as he saw Insemnia. He came and sat beside her, and looked at her. The Senator looked at him and his eye glittered. He leaned forward.

'Commander Jene,' he said, 'you interest me, in my professional capacity. Your measurements are really most exceptional. Allow me to make a few notes for my records.' He opened his notebook and wrote, muttering the entries. 'Athletic type. Seafaring man. Measurements excellent, health and constitution apparently perfect. Brain-power doubtful. . . .'

'I've a mole on my back, if that's important,' said Oliver politely.

'Ah. Whereabouts?'

'Oh, rather low down, actually.'

'H'm. There is nearly always a flaw, a blemish.'

'Perhaps it could be removed, Senator,' said Insemnia, casually. 'Science is wonderful.'

'True, my dear, true. Science can move mountains.'

'Oh, don't made a mountain out of my mole,' said Oliver. 'It's quite small.'

'Ah! In that case we can probably overlook it. Now, at a glance, Commander Jene – at a *first* glance, I must remind you, and subject to error – I should suggest, offhand, in your case one of our most deserving candidates – a one-legged schoolmistress in Oshkosh. New blood is badly needed there. H'm; most interesting.' And he closed the notebook.

There was a brief silence, during which Oliver looked at the Senator, then at Insemnia, and then at Alistair.

'Guv'nor,' he said.

This is one of the strange things about Oliver. He alone is able whenever he wishes, to penetrate Alistair's trances, and to make himself understood. Alistair awoke.

'Yes?' he said. He looked at Oliver and then at Insemnia. He laughed suddenly. 'Oh, er, yes, of course,' he said, and without another word he rose and wandered out. Then Oliver looked at me. I also knew what he meant; he meant 'Would you remove this old gentleman, Grame?'

'Senator,' I said, 'I should like your opinion of a notable wine I have in my room, some very old sherry.'

'Sherry!' said the Senator, and his eye gleamed. 'I haven't tasted sherry for a long time. We have to ban all alchohol from the Institute, you know, ha-ha. By all means, Mr. Grame. Come Semmy, my dear.'

'Oh, I think it would be a little strong for Insemnia, Senator,' I said. 'I shan't keep you a moment. Just a nightcap, you know.'

'A nightcap! Very well, then, just one. Wait for me, my dear; I shall be back immediately. Good night, Commander Jene, if we do not meet again.'

I led him upstairs.

XX

PRACTICE was making me expert in the use of Our Sherry; I was drafting in my mind an article for the *Lancet* about its possibilities as a new and more pleasant form of anaesthetic. Thus I did not need more than ten minutes and half of my second flask to produce amnesia in the Senator. At this point the patient is better, I find, for a little rest, so I took him downstairs, going backwards in front of him myself, with my hands pressed against his stomach, in order that he should not return to his room head-first. As we passed the Bloomsburys' door I heard Lady Bloomsbury sobbing, Lord Bloomsbury upbraiding Harold, Harold expostulating, and Lady Cynthia trying to soothe all three; I judged they would be busy for some time. A gentle pressure laid the Senator once more on his bed and I went on my way, which did not lead to my room, for I felt that work would remain beyond my powers until tranquillity was restored to Number Seven.

Inside the dining-room I heard Insemnia's and Oliver's voices. I turned aside and went into the lounge; I did not wish to disturb them, so I entered and sat down quietly. Unhappily the connecting door was open and I could not but hear what was said.

Indeed, whenever I shifted cautiously in my chair, to make myself more comfortable, I could see them, though they did not see me; the lounge is one of those dark, almost gloomy rooms. They were still sitting at the breakfast table; Insemnia composed and indifferent, as usual, and Oliver turned attentively towards her.

'You're one of those artificial insemination babies, aren't you?' he was saying.

'Ah, so you understand,' she said. 'Everyone else pretends not to. How did you know?'

'Oh, well, the name gave me the clue,' said Oliver, 'and then Mums told me one or two things. She had it a bit mixed, but it was clear enough to me. I tried to explain it to her, but you know what these old ladies are.' (As I say, things that puzzle others always appear simple to Oliver.)

'No, I do not. I cannot understand them. But I am not *one* of those artificial insemination babies. I am the first of them. I was the Senator's first experiment. The Institute grew up around me, and through me a new race of men and women will grow up around the Institute.'

'Gosh, that's exciting for you.'

'You think so? I do not like to be told that I am in any way different from other women. I find it all very boring.' And Insemnia gave her fascinating little yawn.

'You, er, like yawning, don't you?' said Oliver. I gathered that this was not the first yawn, and he sounded a little aggrieved.

'Yes, it refreshes me. But the Committee dislikes it very much. I am always being scolded for it. Why do they argue so much about me here?'

'Well, I've just arrived, and I've only had a garbled version of the facts from Mums,' said Oliver, 'so I don't really know. I did gather there'd been a spot of argument. Wasn't your father, or, er, whatever the correct term is in these cases, a French prize-fighter? Perhaps Lord and Lady Bloomsbury object to that. They're very much opposed to blood sports.'

'But he was a very good prizefighter. His measurements were wonderful. I wish Harold's measurements were better. But the

Committee says breeding is more essential in the second generation, then measurements again in the third. Your measurements are *very* good. It is a pity you are plebeian and unintellectual. You would be very useful to the Cause.'

I heard a note of irritation in Oliver's voice. 'As it happens,' he said, 'my uncle's baronetcy goes back about four hundred years and Lord Bloomsbury was Professor Biggs a few years ago.'

'It is a *new* title?' said Insemnia, showing faint surprise.

'Yes. Not that that means anything. If you went back six hundred years you'd probably find that the Bloomsburys were barons and we were butchers. There are ups and downs in all families and they level themselves out. The process works well in this country. The only trouble is that all families, at all levels, throw up weeds like Harold in great quantities.'

'But when the Senator learns this he will not let me marry Harold and he will take me back to America.'

'I doubt that. A title's a title. Would you be glad if he took you away?'

'I do not know. Harold's measurements are very boring. But it has nothing to do with me. The Senator decides. I wonder where he is?' And she yawned.

'I wish,' said Oliver, and I heard the action-stations note creep into his voice, 'you'd stop yawning.'

'It is my only bad habit. I cannot help it. When I am bored I yawn.'

'Oh, you're still bored! Would anything short of an earthquake amuse you?'

'I do not know.'

There was a pause and as I happened to shift in my chair I saw Oliver lean nearer her. I thought I heard the look-out man call, 'Enemy in sight.'

'I think that's the loveliest dress I ever saw,' said Oliver firmly.

'Yes? The Committee has very good taste.'

'It's very revealing.'

'Revealing?'

'Yes. It emphasizes your femininity.'

'What is there to conceal? I am a woman. I am not dressed to disguise the fact.'

'But there are degrees of emphasis,' said Oliver, leaning still nearer, 'and it's emphasizing the most beautiful woman I ever saw.'

'Yes, the Committee says that . . .'

'Hang the Committee. *I'm* saying it. You're uniquely lovely—your hair, your eyes, your figure. I'll tell you all about them. It's a long story and I won't tell it briefly.'

'Don't tell it,' said Insemnia, 'it is boring.'

Oliver recoiled. 'Confound your cheek,' he said. 'This is your technique. Are you trying to provoke me?'

'Provoke you? I do not know what you mean. Why should I? You are very nice. But I am not interested.'

'I believe you're telling the truth,' said Oliver in the tone of exasperation. 'You *are* different. There's something wrong with you, or something lacking. You're like an empty room, or an unlit candle. Perhaps it has something to do with the way you were made. I wonder if they sent you into the world short of some essential ingredient.' (Oliver, I thought again, does not underestimate his own powers of attraction.)

'I do not know what you are talking about,' said Insemnia, and began, once more, to yawn.

'I warn you,' said Oliver, in his 'Attack' voice, 'if you yawn again I shall do something I shall never regret. Have you ever been alone with a man before?'

'Yes, twice. It was exciting.'

'It *was*! You surprise me. Who was it?'

'The first one was a photographer from *Life*. He came to take my picture.'

'A photographer! I said a man. A photographer is a lens on legs. I am a man, and I'm beginning to feel extremely male. Who was the other?'

'Mr. Grame, last night. I am sorry, I must go now. I dislike all these questions. They are very boring.'

'Well, don't say I didn't warn you,' said Oliver, violently. I heard noises. I leaned forward to look, for fear any harm should befall Insemnia. I saw that her feet were some inches from the floor; he had picked her up bodily and was kissing her as hard as any man could, or any maid could wish. Oliver is a strong lad, and appeared to be exerting all his strength; I thought I heard her ribs crack. He kissed her a very long time and when he put her down I almost wondered if she still breathed. However, neither medicine nor fiction, I believe, record a case of a woman killed by kissing, and, though limp and crumpled, she was alive.

'How did you like that?' asked Oliver in the voice of a ship's commander sentencing a seaman to the cells. She made no answer. She looked frozen. 'How did you like that, I said?' he shouted.

Insemnia's lips parted. 'I liked it,' she said, faintly, slowly.

Oliver looked startled. He plainly thought she ought to like it, and defied her not to like it, but now seemed surprised that she had liked it. 'You did!' he said. 'Then why didn't you say so?'

Again a silence. This girl appeared to examine her feelings closely before she described them. 'I wasn't sure,' she said.

'Oh. In that case I'll do it again, to make sure.' And he did, and put her down again, and stood back. I saw Insemnia slowly sit up, raise her hand to her cheek and then lower it to her heart. For the first time, I saw her really smile, and thought ruefully of my own feeble efforts the evening before.

'Well, there's nothing wrong with you,' said Oliver briefly, looking at her. 'You're exactly like any other woman.'

'Am I?' she said delightedly. 'How marvellous! Mr. Grame said that, too.'

'Did he? I suppose he kissed you too, the old reprobate. Did you like it?'

'I don't know. He seemed to want me to, so I said it was rather exciting.' (Traitor, I thought.) 'But what have you done to me? I am so warm. And my heart is beating.'

'How old are you?'

'Eighteen.'

'Then it's been beating for eighteen years,' said Oliver precisely.

'Has it? I never knew it. Not like this. Feel it.' She took his hand and placed it on her heart.

'Good Lord,' said Oliver, 'did I do *that*?'

'Yes. But what *is* this feeling? I feel happy, and excited, and rather frightened, and I want you to kiss me again and yet I don't want to . . . I can't describe what I feel.'

'Well, I never expected to have to explain the facts of life to a grown female,' said Oliver, 'but perhaps, in your case, there's some excuse. Do you remember Sleeping Beauty?'

'Oh yes. Mr. Grame showed her to me at the waxworks.'

'He would. Well, she was awakened by a kiss. And do you remember Pygmalion?'

'Not bloody likely?' said Insemnia.

'*What!*' said Oliver. 'Oh, I see what you mean. No, not that one. Pygmalion, King of Cyprus, who made a statue of a woman so beautiful that he loved it and called on his gods to give it life.'

'And did they?'

'Yes. The white marble slowly suffused with the tints of life and the statue became a living woman. I didn't think such things happened nowadays, but perhaps they do. You've awakened. You *were* different, you see. You've come to life.'

'And you did it! How clever you are.'

'Don't mention it. It was a pleasure. I suppose it was an experiment, really.'

'Ah, all human progress comes through experiment. The Senator says so.'

'Don't start all that again. I wasn't thinking about the future of the human race when I made that experiment. Come on, let's dance.'

'Dance? But there's no band.'

'We don't need a band for this dance. The only music we want is the beating of your heart—and mine. Come.' Obediently she stood up and I watched Oliver take her in his arms as a seaman should and dance, a very slow and perfect waltz, brushing her forehead with his lips, while she yielded herself to him and the long lashes drooped over her eyes. They were well paired; I thought I had never seen a lovelier couple and had I been of the other sex I do not doubt that some foolish match-making scheme would have entered my head. Behind them, through the big window, I saw Priscilla Grove, sleepy in the sunshine, with old Mrs. Miggins pushing Mrs. O'Bourke in her bathchair and a stray assassin or two passing.

At last they stopped as footsteps came down the stairs and Em Porridge entered the dining-room in search of a belated breakfast. He grinned at them in his customary bewilderment, saying politely, 'Excuse, pleess', as he sat down. Insemnia, as if she suddenly remembered something, said, 'Oh, I must go to the Senator; I wonder why he is so long,' and went quickly out of the room. I came out of the lounge and stopped her at the foot of the stairs. I took a long look at her and marvelled at the change.

'Insemnia,' I said, 'you're wide awake. What a picture you are, for these old eyes. What has happened to you?'

She smiled radiantly. 'I am so happy,' she said, 'I feel so *alive*.'

'I know you are,' I said, 'I know you do, and I know why. But, Insemnia, what now?'

'What now?'

'Yes. Harold? The Senator?'

Her eyes clouded again. 'Oh, all that,' she said. 'I have nothing to do with that. Why do you remind me now?' Then her eyes cleared and she smiled. 'What a lovely day,' she said, and ran away from me and up the stairs; I had never seen her move at anything but a measured walk before. She stopped and looked back. 'I am so happy,' she said, and disappeared.

I went into the dining-room. Oliver looked up. 'Magician!' I said.

XXI

FOR some reason which I could not explain to myself, I felt a little jaded that morning. The atmosphere of the house of trouble which Number Seven was becoming was oppressive, and the unusual number of visitors made it positively uncomfortable; in quick succession arrived a doctor to see Mrs. Barnes, a veterinary surgeon to examine Peggy, and a dentist summoned by Em Porridge, who was suffering from an unaccountable pain in his face. These comings and goings upset the wonted peace of the place and I went out to take a turn in the sunshine of Priscilla Grove. Even there I found little rest. The assassins, smoking innumerable cigarettes which they lit from matches struck on their five o'clock shadow, and the artists, in chattering groups, plainly believed that if they only waited long enough some delightful calamity would transpire and obstinately hung about outside, with their eyes fixed on our doorway and windows. They watched intently, and muttered comments of joyful foreboding, as I questioned the departing specialists, whose arrival had done much to confirm their happy fears for us. The doctor shook his head gloomily when I asked him about Mrs. Barnes. He could find no mortal injury or incurable ailment, he said, but she seemed to be raving, and when he put his ear to her lips he had heard some faint and incoherent babble about a fine day and someone who would come along. The veterinary surgeon, too, was baffled by Peggy. He said he suspected distemper and would swear to bad temper (he displayed a bandaged hand) but he had never before in his experience known a dog change shape. 'Well, you know what women are,' I said, helpfully, but he said no, Peggy was too old for such enterprises; he thought a long-dormant strain of dachshund must be coming out in the old age of what he had always believed to be a thoroughbred Aberdeen terrier. The dentist was uneasy because, having failed to find the cause of Em Porridge's pain, he had, to satisfy that gentleman, pulled a sound tooth; I tried to be comforting, as always, by reminding him that Em Porridge, having so many teeth, would never notice the lack of one; but his professional conscience was not thus lightly consoled.

I always strive to take a detached view of things, and thought I would cross to the opposite side of Priscilla Grove for a survey of Number Seven; being so much in and of it, I had never before contemplated it as a whole. Having done this, I realized that there was some reason, if no excuse, for the morbid curiosity which our neighbours tended to display about it and us. Even from the other side of the street the sounds of upbraiding and defiance in the Bloomsburys' flat could be heard, and the figures of parents and son seen; until Harold, being unable to go home to his mother, since he was already at home with her, shut himself in his own room and began defiantly to sing, in a fine bass-soprano, the marching-song of his discussion-group: 'To the Left of the Left there is always the Left'; which was soon taken up by the sympathizers outside. First at one window, and then at another, the anxious face of Lady Cynthia (with a pipe in it) could be seen as she dashed from room to room with dusters and suction-cleaner; every now and then she looked down at the crowd outside, moaned, and vanished again. Alistair, with his string shopping-bag, came obliviously out and wandered towards the Brompton Road; in the courteous silence which received him he was heard to say, 'Noch nicht ist Polen verloren!' At her window on the top floor Edith sat like a mother of sorrows and looked out into a loveless world with unseeing eyes, the redness of which was visible from the street. After a while she stood up and thereafter was seen moving about in her room; she seemed to be packing something bulky, for there were glimpses of sheets of brown paper and balls of string. The windows of the first-floor flat, alone, were still and empty. I knew why the Senator was not on show, and assumed that Insemnia was resting after an eventful night and morning.

To a man who likes to see others happy, though he does not presume to trespass on their cares, it was a painful sight, and it suddenly occurred to me that it might do me good to take a stroll along the Brompton Road, first to see if the greater world still turned, and next to get another bottle of Our Sherry (for my flask was nearly empty). I found the shop, and the merchant, and he looked at me blankly.

'Sherry, sir?' he said, in the tone of a man whose good humour not even a gratuitous insult could upset. 'Ho no. No Sherry. Ho no.'

'Whisky?'

'Whisky! Ho no. Ho-ho! Ho no.'

'Yo ho,' I said, 'a bottle of rum?'

'Rum! Ho-ho! Oh, ho-ho-ho! Ho no.'

'Port?'

He saw that I, a total stranger, had come to taunt, to wound, to affront him. Until now he had not let himself be provoked, and how many others would have stood as much? Now his manner changed.

'Look 'ere,' he said, 'I don't want to turn ugly . . .'

'I'm sure you couldn't,' I said disarmingly.

'I didn't arst you to come 'ere, did I? I give you a civil answer, didn't I? That's more than what most would 'ave done, isn't it? What do you want to come 'ere insulting me for?'

'I only wanted a bottle of sherry,' I said, 'and you are a wine merchant, aren't you?'

'You – only – wanted – a – bottle – of – sherry!' he repeated in awful mockery, waving to the shelves behind him; it was true that they were empty save for three bottles of Vichy water (which his customers refused to buy until they were cleared of the suspicion of collaboration with the enemy). 'Don't you know there's . . .'

'There's a peace on? Yes, yes, I know,' I said, 'and it's going to be long and hard, but you did once let Lady Cynthia have three bottles of a very good sherry . . .' I broke off, a sudden suspicion having come to me. I had assumed him to be a homely looking man in his own right, or wrong, but now I wondered. That squint; had I not seen its like before? His breath, too. His slightly theatrical good humour at first, and his sudden wrath afterwards. The thickness of his speech, which I had attributed to a rude upbringing or other impediment. I looked to see if his hair was standing on end, but he was bald. 'I believe,' I said, accusingly, 'you've been drinking it all yourself.'

'Wot, me!' he said, focusing both eyes fiercely on the bridge of his nose in an effort to express great indignation. 'I never tush it.'

'*What* did you say?' I asked (I wanted to be quite sure).

'Tush.'

'Not touch?'

'Yes, tush.'

Now I was certain. I leaned across the counter and gave him a gentle push. Like a tree he fell, and lay still and peaceful. I raised the flap, passed through, and looked under the counter. There seemed to be hundreds of bottles, all empty, and I saw that his customers could not reasonably have expected him to supply their wants after he had met his own; among them, however, were three bottles of Our Sherry, one open with a half-filled glass beside it, and the others untouched. I took these two and strolled back to Priscilla Grove, making a few more mental notes for my treatise on the way.

The crowd outside Number Seven was almost gone; it was nearly lunch-time, and even artists and assassins must eat. I went up to my room to wash and met Edith staggering out of hers with a very large parcel.

'Good gracious, Edith,' I said, 'let me carry that. You'll do yourself some injury.' I took it from her, and she leaned against the wall to get her breath. 'It's very heavy. What is it?'

'I'm taking Harold's presents back,' she said, with a quiver of the lip.

'His presents? He's a donor in a big way, isn't he? Is it furniture?'

'No. It's the collected essays of Karl Marx, in fifteen volumes.'

'Oh! You know, I'm really very sorry about all this, Edith.'

'I don't think you are, Mr. Grame. I think you dislike me.'

'Edith,' I said, 'I am among your great admirers, and if I

were not afraid that you would think me a meddler I would like to do anything I could to help.'

'What could you do? What could anybody do? It's all so hopeless.'

'I don't think it is. I have a feeling that all may work out well for you yet.'

'Mr. Grame, you're not hiding anything from me? You don't *know* something, do you?'

'Oh no,' I said hastily, 'not a thing, it's not even my business. But I have an intuition. I think . . .'

But before I could say what I thought Edith's parcel dropped from my numbed fingers on to the landing outside the Bloomsburys' door, which we had just reached; the string burst and the collected wisdom of Karl Marx strewed itself about the floor. It was an exceptionally heavy parcel and made a noise like a thunderclap; and the household was already on edge from a series of loud and unexpected noises. The door opened and Harold's startled face shot out as if he had been waiting behind it for the parcel to arrive in just this manner; a floor lower, the Senator appeared in alarm and came hurrying up the stairs to see what was amiss. Harold looked from the tomes to Edith with an expression which contained no invitation to her to remain; Edith haughtily turned her back and went back to her room. The Senator and I helped Harold to carry in the volumes. He seemed to fear being left alone with his parents and, when we made to go, detained us by reopening of his own accord the subject which had already caused so much wasted acrimony in Number Seven.

'I may as well tell you, Senator,' he said, 'that my parents are still opposed to my marriage. I don't understand their attitude. It savours of the Extreme Right.'

'Good gracious,' said the Senator, 'but this is an affront to democracy.'

'Rubbish,' said Lord Bloomsbury.

'Ah know you're young, Harold,' said Lady Bloomsbury, 'and young people will be young people. . . .'

'I don't think there *are* any young people nowadays,' said

Lord Bloomsbury gloomily. 'They get so old while they're talking about Youth. Why, that last International Youth Rally of yours at the Albert Hall, Harold, was packed with the most decrepit crowd of bald and mumbling octogenarians I've ever seen.'

'Even the Youth Movement must have Leaders, father.'

'Why pick leaders who aren't young and can hardly move? I can't understand . . . '

'Ah've never known two grown men so incapable of keeping to the point. Ah want to know more about this girl.'

'This girl, ma'am! Are you speaking of my ward?'

'If you're against Insemnia because her parents weren't married, Mother, I think you're most reactionary.'

'Weren't married, indeed! Ah understand they never even *met*!'

'Well, suppose they *had* met and then produced Insemnia without marrying,' said Harold astutely, 'would you like that better?'

'Now don't start twisting everything, Harold.'

'Ah cannot reconcile mahself to it. It's all so queer. We don't even know who she is.'

'But, ma'am . . .' began the Senator.

'Let me speak, Senator,' said Harold. 'You *do* know who she is, Mother. Her father was a French prizefighter and her mother an American opera-singer.'

'Ah've only the Senator's word even for that. And these surgeons are so careless – leaving lancets and swabs about in wounds and so on. You don't know *what* might have happened. She might be a . . . Hottentot or something.'

'That's true, Harold,' said Lord Bloomsbury. 'You can't be too careful. They do make mistakes, you know – get the test-tubes mixed up and so on. Mistakes happen in the best-regulated families.'

'Tom, for a public man, Ah think your choice of words is deplorable. Are you holding up Insemnia's . . er . . . pedigree as the model of a well-regulated family?'

'What nonsense,' said Harold. 'These inseminations are under the strictest scientific and official control. You're just raising flippant objections.'

Lady Bloomsbury turned towards the Senator. 'Ah must point out to you, Senator,' she said, 'that we have our position to consider. We have a duty to the title. Ah think our Harold is being very cruel, bringing this bar sinister into the family. . . .'

'Mother! *What* did you call Insemnia?'

'Now, Harold,' said Lord Bloomsbury, 'don't jump to conclusions. Your mother only said bar sinister.'

'Oh, bar sinister. Well, Insemnia's *not* a bar sinister. . . .'

The Senator, who had vainly been trying to break into the dispute, now firmly quelled Harold. 'Harold,' he said, 'be good enough to leave this to me. My dear Lady Bloomsbury, I gather you are strongly opposed to this match.'

'Ah will never consent to it.'

'The trouble is, Doris,' said Lord Bloomsbury, uneasily, 'Harold's mind seems to be made up and he's old enough to know what he's doing. We mustn't say anything we'd be sorry for, without full consideration.'

'Well, my mind *is* made up,' said Harold. 'I think you ought to appreciate the honour that is being done me. As Insemnia's husband . . .'

'Yes, yes,' said the Senator, 'all in good time, Harold. Let me speak, I pray. Now, Lady Bloomsbury, will you please enlighten my bewilderment. What *is* your objection?'

Lord Bloomsbury answered. 'Well, Senator, to put it bluntly, we can't swallow Insemnia. Perhaps we're old-fashioned. . . .'

'She seems so uncanny. Ah keep expecting her to disappear, or have a baby, or something. It's all like Blithe Spirit.'

'Dear lady, you are far behind the times in this old island. But perhaps I can yet reassure you. Is it her parentage that still worries you?'

'Worry is a quite inadequate word for mah feeling.'

'Is it, perhaps, the French prizefighter at whom you baulk?'

'Well,' said Lord Bloomsbury judicially, 'that's *one* thing.'

'Ah believe French prizefighters fight with their feet.'
'Kicking below the belt,' I murmured.
'Yes. Ah think it's disgusting.'
'It's not cricket, Senator,' said Lord Bloomsbury.
'Cricket?'
'Perhaps you should make that a little clearer, Lord Bloomsbury,' I prompted him, 'the Senator is an American. Lord Bloomsbury means, it's not baseball, Senator.'
'Baseball?'
'Must we bring in all these ball games?' asked Harold bitterly.
'I am a little confused,' said the Senator, 'no matter. I gather that, either on social or sporting grounds, you object to the French prizefighter?'
'Ah certainly do, among other things.'
'Then I think I can reassure you,' said the Senator, and for an instant his eye rested on me with a glance of gratitude, 'although to do so I shall have to reveal a secret I meant to carry to my grave. . . .'
'A secret?' said Harold, startled.
'Ee, something else,' said Lady Bloomsbury in grim tones.
'But I must beg you all, on your honour – you too, Mr. Grame, as the family friend, ha-ha – not to betray this confidence to my Committee, or I shall be a ruined man. I did it for the best, but they might not appreciate my motives. Lady Bloomsbury, the French prizefighter was *not* Insemnia's father.'
'Ee, what now?' moaned Lady Bloomsbury. 'Ah'm convinced Ah shall never know the truth.'
'You shall, ma'am, you shall. The story may seem a little strange to you. It may shock some of your old-world notions. You may reproach me. You may say, Senator Vanderboom should never have done such a thing. I do not know. I ask you to hear me and give your verdict. I shall submit to it. I acted for the good of humanity.' I began to feel that the Senator, once he got well started, was apt to be carried away on the wings of his own eloquence; watching him, as he stood with a noonday sunbeam making a golden aureole of his white hair, with his

hand raised in pontifical gesture, and with a benign rapture in his gaze, I felt I could nearly believe him; and not only this, but that he probably believed himself. Even Lord and Lady Bloomsbury, I saw, were held in his spell.

'Insemnia's mother and my Committee,' he continued, 'were insistent on the French prizefighter. His measurements were, indeed, flawless – save for a cauliflower toe. But I realized that physique is not all. Breeding is perhaps more important, and he was of extremely mixed descent. The future of mankind was in my hand. I was determined that our firstborn, Insemnia, on whom the new race depends, should be perfect. I felt justified in overriding the wishes of the Committee and of her mother. I gave Insemnia a different father. I am the only man in the world who knows. At dead of night *I changed the bottles.*'

There was the stricken pause that comes when a moving-picture photographer cries 'Hold it!' I could feel Lady Bloomsbury fighting silently to understand that which the Senator thought he had made completely clear. The Senator looked like one of the prophets of antiquity. Lord Bloomsbury's mouth was open and even Harold looked puzzled. The hush became painful; I thought it should be ended.

'Was the French prizefighter's sacrifice in vain then?' I asked timidly.

For an instant the Senator looked slightly irritable, like a man tripped up in full stride. 'No, no,' he said, curtly, 'I gave him to a Swedish actress from Chicago. It was one of my failures. The result was a girl of inferior physique who gave way to crooning at an early age.'

'Ee,' said Lady Bloomsbury.

Lord Bloomsbury, the chairman fighting against a muddle-headed committee, tried again. 'I don't see that we're getting any further forward,' he said. 'What have bottles to do with all this?'

The Senator raised both hands, soothingly. 'You do not understand, Lord Bloomsbury,' he said. 'There was another man whose measurements were nearly as good as the French prize-fighter's and who was directly descended from William the

Conqueror. He was my choice, and in this supreme matter I could not allow the Committee or Insemnia's mother to override me. It was done in the highest interests of humanity. I made *him* the father of Insemnia's mother's child.'

'But . . . but . . . who *was* he?'

'He was an English nobleman, of one of your oldest families.'

'Was? Is he dead, too? Was he another, er, martyr to your Cause?'

'No, sir,' said the Senator, looking with grief into the past, 'his end was sad. He was impoverished, and used the fee for his great contribution to our Cause to buy back his ancestral abbey. Unhappily it collapsed on him on the very day of his homecoming. He was buried in the ruins. The Institute posthumously awarded him its Order of Merit . . . second class. Now, Lord and Lady Bloomsbury, even you, with your ancient lineage, cannot cavil at Insemnia's descent.'

The Senator beamed at us like a man who had solved all the problems of the universe. At last Lady Bloomsbury spoke, as if speech were a great effort. 'Ah often wondered what it must feel like to go mad,' she said, 'and now Ah know. Ah'm undoubtedly insane.'

'Mother, this is intolerable,' said Harold.

Lady Bloomsbury's iron will suddenly failed her. She had been through a great deal. Dabbing her eye with her handkerchief, she said hopelessly, 'Ee well, what moost be, moost be. Ah've done mah best for mah child. Ah can do no more. Ah chook oop t'spoonge.' (In moments of great stress Lady Bloomsbury's native tongue reasserts itself.)

Lord Bloomsbury went to her and they joined hands, as such good simple folk are wont to do in times of ordeal. He, too, dropped into the vernacular. 'Ee, don't woorry, moother,' he said. 'Coom what coom may, we've got each oother.'

The Senator looked at me in perplexity. 'The Gaelic,' I explained, briefly. 'It means, Lord and Lady Bloomsbury withdraw their opposition.'

He beamed. 'Ah, I knew you would, ma'am, and my dear

sir. Then, ring the bells. On with the wedding. To Westminster Abbey!' He struck an attitude.

Lady Cynthia's head popped through the door. Her face was red and anxious. 'Oh, will you all come down to lunch?' she said. 'I've just managed to get Mrs. Barnes and Peggy off to sleep and I want to serve it before they wake up again.'

XXII

IT was a memorable lunch; it began on a low note of strain and depression but ended on a high one of gaiety and mutual goodwill, a development for which I may perhaps take a little credit.

I went down first to see if I could give Lady Cynthia any help, for I knew that she was overburdened. In the kitchen I found her, Alistair and Oliver walking round the table on tiptoe with plates and pans in their hands and thought I had surprised the Jene family in some ancient druidical rite usually hidden from any strange eye.

'What *are* you doing?' I asked.

Lady Cynthia span round. 'Ssh,' she said.

'What?' I said.

'SSH,' she said, so loudly and angrily that I flinched; and then she whispered, 'We must not wake Mrs. Barnes and Peggy.'

'Oh,' I whispered back, 'right-ho,' and I began to tiptoe with them. 'Can I help?'

'Yes. I daren't use the service lift, it would wake them. We're going to carry everything up. Will you take Edith's lunch up to her? It's on this tray. She refuses to come down. She's heartbroken.'

'All right,' I whispered, 'but it's very difficult carrying heavy trays upstairs on tiptoe. I'll probably fall down backwards.'

Lady Cynthia went pale and clutched her heart. 'Mr. Grame,' she said in a whisper that was like a serpent's sting, 'if you dare I'll close Number Seven for ever.'

'No, no, not that,' I pleaded. 'Give me the tray.' As a man of honour I tiptoed right up to the top floor and found, when Edith opened her door to my knock, that I could not get down off my tiptoes.

'What on earth are you creeping round like that for?' she said, looking at me miserably.

'I can't help it,' I whispered, 'ahrrm, I mean' – I summoned back my normal voice – 'I've got fixed like it. I'll be all right in a moment. Don't take any notice. Why aren't you coming down, Edith?'

'I couldn't,' she said, 'I couldn't bear to face her and see her grin with triumph. Did Harold say anything when I sent back his presents?'

'He was overwhelmed.'

'Was he?' she said, hopefully. 'I don't think he's really bad, you know. He's under the influence of this creature.'

'Are you very much in love with him, Edith?'

'I suppose I am. He's so . . . fine.'

'Who is?'

'Harold, of course.'

'Harold?'

'Yes, Harold.'

'Harold! Oh, I see what you mean.'

'I have so many lovely memories. I keep thinking of our happy Thursday evenings together at the Friendship with Rusher Society . . . and now,' said Edith, bursting into tears, 'it's all over.'

'Don't worry,' I said, 'there will be many more happy Thursday evenings for you – a long vista of them stretching down the years, with the annual Youth Rally shining over your old age like the rising sun.'

She stopped crying and looked at me suspiciously. 'How can there be,' she said, 'if he's going to marry this . . . chemical concoction that he found at some drugstore in New York? Has anything further happened about that?'

'Well, yes,' I said. 'Lord and Lady Bloomsbury have given

their consent, I'm afraid, reluctantly' – Edith broke into sobs again – 'but don't attach too much importance to that. Harold hasn't married Insemnia yet by a long way.'

'Don't you want him to?' she asked, coming out of her handkerchief like the moon from behind a cloud.

'Oh, I have no feelings whatever,' I said hastily. 'It's not my affair. But, I tell you what, Edith; come down to coffee after lunch.'

'Why?'

'Well, I don't know, I may be quite wrong, it's just a guess, but I feel that Harold may be staying in this afternoon while almost everybody else goes out.'

I left her with the light of new hope in her eyes and went downstairs, just in time to see the Jenes tiptoe in Indian file into the dining-room. Save for Edith, the household was fully assembled, and there was, as I have said, a certain constraint. The Senator's sunny good-humour had not yet thawed Lady Bloomsbury's chilly gloom; Harold was restive beneath his parents' look of dumb reproach; and Em Porridge suffered because the dentist, no doubt in a moment of absent-mindedness, induced by the surroundings of Priscilla Grove, had removed a front upper tooth, so that his loss was more noticeable than we had expected and he spoke with a thick lisp instead of his former sibilant hiss.

But the chief cause of the tension was Insemnia. The two other ladies present, with that lightning-like perception which is the gift of their sex, immediately noticed something different about her, and the air was made uneasy by their frantic, though cloaked, curiosity to know the reason. In their condition of deepening anxiety her brighter and lighter manner was a provocation. She looked as if she hugged some delightful secret. Lady Bloomsbury, I guessed, thought that she was exulting about her final triumph in the matter of Harold; this seemed to me an explanation in which none but Harold's mother could believe, yet Lady Cynthia, a good-natured woman, who had been told of events upstairs, seemed also to accept it.

Insemnia, indeed, looked as if somebody had reached inside her and switched on a light. The lifelessness was gone; she no longer resembled the doll of Hoffmann's tale or the Sleeping Beauty. She was vividly awake and zestful, and so much lovelier than before that I did not know which to envy more: Oliver, who had done this, or Harold, who seemed likely to marry her. But when I remembered the kind of marriage it was to be, I thought Oliver was much the luckier. Meanwhile Harold bent over her in the most courtly and loverlike way, telling her fascinating things about Soviet Rusher; while Oliver just stared across the table at her. He was slower in attack than usual, and seemed to be in thrall. The soup was nearly finished before he spoke.

'Miss Vanderboom,' he said, 'will you come for a drive with me this lovely afternoon? I'd like to show you the river at Richmond.'

She smiled dazzlingly, and without an instant's hesitation said, 'I would like that very much.'

There was a pause of consternation. The Senator laid down his spoon and looked at Oliver; Harold looked in amazement at Insemnia; Lady Bloomsbury leaned forward to look at Oliver and then, in silent commiseration, at Lady Cynthia; Lady Cynthia looked from one to the other in surprise. Only Alistair and Em Porridge noticed nothing: Alistair said with quiet decision, 'Literally thousands of square miles of the best timber in Europe, thrown away,' and Em Porridge, leaning towards him, said 'Eckthuth pleeth, I am much intereth for thith queth-tion . . .'

Then the storm broke. 'Insemnia, you surprise me,' said the Senator. 'Young man, my ward is otherwise engaged this afternoon. She goes nowhere without me.'

'Certainly you can't do that, Insemnia,' said Harold. 'If you want to go, the Senator and I will take you.'

'Then I will not go,' said Insemnia calmly.

'Insemnia!'

'Are you unwell, my dear?' asked the Senator kindly.

'No. But I would like to go with Commander Jene.'

'My dear, this is outrageous. What can have come over you? I shall have to send you to your room. . . .'

Lady Cynthia put her oar in. 'Oh, I think it's all a little misunderstanding,' she said. 'Oliver doesn't know about the engagement.'

'I heard a rumour,' said Oliver, 'but what about it?'

'My dear Jene,' said Harold, 'one doesn't usually invite another man's fiancée for a car-ride, does one?'

'Doesn't one?' said Oliver cryptically. 'Oh!'

The weather at the table looked bleak and threatening. I thought I would take a hand. 'What you haven't heard, Oliver, I expect,' I said, 'is that the final arrangements were only made just before lunch. The wedding's to be at Westminster Abbey, soon. . . .'

'At Westminster Abbey?' he said. 'Is that all?'

'Yes,' I said, 'so this is hardly the moment, you understand . . .? As a matter of fact this is a festive occasion and we ought to celebrate it. Now, I've a little champagne in my room. . . .'

Alistair awoke at once. 'Champagne!' he said keenly.

The Senator's attention, too, was caught. 'Champagne!' he echoed, and his eye glittered. Even Lord Bloomsbury looked interested. Only Harold was unmoved; he was looking reproachfully at Insemnia, who was smiling at Oliver.

Lady Cynthia seized the chance to end an awkward incident. 'How clever of you, Mr. Grame,' she said. 'Do go and get it. I'll put out some glasses while Alistair and Oliver clear away and bring the next course.'

It was the work of a few moments to fetch my two bottles of sherry and bring them to the kitchen, where, I knew, were some empty champagne bottles. I took three of them and shared out the sherry among them, adding some soda-water to each; this, I calculated, would give the semblance of champagne without greatly reducing the effect of the sherry.

'What are you doing?' whispered Oliver curiously, while Alistair pottered unseeingly about.

'Ssh,' I said, 'this is a very rare vintage. Er, I wouldn't advise you to have much of it.'

'Why not? I like champagne.'

'Take my advice, and leave it to the others.'

'I say,' he murmured, 'can't you take that old trout to the waxworks, or somewhere? I must get Insemnia away from him.'

'I don't guarantee the waxworks,' I said, 'but I might be able to arrange some little jaunt for him. What are you up to? You're not going to abduct Insemnia, are you?'

'Well, I hadn't thought of that,' he said, 'but now you mention it . . .'

'Don't accuse me of putting the idea in your head,' I said, 'but I tell you one little favour you might do me, to repay some of my kindness to you. . . .'

'What kindness?'

'If you only knew, ingrate,' I said. 'Now, when we're all having coffee after lunch, skip out to the telephone box at the corner and ring Lord Bloomsbury, will you? Tell him the Dean wants to see him at once, at Westminster Abbey.'

As I have said, nothing surprises Oliver. He is always ready to believe that there is a good reason for unusual orders, and, like a good officer, to carry them out to the letter. He grinned broadly. 'That's a grand idea,' he said, 'right-ho.'

I tiptoed upstairs again, and again found difficulty in flexing my toes when I arrived, so that I made a somewhat peculiar entry, which the company assembled took to be of humorous intention, and applauded politely. I was glad to see that the champagne glasses were large ones, and I filled them to the brim, then inviting all to stand up and drink to the health of Insemnia (Harold's health was of less interest to me, and anyway, I wanted him to drink). They did so. 'No heeltaps,' I ordered, and they quaffed the lot; I covered up Oliver's and my own abstention by refilling their glasses before they could take breath. The effect, as I expected, was immediate. A 'Hup! Pardon!' came from Lord Bloomsbury; Em Porridge's ruined smile began to spread; and the Senator's port eye swivelled in search of his starboard one.

'A glorious wine, sir,' he said. 'Dry, very dry.'

'They know me well at Rheims,' I said. 'They've never failed me yet. Your health, Senator.'

'*Your* very good health, Mr. Grame,' he said, and took a pull which made me shudder, though I am not a nervous man. 'Your health, Harold,' I called, 'happy man.' He drained his second glass.

A few moments later I began to wonder, with some alarm, whether I had flattered myself in thinking that I knew the possibilities of Our Sherry to a fraction. I suddenly noticed a change, slight but perceptible, in the good people at the table, and it was a different kind of change from anything I had expected. It started with Harold. Until now he had treated Insemnia solely as a repository for fragments of delightful information about Soviet Rusher, and I felt sure that he had never thought of his coming marriage to her, if this were the correct word for the arrangement that was contemplated, in any light but that of a scientific contribution towards the planning of the world's weal, and beyond that, no doubt, of the future of the firmament.

I did not know all about Our Sherry, after all. I saw with surprise that he turned towards her and looked on her with another gaze. Had I not thought it impossible, in Harold, I would have said that passion burgeoned within him. The smile of the conquering male played foolishly about his lips. Harold seldom knows what to do with his hands, and as he murmured something inaudible in her ear he put them up to correct the time by his bow-tie. Finding that he was not wearing it, he flung them round Insemnia. 'I love you,' he said, in an indescribably inane manner, and for the third time in her life Insemnia was kissed.

She seemed not to notice anything, and indeed there was little to notice in Harold's first kiss, as I thought it must be. But I looked with apprehension at the Senator and the Bloomsburys.

To my astonishment (and I now began to be seriously concerned about the effects of Our Sherry) he merely wagged a roguish finger at Harold and said, 'Now, now, young people, bide awhile, bide awhile!' and laughed loudly, as who should say 'Carry on and good luck to you.' But the Bloomsburys really startled me, hardened though I am to the things Our Sherry does. With their heads on one side and foolishly fond smiles on their faces, they watched in rapture.

'Ee, don't they make a handsome pair, Dad?' said Lady Bloomsbury.

'Ah, it makes you feel young again, Mum,' said Lord Bloomsbury. 'Do you remember our courting days?'

'Oh, go on, do,' she said, giving him a playful slap.

'You were a one, you were,' he said, digging her in the ribs.

'Now, stop your nonsense,' said Lady Bloomsbury, landing a backhander that nearly knocked him off his chair and brought out three loud hup-hup-hups in quick succession.

'All right, my girl,' roared Lord Bloomsbury, rising red-faced with mirth and memories, 'if that's what you want.'

'Now, stop it, Tom,' squealed Lady Bloomsbury delightedly; with joyful squeals she ran round the table.

'Ah'm cooming,' cried Lord Bloomsbury. 'Ah'll have you, you see. Hup!'

'That's the way,' shouted the Senator, 'after her, my dear sir. Attaboy!'

'Yoicks!' cried Lady Cynthia. I turned to look at her, while Lord Bloomsbury chased Lady Bloomsbury round the table, and saw that there was a strange light in her eyes. She jigged up and down in her seat with glee at this amorous display and clearly found it, not only unsurprising, but even enchanting. Odder still, she seemed to be unaware that Em Porridge was ardently kissing her hand. I was even more concerned about Em Porridge than about the Bloomsburys, whom I confidently expected to fall down before anything irrevocable could happen. His combustible Bulgoslav nature, too long damped by the passionless everyday of Priscilla Grove, had plainly been fired by wine and the barnyard scene around. I moved my hand nearer to an empty champagne bottle, in case he should need quelling before Our Sherry took its inevitable revenge. Harold still clung to Insemnia, murmuring, 'I love you.' The Senator made loud noises of encouragement to Lord Bloomsbury, as of a man urging on a horse. Alistair, deep in his memories of Poland, gazed into space and absent-mindedly helped himself to more champagne; I was anxious for Alistair, too.

'We seem out of this,' I said to Oliver, beside me. He was looking dangerously at Harold, and I felt that if he had had a torpedo about him Harold's hour would have struck.

'What on earth did you put in the drinks?' he said.

'Only soda-water,' I said apologetically. 'I can't make it out.'

'You shouldn't mix drinks,' he said accusingly. 'Look what you've done. How on earth are we going to sort this out?'

Lady Bloomsbury solved the problem. With joyful giggles of fear she broke from the round-table chase and darted through the connecting-doors into the lounge, Lord Bloomsbury after her, while Lady Cynthia jumped up (pulling Em Porridge with her, who seemed unable to disconnect himself) and shouted, 'Tally ho! Gone away!'

I stood up. 'Cynthia,' I said firmly, 'this has gone far enough. Think of the good name of Number Seven.' I fixed her with my eye and the light of madness faded in hers. 'Oh dear,' she said, 'whatever's going on?'

'Come,' I said, 'before it is too late.' Lady Cynthia, dimly realizing her responsibility as lady of the house, tried to obey, but was hindered by the obstinate adherence of Em Porridge. She staggered round the dining-room with the movements of a stage comedian trying to rid himself of a piece of sticky paper, and eventually freed herself with a violent wrench; I caught Em Porridge and put him in the chair next to Alistair's. Then we went into the lounge.

Happily we were just in time. Lady Bloomsbury, after a superb final three-times-round-the-sofa, was just sinking exhausted into it with noises of happy anguish, while Lord

Bloomsbury, helped by an especially violent 'Hup!' vaulted over the other end of it. Lady Cynthia resolutely sat herself between her Doris and the pursuant male.

'Doris!' she said. Her tone of rebuke appeared to have little effect, but her physical presence between them quietened the lovers a little. 'I think that's enough for now, dear.' At this moment, fortunately, Edith came in. 'Oh, Edith,' I said to her, aside, 'you make such wonderful coffee. Do go and brew some, and make it as strong as you like.' She went, and Harold appeared, leaning on Insemnia, who guided him to an armchair. He sat down in it, but slipped to the floor, so that his head rested on the seat; he looked happier than I had ever seen Harold look.

'Oliver,' I murmured, 'pop out and make that telephone call.' Without a word he disappeared and I turned to my patients. Alistair had stayed in the dining-room, to commune with himself and the remainder of the champagne; he could wait. The Senator, standing over Lord and Lady Bloomsbury, was urging them to resume the chase. From exhaustion, and Lady Cynthia's restraining presence, they were unable to. Edith came back with the coffee, and gave Harold a startled look. Feeling that she needed refreshment, I gave her a glass of champagne, without explaining the original cause of its appearance. Edith's resistance to alcohol is low. She put down her glass, went to Harold, shifted him so that she could sit down, and took his head in her lap. 'What's the matter, Harold?' she inquired gruffly.

'I love you,' he said.

'Oh, Harold,' she said, not softly, but as softly as she could. I saw the fond and foolish look appear on the Bloomsburys' faces again, and they reached across Lady Cynthia and held hands. The Senator, too, beamed on Edith and Harold. I thought that none of them knew, or possibly cared, that the object of Harold's affection had changed; they merely wanted to look on love. I suddenly remembered that I had never before used Our Sherry in the daytime and made a note for my treatise.

'You have such a beautiful lap, Insemnia,' continued Harold.

'Edith, dear, not Insemnia.'

'Edith? Oh well, I knew it was some such name. I love you. We will go away together, when we are married. We shall see the world, you and I.'

'All of it?'

'Yes. Soviet Rusher first, of course.'

'Oh Harold. All those lovely places! Stalingrad?'

'Yes. And Leningrad.'

'And Molotovgrad?'

'And Vishinskygrad.'

'And Centigrad, and Fahrenheit,' I prompted.

'It's too good to be true,' said Edith dreamily. 'I always wanted to see the golden domes of Centigrad. Oh, Harold.' She stroked his cheek. The Senator, Lady Cynthia and the Bloomsburys watched with red, enraptured faces, like the setting sun in November. The telephone rang. I went to it, listened, and turned to Lord Bloomsbury. 'It's for you,' I said, 'from Westminster Abbey. The Dean wants to speak to you.'

'The Dean?' he said, struggling to get up. I helped him to the instrument, took the mouthpiece from his ear and put the other end to it. 'Hullo. Oh yes. Yes. What, now? Oh certainly, with the greatest pleasure. I'll come at once, hup! In half an hour, yes?' He put down the receiver and turned to us. 'The Dean wants to see me,' he said vaguely but with an air of bemused self-importance, 'hup!'

'The dear Dean?' said Lady Bloomsbury. 'Well Ah never. But we were having sooch foon.'

'The Dean?' said the Senator, groping in the mists of memory. 'Now, didn't you mention something about a Dean, Mr. Grame?'

'Oh, I fancy I did have a word with him,' I said. 'It's probably about the wedding, and Westminster Abbey, you know. I expect you ought to go along too, Senator.'

'Oh course,' he cried, 'the wedding! By all means, by all means.' He beckoned to Edith. 'Come Insemnia, my dear, let us go immediately.'

'Oh, that would never do, Senator,' I said. 'The Dean keeps

very strict purdah. Even his clergy are not allowed to see him unveiled, I believe.'

'Ah!' he said. 'Naturally, naturally. I forgot. Then you must await me here, Insemnia.' He raised his hands in a gesture of benediction. 'Bless you, my children,' he said to Harold and Edith.

'I think I'd better come with you,' I said. 'You may need an interpreter.'

We left Edith and Harold exchanging loverlike nothings while Lady Bloomsbury and Lady Cynthia watched them fondly.

'Can't you picture the moon rising over the Politburo, Insemnia?' said Harold.

'Edith, dear. Did you say Pollittburo?'

'No, Politburo.'

'Oh, Politburo. Yes. I can see it all. How wonderful it must be. You're such a romantic lover, Harold. I don't think there can be another man who makes love quite like you.'

'Dear Insemnia.'

'Edith, dear' (gruffly).

She stroked his hair. Great bliss was on their faces and a lovely vision in their eyes. While I waited in the hall for Lord Bloomsbury and the Senator I gently opened the dining-room door and looked in. Em Porridge and Alistair, with their heads nearly touching, were vigorously disputing something; the champagne seemed to have invigorated Alistair, and his habitual air of remote detachment was gone.

'Here,' he said, banging a fork on the table, 'is the Vistula, and here,' he thumped with a salt-cellar, 'is my forest, and here,' he engraved a line on Lady Cynthia's best tablecloth with the carving knife, 'is the Polish frontier....'

'Excuth pleeth,' said Em Porridge, grinning horribly, 'he ith the eighteen thikthy thikth frontier; he ith not now the Polith frontier.'

'No,' said Alistair firmly, 'this is the nineteen thirty four frontier, the real frontier.'

'Excuth, but in eighteen theventy theven the eighteen thikhthy thikth frontier he ith change....'

'No,' shouted Alistair, 'that was in nineteen theventeen, I mean, nineteen seventeen. In nineteen thirty thikth or theven the eighteen theventy theven frontier wath....'

I moved my gaze from them to the other end of the table. Oliver was bent over Insemnia, and held her hand. She looked at him with bright and happy eyes.

'Where is Richmond,' she said, 'and why should we go there?'

'It's up the river,' he said, 'and there's a terrace there from which you can look down into the heart of England, or one of the hearts, or one corner of the whole heart. There are green lawns and old trees and paths and flowers and lots of good-looking young folk and the river winds and the water's cool and there are shady backwaters and we'll get out the old bus and buzz off and get a punt....'

'A punt? What is that?'

'A punt's a flat-bottomed boat that you push along with a pole.'

'It sounds wonderful.' At this point I knew for sure that Insemnia must be falling in love, which is deaf as well as blind.

'It is. You haven't lived until you've been in a punt' ('with me', Oliver clearly meant).

Insemnia smiled radiantly. Oliver, as if drawn by a magnet, kissed her. 'How clever of you to fix it so that we can get away,' she said, looking at him admiringly. 'How did you do it?'

'Oh, that was easy,' said Oliver. 'I just arranged for the Senator to be called away. You learn about these things in the Navy. Why, to oblige a friend who had an important date I once took an admiral out at night in a bumboat at Plymouth and made him believe he was inspecting the Grand Fleet from his flagship. All he could say was, "It's all lit up, all lit up".'

I do not estimate Oliver to be a sensitive man, but I think even he would have been moved if he had seen the look of reproach I gave him. But he did not see it. He was looking at Insemnia, and to do him justice I do not think I would have been aware of anything in the world about me if Insemnia had looked at me like that. I softly closed the door. The Senator and Lord Bloomsbury came down the stairs.

XXIII

FORTUNATELY the entrances to Westminster Abbey and to the Westminster Parliament are closely adjacent, and in choosing the second of these I felt that I ran little risk of Lord Bloomsbury (and none of the Senator) noticing the difference. Fresh air added to Our Sherry has, in my experience, the effect of diminishing its stimulative effect and still further impairing the faculties. This proved to be the case; by the time we reached Westminster Lord Bloomsbury and the Senator were in a state of languid incomprehension. Only for a moment was I anxious: as we entered Lord Bloomsbury, glancing vaguely at the murals, mumbled, 'This place seems familiar.' As a former member of the House of Commons he knew this place uncommonly well. For that matter, being a peer, he also knew the other place, which adjoined it.

We passed into the Great Lobby amid the salutes of policemen, who knew Lord Bloomsbury by sight but whose welcome the Senator assumed to be for himself. He affably waved his hand to them.

'Who are these gentlemen?' he inquired loudly.

'They are the members of the Swiss Guard, Senator,' I told him.

'Indeed? A fine body of men. Ah, that is an apt phrase; I must remember that. Remind me of it later, Mr. Grame. Did they know I was coming?'

'They are trained to recognize a member of any Upper House at sight,' I said.

'Is that so? I must tell them about this in Washington.'

In the centre of the Great Lobby we paused, with bared heads, and looked around. The scene was that which so deeply, and so rightly, impresses visitors to our ancient Parliament. Some hundreds of the citizenry, come to ask their Member this or tell him that, stood, with hanging heads, looking hopelessly along the small lobby leading to the world-famous Chamber itself. From time to time attendants came slowly out to tell them that Mr. Brown or Mr. Jones had been kept late in the sitting and would not be home to dinner. Now and again, while all fell back in awe, a Member sped out to the row of telephone boxes marked 'Members Only'; in the hush he could then be heard saying in statesmanlike tones, 'I said the three-thirty, not the four o'clock. Yes, five bob, Bob,' and we knew that the affairs of the race were being well looked after. At the post office there was great activity; telegrams were being received and dispatched in scores, and I thought I caught faint echoes of 'Newmarket', 'Gatwick' and other constituencies, the electors of which were clearly inquiring, or being informed, about the progress of the debate, minute by minute.

The Senator looked round, sleepily but with benevolent approval. 'A magnificent edifice,' he said, 'a noble shrine. A hallowed spot. To think that I stand where so many Kings and Queens of England have been crowned. You must see, Lord Bloomsbury, that no other place but this is fit for Insemnia's wedding to your Harold.'

'Ahhrrrahhrmm,' said Lord Bloomsbury. It was a yawn. He looked very tired. I led them both to a bench and we sat down. Without a second's hesitation Lord Bloomsbury fell asleep.

'Senator,' I said, 'Lord Bloomsbury is overcome. It is the customary effect of this place on the members of the aristocracy. The feeling of history and tradition, you know, and the incense. We must give him a few moments to recover.'

'But the Dean?' said the Senator. This was a slight shock to me; I had counted on him forgetting the Dean. Indeed, I had hoped to leave them both asleep there for an hour or two, knowing that elderly gentlemen, asleep, are little noticed and well looked after in these precincts. I saw uneasily that the Senator, a member of a young and virile race, was if anything becoming more, and not less, wakeful, and seemed obsessed with some odd notion about a dean. I did not want to disappoint him.

'Perhaps I can arrange it,' I said. 'Possibly we can settle the matter without Lord Bloomsbury. From what I know of him and his fellow peers he will need a little while to master his emotion. The Abbey always affects them like this.'

'I understand perfectly, sir,' he said. 'I feel the spell of this ancient pile myself.'

'I thought you would,' I said gratefully. 'Then wait here while I see if I can find the Dean, Senator. Er, if Lord Bloomsbury makes a noise, for instance, resembling a snore, take no notice. He will merely be reciting his pedigree to himself.'

I went away and through labyrinthine corridors; I know them fairly well, having in some former life, or dream, been briefly a Member of this House. I passed the Members' dining-room, and the Strangers', and then met an old friend, Humbert, one of the chefs.

'Hullo, Humbert,' I said.

'Hullo, Mr. Grame,' he said, 'nice to see you. Are you In or Out just now?'

'In,' I said. 'How's business, Humbert?'

'I don't know,' he said. 'I haven't looked at the Order Paper to-day. I think there's something good in the way of a Refuse and Sewage Nationalization Bill coming along.'

'You're looking well, Humbert,' I said, and with the words came the idea. He *was* looking well; in his white clothes and tall white cap he looked rather like a pope of the Eastern Church. 'Humbert,' I said, 'I think you can help me. I have a very distinguished guest here to-day, the head of the Dissident Epistophelian Church of America. Er, by the way, Humbert,' I said, looking round, 'I'd like your opinion of this,' and I offered him my flask. He took a long swig.

'Ah, that's grand stuff, Mr. Grame,' he said. 'They don't make whisky like that nowadays.' He staggered a little and shuddered violently. 'Have some more,' I said. He did, and smacked his lips.

'Now, Humbert,' I said, 'you can do me a favour. His Grace wants, if he can, to arrange some little function here, and I think you can advise him as well as anybody.'

'What,' he said, 'tea on the terrace, or something?'

'Well, I think perhaps rather more than that. I'll bring him along. Er, Humbert, your eyes are not bothering you, are they?' I thought he had a slight squint.

'Not me, Mr. Grame, never had any trouble with 'em. All right, you bring his Grace along.'

I went back and collected the Senator. Lord Bloomsbury looked very comfortable. 'You won't disturb his lordship, will you?' I said to the nearest police-sergeant. He smiled broadly, with that all-mankind-loving affability which has rightly caused so many ladies visiting this island to say that our police are wonderful; I always feel that an atom bomb would bounce, abashed, off one of these House of Commons policemen. 'Not me, sir,' he said. 'I'd have my work cut out if I was to start disturbing the gentlemen. Bless 'em, they must get their rest, after all. Why, sometimes we have up to a hundred here, Members, Strangers, permanent staff and all; they just tell us when they want to be called, and if they want a cup of tea. Very nice lot of gentlemen they are too; it's a pleasure to do anything we can for 'em. Of course, it's a bit hard on us sometimes having to come in when the House is not in session to see they're all right, but we feel it's helping the country like, so we don't complain.'

I led the Senator through the maze and as we turned the last corner we saw Humbert standing at the other end of the long corridor, an imposing figure. The Senator stopped. 'Should I approach, Mr. Grame?' he murmured. 'His Grace is unveiled.'

'Oh, I forgot to tell you,' I said. 'This is Midsummer's Day, the only day in the year on which believers are allowed to look on His Grace's face. You are very fortunate.'

'What a privilege!' he said. 'Is that why he is dressed in white?'

'Yes,' I said, 'those are his canonicals for this day, according to the Old Rite.'

'Old Right!' he said, starting, 'What, Reaction!'

'*Rite*; not Right.'

'Ah, *rite*! Right.'

'All right? Good.' We approached Humbert who bowed and said deferentially, 'Welcome, your Grace.'

'Good afternoon, your Grace,' said the Senator. 'This is indeed an honour.'

'You wished to see me about some little function, your Grace?' said Humbert charmingly.

'Ah yes, indeed, your Grace. A wedding.'

'A wedding! Oh, you didn't tell me that, Mr. Grame. I'm afraid we couldn't possibly do a wedding, your Grace. The fact is, we simply haven't the food.'

'The food, your Grace?'

'You see, your Grace, there's the cake to begin with. We couldn't attempt it, in these times.'

'The cake, your Grace?'

'I should explain, your Grace,' I said to the Senator, 'such a ceremony in this place is inconceivable without the cake.'

'Now if it was a little breakfast, perhaps, or even a little supper, before or after, your Grace,' said Humbert, 'and you was set on having it here, why then I'm sure, to oblige a Member, like Mr. Grame here, we'd manage something. Not that we'd be able to supply any wine, that all goes to the Members nowadays, and don't they put it away just, but a tasty sandwich or two, and perhaps a little conducted party round the Sergeant-at-Arms afterwards, just to make everybody happy, why, that we'd do. We always try to please. But a full-dress affair like what you have in mind, your Grace – no, we just haven't the eggs.'

'You must pardon me, your Grace,' said the Senator, sleepily and humbly, 'I did not know the importance of food in your Rite. Ah, the rules of your church are extremely strict, I have no doubt?'

'Church?' said Humbert, squinting gaily. 'Ah, your Grace will have your Grace's little joke. Strick? Strick isn't the word for it. You can't get away with a thing, if you understand me.' A distant bell sounded; I fancied it might have something to do with a division. 'I must go now, your Grace. Sorry I can't help more. The Members will be coming along any moment, and those brothers eat like wolves. And you ought to hear 'em complain when we put another sixpence on the charge.' He withdrew backward, bowing. The Senator retired in the opposite direction, also bowing.

'What an experience!' he said. 'What a privilege! His Grace seemed hardly of this world. There was heaven in his face. What was that bell?'

'Vespers, I think,' I said.

'And the brothers he spoke of? Were those the brothers of his order?'

'No doubt. Well, you see, Senator. It is as Lord Bloomsbury feared. The difficulties are insuperable.'

'I had no idea of these complications. Could I not have food sent from America?'

'Senator! It has to be grown in consecrated ground.'

'Ah, of course. Ahhhrrhhm.' The Senator yawned; he seemed, later than I had anticipated, very tired. We found Lord Bloomsbury, who appeared comfortable, and sat down beside him. I nudged him gently. He did not stir. I nudged him less gently; he gave a little snore ending in 'Hup.' I had to shake him quite hard, under the reproachful eye of the police-sergeant, before he woke. Then I found the Senator was asleep.

'The Senator is not very well, Lord Bloomsbury,' I said. 'I think we should give him a moment to recover. Er, I saw you were tired and took the liberty of sending in your name to the Dean. I'm afraid I have bad news for you.'

'Hup!' he said. 'Pardon. You have! What is it?'

'Well, it's a most extraordinary thing, but the Dean, who asked me to convey his warmest compliments, says he did not send for you.'

'What!' he said, starting indignantly. 'Well, who did then?'

'That is the mystery,' I said. 'It seems to have been some monstrous joke. Scotland Yard are very much alarmed about it.'

'But who could have done it?'

'Well, after all, you are a public man, Lord Bloomsbury, and public men have enemies. Remember Booth.'

'Booth. I've never done anything to upset the Salvation Army.'

'No, I mean the other Booth, the one who killed Lincoln.'

'Lincoln! The fellow who used to be an M.P.? I thought he was a Buddhist monk in Tibet now, or something.'

'President Lincoln,' I said patiently, 'President Lincoln of America. He was *killed*.'

Suddenly Lord Bloomsbury became quite awake. 'Did you say killed?' he asked, looking nervously around. 'My dear Grame, you don't think this was a trap?'

'No, *I* don't, Lord Bloomsbury,' I said soothingly, 'but the Yard, of course, have to consider all possibilities. I think it was just a practical joke, in very bad taste. I don't want to say anything I shouldn't, but personally I suspect the Lord Chancellor.'

'I don't believe it. He seems perfectly normal.'

'Sitting on the Woolsack sometimes produces very curious effects,' I said, 'like softening of the . . . well, some form of mental disturbance. Anyway, I've been hearing some queer rumours about him lately. I know for a fact that Black Rod caught him writing some very odd things on the wall of the Lobby during the last vacation – "Herbert is a sneak", and all manner of unintelligible nonsense. . . .'

'Grame,' he said, clutching my arm, 'wake the Senator and let us get out of this place. The Abbey always makes me feel uneasy.'

'Yes, perhaps we should go,' I said. 'Anyway, I think I have some good news too, Lord Bloomsbury. I was able to see one of the canons, who persuaded the Senator that a wedding at the Abbey could not be arranged.'

'Thank the Lord for that,' he said sleepily.

We had to enlist the help of the police-sergeant to wake the Senator, and he was loath to give it, never having been asked so strange a service before. Lord Bloomsbury seemed ill at ease until we were all in a taxi-cab on our way home, when both he and the Senator went to sleep again. At Number Seven I managed to wake them and steer them into the lounge where, as we opened the door, we found Harold asleep in the sleeping Edith's lap, and Lady Cynthia and Lady Bloomsbury, also asleep, propped up against each other on the sofa. The Senator and Lord Bloomsbury took an armchair apiece and fell asleep immediately. Feeling that I was the odd man in, I thought I would go out, and was tiptoeing to the door when Harold awoke.

'Oh, Insemnia,' he said, 'I love you.' Receiving no answer, he looked round, and jumped. 'But you're not Insemnia,' he said.

'Ssh, Harold,' I said, 'of course it's not Insemnia. It's Edith.'

'But why is my head in her lap?' he said querulously.

'Harold,' I said, 'you will do it. I've warned you before. You will take the thimbleful too much, and you simply cannot hold it.'

'Oh dear, dear,' he said, 'what did I do?'

'I wouldn't like to tell you. I only hope your parents may have forgotten all about it when they wake. I'm afraid Edith won't have forgotten anything, though.'

'But I don't want Edith,' he wailed, 'I want Insemnia. Where is Insemnia?'

'Who knows?' I said. 'She might be in her room. Well, so long Harold.'

'Where are you going?' he said.

'It's such a lovely afternoon,' I said, 'I thought I'd get out of London for an hour or two. I might run down to Richmond. See you later, Harold.'

XXIV

AT Richmond, just above the bridge, I found a boatman and a punt. It was more wars ago than I cared to remember since I had used a punt and I entered it anticipating that my voyage would have a Jeromesque and watery end, in which I should be parted either by the pole from the punt, or by the punt from the pole. The boatman had that reassuringly time-defying look about him which such occupations give; as long as a small piece of the planet remained, and Richmond were included in it, I felt, he would be there, watching old father Thames roll to the mighty sea.

'Would you kindly direct me to the first backwater?' I said to him.

'Straight on,' he said, absent-mindedly and automatically, 'you can't miss it. If you miss it, ask again' (this reply, for some reason hidden from me, appears to be taught to the children of our island schools together with the alphabet and the rule of three; at all events, it is the invariable answer to any inquiry about the way).

Then something seemed to occur to him and he peered suspiciously over my shoulder at the empty punt. 'You alone?' he said.

'Yes,' said I.

'What do you want with backwaters then? Not one of these peeping Toms, are yer?'

'Do I need a backwater permit?' I asked.

'Not yet,' he said grudgingly, 'but it'll come.'

'Good-bye,' I said, 'I shall find it myself,' and I pushed off. Knowing Oliver's naval tactics so well, I felt certain I *should* find him; a straight course to the objective – I couldn't miss it. I found that my course was more serpentine than straight and that a great deal of water from the pole ran down my sleeve, then into my shirt and out again at my trousers' ends, but I contrived to accompany the punt, and to keep the pole with us both.

It was strange to be on the river at Richmond again. Now I came to think of it, I had not been there since my youth, when motor cars were new and aeroplanes hardly thought of, when the future stretched before me as smooth and golden as the stream itself. None of us who punted then had imagined the tortuous journeyings that lay ahead; such ploddings through French mud and African sand and Burmese jungle; such hoppings into and droppings from aeroplanes; such fussy, hurry-scurrying in an endless circle. I wondered, as I poled towards Insemnia and Oliver, whether any of those flannelled youths who had shared the river with me forty years before were now, like myself, punting upriver again from Richmond Bridge. I hoped some were, for it had been a fine cruise, from the nineteen-hundreds to the nineteen-forties, and I would not have missed a moment of it, and it was good to find that it led back, in spite of all the pother, to the river at Richmond. I looked at the other punts around me. The young men in them, I thought, were somewhat under standard, but the girls seemed prettier than ever; on looking back, however, I realized that I had always found them so. The sight of them took my mind to those who once had occupied the place, now empty, in my punt; where were they now? I wondered, Kathleen and Lilian and Frances and the rest. What an abyss of time, somehow, seemed to lie between Frances, with her starched white frock, tight waist and long skirt, and the artificial girl, Insemnia! How fast we moved, in this century, and whither? Well, well, I thought; I wish Insemnia were in my punt now, anyway.

In the first backwater on the right I found them, as I knew I should. It had a narrow entrance, screened by tall grasses, and within was a shady pool, overhung by weeping willows. Not for nothing had Oliver studied the fjords of the Norwegian and the coves of the French coasts. The cushioned seat-back was up and hid them from the river, and indeed from all save any who came right alongside: the slap-slap of tiny waves against their punt prevented them from hearing the only sounds of my stealthy approach, which were those of water dripping from the pole as I gently entered. I could not see them but I heard their voices.

'I like this punt,' said Insemnia's voice. 'It is much nicer than the *Empress of Poland.*'

'You don't like the big ships? They have their points. Personally, my ideal of domestic bliss would be to have you with me in the captain's cabin of a Hood-class battleship; when I came home in the morning, tired after a hard night's work in the wardroom, you would be waiting for me with my rum-toddy warming before the fire . . . lovely. But I have always been pro-punt. I don't deny it. When the anti-punters look at me and mutter behind their hands, "Oliver is pro-punt", I just laugh and snap my fingers. Let them say. Give me a punt – and you.'

There was a long pause. Then, 'You are making my heart beat again,' said Insemnia.

'You know,' said Oliver, 'I think I must be good. I've long suspected it. I believe I've even cured your yawning. Where all Harley Street failed I have succeeded.'

'I wonder if you have. Let me try. No, I can't yawn now when I try.'

'You're so lovely. Would you be bored now if I told you about your dress and your figure and your eyes and your lips?'

'No, I want you to.'

'You've changed so much since I first kissed you. You seemed so . . . lifeless, so cold. Now you remind me of that moment at dusk when all the lights go on together.'

'I feel like a clockwork toy that's been wound up. I want to run about and buzz. Oliver, I can't explain, but I don't think I shall like to marry, Harold.'

'Marry Harold! Who put that idea into your head? You're not going to marry Harold.'

'But then I shall have to go back to New York.'

'You're not going back to New York.'

'But the Senator will take me.'

'Oh no he won't,' said Oliver calmly. 'I shall forbid these banns. I have a proprietary interest in you now: I completed the product. It's what they call the finishing process – highly skilled labour. You see, the kind of busybodies who, er, manufactured you, my beautiful, think they are very clever. They know how to distil a million synthetic human beings in one laboratory and destroy a million more in another; that's what they call progress. They think they can raise a race of bottle-bred puppets and control them from the test-tube to the grave. In a way it's the old story of the invincible armada over again. Drake and Nelson didn't agree with the old invaders; Oliver Jene doesn't agree with the new ones. Their calculations reckon without the unknown quantity.'

'What is the unknown quantity?' said Insemnia.

'Well, it's a hackneyed word, but nobody seems to know a better one. They call it love; and it takes several forms – love for a faith, love for a country, love for a woman.'

'You put the woman last.' (Insemnia, I thought, was coming along fast.)

'Just now I put this woman first.' Insemnia, I gathered, was being kissed again. 'I'm going to cut you out.'

'Cut me out?'

'Oh, I forgot. That's English. In American, I'm going to cut in.'

'I would like that. I never wanted anything before. Since my heart began to beat I want so much. But I do not know how you can take me from Harold, the Senator and the Committee.'

I leaned gently on the pole and my punt slid silently alongside. 'Well, my children,' I said, 'here you are then. I thought I saw your car by the boathouse, Oliver.'

'Grame,' he said, 'you old snooper. What are you doing here?'

'Well, it was such a lovely day,' I said, 'I thought I would revisit the haunts of my youth. Insemnia, you look indescribably lovely. Would I were young Doctor Faust and had his connections in low places; I would cut Oliver out.'

Insemnia was neither embarrassed nor perturbed; she retained that much of her earlier immunity from the emotions of other women. 'You were right in what you said about other men's kisses,' she said happily. 'I did not know life could be so exciting. Oliver is a good teacher.'

'The best, I fear,' I said, 'but Oliver, don't forget that this isn't going to be quite like warfare at sea. There are obstacles that land-lawyers know and sea-lawyers may not.'

'What do you mean?' he said.

'Well, the first thing is, what do *you* mean? I am here, in a sense, as your fairy godfather. . . .'

'Are you?' he said. 'I don't see it.'

'You wouldn't,' I said bitterly. 'I suppose you think you contrived this all by yourself?'

'Of course,' he said blankly, 'it was quite simple. Why, it's nothing to what I did with the Fleet Admiral. . . .'

'At Plymouth?' I said. 'Yes, yes, I know.'

'I believe you were listening.'

'I was. Anyway, this is different. Of course, I'm the last man to interfere, but I wonder if you've thought it all out. I know your intentions are honourable, as becomes a Jene, but what *are* they?'

'I'm blowed if I see what it has to do with you.'

'Well,' I said, 'I just take an interest, that's all. I'm not sure that I didn't help a little towards the awakening of Insemnia. What do you say, my dear?'

'Yes, you did,' she said. 'I had my first taste of life with you. It was a lovely night out.'

'Look here,' said Oliver, sitting up, 'what went on between you two?'

'Nothing,' I said, 'that you wouldn't have done yourself.'

'That's different.'

'Oh no. Whenever I look at you in future, Oliver, I shall think, there, but for his own self-sacrifice, goes George Grame. And what, if I may ask again, *are* your intentions?'

'I'm going to marry Insemnia, of course.'

'Now that's just what I thought,' I said. 'What do you feel about it, Insemnia?'

'I would love it, but . . .'

'You would!' I said. 'You're coming along very quickly, my dear. Isn't this rather sudden?'

'What if it is?' she said. 'As soon as Oliver explained it all to me I knew that I wanted nothing else. Nobody else ever explained things to me like that before.' She looked at Oliver admiringly. 'Of course, nobody ever had the chance to. But he's so clever.'

'Oh dear,' I said.

'Still, I don't see how he's going to do it. The Senator will never allow it. It would upset all his plans for the future of the Institute and the race. I expect Oliver would want to live with me.'

'Yes, that's a distant possibility, I imagine,' I said, 'and that is the point, Oliver: *how* are you going to marry Insemnia?'

'How?' he said, staring. 'Why, just take her and marry her, of course.'

'Look,' I said patiently, 'after this escapade neither the Senator nor Harold, if I judge them right, will let her out of their sight again until she's married to Harold. Apart from that, Insemnia is a ward, and she's under age.'

'Oh, that's an easy one,' said Oliver calmly, 'we only need a special licence. I know all about it; I went with a friend to get a special licence once. We can be married in forty-eight hours.'

'As I say,' I explained, 'I don't think the Senator will let her go again. And even if you eloped with her, I'm not absolutely certain how these things are, but the Registrar might need a birth certificate showing that Insemnia's over twenty-one. She doesn't look it, and Registrars are suspicious men. You'd be completely foiled if he raised that point. You know, Oliver, I'm inclined to think you've only one chance.'

'What's that?' he said.

'Not to come back home at all,' I said. 'The best thing would be to park Insemnia in a hotel – I'll arrange that – for forty-eight hours, and when you stand before the Registrar with her, to bluff the thing out. If he *should* raise the question of her age you must simply defy him. As a matter of fact, I think Insemnia might help there.'

'I?' she said. 'How could I help?'

'Well, I think if you looked at him just like that not even the greatest curmudgeon of a Registrar would refuse to marry you.'

'What, like this?' she said, looking at me.

'If you looked at him like that,' I said, 'he'd probably have Oliver removed and marry you himself. I would.'

'Ah, you notice that, Grame,' said Oliver keenly. 'It is the mother and father of a look, isn't it?'

'What is there about it?' said Insemnia inquisitively.

'Well,' I said, 'if you know what I mean, it's *exciting*.'

'Oh, I know all about that,' she said. 'Oliver has been explaining it to me.'

'A murrain on Oliver,' I said. 'Well, that's how it is, Oliver. You know, that's really why I came along. Loath though I am ever to meddle, I had a feeling that you might need a little advice. If you ask me, your only chance is to confront the Senator and his Committee with an irrevocable fact. Nothing in life is so insuperable as an accomplished marriage – not even death. I don't think any court in the world would undo it for less than about five million pounds, once it was done, and I doubt if the Senator has so much. If I were you, I should disappear, both of you, until you are married and then appear before the Senator hand in hand. If you don't do that I doubt whether you'll ever be married. And now the sherry's finished I shan't be able to help you any more.'

Insemnia laughed for joy; this was the first time I had heard her laugh aloud. 'Oh Oliver,' she said, 'won't it be lovely? To think: I've only been here a few days and I may be married in two more. It's getting more exciting every moment. And I can go away and forget all about the Senator and the Committee and Harold for ever more.'

'I thought you'd like the idea,' said Oliver modestly. 'That's fine. We'll go right back now and find a hotel for you. I've lost far too much time already trying to explain everything to you. You'll have to sign at the hotel as Insemnia's father, Grame. There'll be no difficulty there; they'll never suspect anything wrong at your age.'

'Thank you,' I said, 'but wait a moment. This is going to be even more complicated than I thought. It just occurs to me that this is Thursday afternoon, and you can't get a licence until to-morrow morning. That means you can't be married, at the best, until Monday morning, and that's a long time to keep Insemnia hidden.'

'Oh, that's all right,' said Oliver easily. 'I slipped out and got the licence this morning. We can be married first thing Saturday.'

'Isn't he clever?' said Insemnia adoringly. 'He thinks of everything.'

For once I was lost for words for a moment. Then, 'You did?' I said to Oliver. 'Well, I must admit that you work quickly on occasions.'

'You don't think I was going to waste any time once I'd met Insemnia, do you?' he said.

'I suppose not. You were quite sure she'd be pleased about it?'

'Oh, I thought I could probably get round her,' he said. 'So you see, all we've to do is to keep the Senator off her track for just over twenty-four hours. We'll get married on Saturday morning. You can be best man if you like.'

'You think I deserve it?'

'Oh yes, that's all right.'

'What age did you give for her?'

'Twenty-two. I thought I'd better be on the safe side.'

'But what about her parents?'

'Oh, I gave her a couple of dead ones – of good British stock.'

'You think of everything, Oliver,' I said. 'Insemnia, a day seldom passes without somebody giving you some new parents. I daren't think how this tangle will ever be straightened out if it ever comes to light. I wonder what the position is if you never had any parents at all; I'm ready to believe anything now. I wonder if the law provides for the marriage of persons whose entry into this world can't be proved at all. It's an interesting point. Well, I only hope you can make the registrar believe it all, Oliver. I wouldn't. I daren't think of meeting his eye.'

I had never expected to hear Insemnia squeal. But she did now. She literally squealed with delight. 'I'm going to be kidnapped,' she said, squirming with happiness; and she threw her arms round Oliver and hugged him.

'Well,' I said, 'I should say we ought to be going. Every moment you keep her out now increases the risk of being caught. If the Senator once lays his hands on her again you'll never get her out of them, on Saturday or any other morning.'

Just then I heard the engine of a motor boat, much closer to the backwater than the others which were passing upstream and down. I looked round. The prow of a white motor launch came nosing into the narrow entrance, completely blocking it. Three heads showed above it; they were those of Lord and Lady Bloomsbury and Harold.

'Good heavens!' I said.

'What is it?' asked Oliver, raising himself on his elbow.

'Something I never expected to see,' I said, 'a boatful of Bloomsburys. Harold is sharper than I thought.'

Oliver jumped up to look, and Insemnia followed. As her head came in sight of the launch a piercing cry, of triumph mingled with reproach, came from one of the heads (Harold's). 'Insemnia!' he wailed. Immediately the heads of the Senator and Lady Cynthia shot up behind his; anger and astonishment were written on their faces. The motor boat thrust gently into the backwater and came alongside our punts; I saw two peaked hats at the stern and realized that our pursuers had enlisted the help of the River Police.

The Senator stood high above us, glaring down. He looked even bigger than he is, like that, and wrath inflated him still further. He seemed to swell until he obscured the weeping willows behind and the summer sky above. Justice and retribution, in awful human shape, loomed before us. It was as if the sun went out and the blue heaven clouded over. The others, clustered round him, were just extras in a crowd scene. Time, as they say, stood still. I suspected the Senator of having stage experience; he did not break the silence a moment too soon or an instant too late. When the suspense was almost unendurable he spoke.

'Insemnia,' he said, 'this will break the Committee's heart. To think that you, the first of the line, should betray the Institute thus! After all that has been done for you. Would you jeopardize the whole future of the race to wanton with this youth in a punt? Come here!'

'I won't,' said Insemnia calmly.

'COME HERE!'

'I won't,' said Insemnia, but not quite so calmly.

'Why should she?' said Oliver stubbornly. 'She wants to stay here with me.'

'Insemnia!' wailed Harold.

'Insemnia, for the last time, I order you to come here.'

'Well, she's not coming, because I won't let her,' said Oliver.

For a moment I thought there was to be a naval engagement. It looked as if we were to be boarded by the whole attacking force, led by the Senator. But then a calm, impersonal figure in uniform stirred in the stern of the launch, came forward, leaned its elbows on the rail, tipped its hat nonchalantly back, and spoke. 'Now, what's all this about?' it said in a voice friendly, winning and deep.

I never can sufficiently admire Our Police, and wish they could be entrusted with the care of the planet for a decade or two; there would be perfect peace. Gentle as lambs in manner, firm as lions in purpose, they can make order out of chaos with less expenditure of effort than a woman smoothing a crumpled pillow.

'Now then, miss,' said the voice, like balm pouring from a steel cup, 'it's a fine day on the river and we don't want any trouble, do we?'

'No,' said Insemnia faintly, as if mesmerized.

'*That's* right,' it said (it was as if honey were being spread with a sword), 'not with a pretty young lady like you, we don't, and I never saw a prettier on the river, did you, Dick?' ('Not me!' said another human 'cello from the steering wheel.) 'Now, is this gentleman your guardian, miss?'

'Yes.'

'And are you his ward?'

'Yes.'

'And is your age eighteen?' asked the voice charmingly (as who should say, 'This is the way to reduce a simple problem to its simplest component parts').

'Yes.'

'*That's* all right, then. Now come along, my dear.' One arm detached itself from the railing and reached down a helping hand.

Even Oliver was too stricken to protest. Insemnia took the hand and tried to raise one foot to the launch's deck. It was a long step and her skirt was tight. More and more leg appeared, until there was hardly any more to appear, as she strained to make the ascent.

'And very nice too, if I may say so,' said the voice, in the tone of a silken surcoat being drawn over chain-mail. 'Upsadaisy! There we are! That's a good girl.'

'I'm very glad you arrived, Senator,' I called. 'You were only just in time. I couldn't persuade them to come back.'

He made no reply but bowed severely to me. His companions seemed dumbstruck with horror.

With a soft chug-chug the motor launch withdrew backwards, disappeared in reverse, and then crossed our narrow field of vision again, going downstream. Four accusing faces briefly glared at us; on the fifth (Lady Cynthia's) I thought I caught a less hostile look; Insemnia's head was turned from us. The chug-chug died away. We were alone, beneath the weeping willows. All was still.

'Your police are truly wonderful,' I said at length, turning to Oliver, 'and I might have known.'

'You might have known *what*?'

'That Insemnia would have a leg like that. To think that she must have another just like it! Well, Oliver, you see what you've done. Careless talk, my boy, careless talk in port has cost many a promising young naval officer his prize and his career. I sometimes wonder how the Royal Navy wins all its wars. Don't you know that the first rule of convoy work is not to talk about your destination when enemy ears may be listening? Lord, what an admiral was lost in me.'

'You mean that ass Harold guessed I'd come to Richmond?'

'And that you would anchor in the first backwater,' I said, 'of course. Why, it would shame the R.N.V.R. Well, I'm hanged if I see just how you'll get Insemnia now.'

'I'll manage it somehow,' he said obstinately.

'That's the spirit, but it will need much better staff-work than you've shown so far.'

'Why did you put your oar in?' he asked curiously.

'My oar?'

'When you told him you'd been trying to persuade us to go back.'

'But, Oliver, were you never taught tactics and strategy? What hope would you have if the Senator thought I'd been here as an accomplice?'

'Oh!' he said. 'I hadn't thought of that.'

'You wouldn't. I only hope he believed me, but if he didn't I may yet be able to convince him. Shall we punt a little, Oliver? Then you shall drive me back to town.'

Side by side we punted absent-mindedly downstream. I admired Oliver's strong stroke and perfect control; not a drop of water went up his sleeve, I saw, while I was so wet all down one side that I might have fallen half into the water and been pulled out before the other half could submerge. He is a fine lad and I would have liked to see Insemnia in his punt, since I could not have her in mine. Ours seemed the only empty punts (for a punt with but one man in it *is* empty) on the river that lovely evening. There were more uninteresting youths and more pretty girls on the water than ever before. Somehow, I found the journey a trifle sad.

At last we came to old Richmond Bridge, mellow in the evening light, and disembarked.

'Oliver,' I said, 'I need comfort. Shall we have one for the road before we take to the road?'

'If we can get one,' he said, 'which I doubt.'

XXV

I DID not think it wise to return to Number Seven in Oliver's company, so we stopped the car at Gloucester Road.

'I'll walk home from here,' I said. 'It won't do for us to go in together. In fact, I should think your best plan would be to lie low and not let the Senator see you at all.'

'Well, don't let him pack up and go home with Insemnia while I'm lying low.'

'No,' I said thoughtfully, 'we can't have that. But if he saw you about it might put the idea in his mind; I've a notion he looks on Insemnia as an investment. I tell you what, Oliver; go and get a room at the Rembrandt and stay at the end of the telephone.'

'But he might get her married to Harold before I can arrange anything,' he said.

'I don't think so. He couldn't do it under forty-eight hours at the least, but I believe he's so keen on a spectacular wedding, for publicity and dividend purposes, that he would never agree to a registry office ceremony anyway.'

'Well,' he said briefly, 'just you arrange it somehow that he's out of the way on Saturday morning; then I'll collect her.'

'You have complete faith in my powers?' I asked.

'What, in a little matter like that?' he said, in surprise. 'Of course. I just give you the main outline of the operation and it's up to you to work out the petty details.'

'Thank you,' I said gratefully. 'By the way, I suppose it will be all right with your parents?'

'Oh lor, yes. Mums will do what I say. Anyway, she'll love Insemnia as a daughter-in-law. The Guvnor may be a bit jealous, but he's married already so he can't complain.'

'You'd better ring me from time to time, in case I've any news or orders.'

'Right you are.'

In a cloud of blue smoke from the old bus Oliver disappeared. I walked home. In the hall of Number Seven, where there were no external signs of trouble, I met Lady Cynthia coming out of the dining-room.

'I can't make it out,' she said, 'Alistair and Em Porridge are in there fast asleep with their heads on the table and I can't wake them. I'm sure there's a curse on this house. They seem to have been playing some childish game with the table things.'

'Let me have a go at them,' I said. 'I think I know how to wake them.'

'Mr. Grame,' said Lady Cynthia; and I noticed an unusual coolness in her voice, 'why did you follow Oliver and Insemnia to Richmond?'

'But, Cynthia,' I said, 'it was in the interests of all concerned. I feared that something of the sort might happen and I didn't want fresh trouble to come on you. Also, I couldn't bear to think of Harold's disappointment.'

'You're an interfering old gentleman,' she said. 'Weren't you young yourself once?'

'Cynthia!'

'Well,' she said, 'I think that nice girl's much too good for Harold, and Harold needs a lesson anyway, after treating Edith like that.'

'After this nothing will ever surprise me again. Do you mean that you would welcome Insemnia as your daughter-in-law?'

'Why not? She's quite lovely, and extremely wealthy.'

'Wealthy!'

'Obviously. Those tiaras must be worth a fortune.'

'Aha,' I said, 'yes, if they're real, they must. Of course, they may be the property of the Committee. Well, I must say I didn't expect this from you, Cynthia.'

'I didn't expect it of *you*,' she said, going down the stairs. 'Peeping Tom!'

The female of the species, I thought; mother love is an incalculable thing. I went into the dining-room. To my joy, there was half a bottle of champagne left. I decanted it into my flasks, woke Alistair and Em Porridge by saying 'Poland!' loudly into each of their ears, and went upstairs. In answer to my knock the Senator himself opened the door. He looked at me doubtfully.

'Ah, Senator,' I said, 'I have just returned and felt I must congratulate you on the way you handled that difficult situation. I never saw anything like it. It was masterly.'

'You think so?' he said.

'Magnificent!' I said. 'I could do nothing with them. I noticed when we returned from the Abbey that Commander Jene and Insemnia were missing and was rather concerned on your account. You seemed a little preoccupied, probably as the result of your interview with the Dean – the incense, you know, and all those cardinals – and I thought best to follow them myself. I was trying to bring them to their senses when you arrived.'

'Ah, I see,' he said. 'Come in, Mr. Grame, come in.' He led the way.

'How did you find them?' I asked.

'That was Harold's idea,' he said. 'It was extremely astute of him, extremely astute. I knew I was right about his intellectual powers. I am convinced that the children of this union will be physically and mentally of such quality that the Cause of Selective Parenthood will be established for ever in the eyes of the world.'

'And where . . . er, how is Insemnia?' I said.

'She is locked in her room, sir,' he said grimly; and then, with one of his curious lapses into the vernacular, 'and I guess she'll stay right there until I've seen this thing through. If she thinks she can double-cross me she's got another think coming.'

'I beg your pardon,' I said, 'I fear you have been studying our English films, Senator.'

'Ahrrm,' he said, 'I mean, Mr. Grame, this has been a very great shock to me. Picture it to yourself: all my plans, the whole reward of twenty years of labour, might suddenly have been brought to nothing, if I had not found Insemnia in time. Think of the shame it would have brought on the Institute!'

'Awful,' I murmured.

'Now that we have, in years of experiment and research, produced this perfect, this unique human being, on whom the future of the whole race depends, my entire work might have been jeopardized by the intrusion of this young man.' He grew heated. 'Gee, when I think of it I get that sore I could forget myself . . . ahrrm, that is to say, you can see how much turns on this, Mr. Grame. The whole future of the Institute and the Cause demand that Insemnia should make a sensational, that is, I mean, a suitable marriage.' His eye grew bright, and he seemed to forget me again, as he looked into the golden future. 'Why,' he went on, as if to himself, 'the publicity alone would be worth a million bucks. Every sucker in New York would be knocking on the door with a wad as thick as a coupla hamburgers put together. Oh boy,' (he appeared to change into the tones of the deep south) 'Ah jes caint wait ter git mah hands on dem dollahs. . . .'

'Senator,' I said, gently.

'What!' he said, looking at me vaguely, and returning from the south to the north. 'You see how it is, pal, they's too many in this racket now, see, it ain't what it was, see, it was good once, see, but now every crook in New York thinks he can schnozzle in, see, 'n what will the harvest be? ah jeez. . . .'

I noted mentally that Our Sherry has certain delayed-action effects. 'Senator!' I said, less gently and more firmly. He blinked, came out of his reverie, and crossed the Atlantic.

'And so you see, my dear sir,' he boomed, 'our little girl, our first born, our immaculate princess is a precious jewel to us. We cannot afford, indeed it is our duty to humanity to prevent, any wanton interference with our plans.'

'Of course,' I said. 'Obviously Insemnia must make a carefully planned marriage. I think you have made the perfect choice for her, Senator. A man of rank and intellect, not wealthy, of course. . . .'

He started a little. 'Ah, perhaps you would confide in me about that, Mr. Grame,' he said. 'I confess I found these surroundings a thought humble for people like Lord and Lady Bloomsbury. However, I know the ways of your English aristocracy, ha-ha. No outer show; everything under the counter . . . I mean, under the surface. Of course, money is indifferent in this matter. Insemnia's dowry from the Institute will be more than ample to support her in the manner to which the Committee has accustomed her. Nevertheless, her future husband's financial standing is not without interest for us. . . .'

'I see what you mean,' I said. 'Well, the Bloomsburys are certainly not affluent.'

'Not?' he said, with some appearance of concern. 'I thought

the members of the English nobility were all opulently wealthy.'

'Oh no,' I said, 'they vary. The Bloomsburys, for instance, have much priority but little cash. They have not had time to become rich, I suppose.'

'How do you mean, not had time?'

'Well, it is a very new title.'

'A new title? I thought all titles were old.'

'By no means. New ones are constantly being added, in order to diminish the deadweight of reaction among the older families. I believe it may be necessary to create several hundred thousand new peers at the next election, to ensure the victory of democracy.'

'This is a great shock to me. . . .'

'It's quite a day of shocks for you,' I said sympathetically.

'Harold did not tell me.'

'Did you ask him?'

'Why, no. As I say, I had no idea that such things happened. It is the common belief with us, Mr. Grame, that your titles are hereditary.'

'They are. But even heredity has to have a beginning.'

'Dear me. Ah, tell me, Mr. Grame, I suppose this would all have to come out?'

'Come out?'

'In the publicity.'

'You mean, about Lord Bloomsbury having been Mr. Biggs a year or two ago? Well, I know and respect the restraint of your New York columnists, Senator, but I imagine one of them might think that worth mentioning. "Insemination Institute's Weanling Weds Labour Lordling: Biggs Boy on Broadway." I should think those would be the headlines.'

The Senator seemed to retreat from me in spirit; his soul winged its way across the ocean to his native land. 'Aw jeez,' he said bitterly, 'this hadda happen to me. Dey jes caint gimme a break.' Fearing he might go too far south, and break into Spanish, I interrupted him.

'Senator,' I said, 'I hear the dinner gong. We should go down.'

He took no notice, save to travel a few hundred miles northward. 'They can't *do* this to me,' he said. 'It's a frame-up, see. I'd have every con man from Alcatraz to Sing Sing laffing at me. . . .'

I took out one of my flasks, unscrewed the cap and held it under his nose. 'Senator!' I said sternly. He shuddered and came to.

'Mr. Grame,' he said, drawing himself up and resuming the mien which, I felt, must have sold many gold bricks, 'I am most grateful to you. I admit that what you tell me has somewhat surprised me. Insemnia, after all, is virtually a princess of the blood royal, and I had counted on a consort of equal rank for her. I fear I assumed that Harold was of Stuart or Tudor descent, at the least. . . .'

'You're not going to call it off, are you?' I said. I wondered if I had been precipitate; Saturday was still far off.

'I must consider the matter,' he said gravely, and then he startled me, as he had done once before, with a sudden roar of 'Insemnia!'

'Isn't she locked in?' I said.

'Ah yes.' He went out and I heard a key turn; he came in again with Insemnia. His head was turned from me and I lowered my right eyelid gently as her gaze met mine. I saw a responsive glint, like the answering light of a ship acknowledging a signal.

'My child,' said the Senator, looking once more like Moses on the mountain, 'this is a bitter day for me.'

'I told you, my dear,' I put in gently, 'how your behaviour would hurt the Senator. How could you do it? Why would you not follow my advice and come home with me?'

'I don't know,' she said meekly. She was wearing a pale green housecoat with a wide and flowing skirt and looked lovelier than ever. Her timidity seemed to provoke the Senator, so that his mind set off on its wanderings again.

'Lookithere, babe,' he said roughly, 'I been getting the low-down on dese boobs from dis guy, see, 'n it's a frame-up, see? Dey ain't gonna be no weddin' in Westminster Abbey, see, 'n dey ain't gotta bean, see, 'n dey ain't no blueblooded aristocrats, see, 'n I guess we're gonna hit the trail for home, see. . . .'

I saw that Insemnia had not known the Senator in this vein before; the delayed-action workings of Our Sherry are curious. She looked startled and almost frightened. I thought it time to intervene.

'Senator,' I said inquiringly, 'boobs? Guy? Frame-up? Trail? Would you explain?'

Once more he paused and looked at me vacantly (he had been through a great deal one way and another). Then he swayed a little, passed a hand over his forehead and pulled himself together. 'Ah, Mr. Grame,' he said, 'pardon me. Was I communing with myself? Now, where was I?' He drew himself up. 'The events of this day have unnerved me. I am a little distraught. The Cause is very dear to me; and all is at stake. I must consider what I have to do. I feel that I have been badly treated.'

'Oh, Senator!' I said.

'Come, sir,' he said, 'come, Insemnia. Make yourself ready, my child. We must go down to dinner.'

XXVI

NOT since the Commissar had Lady Cynthia's nerves been so sorely tried as they were at dinner that evening. For one thing, although it was still broad daylight we had to dine with the curtains drawn and the lights on. The reason was that the telepathic vibrations which appear to communicate news of what goes on in Number Seven to our neighbours in Priscilla Grove had once again caused a considerable crowd to gather outside. The artists, in particular, seemed to be convinced that a crime of passion would be committed at Number Seven one day and were resolved to be in at the death. The Balkan exiles at the other corner probably expected a political assassination, and fond memories of their homelands drew them irresistibly to the likely scene of so familiar and pleasing an event. On the other hand, I could not guess what dire rumour had reached old Mrs. O'Bourke, that she should have had herself pushed out by old Mrs. Miggins at an hour of the day when no human eye had for many years beheld her outside her own four walls. Anyway, there she was, firmly encamped on the opposite pavement with field glasses; and her thermos flask and sandwiches showed that she was prepared to wait a long time for the worst to happen. The artists and the blue jowls, grouped on either side of her, stood on tiptoe, or even jumped in the air, in their efforts to keep her supplied with news from the front room of Number Seven.

The good people in that room, already distressed by the events of the day, by anxiety for loved ones, or (in Lady Cynthia's case) by the fear of further retribution for crimes not yet fully expiated, were made still more nervous by this demonstration outside; and the soup was barely served before Lady Cynthia asked Mrs. Barnes to lower the blinds and close the curtains. In the manner of a sexton tolling funeral bells, Mrs. Barnes did this, thus deepening the gloom. Though she had received no mortal injury, she behaved as if she had suffered one, and clearly held each of us equally accountable for it; no serving-maid at a supper party of the Borgias could have handed the rissoles with a more grimly confident air of calamity to come.

We were a smaller party than usual, Em Porridge and Alistair having gone to bed. Edith, though unwell, had come down, refusing to be deprived, I guessed, of the chance of fixing Harold with a gaze which said, 'How can you treat a poor maiden so?' She had little success, however, in catching Harold's eye, which was directed with similar reproach on Insemnia. Lord and Lady Bloomsbury equally conveyed with martyred looks that they had been ill-treated by someone or other, while the Senator, sunk in himself and silent, was the gloomiest of all.

I have seldom known the air of Number Seven so oppressively laden with feelings of mutual accusation. The loveliness of Insemnia, which should have cheered any scene, now only added, I felt, to the misery of most of those present. Had I been able to spare a little of my small store of sherry, I would gladly have given it to uplift them, but I felt I should keep it for a greater need. In the circumstances, although Lady Cynthia climbed the ladder of vivacity, and nearly touched the top rung of hysteria, her efforts, and my own humble ones, to get the party going were vain, and we went into the lounge for coffee like mourners following a coffin, while Mrs. Barnes, at the opened doors, stood with folded hands and upcast eyes.

Lady Bloomsbury sat down with a sigh that said more than many words, and Lord Bloomsbury with the grunt of the elder statesman tired. The Senator strode restlessly about; he looked to me as if he were turning something over in his mind. There was silence while Lady Cynthia fussed with the coffee-cups.

'Ahrrm,' said Lord Bloomsbury; or rather, he cleared his throat in the way in which elderly gentlemen seem to say something. We waited, but nothing followed.

'Oh dear, dear,' then said Lady Bloomsbury, in a kind of moan. We looked towards her, but she added no more.

In the silence Insemnia yawned, amid indignant looks. Then everybody spoke at once.

'Is your cof . . .?' said Lady Cynthia.

'May I have some sug . . .?' said I.

'I was going . . .' said Lord Bloomsbury.

'Ah think Ah . . .' said Lady Bloomsbury.

'Sorry,' said Lady Cynthia.

'After you,' said Lord Bloomsbury.

'What were you going to say, Cynthia, pet?'

Before we could straighten out the tangle the Senator stopped pacing and turned, holding the thimblelike coffee-cup in his massive hand, to Lord Bloomsbury. I felt he had made up his mind about something, and wondered what it was: his sell-you-a-gold-brick manner was with him again.

'Ah, Lord Bloomsbury,' he said, in the tone of a bass-violin, 'we must discuss what we are to do about the wedding. It has been a grievous disappointment to me that it cannot be at the Abbey.'

'Well, I told you, Senator, the Abbey is only used for royal weddings.'

'Reaction!' exclaimed Harold bitterly.

'Insemnia, my dear sir, is after all virtually a princess of the blood royal, of the best Norman descent.'

'I'm afraid the Dean would need a lot of convincing about that, Senator.'

'Ah'm sure,' said Lady Bloomsbury peevishly, 'he would want proof about that story of the broken bottles. . . .'

'*Changed* bottles, Mother.' Edith and Lady Cynthia looked in bewilderment from Harold to the Senator and Lord Bloomsbury.

'However, what cannot be, cannot be. Since a wedding at the Abbey is out of the question, Lord Bloomsbury, what suitable alternative is there? Ah, may I ask where your own nuptials were performed?'

'At Caxton Hall,' said Lord Bloomsbury.

'What is that? An annexe to the Abbey, perhaps?'

'It's a Registry Office, Senator,' explained Harold.

The Senator started. 'A Registry Office?' he said, drawing himself to his full height. 'This is most unfortunate.'

'Unfortunate!' said Lord and Lady Bloomsbury together.

'Dear me,' said the Senator, 'did you hear that, Insemnia?'

'Yes, Senator.'

'Oh dear. This is more than unfortunate.'

'*What* is?' said Lord Bloomsbury.

'Ee, what's the matter now?' said Lady Bloomsbury.

'Oh, I may have to cable the Committee about this,' said the Senator, in the voice of a man faced with unimagined crisis. There was a short silence, in which, once more, I had fears for Lord and Lady Bloomsbury. Then, in percussive tone, Lord Bloomsbury spoke.

'Damn the Committee!' he said. 'What *is* it?'

Even Harold was impatient. 'What's the matter, Senator?' he said.

'Lord Bloomsbury, this is a serious matter,' said the Senator. 'Insemnia's father . . .'

'Ee, which one?' asked Lady Bloomsbury fretfully.

'The English one, ma'am. Insemnia's father made it a condition of his sacrifice for Our Cause that Insemnia should be brought up a Catholic and his last wish – as it proved to be – has been faithfully observed. Now, in the sight of the Church, you are practically living in sin. . . .'

'Ooh,' cried Lady Cynthia in terror.

'In sin! Eee . . .' moaned Lady Bloomsbury, reaching out for her Cynthia's hand.

'In sin!' cried Lord Bloomsbury, rising. 'Look here, I've had about enough of this. . . .'

'To think Ah should have to listen to it. Oh, Tom. . . .'

But the Senator was in his stride. It is an illusion that age saps a great man's powers. He had never been as good as he was at this moment. He seemed to grow taller and wider. I could have sworn I saw the aureole round his white hair again. Every con man on Broadway, I thought, would have fallen back in awe, could they have seen him now, and admitted, 'He's still the chief.' He could at this moment have sold a gold brick to a blind elephant.

'I am not sure,' he roared, 'how this affects the standing of Harold in the eyes of the Church.'

'Oh, really, Senator!' said Harold.

'How can you let him talk to your father and mother like that, Harold?' said Edith, unable to restrain herself any longer.

'Tom,' cried Lady Bloomsbury, 'how can you stand by and hear Harold called a bar sinister?'

'Mother!' expostulated Harold.

But there was no stopping the Senator now. 'Harold,' he said, 'you should have told me of this. Insemnia's name must be guarded against all smirch or blemish. . . .'

'Her name!' said Lady Bloomsbury. 'She hasn't a name.'

'Then her good fame, ma'am. Really, Lord Bloomsbury, I did not think such a thing possible in a family like yours. . . .'

Lord Bloomsbury began (as he, not I, would have said) to look ugly. 'If you don't like it, Mister Vanderwhatsyername,' he shouted, 'you know what to do.'

'If our family is good enough for the English peerage,' wept

Lady Bloomsbury, 'it's good enough for anybody. Too good for most.'

'Oh, please don't talk like that, Mother,' said Harold. 'It's pure Fascism. . . .'

'If you don't shut up, you young prig,' roared Lord Bloomsbury, 'I'll box your ears. How dare you speak to your mother like that? . . .'

The Senator compelled silence with a raised hand. 'Lady Bloomsbury, Lord Bloomsbury,' he said, in pulpit tones, 'Harold, I beg you. This is most painful to me. And to our princess here. . . .'

'Princess!' said Edith with venom.

The Senator quelled her with a look. 'Princess, I said, young lady, our Insemnia, the firstborn of Our Cause. There can be no frivolous giving-in-marriage for her. Too much depends on it. I can take no chances with the future of the race. Harold, it hurts me more than it hurts you when I do this, but I fear I must withdraw my consent.'

There was a long hush. I made a rapid mental calculation; the Senator might remove himself and Insemnia the next day, and that would completely foil Oliver. I looked across at Insemnia. She had been listening with her usual indifference, but now her eyes imperceptibly turned to mine; I saw alarm and questions in them. I did not know the answer, but again I slightly lowered one eyelid, and saw the light of reassurance; she seemed to have more confidence in me than I felt myself. I looked at the others, and in their eyes saw the look of thankfulness and hope reborn. There was no doubt about it: Lord and Lady Bloomsbury were content, Lady Cynthia was happy and Edith was delighted. Nobody was looking at Harold; the Senator was much too dominant in the scene. At length Lord Bloomsbury spoke.

'Well,' he said, cautiously, 'if that's how it is, and if we don't suit you, Senator, good day.'

'Ah'm sure our Harold's not good enough for the princess, Senator,' said Lady Bloomsbury happily.

Lord Bloomsbury rubbed his hands. 'Of course, I'm sure he'll always be a brother to her – or to the Committee,' he said; and then, to Lady Bloomsbury, 'I told you to leave this to me, Doris.'

'Oh Tom, you're so clever.'

We all jumped as Harold sprang to his feet; we had not known he could spring. 'Senator,' he cried, in soprano indignation, 'I won't have it. I'm not going to have my affections trifled with. The old feudal days of parental bans are over. I'm of age, I love Insemnia, and I'm going to marry Insemnia.'

'Ooh,' said Edith.

'Eee,' moaned Lady Bloomsbury, 'just when we'd got you well out of it.'

'Harold,' said Lord Bloomsbury, 'after all that has been said to your mother in this room, you're not going to marry this . . . woman.'

'Father, how dare you call her a woman.'

'But Harold,' pleaded Lady Bloomsbury, 'the Committee won't consent now that they know . . .'

'I defy the Committee!' said Harold.

The Senator intervened. 'My boy,' he said, 'you can't do that. My authority is absolute in this matter. You must accept my decision. Insemnia has been brought here, as you may say, under false pretences. . . .'

'Senator,' shouted Harold, 'if you try to come between us now I shall tell the Committee you changed the bottles!'

Over the Senator came a change awesome to watch. He seemed to deflate and shrink. The air of mastery passed from him and he became a scared old gentleman. A vacant look entered his eyes, he swayed a little and put his hand to his head. He sank into a chair. Harold, by comparison, seemed to grow and assume almost masculine traits: Edith watched him with glory, and yet with the look of infinite loss, in her eyes. After a while the Senator spoke. Even his voice was changed.

'You wouldn't do that, pal,' he muttered, 'you wouldn't put me on a spot. I'm a good guy, see, 'n I haddalotter tough breaks lately, see, 'n . . .'

Harold was so carried away by his conquest of the crisis that he appeared not even to notice the transformation in the Senator.

'I warn you,' he said, wagging a menacing forefinger, 'if you try to interfere any more I shall elope with Insemnia.'

'Eee,' whimpered Lady Bloomsbury. She staggered to her feet and once more made her way from that fateful room. Lord Bloomsbury and Lady Cynthia went to help her. 'If my poor old dad could only see this,' said Lord Bloomsbury hopelessly as they went through the door.

The Senator looked as if he had had a stroke. 'You'd better get him upstairs,' I said to Harold.

'Why don't you?' he said; he was intoxicated with success now.

'He's not my father-in-law, or whatever his status will be,' I said, leaning farther back in my armchair.

Seeing nothing else for it, Harold lifted the Senator out of the chair and supported him. It was time he went; he was babbling incoherent things about 'a rap' and 'a frame-up'.

'Come, Insemnia,' called Harold imperiously, looking back over his shoulder.

'I shan't,' said Insemnia flatly.

The Senator moaned. Harold looked as if he would like to drop his burden and fetch Insemnia, but did not venture. With a glare of rebuke, he disappeared upstairs, holding the Senator under one arm.

I was left alone with Insemnia and Edith and was about to soothe them with small talk when the telephone rang.

'Hallo,' I said, into the mouthpiece.

''allo,' said a strange, gruff voice, 'ees zat Meester Grame?'

'Yes,' I said. 'Who is that?'

''Ow is Insemnia?' said the voice. 'Ees aiveryting ollrite?'

'Oh, it's you, Ol. . . .'

'Shut up, you fool,' shouted the voice so that I hastily took the receiver from my ear, 'I'm talking in code, so that nobody suspects. Ees aiveryting okay? Ees she steel thairrrr?'

'Oh yess,' I said, 'aiveryting ees olwrong. Zee bird, she ees going to fly avay.'

'What!' said the voice. 'Why on earth are you talking like that? Is something up?'

'Yess,' I said, 'somezing is oop. I tink you better coom bimeby, yes, no. Allee litee?'

XXVII

I AM not the man to stay where I may not be needed, or to thrust myself on others, but I thought on balance that I should remain to bear Edith and Insemnia company. They had not been alone with each other before and there might, I thought, be some constraint which I could ease; or Edith, a moody girl at times, might not show that unlaboured courtesy, towards a visitor to this island, which is the charm of the British and the envy of others. Indeed, the look she bent on Insemnia was of those which, if they could kill, would inflict a painful and lingering death. This woman had torn her Harold from her lap and been pursued by Harold to a shady riverine glade; what, Edith clearly asked, could be fouler than that?

Insemnia, I saw, looked a little unhappy, as if something were on her mind. I tried to comfort her.

'Are you worrying about the Senator, my dear?' I said. 'I think it is but a passing faintness. Harold will soon put him right.'

'I'm not worrying about the Senator,' she said, thoughtfully, 'I'm worrying about my father.'

'Ah, the Senator has told you,' I said gently, 'bear up. It is very sad to lose a parent suddenly like that, but after all, you never knew him.'

'He was very real to me, somehow, and his measurements were wonderful. I was very fond of him.'

'But the Senator has at least given you another father.'

'I know, of English royal blood, but it does not seem the same.'

'What are you talking about?' snapped Edith, whose curiosity appeared to overcome even her antipathy to Insemnia; also, she probably thought (I imagined) that the more she knew about Insemnia, the stronger her armament would be, and I doubted if she had given up hopes of Harold.

'There has been a slight readjustment of Insemnia's pedigree, Edith,' I explained, 'and she is suffering from the sense of bereavement.'

'What's this nonsense' – Edith is one of those girls, who, unforgivably, speak their minds – 'about royal blood?'

'It is best,' I said mysteriously, 'for you not to ask, and for me not to say, anything more. Several of the leading Royal houses are involved, and the secret is closely guarded. Their agents are always on the track of those who Know Too Much.'

'Rubbish,' said Edith.

Insemnia yawned. 'I suppose the Senator will want to lock me in my room again when he is better,' she said. 'I am so tired of my room. There is nothing to do but read, and I have finished all the books there.'

'I'll lend you one,' I said.

'She ought to try the *Origin of Species*,' said Edith, venomously.

'Is that interesting?' asked Insemnia languidly.

'It should interest *you*. It's about people descending from monkeys.'

'Oh, not quite that, Edith,' I said hastily. 'It merely argues that we all started from scratch.'

Insemnia yawned. 'This is a very boring house,' she said. 'I do not understand all these disputes and disturbances. There was nothing like it at the Institute. I think everybody in this house is mad. I wish Oliver were here.'

'Insemnia,' I protested.

Edith's self-control gave way. 'You are shameless,' she positively hissed. 'I suppose it was just your brazen lack of womanly delicacy that appealed to an inexperienced boy like Harold. Why did you have to pick on him, out of all the world?'

'But I have told you I did not choose Harold. The Committee chose him. I do not like his measurements very much.'

'His measurements are too good for you. And don't tell lies. You know very well you're after his title.'

'Oh no. Harold is plebeian. The Senator was very angry about it. He would take me back to America but that Harold threatened to tell the Committee.'

'Tell the Committee *what?*' said Edith, in harnessed exasperation. 'What is all this piffle about?'

'Ah, now that's the point you shouldn't inquire into, Edith,' I said.

'I think she's mad,' said Edith bitterly.

'No. *You* are mad. You say "Spanish bullfighter" to people and then you strike them. The Senator thought it was very odd....'

'If you think you can talk to me like that ...' began Edith dangerously.

'Why are you so angry with me, and why do you shout at me?' asked Insemnia.

'You hypocrite,' said Edith. 'You know very well I was practically engaged to Harold before you ... escaped from your laboratory.'

'Do you love Harold?' asked Insemnia, in real and deeply wounding surprise. She smiled suddenly, as if she remembered something. 'That is very strange. I cannot imagine anybody loving Harold. He is not ... exciting. And his measurements are poor.'

'You... foetus!' exclaimed Edith, half-rising. 'How dare you talk about Harold like that! Do you think you're too good for him? He's ruining himself by marrying you.'

'But I do not want him. You have him. Please! The Committee will be very cross when they learn about the circumstances of his birth, anyway.'

'Rabbits,' said Edith, 'are thoroughbreds compared with you.'

'Besides,' said Insemnia calmly, 'he is probably mad. Everybody is mad in this house; Oliver said so. You would be well-matched. You could say "Spanish bullfighter" to each other and slap each other's faces. . . .'

There was a sharp report, as Edith jumped up and smacked Insemnia's face. Harold, looking agitated, came in as she did so, and started. 'Good heavens!' he said, placing himself protectively by Insemnia. 'Why did you do that, Edith? Did she say "Spanish bullfighter" to you, Insemnia? My poor darling. It's obviously some quite new form of insanity. . . .'

'Harold!' Harold turned to find Edith advancing on him with mien so terrible that he shrank from her.

'Get her out of here,' said Edith with awful calm.

'What!'

'GET HER OUT OF HERE,' roared Edith suddenly, so that we all recoiled.

'Oh, I see. Er, Insemnia, I think you'd better go to the Senator. He's in a very strange state. I don't think he's quite lucid. He keeps muttering something about somebody pinning a rap on him, it seems to be some kind of code. And he's yelling for you. I can't answer for him if you don't go to him.'

'I won't go,' said Insemnia stubbornly.

'I think perhaps you should, my dear,' I put in coaxingly. She looked at me, and again the signal-lamp in her eyes answered my slightly lowered eyelid. She rose to go. Harold moved with her.

'HAROLD,' said a voice, 'STAY HERE!'

Harold looked round. Fear entered his eyes and he stopped. Insemnia slipped through his fingers like water and went out of the door. I had never seen Edith so formidable; or, indeed, dreamed that she could look so. With a gun in either hand, she could not have been more compelling. I began to realize that, if Harold ever became her husband, he would not have it all his own way; the name beneath those innumerable letters to the *New Statesman* might be his, but the power behind the pen would be Edith's.

'SIT DOWN!' said Edith. The door closed behind Insemnia and Harold sat down. 'Harold,' said Edith, 'I will not be trifled with.

This afternoon you told me, in the presence of witnesses, that you loved me, and discussed our honeymoon. This evening you said you were determined to marry Insemnia. I demand an explanation.'

Harold stirred mutinously. I saw that, however strong her will, Edith would not be able to shake him in this. His mind was set on Insemnia, and I began to think that even Harold, now, was thinking more about the physical Insemnia than the abstract Cause.

'I didn't know it was you,' he said peevishly.

'Didn't know *what* was me?'

'I didn't know your lap was yours, I mean, you.'

'A likely story,' said Edith pitilessly. 'I should like to see any court in the country that would believe it.'

'Court?' asked Harold nervously.

'I said court.'

'Oh dear,' said Harold.

'I told you, Harold,' I put in, 'you should leave it alone.'

'Mr. Grame,' said the awful voice, 'kindly keep your opinions until they are invited. Harold must be saved from himself.'

'That shouldn't be difficult,' I said, mildly. 'You mean, from Insemnia, surely?'

'Anyway, he must be saved.' At this moment there was a ring at the front door. Guessing that Mrs. Barnes had gone home, and that Lady Cynthia was busy ministering to Lady Bloomsbury – indeed, that I was the only person in the house capable of attending to these small matters – I answered it. On the doorstep stood a figure in grimy dungarees, with a bag of tools, cap pulled down, bushy moustache and toil-stained face.

'Good evening, sir,' it said. 'I've come to see about the lights.'

'At this hour?' I said. 'That's very conscientious of you . . . Oh hullo, Oliver, it's you.'

'Shut up, you ass,' he muttered. 'Don't you see I'm in disguise?'

'But why?'

'It's the only way.'

'Is it?' I said. 'Oh well, if you insist, come in. But the lights are all right.'

'I'll soon have 'em all wrong,' he said hoarsely.

'You're picking up the tricks of the trade quickly,' I said. 'Which lights do you want to put wrong?'

'Where's Insemnia?'

'She's upstairs, with the Senator.'

'Locked in?'

'I expect so, by now.'

'What's up? You said something was up.'

'Oh, there's been a great rumpus. In my well-meant way I told the Senator the Bloomsburys were poor and a new title, thinking he'd throw Harold overboard. He did, but Harold turned unexpectedly male and refused to give Insemnia up. He threatened to expose the Senator – I'll tell you about that sometime – and said he'd elope with her if anybody tried to interfere.'

'Harold did? Good heavens!'

'I know. Unsuspected depths, you see. Practically everybody in the house has been having hysterics.'

'Well, you've made a fine mess of it again, haven't you?'

'I? I like that, Oliver.'

'Oh never mind, I'll sort it out somehow. The chief thing is for me to be in the house, so that neither the Senator nor Harold or anybody else can run off with Insemnia before Saturday morning.'

'Don't you think you're rushing this a bit, Oliver? My advice would be to keep out of the way until Saturday morning and leave it to me to keep an eye on her.'

'No, I can't trust this to anybody else. Let's go into the lounge.'

'But Harold and Edith are in there. I may tell you, if you leave well alone there's a good chance of Edith abducting Harold before Harold can abduct Insemnia.'

'Doesn't matter, I want to be on the spot. We can't stand out here. Let's go in and I'll find something to fiddle about with.'

We went in. Harold was still cowering in his chair, with Edith standing over him, but I saw that he was not yet conquered. Though frightened and at bay, he was obstinate, and Edith looked near tears.

Harold glanced at us. 'Hullo, Jene,' he said absent-mindedly, and then started. 'I say, what are you doing here, and why are you dressed like that?'

'I've been messing about with the lights, in the basement,' explained Oliver, quickly covering up his discomfiture. 'There's a fault in the cable.'

'The lights? There's nothing wrong with them.' Harold jumped up; like many of his type he has a feminine intuition in some things. 'I don't believe it,' he said. 'You're up to something. You're after Insemnia again. I won't have it. I shall go up and sleep outside her door all night.' And like a flash he was gone.

'Oh, Mr. Jene,' cried Edith, falling into her chair and bursting into tears, 'how could you? Why did you come in just at that moment?'

Even Oliver was shaken. 'I'm sorry,' he said, 'I didn't know . . .'

'Well, you know now,' I murmured. 'Now you've done it. I told you so.'

XXVIII

I HAD much difficulty in getting rid of Oliver that night. The years he spent raiding enemy coasts at dead of night, and transporting to or retrieving from them soot-blackened Commando-men with knives between their teeth, have left a deep mark on him. The Services mind, notoriously, is apt to run in a groove, and Oliver is inclined to think of every enterprise of the day, simple or complicated, as a Commando operation. Nothing would satisfy him now but that he should remove Insemnia from Seven Priscilla Grove forthwith and keep her in hiding until the moment when they could stand before the Registrar together.

He had a highly involved plan to this end, which, I believe, entailed the use of smoke and a diversionary movement in which I was to play some part; I think he wished me to draw off the garrison to the top floor, while he abducted Insemnia, by shamming a fit in my room.

It was not easy to deter him (his impatience to see Insemnia again seemed as ardent as any girl could wish) but gradually I convinced him, first, that Harold, on guard before her door, would probably remain quite indifferent to my sufferings upstairs; second, that he would in any case be unable to slip quietly away with Insemnia, in view of the considerable crowd still gathered before Number Seven; and third, that it would be much better to collect her at the last moment than to give Harold and the Senator a whole day in which to set every Registrar in London, to say nothing of the police, on the watch for her.

'Curb your ardour, Oliver,' I said. 'We of the Crimean war also know a thing or two. Let suspicions subside. Get them off their guard. Give them a day to cool off. I don't see myself how you are going to get past the Senator, to say nothing of Harold, even on Saturday morning, but you'll only make matters worse by rushing in now.'

'Can I trust you to see that they don't spirit her away to-morrow?' he said.

'If you'll only keep out of the way,' I said, 'I think I might manage it.'

'That's all very well,' he complained. 'How would you like to be told to keep out of the way of a girl like Insemnia?'

'There's a lot in that,' I admitted, 'but if you don't you'll probably ruin everything. The Senator will put her right beyond your reach if you show your face again. He's a pretty tough customer when he's fit and I've an idea he will be at his best again by to-morrow.'

'Well, don't let them out of your sight,' he said, 'and if you want me I won't be far away.'

'Don't be too near, Oliver,' I begged. 'There's something unnerving about your close proximity at the moment.'

So he went away, though I am not sure how far; it was now dark, but looking down from my window I could see that there was still a fair crowd in Priscilla Grove. The muffled hum of talk came up to me and the red tips of cigarettes bespangled the night. Knowing Oliver, I guessed that he might be among these watchers. As I went upstairs I passed Harold, sitting on a chair outside the Senator's flat; he looked a little scared, Edith having paused on her way up to make him further reproaches, but nevertheless he seemed determined to keep watch all night. Farther up, Lady Cynthia passed me, coming down. She merely said, 'We've got Lady Bloomsbury to sleep at last; I'm *sure* there's a curse on this house,' and disappeared basementward, taking a more than usually haunted look with her. After that peace fell on Number Seven. All in it had had a hard and wearing day, myself included, and I fell into a deep sleep the moment I reached my bed.

I was wakened very early (at least, it seemed very early) by Mrs. Barnes, who with lugubrious satisfaction told me that a foreign gentleman was asking for me on the telephone. 'Mind you don't fall over Mr. 'Arold,' she added, with the air of a woman whom nothing more can surprise, 'he's asleep on the mat outside the Senator's door. I told Lady Cynthia, but she said she knew. I don't know what this 'ouse is coming to.'

Hastily throwing on a dressing-gown I went downstairs, stepped over Harold, and made my further way to the telephone. 'Look here, Oliver,' I said, 'why call me at this unearthly hour? I need a little sleep.'

'Why, it's eight o'clock,' he said. 'You should have been up and about long ago. You're a fine friend. Insemnia might have been carried off while you lay snoring. Fortunately I've been watching outside. I thought you'd probably be neglecting your duties, that's why I rang. What's the position now?'

'Bad, Oliver, bad,' I said. 'I don't know how you're going to get at Insemnia. Harold's permanently on guard outside the door, the Senator's in the next room to hers, and I'm pretty sure he's locked her in.'

'Do you think you can get to her?'

'I expect so,' I said. 'I am held in great esteem by all concerned. But I don't see how that's going to help you.'

'Well, you go and have a talk to her and find out the lay of the land,' he said. 'Tell her I'll be round to see her sometime during the day and not to go out. . . .'

'Oliver,' I said, 'for goodness' sake stay away until to-morrow morning. You'll spoil everything.'

'You leave that to me and do as I tell you,' he said. 'I'll ring you again in an hour for news.'

Sighing, I put down the receiver and went upstairs to dress. I saw from my window that Priscilla Grove was empty save for one listless assassin, with a cigarette dangling from his lips and an exceptionally blue jowl, who lounged against a gatepost opposite. I was turning away when a thought struck me and I took another look at him. He raised his eyes to my window, saw me, and winked.

'Oliver, Oliver,' I murmured to myself, 'why will you do it?'

After just an hour, while I was still eating a lonely breakfast, he rang again. 'Well,' he said eagerly, 'what's the news?'

'The news is that I'm just finishing breakfast,' I said.

'But what about Insemnia? Haven't you seen her yet?'

'You're going to marry this girl, Oliver,' I said, 'not I. Give me a chance. I shall try to get in to see her during the morning. Ring again to-morrow.'

'To-morrow,' he almost screamed. 'Don't fool about with me, Grame. If you don't go and see her now I'll come across and batter down the door and slug Harold and the Senator. . . .'

'Oh, all right, all right,' I said, 'for heaven's sake don't start any raids. Think of your mother. You may have her death on your conscience if you cause any fresh trouble. I'll go up and scout out the land in a moment. Ring again about midday.'

'I'll ring in an hour,' he said, 'and if you haven't . . .'

'I will,' I said hastily, and rang off.

A little later I went up. Harold, in a sleeping-bag, lay across the Senator's door. He was awake and was drinking a cup of tea brought to him by Mrs. Barnes.

'Good morning, Harold,' I said. 'Comfortable? Sleep well?'

He ignored my questions. 'Is that fellow Jene still hanging about?' he said.

'Oliver? Oh no. I think you scared him badly last night, Harold. He hasn't been seen since. I imagine he's run away to sea.'

'Well, I don't. I think he's lurking somewhere near until I'm out of the way. Then he'll try to get Insemnia to go out with him again. He's just the kind of adventurer an inexperienced girl like Insemnia needs to be protected against.' He yawned; I gathered that he had not slept well.

'If that's what you think, Harold,' I said, 'what are you going to do about it? You can't stay here for ever. Life on a landing is notoriously hard and thankless. Besides, Edith passes this way a great deal, you know.'

'It won't be necessary,' he said calmly. 'Insemnia and I are going to be married to-morrow.'

I jumped. 'What!' I said. 'How do you know?'

'I took out a special licence yesterday,' he said. 'I could see the only thing to do was to cut through all the argument and act. I just need to keep an eye on her for the rest of to-day and then I can snap my fingers at Jene and everybody else. I've already arranged for the Society Editress of the *Daily Herald* to act as best woman.'

'Well,' I said admiringly, 'I shouldn't have thought it of you, Harold. I begin to see why Insemnia couldn't resist you....'

'Oh, I don't know,' he said, archly.

'But what about the Senator? Didn't he withdraw his consent last night?'

'He can't. I shall ruin him if he tries to come between us. It would be the end of the Institute if I were to publish the facts about that disgraceful piece of juggling with the bottles. What right had he to interfere with Insemnia's parency and give her a reactionary taint? It was the most undemocratic thing I ever heard of.'

'Pure Fascism,' I agreed, 'the fifth column in the bloodstream. Shocking. Well, it looks as if you have the Senator in the hollow of your hand, Harold.'

At this moment Edith came downstairs on her way, probably not to breakfast, for she bore that unbearable look of universal reproach with which a woman like Edith says 'If I were to try to eat a mouthful it would choke me,' but to the chance of another discussion with Harold.

'Have you been here all night, Harold?' she asked in tones of deep contempt.

Harold flinched a little. Bold spirit though he is, Edith's air of awful accusation was enough to strike fear into any heart, and he shrank a little into his sleeping-bag, so that he looked like a turtle. However, he answered resolutely enough.

'Yes, I have,' he said, 'and I must ask you to mind your own business, Edith.'

He could not have said anything worse. 'My own business!' echoed Edith, with a grin of hideous mirth. 'Perhaps you haven't realized yet that this *is* my business, Harold. You cannot play fast and loose with me. I am going to my solicitor this morning to instruct him to take action for breach of promise. Other women must be saved from you.'

Harold shot half out of his sleeping-bag. 'What!' he cried, 'what promise?'

'I have witnesses, Harold,' said Edith warningly.

Harold's trouble was that he did not know to what, exactly, Edith had witnesses; indeed, I believe I am the only member of our household who was quite clear on that point. However, he did not give way.

'Nonsense,' he said, 'you can't prove a thing.'

'Oh, is there something to prove?' I asked, with interest. Edith turned on me with menace in her eyes. I had intended to visit the Senator but now thought it wiser to postpone this. I made a graceful retreat downstairs, leaving Harold to her mercy.

Oliver's next call was due, anyway. In the lounge I found only Lady Cynthia, whom Mrs. Barnes was plying with cups of tea and words of hopeless compassion.

'Oh, hullo, Mr. Grame,' she said. 'Is there any more bad news?'

'None at all,' I said. 'Edith is threatening Harold with an action for breach on the landing; that's the only fresh development this morning.'

'If only Harold hadn't sent those terrible people here,' she said, 'and yet I don't know. If it hadn't been them, it would have been somebody worse. I'm certain there's some evil presence in the first-floor flat. I wonder where Oliver is?'

'He probably thinks it tactful to keep out of the way for a bit,' I said, and as I spoke Edith came in, with a very red face, and the telephone rang. I answered.

'That you, Grame?' said Oliver. 'What's the news?'

'Oh, yaiss, yaiss,' I said, 'ze balloon, he go up.'

'Oh, there's somebody there, is there?' said Oliver keenly. 'I understand. Come out; I'll be waiting at the corner.'

'What a funny way you were talking, Mr. Grame,' said Lady Cynthia curiously as I went out. At the corner house I saw a listless figure, with blue jowl and hat-brim pulled down, propped against some railings, and went up to it. 'Not here, Oliver,' I murmured warningly, 'let's get out of sight.'

'Pardon!' said the figure in surprise, and at the same moment I heard a hissing 'Psst . . .' I looked round and saw Oliver's head protruding round the end of Priscilla Grove. 'Sorry,' I said, raising my hat, and passed on. 'Oliver,' I said, when I reached him, and as we walked together towards the Brompton Road, 'do drop these disguises. You're making me quite confused. I shall be giving the whole game away to the postman, or something, if you go on like this.'

'Oh, we can easily get round that difficulty,' he said, 'we must have a password.'

'We won't,' I said. 'Now listen. The thing's getting more and more complicated.'

'What's happened?' he said. 'Did you see Insemnia?'

'No. I went up to try and get in to her but Harold is firmly encamped on the rug outside the door and says he's going to stay there until to-morrow morning, so that you can't get up to any more tricks with her. Not only that, but he too has a special licence for to-morrow, and I expect all the information on it is in order.'

'Oh lord,' he said, 'but that won't help him now the Senator's withdrawn his consent.'

'Well, I don't know,' I said. 'Harold's nearer to Insemnia than you are and he's proving unexpectedly stubborn. He's in a strong position, too. He may be able to get his way. He knows something about the Senator, and, as I told you, threatens to expose him if he tries to withhold his consent now.'

'What does he know?'

'Oh, that's a long story....'

'Well, tell it briefly for heaven's sake.'

'It seems – mark you, I only say seems, for I think the true facts of Insemnia's birth, if she *was* born, will remain for ever a mystery – it seems that the Senator secretly changed her father at the last moment. The French prizefighter wasn't her father at all. It would ruin the Senator and his Institute if it were known.'

'Ah, I see,' said Oliver alertly, 'I suppose he changed the bottles for some silly reason of his own.'

As I say, Oliver, a simple lad in some ways, has this remarkable gift for understanding things which are even somewhat beyond my perception. 'How did you guess that, Oliver?' I asked in surprise.

'Oh, it's obvious,' he said airily. 'Who *is* her father, then?'

'*Was*,' I said. 'He was a Royal duke, according to the latest communique, and subject to correction.'

'Oh well,' he said impatiently, 'it doesn't matter, anyhow. The point is, that I'm now up against Harold, and the Senator is against Harold and against me. I don't see that it makes any difference. The essential outline of the operation' – his mind sailed the seas again – 'remains the same. All you have to do is to see that Insemnia isn't spirited away by either of them before I can collect her to-morrow morning. Can't you give the Senator and Harold some knockout drops?'

'I suppose you imagine that I can just walk into any chemist and ask for knockout drops? All I have now is a little sherry and I don't think I'll be able to persuade Harold to take any more. The Senator *might* be induced.'

'That's all right, then. Harold's safe, anyway; we can just leave him on the mat. You look after the Senator somehow and see he doesn't get away with her.'

'Well, I promise nothing, Oliver,' I said, 'but I'll try.'

The morning was well advanced before I made my next attempt to see the Senator. I explained to Harold that someone ought to see how the old gentleman was and he watched indifferently as I knocked on the door. After a few moments the Senator opened it. He appeared to be quite himself again, but I thought I saw the look of a trapped animal – a dangerous one – in his eye. He gazed in surprise at Harold, who was seated in a chair on the landing, but made no comment.

'May I come in, Senator?' I said. 'I should like a word with you.'

'Come in, Mr. Grame,' he said, with his wonted booming affability, and then, as he closed the door, 'What is that young man doing there?'

'Harold,' I said, 'is resolved not to stir from the spot until he accompanies Insemnia to the altar, or the desk, or whatever Registrars use. He refuses to accept your withdrawal of consent.'

'Is that so?' he said thoughtfully, leading me into his room. 'That is most regrettable. However, I have decided that the wedding shall not take place. I am preparing to take Insemnia home.' I looked round and saw with anxiety, on Oliver's account, that he was.

'You are packing, Senator?' I said. 'When do you think of leaving?'

'At once, sir,' he said, 'to-day.'

'But,' I ventured, 'will that not lead to unpleasant consequences? You remember Harold's threat to reveal your, ah, sleight of hand with Insemnia's various fathers?'

'As to that,' he said dangerously, 'I shall deny everything. It is but his word against mine.'

'His and that of one or two other persons who were present,' I objected mildly. 'Senator, you look pale. All this excitement has been a trial for you. Will you try a little stimulant?' I offered him a little – a very little, as I needed to keep a reserve – from my flask.

'What is it, Mr. Grame?' he asked greedily.

'Try it,' I said simply.

He drank and seemed refreshed, but absent-minded. 'He's crazy if he thinks he can do this to me,' he murmured. 'I got all those newspaper boys on my side, haven't I? I always treated 'em good, didn't I? They know where to come when they wanna story, don't they? Aw, he'll get a shock when he reads what those boys'll say about him. They'll ride him. They'll say he st . . .'

'Don't say it, Senator,' I begged. 'I always think the word unworthy of your fertile American imaginations.' I gave him a little – a very little – more. 'Look, Senator,' I begged, 'don't go to-day. A few hours more won't make any difference. We like each other, you and I, indeed, I think I may say we understand each other. I do not want you to go with a bad impression of our English hospitality. You have never had an opportunity to learn to know London at its best since you have been here. Now, let us have just one night out together before you go.'

His eyes glittered. I saw that I had found the key. 'A Night Out,' he said, 'oh boy! Can we go to the Tiv?'

'The Tiv?' I said.

'Yes, I always wanted to see the Tiv. Or the Pav.'

'You shall. For that matter, I can even take you to the Emp.'

'No, I've always heard the Tiv is the place, or failing that the Pav. The proms are better there.'

'The proms?'

'Yeh, you know. Where the dames are.'

'The dames? In the proms? At the Pav? Oh yes, of course.

Of course! I think you may find the prom at the Pav a little changed but the dames are as good as ever.'

'As *good*? No!'

'Yes,' I insisted, 'quite as good, if not better. You shall see them all, Senator. Nothing of the gay night life of London shall be hidden from you. I warn you: be ready for anything.'

'I will,' he said, squinting in anticipatory delight, 'oh boy, oh boy!'

'But you must rest now, Senator,' I urged. 'You will need to be fresh for this evening. Even your constitution may not be equal to the strain, you understand? Now, if I may advise, stop your packing and lie down. Have a good sleep, so that you may be equal to the dames and the proms. I will call for you in the late afternoon.'

'Sure, Mr. Grame, sure,' he said, 'I'll do that. I don't wanna miss this. I saw you was a good guy from the first, Mr. Grame. Between you and me, it's been a bit dull here.'

'Dull?' I said. 'You surprise me. Before I go, and you lie down, may I have a few minutes with your lovely ward? I shall not have another chance to say good-bye to her, I expect.'

'Sure,' he said, 'sure,' and he led me to her room and unlocked the door. She was standing at the window, looking out on to Number Seven's little rear garden, as we entered and I thought she started a little. 'Here's Mr. Grame to say good-bye to you, my child,' he boomed. 'We're not leaving until to-morrow morning, after all. I shall go and rest a little, my dear. Lock the door when you leave, Mr. Grame.'

'I will,' I promised, and the Senator, squinting happily, withdrew. I lowered an eyelid as Insemnia came towards me and sat down. She was wearing her beige suit and the sight of her was too much for the twenty-year-old George Grame who lives inside the ageing husk of Mr. Grame of Priscilla Grove. As the door closed I took her in my arms and kissed her very hard. She kissed me back, in the manner, I noticed with regret, of a daughter kissing her father.

'Well, my dear,' I murmured softly, 'here you are at last. How lovely you are.'

'Where is Oliver?' she whispered, disengaging herself gently; and she was right to do so, because I should not have let her go. 'I have been so frightened.'

'Don't worry,' I said, 'he's not far away. Why have you been frightened?'

'There's such a funny old man outside in the garden,' she said, 'and he's been making faces at me.'

I went quickly to the window. In the tiny paved rectangle, with one or two straggling bushes, which is the rear garden of Number Seven was a figure of toil; it wore an apron of sacking, and an old trilby hat pulled well down and on its face was what appeared to be a week's growth of beard. The face was turned up and one of the eyes winked at me.

'That's Oliver,' I said bitterly. 'He'll ruin everything yet.'

'Oliver!' she exclaimed, and ran to the window. Smiling delightedly she waved and blew kisses. I saw the revolting figure wave back and kiss its hand. I shook my fist and made energetic gestures of dismissal. After a long period of blank incomprehension the figure withdrew under the lee of the house. I drew Insemnia away from the window to a chair.

'Insemnia,' I said, 'never marry a naval officer with a commando complex. Your life will be hell. Why not marry me instead?'

'I'd sooner marry Oliver,' she said candidly. 'What has been happening?'

'Practically everything,' I said. 'You know that the Senator means to take you home. Meanwhile Harold is standing guard outside the door. He's determined not to let you go and he's got a special licence, all ready to marry you to-morrow morning. It seems clear that you're not going to leave this house without getting married to somebody, but who it's going to be, time alone can show. I only hope it's me. But meanwhile, I've persuaded the Senator to stay until to-morrow and I'm going to get him out of the way. I'm taking him for a night out.'

'Are you going to leave him at the waxworks?' she said joyfully.

'I don't know yet,' I said, 'but I'll fix him somehow. Do you know if he carries his boat-tickets on him?'

'Yes, they're in his wallet.'

'Good. Then I may find a way to dispose of him.'

'But this still leaves Harold. How will Oliver get past Harold?'

'I can think of methods,' I said, 'but I hope it won't come to that. Oliver may come down the chimney.'

'He can't,' said Insemnia, contemplating the fireplace seriously, 'it's blocked up.'

'So it is.' The fireplace was indeed bricked in, and an electric fire stood before it. 'Well, then he'll either come up through the floor or down through the ceiling, I expect. Anyway, one way or another we'll manage it. Now, all I want you to do is to stay here and refuse to leave your room in any circumstances until we come for you to-morrow morning. Say you want your meals sent up, or you're unwell and don't want anything. Just stay here and don't budge.'

'I will,' she said obediently, 'I shan't mind at all if Oliver's in the garden.'

'Oh lord,' I said, 'I hope he won't be. Good-bye, Insemnia. This *is* the last one, I'm afraid. But it's the fourth, so I can't complain.'

I locked the door on her, went out, ignoring Harold's inquiring look, and went downstairs, humming softly to myself a few lines of a song I once knew – was it in Berlin, or Prague, or Vienna? I could not remember, but the words came back to me:

> Hab' keine Angst, vor dem ersten Kuss,
> Weil es schliesslish einmal kommen muss;
> Hab' lieber Angst, vor dem letzten Kuss –
> Weil es auch 'mal kommen muss!

'Eheu fugaces,' I thought, as I went into the lounge; 'lang ist es her, lang ist her!'

XXIX

FOR the rest of the afternoon all was quiet in Number Seven save for the sound of footfalls on the stairs. These belonged variously to Mrs. Barnes, gloomily bound with meals for Insemnia or cups of tea for Harold; or to Lady Bloomsbury, descending to cast a mother's despairing eye on her stubbornly wayward son; or to Edith, going up and down under various pretexts, but always with the purpose of resuming hostilities on the first-floor landing; or to Lady Cynthia, desperately seeking to spread comfort in a doleful house. Alistair, vaguely sensing that trouble was afoot, was taking a walk; Em Porridge, now recovered, had gone to relieve the anxiety felt, on account of his absence, by his colleagues of the Bulgoslav Cultural Society. So quiet, and yet disquieting, was the atmosphere that I would have retired to my room, had not my duty to Oliver and Insemnia dictated that I should remain below, on watch for any surprise departure by the Senator or abduction by Harold. Priscilla Grove, heavy in the heat, was unwontedly empty. Our regular spectators, apparently exhausted by their long and fruitless vigil, were absent.

As soon as the clock showed an hour which could by any stretch be called evening I went up for the Senator. Harold, with several volumes of the collected writings of Stalin beside him, was preparing himself for his approaching nuptials and seemed refreshed and carefree.

'I'm going to take the Senator out for an hour or two,' I told him. 'He needs fresh air. Take care of Insemnia while we're out.'

He looked suspicious for a moment and then his doubts cleared; with the Senator out of the way, he obviously reflected, Insemnia would be safe from one of the two who threatened to stand between Harold and his happiness. 'I will,' he said briefly. The Senator answered my knock with his customary 'Come in, sir, come in,' and gave Harold a look of deep dislike. 'In my younger days, sir,' he said, as he closed the door, 'I would have thrown that young man downstairs.'

'Do it to-morrow morning,' I suggested, 'I have always felt that Harold needs it.' While the Senator prepared himself, I prepared the evening. I calculated that a tumblerful of Our Sherry remained in my flask, and thought the maximum effect would be achieved if I gave it him in two doses; I had remarked that the patient's resistance became less as the treatment proceeded. Taking a glass from the sideboard I half-filled it and gave it to him.

'What is that, sir?' he said, looking at it inquisitively.

'A little something for the road, Senator,' I said. 'It is an old English custom to lay a good foundation for a night out with malmsey. It is our way to quaff it at a draught. Bottoms up!'

'Bottoms up!' he said, and drained the glass.

'You take me too literally, Senator,' I said, exerting all my strength to pick him off his face and restore him to his feet. He swayed for a moment or two, while I held on to him, and then gradually rocked to a standstill. A mad light suffused his eyes and suddenly he roared, 'Yippee!'

'Come, Senator,' I urged. I tapped on Insemnia's door. 'What is it?' I heard her answer. 'The Senator and I are going out for a little while, my dear,' I called. 'We shan't be long.' 'Very well,' she said. I winked at the closed door, and we passed out. Harold ostentatiously did not look up as we went.

It was a matter of some difficulty to get the Senator to the Brompton Road; he was stiffening and shot his inflexible legs out in front of him like a pre-1914 Prussian drill-sergeant. Fortunately we found a taxi-cab with the hood down and the Senator, standing in it with his head in the air, was able to have a good look at London on his last night in it. This was even a little embarrassing when we arrived at the Pav, because that establishment wore on its façade a poster of an almost naked lady, some hundreds of times lifesize, who lay on her back and appeared to be expecting assault, or to have just suffered it. It was one of the more tasteful exports of Hollywood, and to the Senator, no doubt, seemed appropriate and promising. His tall figure, contemplating it blissfully from the interior of a taxi-cab above which he towered giantlike, attracted some notice locally, however, and I was glad when the driver and I were able to extract him and propel him towards the entrance, where I purchased two seats.

Within, the Senator's anticipations were more than fulfilled. We entered a dark corridor where a beautiful maiden suddenly appeared, but dimly seen in the gloom, who shone a dazzling beam of light in his eye, and said, 'Follow me.' She then sped away, and the Senator tried to obey the invitation. Fortunately the rigidity of his limbs prevented him from catching her, and I was able, as she disappeared in the darkness, to head him round a corner, where another sprite popped up close in front of him. Flashing another searchlight in his eye, the reflected radiance of which enabled him to see that she was fair to behold, she said, 'Follow me,' and ran away. The Senator did his best to catch her, but could not, and I led him, breathing hard, up some stairs, at the head of which a third lovely creature materialized, blinded him with light, called, 'Follow me,' and vanished. In this way I was able to keep the Senator running, or at any rate, moving jerkily, after a series of lamp-flashing dames, along passages, through corridors and up and down stairs, for a full quarter of an hour, and he enjoyed himself immensely, though his breathing became rather stertorous and out of the darkness around ssh-ing sounds came towards him. At last we came to a rather wider corridor or passage, which was dimly lit, and had two or three magnificent sofas in it. It was quite empty, and for all I know may once have been a prom; I think probably that was the story of its past.

I guided the Senator to one of the sofas and he fell into it, panting. I was a little short of breath myself and was glad to sit down beside him.

'Ah, glorious, sir, glorious,' he said, chuckling and mopping his forehead. 'What a night! This is like the old times.'

'Isn't it?' I said. 'And this is only the beginning. We can go on all night like this.'

'No!' he said. 'But tell me, dear Mr. Grame, why do they run away from me? Why don't they let me catch them?'

'Ah, the evening is young,' I said, 'there is plenty of time. That is the art of their calling, these *mädis vom Chantant.* They are spirited girls, they like to be pursued. The zest of the chase, you know, Senator, ha-ha. The lights they flash are symbolic of the will-o'-the-wisp, love. They find it pleases their patrons. The more they run, the merrier the fun. Fast and furious is their motto. They develop an incredible turn of speed sometimes. Why, I believe some of them have run for England at the Olympic Games.'

'England!' he said in amaze,

'Was it England, or France?' I mused. 'Probably France. You know what the French are, Senator.'

'Well, well,' he said, 'I am extremely grateful to you for this experience, Mr. Grame. There is something irresistible about a night out, even at our age. . . .'

This shook me. '*Our* age, Senator,' I said.

He laughed loudly and dug me in the ribs. As he could not flex his fingers it was painful. 'You're a gay dog, Grame,' he said, 'but tell me, why is the prom so empty?'

'As I say, the night is yet young,' I told him. 'You must be patient, Senator.' Then I saw that his attention was not with me; his gaze was directed elsewhere. I turned and found that it was fixed on a door bearing the legend 'Dames'; another, not far away, was marked 'Messieurs'.

'Mr. Grame,' he said triumphantly, and striving to rise, 'you see that. That's where they are. C'm on! We're wasting our time. . . .'

I took him by the shoulders and pressed him back. 'No, no, Senator,' I said firmly, 'that is the green room.' I saw that it was time for the second dose and poured it out for him. 'Bottoms up, Senator,' I said, holding him down. He drank, and with awe I watched the hair on his head stand straight up. I thought it time to change the conversation.

'Senator,' I said, 'now that we are alone for a moment, will you tell me something I very much want to know. Who is, or was, Insemnia's father?'

Whether the name Insemnia recalled him to his cares, or whether he was passing through another phase in the effects of Our Sherry, I know not, but a sudden change came over him. The wind seemed to go out of him, he shrank and shrivelled, and the cunning look came over his face. He looked furtively from side to side and bent his head towards mine.

'Aw, listen, pal,' he said, 'it ain't no good asking me, see? I'm a con man 'n I've always been a con man, 'n they ain't another con man on Broadway kin sell oil stock like old Uncle Lester Vanderboom, see? But I ain't no office executive, see, 'n I never did understand card indexes 'n bookkeeping, see? Waal, when I started the Institute it wuz a good racket, see, 'n it kinda ran away with itself, see, 'n all those bottles 'n labels got kinda mixed up, see, 'n before I could get it *organized* they wuz a lotta funny things happened, see?' And he leaned back, with the air of a man who has unbared his soul.

I thought a moment. 'Then what you mean,' I said, 'is that you don't know who her father was or is?'

'Pal,' he said, 'I jest haven't a notion.'

'But at least there's no doubt who her mother was?'

'Now it's kinda funny you should mention that,' he said, 'because, as I tole you, we haddalotta trouble when I was starting the Institute, see, what with mothers and fathers linin' up outside, see, with their wads in one hand and application forms in the other, see, on account of they wanted the publicity, see, 'n I kinda had to do the best I could as we went along, see? Well, in those early days, before I got it scientikif . . . scientishif . . .'

'Scientifically?' I suggested.

'Yeh, that's right, scientishifically organized, they wuz a lotta funny things happened, see . . .'

'Yes, you told me that,' I prompted him.

'. . . 'n doggone me, but I had to do the nursing *myself*, see, 'n all those kids looked jest the same to me. . . .'

'You don't know who her mother is or was, either?'

'Pal,' he said, 'I know within about twenty, 'n that's all. It wuz a good racket, the best racket Broadway ever saw, but I made one mistake. I oughta had a business organizer in with me from the start. But I'd always worked alone, see, dey all know me on Broadway on account of I always worked alone, see, 'n I reckoned I could keep it to myself, see, 'n why should I let some other guy muscle in, see. . . .'

We sat silent for a moment while I pondered the mystery of Insemnia's birth. How strange, I thought, was the way that had led her to Oliver. Was there a Purpose in the universe, a higher scheme of things, or no scheme? If there *was* a scheme, did it provide for such interferences as that of the jovial old ruffian at my side? Did it include them, merely in order to rectify their intrusions in its own way and time, so that it might show what it could do? If there was *no* scheme, would it be possible for a small coterie of such ruffians, tricksters calling themselves scientists, to disrupt all the processes of human faith, human love and human procreation which our little planet, during untold aeons, had come to believe the natural order of life? Was there a meaning? Was there no meaning?

My reverie was cut short; its prolongation would not have led me to the answer, anyway, for I have thought much about these things since and have found none. We both started as two ladies came through a swinging door and sat down on another sofa. The Senator nudged me.

'Pal,' he said, 'here they come!'

'Who?' I said absent-mindedly.

'The dames.'

I looked and pulled myself together. They were two good ladies from who-knows-where, but not very far away: from Wimbledon, Wapping, Walthamstow or Willesden. They were plump, fiftyish, behung with handbags into which they now half-disappeared. I saw that some fate much worse than death must have befallen the lady of the placard outside; they were red-eyed and agitated and wished to compose their feelings and features. They patted and powdered, grimacing into little mirrors and talking volubly to each other between pats. Presently a bus or tube would restore them to little homes-in-a-row; meanwhile they lived in a twilight world, between the real one they had just left and the unreal one they would return to. Like the Empress Elizabeth stealing from the masquerade, they were putting off love, fear, sorrow, joy, horror, passion, lust, and putting on their empty daylight faces.

'Ooh, Audrey,' said the one, 'wasn't it *awful*! I didn't know where to look!' (yet I surmised that she had looked).

'I don't know what they'll show next, Patricia,' said the other. 'Shall we come next week?'

'Come on, pal,' said a voice in my ear. Before I could remonstrate the Senator stood up, strode stiffly to them, bowed (happily without falling) and said, 'Good evening, ladies. I do not wish to intrude on so much beauty, but may I join you?'

We have always something to learn, and I was mildly surprised by what happened next; afterwards I reflected that the two ladies saw an irresistible opportunity to dally a while in the land of romantic twilight, which they would all too soon have to leave for Willesden, Walthamstow, Wapping or Wimbledon.

The Senator, at his best, is a fine-looking man, and the presence of these dames stirred him to put his best face foremost. He looked really noble as he leaned deferentially towards them, rocking slightly. I saw two large red faces express first consternation, then doubt, then forgiveness and then beaming pleasure. Willesden could be forgotten for a little while yet. With those wriggling movements which large ladies make when they are seated and wish to change their position, they made room for him between them. The Senator sat down and placed a courtly arm around each. They yielded with gleeful struggles. The Senator had reached the haven where he fain would be.

I was mildly interested to know the fate of the lady on the placard and, seeing that the Senator might safely be left for some time, went to watch the film. It was disappointing; the lady in question, had she followed the precedent set by Mary Pickford in the dear silent days beyond recall, might have proclaimed herself to be The World's Bosom Friend, but as she did nothing save display her admittedly exceptional charms, she palled in time and I went to sleep; I had still a good deal of sleep to recover. When I awoke the lights were on and everybody was going home. I hastened to the prom, where I found the Senator, alone. The last bus to Willesden had evidently gone and he was fast asleep on the sofa with one of the *mädis vom Chantant* bending over him and thumping him with her torch.

'Ah, leave him to me, my dear,' I said. 'He is my friend.'

'Your friend, is he?' she said, looking at me. 'Well, I think he's had one over the eight. He woke up just now and tried to get up and chase me round the room. "My will-o'-the-wisp," he called me. Then he fell back and went to sleep again.'

We had some trouble in waking the Senator sufficiently for me to get him downstairs (the heavy week he had behind was beginning to take toll of him now) and it cost me much more money than I thought him worth to find a taxi-cab driver willing to put the hood down, so that we could get the Senator into his cab and drive to Waterloo. However, we did accomplish this; and on the way I relieved him of the key to the first floor and of his wallet, which I found to contain several hundred dollars. I kept a hundred dollars and his boat-tickets and restored the wallet.

At Waterloo I put him in a sleeper. The attendant was one of the old type: a man with the Mons Star whom nothing could startle or ruffle. 'Friend,' I said, 'this gentleman, who is in a lamentable state of intoxication' (the Senator was now fast asleep, in his berth) 'has to catch a ship from Southampton. I believe it is called the *Empress of Poland* and is sailing in the morning, I hope. It is a matter of life and death that he should not miss it. Will you see that he sails? This is for you, and there will be as much again if you get him to the *Empress of Poland* before she leaves. Here are his sailing tickets.'

'Fifty dollars,' he said, looking at the notes, 'that's a lot of money. Thank you, sir. You leave it to me, sir. I'll see he don't miss it.'

I watched the lights of the train disappear, and heard the roar of its passing dwindle, leaving Waterloo Station deafeningly quiet. The man of destiny was gone. 'Bon voyage, Senator,' I murmured after it (I had grown rather fond of him in my way). 'You had a big idea, but the best-laid plans . . .'

It was very late when I returned to Number Seven. I had that eerie feeling of being followed or watched which comes on the least nervous of us sometimes, in a dark and empty street, and thought that Oliver was probably somewhere about, but I did not see him.

Inside, all was quiet. Harold snored faintly on the mat, but did not stir as I went to my room.

XXX

I WOKE early, dressed quickly, and stepped across to Edith's room before I went downstairs. In answer to my tap on her door she appeared, looking rather startled, with her hair in curlers and herself in a revolting pink housecoat.

'Psst, Edith,' I said warningly.

'What do you mean, psst?' she said in quarrelsome tone.

'Oh, don't start arguing about that now,' I said. 'I meant that walls have ears.'

'Well, why shouldn't they have? I've nothing on my conscience.'

'Edith,' I said, 'do stop splitting hairs. This is a day of crisis for us all, for you, for Harold, and everybody. Now, will you help me?'

'You asked me to help before and it didn't get me anywhere. Everything is much worse now than ever it was.'

Even a pretty girl loses her looks when she cries, and Edith is not pretty at any time. I began to dislike her habit of tears. They seemed always present in her eyes.

'It's all working out for the best,' I said mysteriously. 'I can't tell you more now, but if you lend a hand I think we may be able to . . . er . . . prevent Harold from marrying Insemnia.' I did not wish to tell Edith too much; one never knows how a woman's mind will work.

'I doubt it,' she said. 'Anyway, what can I do?'

'Can you get Harold away from that door?'

'No,' she said. 'While you were out last night everybody in the house was trying to get him away, and he wouldn't budge. Lady Bloomsbury had a heart attack and we had to send for the doctor.'

'Well, get him away if you can,' I said, 'and if you can't, keep him talking.'

'Why?'

'I can't tell you why, but do it.'

'When?'

'Ah, when?' I said. 'Now that's a bit of a problem.' I wondered at what time Oliver would start his raid. 'Well, let's say, at nine-thirty. They don't open until ten.'

'They don't open until eleven-thirty.'

'When, I said "they", I didn't mean *they*, Edith,' I said, 'and I'm surprised that you should know when *they* open. I was thinking of something else. Anyway, you begin operations about nine-thirty, will you?'

'All right,' she said, 'but it sounds like nonsense to me.'

'Not a bit of it,' I said, 'just you wait and see.'

Leaving her with curiosity written on her face I went downstairs and out and telephoned the Rembrandt Hotel from the telephone box at the corner. I was put through to Oliver and told him that the Senator was out of the way, but Harold still in it.

'Oh, that's all right,' he said carelessly, 'he doesn't matter.'

'Why, what are you going to do?'

'Wait and see,' he said, 'I've got it all teed-up.'

'But you'd better tell *me*.'

'No. No careless talk,' he said, 'just you see that Insemnia stays in her room.'

'I suppose you're up to some ridiculous stunt,' I said. 'Anyway, what time to you propose to start operations?'

'What time?' he said, guardedly. 'Oh, that's a top secret. Good-bye.' And he rang off.

I went back and found Priscilla Grove placid and almost empty. Mrs. Barnes was even washing the front steps and crooning 'One Fine Day He'll Come Along' faintly to herself. Peggy, with a wary air, was sunning herself on the pavement. I went upstairs. Harold's head once more protruded from his sleeping-bag like that of a turtle from its shell. He was just awake.

'I didn't hear you come in,' he said sleepily.

'You were sleeping very soundly, Harold,' I said, opening the door with the Senator's key.

'Hi!' he said, sitting up. 'Where did you get that key?'

'Shush,' I said, 'as a matter of fact the Senator was rather unwell when he came home last night and didn't wish to be roused too early this morning, so he gave me the key.'

'Oh,' he said, lying down again, 'tight again, I suppose.'

'Coming from you, Harold,' I said rebukingly, 'that is a most improper remark.' Leaving him to worry it out I went in and closed the door behind me. Then I knocked softly on Insemnia's door. 'Who is it?' she called. 'It's I,' I answered.

I unlocked the door and stood entranced. Insemnia had only begun to be interested in getting married forty-eight hours earlier, but now a blind man would have known that she was to be a bride. She wore a plain black suit; indeed, nothing in her clothes was bridal or in any way different from everyday. Yet something about her said 'Bride'; something in her eyes, her colour, her whole radiant expectancy. I could not help myself or resist her. 'There,' I said, 'that really is the last one,' and I let her go.

'Where's the Senator?' she asked softly.

'He's gone, my dear,' I said. 'By now he should be on his way to America – I hope. Anyway, he can't interfere with us to-day. His plans for Selective Parenthood have been taken over by others.'

'Has he really gone?' she said, looking for a moment bereft, and then, 'Oh, I am glad. For the first time I feel free. What a wonderful thing that is, to feel free.'

'There's nothing else like it in the world,' I told her, 'not gold or jewels or all the wealth of Croesus – nothing.'

'And where is Oliver?'

'I don't know, but I expect he's on his way here. I don't even know what he's going to do, but he swears that he knows. He may be going to murder Harold and break the door down. . . .'

'Is Harold still there?'

'Yes, and he thinks he's going to marry you this very morning. I have a feeling something dreadful is going to happen in this house very soon.'

'It won't be dreadful if only Oliver comes quickly.'

We both jumped as a tap came on the window. Outside appeared a figure on a ladder with a wet rag in one hand and a bucket in the other. It wore a cap and began to clean the window. As it did so, its face asked unheard questions of us. 'Is the coast clear?' it plainly said.

'Oliver!' cried Insemnia joyfully.

'Oliver!' I said with deep resentment. I went to the window and opened it. He climbed in. 'Oliver,' I said, 'if you don't lose Insemnia, it won't be your fault. What on earth do you want to dress up like that for?'

'It was the only way to get in without attracting attention,' he said. 'Where's the Senator?'

'On a ship by now – I hope,' I said.

'Not bad, for you,' he said. 'Where's Harold?'

'Outside that door and probably armed,' I said.

'Fine. Then everything's all right.' He took no further notice of me; indeed he seemed suddenly to forget that I was there. He turned to Insemnia and took her in his arms.

'Insemnia!' he said.

'Oliver!' she said.

'My beautiful.'

'My darling.'

'Oh lord,' I said; but they did not hear me.

'Now for a real experiment,' said Oliver, looking deep into

Insemnia's eyes, 'an old-fashioned one in selective parenthood—they call it an elopement.'

'How exciting!' said Insemnia. 'I have read about elopements – by coach and four to Gretna Green.'

'Well, by taxi to Maidenhead is the modern equivalent,' said Oliver. 'This is an elopement with several differences.'

'What other differences?'

'Well, for one thing, your parents can't pursue us, can they?'

'My poor parents,' said Insemnia pathetically, 'I wish I knew who they were. Ought we not to have their consent?'

'If you expect me to go rummaging about among a lot of broken bottles,' said Oliver. 'I say, this is not the time. Anyway, I can supply you with parents-in-law. Mums and the Guvnor will love you.'

'You know, Oliver,' said Insemnia thoughtfully, 'there's just one thing spoils this for me.'

'There is!' he said, staring. 'What is it?'

'Well, I feel that I'm letting that cat Edith have her own way. She was trying to take my Harold from me.'

Speechless for a moment, both Oliver and I looked at her. Then we saw that Insemnia had learned much more than we thought in the past forty-eight hours. Oliver suddenly laughed and kissed her.

'Come on,' he said, 'time's a small place and the world's flying. . . .'

I was getting nervous and wished they would go, but Insemnia seemed to be enjoying herself so much that she did not want Oliver's arms to loosen about her.

'What I adore about this,' she said, 'is that it's all so sudden.'

'It isn't really,' said Oliver, 'most lovely wife, it's all part of the Great Plot, or Plan, or what you will. You were sent wandering down the corridors of time for a million years just so that you should come and stay at Seven Priscilla Grove when I was due on leave.'

'I'm so glad the Committee chose Harold and sent me. They're a lot of silly old men; I never really liked them until now.'

'Silly, and yet the instruments of wisdom,' said Oliver, 'but for them you wouldn't have come here just at the right moment.' He smiled, then laughed; Insemnia laughed with him. Then she stopped and said, 'I wonder why we are laughing.'

'I was just thinking of the Committee, rushing in,' said Oliver. 'They manufacture human beings. Some other Committee, somewhere else, arranges to atomize them. Isn't it a snigger.'

'It's excruciating,' said Insemnia.

'But they can't stop boy meeting girl.'

'But why do they want to blow us into the world and then blow us out of it?'

'I can't think. But isn't it funny? I suppose they think they've a trump card in the atom bomb, the silly old goats.'

'A last-trump-card, you mean,' laughed Insemnia; but then she became grave again. 'I have just thought of something.'

'What?'

'I do not want to be blown up, now that I have met you. I want to be with you for years and years and years. . . .'

'Don't worry,' said Oliver, pressing her to him, 'we shall always be together. When they vaporize us both our atomic dusts will spin round among the stars for another million years until it collects itself into Insemnia and Oliver again and you walk in at one door as I come in by another . . . By the way, what is that delightful scent of yours?'

'It is my perfume – wood violets.'

'Then my dust will always know yours by its scent – wood violets.'

'And what will your dust smell of – tweed and tobacco?'

'If the last-trump-card should happen to be played during a cocktail party it might smell strongly of gin.'

'I do not think I shall like to be dust,' said Insemnia unhappily. 'It is so . . . humiliating to be flicked off the ends of cigarettes . . .'

'And sucked up by Hoovers. I know. Never mind, in the course of time we shall take shape, meet again, and have a wonderful series of lives together – until the world has another attack of progress. We shall have a lot of trouble then.'

'I shall not mind,' murmured Insemnia, 'if we are together.'

'We shall be, for ever. We always were. We are. The planets will get to know us as we spin by.'

'I shall be jealous. Venus will say, there goes that nice Jene man again, how I love the smell of tweed and tobacco.'

'I hope Venus likes the smell of gin. I shall have more cause to be jealous. I can just imagine Mars sniffing and saying, Hm, wood violets, that must be that lovely Mrs. Jene.'

'And my dust will always be saying, I love you.'

'And mine, I adore you.'

Obviously they were going on like this a long time. They had quite forgotten me, the day, the ladder—everything. 'Oliver,' I said urgently, 'Insemnia . . .'

'What's that?' asked Oliver. But before I could answer there came a loud hammering at the outer door and Harold's voice, shouting 'Grame! Grame! Let me in.'

'Oh lor',' said Oliver. 'Grame, you hold him off a moment while we get away.' He stooped down and took Insemnia over his shoulder, put one leg over the window-sill, and said, 'Good-bye, old man.'

'Good-bye,' I said, 'bless you my children. Good-bye, Insemnia. You'll have to find another best man.'

'Good-bye,' she said, and blew me a kiss, a rather difficult thing to do in her position.

They disappeared from sight. I closed the window. The noise on the door grew louder and I heard Lady Bloomsbury's and Lady Cynthia's voices as well as Harold's. I went into the hall, closing Insemnia's door behind me, and opened. I expected an invasion of Insemnia-seekers. Instead Harold rushed in with fierce indignation on his face, waving what appeared to be letters.

'Look here, Grame,' he cried, 'I won't have it. What is all this?' And he thrust the letters under my nose.

'I don't know. What is it?' I said in perplexity.

'Bills!' he stormed. 'Five pounds for a box, ten pounds for a car, twenty-five pounds for a banquet. Who gave them my name?' Over his shoulder I saw the equally indignant faces of Lord and Lady Bloomsbury and Edith, and behind them Lady Cynthia's, with a pipe in it. Then Harold broke off. Looking past me through the open door of the Senator's room he saw an empty bed. Astonishment spread over his face; then suspicion. He rushed in, and out again.

'Where's the Senator?' he cried wildly.

'Isn't he there?' I said.

An awful doubt dawned in his eyes. He looked at me accusingly, then ran to Insemnia's door, opened it, and burst into the empty room. He glanced around for a moment and hurried to the window. Coming up from behind I could see Oliver lifting Insemnia over the rear wall; on the further side a narrow passage ran into a little mews where, I guessed, the old bus waited. Once again we saw Insemnia's lovely leg. Then she disappeared over the wall and we saw only two bobbing heads, whose owners ran towards the mews. Harold got the window open just before they vanished.

'Jene!' he roared, shaking his fist, 'you . . . Fascist!' Then he turned and dashed out of the room and down the stairs. He was too late, I knew; in the distance I heard the old bus start up and from the direction of the mews a cloud of blue smoke rose and drifted over the gardens. I came quickly out of the room and met the whole household clustering towards me with faces anxious, inquisitive, alarmed and baffled. Only one of them was hopeful: Edith's.

'What is it?' they said.

'I'm not sure,' I said, 'but I think there's been an elopement. I think Oliver's run off with Insemnia.'

They stood looking dumbly at each other and then I saw relief appear on their faces: Lady Cynthia looked positively happy, Alistair quite pleased. Only Em Porridge looked more perplexed than ever.

I made my way through them, down the stairs and into Priscilla Grove. There was a sound of running footsteps, dwindling; Harold disappeared round the corner in vain pursuit.

From the corner houses, as if in answer to a call, came the artists and the assassins, their eyes big with curiosity. Priscilla Grove had never looked so much like a stage-set. Mrs. Barnes, standing with damp rag in her hand in the attitude in which Harold's sudden dash had surprised her, slowly relaxed and bent to her work.

'One Fine Day He'll Come Along,' she sang. Old Mrs. O'Bourke, pushed by old Mrs. Miggins, appeared from her garden gate. I turned back into Number Seven, absent-mindedly handed Mrs. Barnes her truant half-crown, and began slowly to mount the stairs to my room. Now, I thought, I might be able to get some work done. I was happy that I had not meddled in these tangled events and that all had nevertheless worked out well.

In the next room to mine I heard Edith; she was humming happily to herself.